MESSENGERS
WATER AND EARTH

A.L. Mundt

Orange Hat Publishing
www.orangehatpublishing.com - Waukesha, WI

MESSENGERS
WATER AND EARTH

A.L. Mundt

Orange Hat Publishing
www.orangehatpublishing.com - Waukesha, WI

MESSENGERS BOOK 1: WATER AND EARTH
Copyrighted © 2016 A.L. Mundt

MESSENGERS BOOK 1: WATER AND EARTH by A.L. Mundt
ISBN 978-1-943331-36-9

For information, please contact:

Orange Hat Publishing
www.orangehatpublishing.com
info@orangehatpublishing.com

Cover design by Therese Joanis
Birds imagery: Andrey Tiyk/Shutterstock.com
River imagery: Burdov/Shutterstock.com

Printed in the United States of America

www.orangehatpublishing.com

This book is dedicated first and foremost to my oldest friend, Sunny—thank you for allowing me the use of your brilliant, adorable characters, your dazzling plots, and for humoring me each time I laid on your floor with my notebooks and complained about weather motifs. There is no way in any parallel universe that this story would exist without you.

Special thanks also to Mom and Dad, for helping me comb through and improve each agonizing draft, and for sticking with my "elemental nonsense" all these years.

And to Grandma, who came up with titles, and to Sam, who helped little high-school me believe I might actually be good at this, and to all my other family and friends, for their ongoing support—I am so unfathomably grateful.

Lastly, a huge thank you to Shannon and the team at Orange Hat: you're making a lifetime dream come true!

PRONUNCIATIONS
In order of appearence

Aletta (Letty) Skylark – Uh-LET-uh (LET-ee) SKY-lark
Komi – KOH-mee
Majest (Maji) Skylark – Muh-JEST (MADGE-ee) SKY-lark
Lunesta Skylark – Loo-NEST-uh SKY-lark
Maxine (Maxi) Skylark – Max-EEN (MAX-ee) SKY-lark
Dagur Sigurðsson – DAH-guhr SEE-guhrth-sun
Seti Sinestre – SET-ee Sin-EST-ruh
Chami – SHAM-ee
Shayming – SHAY-ming
Shatter Seacourt – SHAT-ur SEE-cort
Soti Sinestre –SOH-tee Sin-EST-ruh
Raizu Capricorn – RYE-zoo CAP-rick-corn
Amitu – AH-mitt-too
Sira Sinestre – SEER-ah Sin-EST-ruh
Caiter Mandle – KAY-ter MAN-dull
Ohanzi – Oh-HAHN-zee
Malory – MAL-or-ee
Kallica – KAL-lick-uh
Coda – CODE-uh
Sylver– SILL-ver
Arathiel Capricorn – Uh-RAH-thee-ELL CAP-rick-corn
Nafuna – Nuh-FOON-uh
Charan – CHAIR-en
Donec – DOH-neck
Sedona Seacourt – Sed-OH-na SEE-cort
Sunni Seacourt – SUN-ee SEE-cort
Vosile Masotote – VAH-sile MASS-oh-tote
Vari Nyght – VARE-ee NIGHT
Rapple Ardyn – RAP-pull AR-din
Acillia (Cilli) – Uh-SILL-ee-uh (SILL-ee)
Jay – JAY
Raylea – Ray-LEE-uh
Quell Souleia – QUELL Soh-LAY-uh
Idyllice Souleia – EYE-dill-eece Soh-LAY-uh
Cydinne Floodleaf – SID-een FLUDD-leef

PROLOGUE

A high-pitched whirring shook her from her dreams. Where imaginary friends and unconscious fantasies had woven their threads through a sleepy mind moments before, a tall figure in a sweeping gray cloak now stood, its expressionless face a mask of overpowering, enigmatic uncertainty.

The girl stared in horror, tiny hands balled into fists. *Am I still dreaming?* Her thoughts were blurs, crushing her mind into wonder and perplexity. She had never had a dream such as this.

The world around her was in unbridled chaos. She could hear voices, screaming as if from a distance, their shrieks muffled by the dense fog that swirled in a spiral shape around her and the stranger. There was no visible sky for reassurance, though the air spun with glowing specks of light—some sort of odd, twinkling stars.

The girl looked down at her bare feet and discovered with a shock there was no solid ground beneath them; she was standing on emptiness, and between her toes stretched a void of mottled azure.

The whirring sounded again, and she covered her ears with a squeak of surprise. The figure took no notice of the sound or the girl's reaction, instead reaching out a beckoning hand.

Mystified, the girl took a shaky step forward, eyes fixed on the cloaked figure.

"Are there others?"

A jolt of surprise shook her as the figure spoke. It was a cavernous voice, like an echo into an uncertain sky, and although the face it belonged to was inhuman and strange, with blank lapis eyes and streaks of blue and red painted across silver skin, the girl was convinced it had to be a man. Nevertheless, she still didn't know what was happening, or for any matter, what to say.

"Others?" The girl forced the words to come from her throat. Her voice sounded weak and frail in comparison to the stranger's, and she shook herself. "Where am I? Who—who are you?"

The man blinked his round, alien eyes. "My name is Komi," he said, and he left the girl repeating his words under her breath. *Komi, Komi.*

"Some time many years ago, a whole humming world roamed the land not far from you, Aletta Skylark," Komi continued, his voice a powerful drawl that pulled the girl forward as if he had her captivation on a string. "That was the time where there was road beneath shoe-shined feet, a time where tall men worked in smoky factories and toppled whatever was unfit to their way—before the war, The End, when their grapple with the unknown drove them to tear their land apart."

"The End?" she restated, the end of her words lifting into a question.

Komi looked at her gravely, as though he pitied her for not knowing. "The gods intervened to halt the human destruction—but when the gods come to your vulnerable earth, demons are sure to follow, to prey, to fight. And so we fought, and so we saved the last helpless scraps of humanity and banished the demons back to Hell to lick their wounds, and so this planet rebuilt, frozen and tougher, accelerated under the blanket of our postwar dust. Have you never heard the stories?"

The girl didn't understand a word he was saying. She crinkled her nose, said in a tone coated with disbelief, "My mother and father were born in the time before mine. They fled from that war; they never said anything of *gods,* or *demons.* Is that what you are? A god? What do you want from me?"

Komi shook his head. "Enough of this talk. It is not what I came here to do." He lifted his hands to the dark cloud above his head, closing his eyes and arching his back like a great cat unfurling from its perch.

The girl—Letty Skylark, her mother's hair and her mother's last name—watched in incredulity as silver wings, glittering with an unseen force, unwrapped themselves from Komi's back and ascended to their full volume, extending into space like two twin feathery stars. They were massive and foreign and filled her mind with exhilarated fear.

"I don't—I—" Letty stammered, eyes growing even wider. She was almost positive she was dreaming. And if she wasn't, she was beginning to wish it, simply so she could awake from this madness, blame it on an unsettled lunch or an overactive imagination.

"Are there others?" Komi asked, his eyes searching Letty's. His gaze made her blood run cold with a sort of astonished, restless fear.

"Others of what?" She didn't dare raise her voice, even if it were just a dream.

"Your kin." Komi looked almost impatient, his brow furrowing in a rather humanlike gesture. "I come here seeking not only yourself, but family your age."

Letty thought for a moment. She was still young enough to not understand everything said by those older than her. Was he asking about her siblings? She had two: one brother, Majest; and a much older sister, Lunesta. But Komi had asked for someone her age, and only Majest still was a child, with the looks of someone no older than a decade.

"I have a brother," she began.

Komi dipped his head. "Bring him to me," he said.

Before Letty could formulate a reply, she felt the invisible ground give way beneath her, and with a scream, she was sucked into a tunnel of blackness. She couldn't see or hear anything; all she could do was howl while writhing about inside the tornado, teeth rattling and hair whipping like frayed rope.

She bit her lip to keep from crying out again. *Dreams aren't supposed to be like this!*

Letty resurfaced in a small bedroom. There was a dusty dresser on her right, and straight in front of her lay a small, fur-covered bed. Various sketches lined the walls, dotted in her father's foreign script, and on the floor was an old slingshot made from the bark of a young spruce.

She froze as she recognized her brother's room. *Bring him to me,* rang the words in her head. On shaky feet she moved forward until she reached the bedside.

Majest was asleep; his hands were tucked in close to his chest, his breathing slow and even. Brown hair streaked with faded green was strewn around his face, his evergreen eyes closed but twitching with the inklings of dreams.

Letty put a hand on her brother's shoulder and shook. "Maji," she whispered. "Maji, you've got to wake up. Something strange is going on."

Majest's eyes fluttered open, face contorting into a tired stretch. He brushed the hair from his face with one hand and blinked groggily at his sister, whose head didn't even reach the pillow. "What?"

"I had a dream," Letty whispered. "A dream about a man named Komi, but he wasn't human. He spoke of the past, and a great war of demons and gods, and then he told me to bring you to him. He wanted something from us."

Majest made a face. "It was just a dream, Letty. Go back to sleep." He rolled over and closed his eyes again, pulling a seal-fur blanket around his face.

"No," Letty protested, yanking it off. "This is too strange; you need to help me!"

Majest turned his head to glare at her. At most hours, he was good-natured and humorous, but in the dead of night, interrupting his deep slumbers was like waking a bear from hibernation. "You can tell me more about it in the morning. Right now I've got to get some rest—Mother wanted me to go out tomorrow and hunt. I can't do that if I'm exhausted."

"You hunted yesterday," said Letty, growing impatient. "And to be frank, repeating yesterday's '*success*' wouldn't exactly fill any of our stomachs. You're too young to be hunting with Father anyway, so he's not going to be angry if you're tired. You have to come with me *now*."

4

Majest scrutinized her with sleepy eyes, seeming to sense his sister wouldn't have come into his bedroom for just any ordinary dream. "You're certain about this?"

"Yes," Letty insisted, eyes roaring twin waterfalls. "I promise."

"Alright." Majest heaved himself out of his bed, the wooden frame creaking in protest. Still in his sleep-clothes and with his hair stuck into the air, he was barely presentable, but it didn't matter.

Confident now that she had her brother's attention, Letty turned back to the doorway, pursing her lips. "Um," she stammered, looking this way and that, "well, I got here by some sort of tunnel, so I don't know how we're supposed to get back."

At once there was a sort of laughter in her head, which startled her until she jumped, as if static shock had grazed her skin. The laughter, Komi's, grew louder and louder until it was all she could hear, and then she felt herself falling again.

This time, Letty didn't even think to scream, and she fell through endless mismatched levels of darkness and light in breathless silence. She heard Majest cry out in surprise and tried to reach him, but before she could do anything of the sort, they landed on their feet amongst nothingness, as though they had never fallen, as though they had been there all along.

"Wow," Majest breathed, eyes huge and green as he searched the swirling chasm. He wasn't afraid, he never was, but his gaze faltered with disoriented shock. "What is this place?"

Whatever Letty was going to say in response was cut off as Komi reappeared in front of them like a ghost, his wings light and mystical, flowing in a satin cloak around him.

Majest gasped and took a shaky step back. "Letty, what—?"

"Aletta Skylark, welcome back." Komi cut him off and nodded in greeting. "This must be your elder brother. I see he looks just like you."

It was true—despite the divergence in hair and eye coloration, Majest and Letty both had the same square jaw set boldly, the same angled nose, the same faint spray of freckles. Side-by-side, they looked nearly like twins.

"Komi," Letty said, the name still foreign on her tongue as she played along, "why have you brought us here? And won't you tell us who you really are?"

Komi spread his wings wide, blotting out much of the darkness. "I am the Deliverer. My duty is to bestow power in times of strife, in hopes it will fight back against the dark, in hopes it will bring the message of peace. My duty is to see that the world is protected by godly force."

"Then why did you allow the world to be destroyed, like Father always talks about?" Majest challenged, though his voice was small and bewildered.

Komi blinked, clearly not taking offense. "I was forbidden by my superior from interfering with gifts of power any longer." He shook his wings, sending feathers and stardust flying.

Letty looked at Majest, mouthed *"forbidden?"* curiously. He shrugged.

"The End has allowed me to convince the gods to strive for that elusive peace once more," Komi continued, "in hopes that this frozen world has grown back stronger than the fragments of the time before it, in hopes that it can protect itself as well as I can. And so in my duty as Deliverer, I have come to make the two of you, the elements' chosen, Messengers. If successful, you will bring to this earth the truth of how humankind is intended to be, free of darkness. You will bring news of a fresh world as those before you were unable to."

"Messengers?" Majest echoed. "What's this about? Forbidden power, peace—and you want us to help you with that?"

"Majest Skylark," Komi said, not answering.

"Yeah, that's my name. You know, Majest, like, 'majestic'—but not like 'majesty.'" Letty saw her brother's lip tremble. He refused to lose his casual tone, clutching it close. "Spelled like it sounds."

"Do you believe you can contain the force of what I am about to bestow unto you?"

Majest was confused and shaking, but he was brave as always. "Sure?" Though his expression bled uncertainty, he didn't hesitate; his voice didn't shake. "I mean, I can handle anything."

"Then by the powers of many years long since passed, the four elements and their heavenly brethren, I present to you your gift." Komi fixed him with unnerving jeweled eyes and continued:

"You are gifted with the force of the land which runs under your feet. The force spread across our meager planet to keep the circle of life in balance, the one and only strength that understands the forces of nature and all who dwell inside it, large and small, plant and animal."

As Komi spoke, a glowing green light rose up around Majest, whose eyes were wide and just as bright in color, face feverish under the glow. He was shaking now, knees wobbling in an earthquake. "What—?"

Komi turned his endless blue gaze to Letty, who was beside herself with anticipation and fright. If this dream had such an effect on her brother, what might happen to her?

But Komi's eyes were soft, almost kind as he brought them to Letty's face.

"And Aletta," he began, *"you are gifted with the greatest force known to your planet. The one force that can quench all others in a single breath. While thought to be uncontrollable, you will have its strength at your beck and call whenever it presents itself to you."*

A bright blue-black light shone around Letty at the words, making her quiver all over as though someone had prodded her with needles, pinching and sewing her from the inside out. She sank to her knees as some blurry strangeness wove between her seams, unfamiliar and terrifying. Unable to help it, she cried out, limbs petrified and mind bewildered, screaming until all she could hear was a mad roaring in her ears, a pulsing wave like the beat of the world's heart.

Then she realized that Komi was gone, the swirling world was gone, and most frightening of all, Majest too had disappeared. Letty had never been so afraid in her life; she had never known less about who she was and what she might become.

And then she awoke.

I. SLEEP

It was dark. Darker than it had been since Majest could remember. Even in the dead of wintry nights after a day of no sun, there had always been at least the light of the moon to guide the footsteps of all who passed through the land. Even when it seemed as if the cold habits of the northern regions would sweep away any last shreds of hope, there had always been a glimmer of light on the horizon—something to at least give one the impression he or she was not alone.

Now there was nothing—not a star in the sky, not anything but the vast, eddying black clouds that hovered above the heads of the Skylark siblings. They watched from inside their cottage with a nervousness pooling in their stomachs like water poured into two unstable cups.

The darkness was unavoidable this time of year, and yet it still felt like a bad omen to be trapped under lightless skies the night after such an unsettling incident. Majest couldn't free his mind from thoughts of Komi and the land of stars that weren't quite stars, godly words of element and power—and the notion that such words might have followed Majest here and now, to the waking world.

That thought was the most uneasy of all.

He was sitting in the kitchen, Letty next to him, picking at the ends of her hair and occasionally taking a fidgety sip of water. Majest didn't have the heart to tell her to get herself to sleep, not tonight. Especially when their mother herself was awake at this hour, winter coat pulled over her nightgown as she stood vigil just outside the door, just like she did most nights their father was away hunting—stubbornly ignoring the frozen tips of her nose and ears and the drowsy tug of her eyelids. She would always wait for him to come home.

And tonight, Majest and Letty waited with her, cloaked in darkness.

"You think we should tell them?" Letty whispered suddenly, passing her cup between her hands and tapping her toes slightly against the wood floor, as if she didn't know how to control her movements.

"Tell who what? Tell our parents about Komi and the dream?" Majest let out air through his nose, but sat still. "I mean, that sort of thing—the gods, the heavens, myths of prophecies and greatness—that's the sort of thing *Faðir* always taught us to believe in, so at the very least, he wouldn't think us insane."

Letty studied him, blue eyes like dark glass with only a small candle's flame fluttering behind them. "Who's to say Komi would want us to tell Father, or Mother, at all?"

"Well, he didn't say it was a secret," Majest noted. "And none of that matters if it ends up being only a dream."

"I think you know it wasn't only a dream," murmured Letty, words flickering. "We both were there. We both saw it."

"You're probably right. My brain isn't at a high-enough level of creativity to come up with something like that, anyway." Majest grinned, and Letty glared at him.

"Be serious."

"I am! You think it was real? That we have some sort of supernatural, god-given powers now?" Majest swallowed hard at the words, all joking aside. They were too young for *any* sort of responsibility, let alone a mythological one; Letty was merely ten years of physical age, while Majest was twelve—time flew by at double the pace in this restarted world; he had only been born six years ago, though he had the demeanor and body of a boy twice that number.

"We might have powers!" Letty sounded almost accusatory, as though daring her brother to believe that their world might be

9

flipped on its head. "And what if they turn out to be dangerous? What if Komi's an evil spirit using us to do his bidding?"

Majest snorted. "Alright, now *you* be serious."

"Serious about what?" A new voice cut in: lower, older, coming from the doorway.

Majest turned slightly, and his older sister's frame came into view, all slender limbs shadowed just out of reach of the candle. And yet, she flickered in the dark, leaning up against the doorframe for support as she spoke.

Letty paled slightly. "It's a secret, Lunesta."

Even in the dark, Majest could tell Lunesta was rolling her eyes, short hair in blue-black curves around her face. "Of course it is," she said sourly.

"Why aren't you asleep?" Majest asked her, trying to steer the conversation away from any and all secrets—the last thing he needed was their bad-tempered older sibling sticking her nose into their mystery.

"It's hard to sleep with you two banging about in the kitchen," said Lunesta.

Now it was Majest's turn to roll his eyes, though he didn't have time to fabricate a response.

There was a soft thudding and shuffling coming from outside, and all three siblings turned toward the sounds like mice turning toward a suspicious crack in the undergrowth, eyes widening, senses alert for danger. The sounds grew louder, closer, and were accentuated by a muffled cry from their mother and the thumping of Majest's heart building up rampant in his chest.

Majest and Letty only had to exchange one quick, loaded glance before they were tearing through the kitchen without thinking, their candle waving after them as Majest yanked open the front door with a *creak* loud enough to wake the dead—or scare off any wild beast or intruder who may have stumbled upon their home.

But instead of finding a possible threat or peril behind that wooden divider, Majest was instead met with a pair of eyes that twinkled like the night sky above and peeked out from behind a familiar tangle of dusky brown hair and matching stubbly beard. It was a sight of home.

"You're back!" Majest cried in glee, and flung himself into his father's arms.

He was caught with a low, surprised sound of *oof* before his father chuckled and spun him around like he weighed no more than a couple of feather-fluffed pillows. Majest was breathless and flushed with cold wind as he was set back onto his feet next to Letty.

"We thought with how cold it's been getting that you might not make it back until tomorrow!" Majest blinked up at his father with a huge grin, his concern over Komi temporarily brushed aside as though it were made of mist rather than stone.

His father never stopped chuckling, and he pulled a sack from his shoulder that looked heavy with fresh meat, depositing it in the icebox on the porch. "I keep telling you, we from Ísland, we do not feel so much cold. This Canada—Cognito now, whatever it is called—is nothing. There is no storm that can get the better of me. I have always seen worse." He winked at Majest and Letty, who giggled. The rough voice, the accent, the jokes—it had all been gone for days, and Majest had missed it with everything he was.

"I'm sure even Icelanders have to take cover sometimes, Dagur," their mother reprimanded, though she was smiling, too, shivering with her boots poking out almost comically from underneath her thin cotton gown, red hair in a loose knot. "You still have to be careful out there."

Dagur sighed with false dejection. "Maxine, *elskan*, you worry so much. Are you not happy to see me?"

She swatted him with her sleeve in a gesture that made Majest laugh. "You know I am, as we all are, you old goof. Now let's get you inside, hmm? You've got to be just about frozen solid."

"Yes, ma'am," said Dagur cheerily, and began to follow his partner inside.

As they moved, Majest and Letty were left alone on the porch, and Letty caught Majest's eye. The look on her face was blanched and nervously questioning, and Majest remembered their earlier conversation with a mental flash, realizing what her expression was asking.

He nodded to her as they followed their parents inside. "We will," he said to her unspoken question. "Right now."

Through the door once more, Maxine was starting a small fire on their stovetop, likely to warm the room, and Dagur was discarding his gloves and boots and shaking the ice from his hair like a wolf shaking water from its coat. He always looked so young when he did that, Majest thought, but then again, everyone in Cognito was stuck as bugs in amber, young forever, at whatever adulthood age their body decided to freeze—this whole landscape; it was all frozen, immortal and bitter with no end, just trees and horizon.

Though rarely could anyone cling to survival for long out here between the blinding white of the snow and the sky—especially this far north.

Maxine turned to her son and daughter as they entered, hair now escaping its hold entirely and falling in ribbons over her shoulders, just as Letty's had a habit of doing. "You two look thoughtful," she commented. "Something on your minds? Maybe you should get some rest; I'm sure your sister's already in bed."

Majest swallowed, and Letty said, "We do—we do have something to tell you."

Dagur raised an eyebrow. "Not bad news, I hope?"

"We hope so, too," Majest said, with a sort of nervous laugh that made his shoulders quiver.

Now their parents were both staring at them.

Majest looked at Letty. "Well, go on, it's your dream," he murmured.

"Yes, I—I had a dream. Last night. Well, Maji and I both did." Letty was back to kneading her hands together, as though trying to form something between them. "It was a lot to process; we're not sure if it—if it means something—"

"All dreams mean something," Dagur interrupted gently, and reached over from the table to squeeze Letty's hand. His eyes were soft, without any of the outside chill. Maxine's were the same way, glowing green and orange by the fire, her freckles like sparks. Of course Majest and Letty could trust them with whatever this dream might hold; they were family; this was trust in its most infinite form.

And so, together, Majest and Letty told them: about Komi, Komi and his wings that shimmered like starlight and smoke, a war of mortal and immortal where immortal had left victorious, and most of all, of Messengers, of elements, of power that was presently little more than a tremor of the imagination.

Majest expected a lecture from his mother, of eating less before bed or not reading so many of his father's old mythology books, but Maxine was staring at them in a quizzical, dumbfounded silence, the dancing shadows on her face the only move she made.

Dagur, on the other hand, looked positively *enraptured.* "Messengers?" he exclaimed, the second Letty dropped the dream's finale in favor of clamping her mouth shut, punching her worried gaze through the floor instead. "Messengers, you are *serious?*"

"Yes?" Letty's voice was small, brow still furrowed as though she expected some sort of punishment.

Majest held his breath as his father jumped from his seat at the table with a startled creak from his chair, eyes shining like nothing Majest had ever seen before. "My children are Messengers?"

Maxine snapped out of whatever trance she had been in and swung her gaze toward him. "You know what this unconscious fairytale *means?*"

Majest felt something fluttering in his chest, something he had not known existed, like it had been in hibernation and all his life had been one endless winter. "He thinks it's real," he whispered to Letty, who had shifted closer to him as if to take his hand.

"I have heard of it—of them," Dagur said, almost urgently, sitting back down when he seemed to realize his clothes wouldn't dry if he didn't sit by the fire. He was stammering; his English clearly couldn't come fast enough for his thoughts. "Messengers—four chosen by gods for the power of four elements, just as prophets are chosen, and guardians, and—"

"Again with all of these myths? They're just myths, Dagur; no one's ever *seen* any of these people." Maxine was speaking sternly, though her words were not convincing.

13

"You know we have," Dagur argued lightly, and his bright eyes never left the two young freckled faces in front of him. "It's real, it is all real."

Real? The word echoed through Majest's brain, tossed back and forth as if by a particularly violent wind. He felt like he might fall over from the weight of it as it bore into him, but it was hard to feel the uncertainty and fear jutting through his chest when his father was staring at him like he had found a path to the heavens. And maybe, somehow, he had.

"Maji, Letty." Dagur was reaching two callused, ungloved hands out to them now, and they each took one. "I do not know much of this, not much at all, but if you might have this power, won't you let me help you…what is the word…unlock it?"

Majest tried to let out a laugh, though he could not completely deny the uncharacteristic panic that made his voice shake. "What, right now?"

"None of you are going anywhere right now," protested Maxine, and put her hands sternly on her hips. "It's the middle of the night, and you all need your sleep. If you want to explore the inner corners of your subconscious, you can do it when there's a sun in the sky and a full night's sleep in your bones, alright? Don't get ahead of yourselves."

And for the first time, Dagur hesitated. "Alright, Maxi, you're right." He blinked, and his gaze against Majest's was like a magnet, pulling him in, snapping him to attention. "Tomorrow?"

"T-tomorrow?" Letty repeated, looking rather put on the spot.

"Absolutely."

"And you believe us, believe in what this Komi told us?" Majest hoped it didn't sound as though he were searching for a way out.

"I believe in you, yes." There was no escaping from the conviction in Dagur's voice, in the deep blue of his eyes, in the firm squeeze of his hands. "We may not know for certain, but if this is how the gods say it is, this is how it is."

Letty made a small, choked sound. "But why would anyone, any gods, go around asking random children in the middle of the woods to hold power? What are we supposed to do with it if we have it, use the trees and the rivers to unlock some hidden full potential? It was just a stupid dream—"

"Your questions are questions for tomorrow," Dagur said and stood up, hands still wrapped firmly around Majest's and Letty's. "Your mother is right, and I am very tired. Off to sleep, all of us."

With his blood pounding and thoughts churning faster than ever, Majest conceded in a yawn, and trailed after his family to where seal blankets and hopefully god-free dreams were waiting. Letty, behind him, put out the fire and blew a wispy breath onto the candle, which smoked a protest of gray tendrils in her wake.

Majest swore he brushed past another figure on his way out of the kitchen, and perhaps heard a low growl of distaste, but if it had been Lunesta listening in on the conversation or merely a shadow against the wall, Majest had forgotten all about it by the time his head brushed the pillow, and sleep took him.

He dreamed of the force of the land which ran under his feet.

During Cognito winters, the sun was not only fleeting, but deceiving—it shone with all the fierce slant of a summer day balmy and clear, though in reality, it did nothing to ease the bitter northern winds or the chill straight through to the bone; it just gave false hope.

Letty was wearing three extra layers under her fluffy fur jacket, feeling less like a potential candidate for heavenly power and more like a waddling seal. She still shivered, even in her protective cocoon: less from the cold, and more from the reason she was gathered in the front yard with Majest and their father, whose enthusiasm was equal parts consoling and unnerving.

She didn't want power, she kept thinking, and smacked her gloves against her thighs until feeling crept back into her fingertips. Power, responsibility, *control*—wasn't it all too much for someone her age? And what was the *point?*

Dagur's softly rumbling voice wafted through the concoction of fear and skepticism brewing hotly beneath her ribs, and Letty realized he had been speaking for the past few minutes. She shook herself to attention as best she could. She had to at least follow along for his sake, if pretending to unlock a dream would entertain him.

"There is a key to focus," Dagur said, his hair shining a rich brown under the cold sun. "It is a key that can unlock almost anything, and perhaps it can help you, too."

"What's that?" Majest asked, who was bouncing around on the balls of his feet to keep warm. He didn't look troubled, Letty noted, and tasted metal in her mouth.

"To not feel distraction," said Dagur, adjusting the top button of his coat. "To reach inside your mind without the worry, without the fear. Without feeling."

Well, that's not going to be possible, thought Letty with a glum purse of her lips. *All I've done for two days now is worry and fear and feel.*

"Close your eyes, both of you," their father instructed suddenly, waving a vague hand at them. "It is much easier to find what you are looking for if you cannot see it at all. Close your eyes, and breathe, until you feel all of yourself, and nothing more."

Letty frowned, but obeyed, and then she was both cold and dark, feeling rather lost in the abundance of space somewhere beyond the earth's protective surface. She didn't feel herself; she felt the chill; she felt alone.

"This is an old family trick of mine," Dagur told them. "Usually for meditation, for an attempt to reach the gods, or peace. I thought it could be of some help if your minds have new doors to unlock."

Letty squinted one skeptical eye open to see Majest's face wrinkle, mouth open in a question. "But how do you know anything about Messengers in the first place? You never—never said anything to me."

Dagur usually passed his history onto Majest, Letty knew, because Majest soaked it up like a tree soaked up the sun. He taught him Icelandic and old-world myths, but clearly, whatever their father knew of supernatural abilities, he had thus far kept it to himself.

"It is not a particularly well-believed piece of history," Dagur replied. "And Letty, keep your eyes shut, please."

She slammed her eyelids together, feeling her cheeks burn. She had no intention of looking like as much of an idiot as she felt.

"But my family, we did know of many unbelievable stories—of gods picking sides in human wars, and fighting along with them for lost causes. There were those who claimed to be prophets, and they were ignored, laughed off. There were rumors of elemental power, but no one could prove it, and no one could determine a possible purpose for it. But I read all the stories anyway—perhaps you would like to read some? After all, you may become stories one day, too."

Letty swallowed the coppery taste from her teeth and tongue, tried to imagine her eyes poring over the stories of those who could have been just like her. She wondered if they had been scared, when they had started having dreams of stardust and history. She wondered if, like her, they hadn't wanted any of it to be true.

"Now focus," Dagur went on, voice hushed, and he was addressing them both. "Block out everything but who you are. Try to open new doors in your mind—break them down if you must."

What if I have no idea who I am? Letty wanted to protest, but she kept her mouth clamped shut. She couldn't say the same for her eyes, however; she had to know how Majest was doing, if he understood, if he could focus.

Through the infinitesimal line of her blurred vision, Majest certainly looked as though he were deep in concentration—his brow was furrowed and trembling like an earthquake, mouth pulled taut, not a hint of the day's reality penetrating the rings of his lashes. At once, Letty was reminded that he was physically two years her elder, and he was never scared. She bit her lip.

Dagur cast a whisper in Majest's direction, completely entranced in his son's focus. "Now, try moving your hands."

Majest set his jaw with an audible huff of air, and after a moment, struck a pose with a low grunt, hands flying out in front of him, body twisting like a fish. Letty almost giggled; he looked ridiculous. And there were no signs of anything suspiciously elemental, which sent an odd pang of relief through her gut.

With a frown, Majest opened his eyes, giving his father a dejected stare. Clearly, he was disappointed. "Nothing."

Dagur chuckled. "Well, it is a rare thing for success on the first try."

"But this might not even be *possible*. These powers might not even be *real*."

"They're real," Dagur said shortly, and Letty wondered how he could have so much faith in stories that chilled her to the bone. "They must be. *Reyndu aftur,* Maji. You'll get it."

Letty hadn't the faintest clue what her father had just told him, but she figured it was something along the lines of "don't give up", as Majest was retreating into his former position, hands open and still at his sides, every line in his face pursing in deep concentration.

Then he shifted with his hands up once more, and apart from the gust of wind that stung Letty's face with a whip as it passed over her, the land once more had no reaction to Majest's attempts.

Majest opened his eyes with a frustrated growl, but Dagur's eyes widened, and he turned his gaze to the treetops. "Wait," he said. "Did you feel that?"

"Feel what?" Majest and Letty exclaimed, Majest in hope, Letty with a nauseating worry.

"I think the trees, they rustled."

Majest let out a long, grumbling breath through his nose. "That was just the wind. Why would I have any effect on the trees?"

"Komi said you have the force of the land." Dagur's words were firm as ever. "That what you have *understands the forces of nature and all who dwell inside it, large and small, plant and animal.* Right?"

A sudden light seemed to flash inside Majest's head, and he nodded. "If I have an element, it's Element Earth, isn't it?"

Dagur nodded, and Letty's eyes narrowed into slits. *What about me? What might my probably-fake power be? What if this is all danger with no gain?*

By the time Letty arose from her bitter thoughts, she realized her father had found a stone and brushed the snow from its body, holding it out to Majest as though making an offering to the gods.

"Try breaking this," he told him. "Focus on it, this time, and yourself, and what you want—focus on the break."

"A-alright," said Majest, very obviously trying to pin down his thoughts before they could fly away and create a whirlwind. He took a deep, steadying breath that stilled his entire body, and Letty was appalled and reluctantly amazed at his complete and total concentration. She knew she couldn't do that.

She watched for a third time as Majest turned to marble in front of her, a gangly statue with lines of focus in his face and a carved pose trembling with potential energy. Dagur held the stone in his open palms before him, and this time, when Majest lifted his hands, he pointed them in his father's direction, a bead of sweat running down his temple that hadn't been there before.

Letty leaned forward as she heard and saw nothing, daring to hope. She held her breath as Majest's hands shook, eyelids smashed together, a gasp of exertion escaping between his teeth.

But then there was a crack, just a small creak, like the earth had decided to twitch in its sleep. The rock fractured in Dagur's hands, splitting into fragments, and Majest was panting like he'd just sprinted the forest end to end.

Letty's eyes widened from crescents to full moons, and Majest was jumping with an exclamation of delight that broke his face into a grin that shone with the sun.

"You did it!" Dagur was exclaiming, and clasped his son in an enormous hug. "I knew it, of course you could!"

"It's real," Majest said through his grin, and stepped back to stare at his hands, then at the rock Dagur had let crumble to the snowy ground. "I—it's *real*. I did that." His eyes swung to meet Letty's, and she fought the sudden and terrible urge to look away. "Letty, you *have* to try! It wasn't just a dream!"

Letty could feel her heart sinking to her feet, nestled between her toes. But all the same, an unexpected rush tunneled through her, and it was the rush of adrenaline, and of something beyond that, something she could not touch or comprehend. It was the "what if" again, but this time asking, "what if I can do that, too?"

The notion drowned out all others, and she nodded, hands

shaking violently as she balled them at her sides, clenching her fingers in a failed attempt at controlling their trembles. She could feel Majest and Dagur still as they turned to her, tried not to let her face burn.

Her eyes fluttered shut, and then she was on her own. She burrowed through herself, digging and tunneling without any way of knowing where she was going, and she felt herself grunt in exasperation. Concentration didn't feel like power, like possibilities. It felt like walking straight underground without a guiding lantern or a sense of direction.

And yet Letty focused, focused all the way down to her fingertips, but as much as she blacked out the world around her, she couldn't erase the way her heart thumped with worry, pulsing a sickly fear into her veins with every beat; she couldn't escape the tremble of her limbs or the panic clouding her thoughts. She was unable to find her way through the tunnels of her mind, lost in the dark, lost in trying to find what was outside of herself, what lay in the blackness. She heard herself as if from a distance, crying out in a howl of fury.

Then there was a hand on her shoulder. Majest's. "Hey," he whispered, and Letty opened her eyes slowly, allowed the fists at her side to unfurl. "Letty, it's alright."

Letty shook her head to clear the last of the darkness, and glared at the blinding white of the snow under her boots. "It's not, though. It's not alright."

"*Of course* it is," Majest told her, and he was smiling—*of course* he was, *of course*. "We know now that these powers are for real, and now we can work on unlocking them. You don't have to worry, or strain yourself."

Letty glowered. "But I don't have any of this power, any control over my thoughts. I can't find my way to what seems to come so naturally to you. Maji, I can't."

"But you will," he said gently. "It's tough the first time, but you'll figure it out—I did."

At that, Letty whipped her head back to stare at him with an incredulous sort of fury. "You didn't even know if these powers were real a few moments ago, and now you think you have a right to act like you're the master of them just because you broke a *rock?* Anyone can break a rock. Don't talk down to me like that."

Majest frowned, looking a little hurt, but mostly concerned. "Letty, I'm sorry, I—"

Letty sighed, the sound loud and aggressive. "Don't worry about it. I'm going to take a break. Have fun with your rocks."

With that, she turned and marched herself back to the front door, ignoring the two voices that strained in encouragement behind her, for she didn't want to hear any of it. Her mind felt like it sat above flames on a stove, trapped bubbling and roaring inside the confinement of a pot, burning alive. She couldn't take it. She couldn't take having power, but she couldn't take *not* having it.

Hot tears spilled over her cheeks and she gritted her teeth as she stamped into the kitchen, embarrassment coloring her cheeks as red as what smoldered beneath her surface. She wiped at her face and shucked off her boots, unable to help the irritable stream of grumbles that poured like steam from her lips. She was scared; she was furious. She didn't want any of this, and it overwhelmed her, overheated her.

Maxine caught her before she could reach the hallway, calling her back with the sharp, worried tone Letty could recognize from a mile away.

"Aletta," it said, and Letty ducked her head, hoping her mother hadn't seen the tears. "What's wrong? I thought you were out... *experimenting* with your brother?"

Rubbing her face with her sleeve, Letty turned, and found her mother and Lunesta seated at the kitchen table, Maxine sewing a hole that had been in one of Majest's shirts, Lunesta pretending to read a book with a scowl.

"Um." Letty cleared her throat. "Yeah, I was. I needed a break."

Two green eyes flicked up to her face and held steady and challenging there, clearly not satisfied with her response. Lunesta didn't even acknowledge her sister's presence, though Letty could tell she was listening by the tightening of her hands to her pages, the slow way she bit her lip.

21

"The powers…they're real," Letty said, and didn't know why she hesitated to say it. Perhaps by saying it aloud, there was nowhere to hide from its truth any longer.

Lunesta's eyes snapped up, like those words had set off a trigger to break her from her consistent glowering slumber. Her face was still fixed in an ugly glare, and her short dark hair was falling over one eye in an act that seemed almost deliberately rebellious. "You're kidding," she deadpanned.

Maxine blinked, processing it. "Well, I can't say I'm too surprised, the way Dagur went on about them. Maybe that's a normal thing for Cognito now—we're ageless, mutated, and now we have special powers like we're straight out of a storybook."

Letty felt short of breath. "But I can't use them," she said, and after that, her words came out in a trembling, broken flow. "I can't use my powers. I don't know what they are, but I can't use them. Maji can. He broke a rock. He can concentrate. He can do anything."

Lunesta opened her mouth as though she were about to say something—likely something nasty—but Maxine held up a warning hand in her direction, staring at Letty with enough concern to fill the seas. "Come sit down," she said. "I want to tell you something."

Letty blinked, hesitated, but there was no question awaiting an answer in her mother's eyes; this was a demand. And so she sat, on the far side of the table, feeling Lunesta's gaze cutting her like tiny knives, just barely pinching her skin. She wondered why no one else seemed willing to make a big deal out of this.

"Power," Maxine was saying, before Letty had even adjusted herself on the seat of the chair, "is like the snow, Letty. You see it so often, falling in gentle sheets, just the tone of someone's voice or the strength of someone's legs when they run—you forget how dangerous it can be, too. You forget the blizzards, and the avalanches."

Letty frowned, not understanding. "So what are you saying?"

"I'm saying you might be sad you can't make snowflakes, but you certainly don't want to make a snowstorm. I'm saying, it might not be such a bad thing that so much potentially-explosive power doesn't come naturally."

"You think our powers could be dangerous."

"Not just the powers themselves, Letty—but at the same time, what some might do when they fear your power for the danger it possesses." Maxine tucked a stray lock of red behind one ear, and her gaze had a quality like a single flame in the dark; Letty couldn't look away. "I once knew a woman who was always on the run, always frightened someone would catch up to her who meant her harm."

"Why?" Letty asked, though she believed she already knew the answer.

"She had so much power," Maxine said carefully, "and there are many who believe that there are no such things as peaceful blankets of snow—only the pounding, perilous storms."

Lunesta made an unimpressed scoffing sound. "Your friend sounds more *guilty* than afraid. Only the guilty run."

Maxine silenced her with a harsh look. "Power is everything, no matter what kind of power it is. Power determines your friends, and your enemies, and yourself. I've seen power used for good, and I've seen power used for evil. Perhaps we don't know what your powers mean yet, but you should be careful, and you should not be discouraged."

"How can I not be discouraged, when there's a stack of potential problems waiting for me whether I can unlock this thing or not?" Letty blurted, her frustration peeking through the cracks.

"If you're meant to get this right, Letty, you'll get it right."

And her mother said nothing more than that, just let the snow fall outside the window from the thick gray sky, and Letty wondered how it would feel if her power could coat the land like winter could.

II. CALLING

Despite what her mother had said, Letty didn't get it right.

The sun and the moon traded places in their unending dance, again and again, but the more days Letty spent attempting to find the right sort of concentration, the more her focus slipped from her mind, as though she were trying to catch the rain with nothing but her bare hands.

She followed Majest's footsteps out to the woods encircling their cottage, day after day after short, withering winter day, only to watch as her brother conquered his element—to move stones, bend branches, and be hooted at like an excited owl by Dagur—while Letty stood and balled her fists, gritting her teeth and setting her feet firm and steady, but could never do what Majest did.

It wasn't that she was jealous, Letty decided. She was just angry, angry she couldn't pull anything more out of herself than growls of frustration.

And so she stopped going outside with Majest and their father, instead getting to listen to the stories every night when they came in from dinner, stories of smashing stones into fragments or twisting trees into knots. Letty at least tried to be happy for him, smile and nod—which was more than she could say for Lunesta, who would instead plaster a look on her face like she had smelled something foul.

Majest was gone again today, and he hadn't even batted an eye when Letty had told him she wouldn't be attending his session for the third time that week. She had told him she wanted to help her mother sew, but that was a lie; she was far too distracted for needles and thread; she wanted adventure in dirty crescents under her nails and flooding her lungs in a thousand ice crystals.

She took advantage of what daylight this day could bring her, sneaking her way out the back door and ignoring a jeer of "where are *you* going?" from Lunesta, seeking solace in the aching creak of the door as it granted her wish for an escape.

Outside it was foggy, the wet and thick kind of fog that turned the trees into hazy blurs that could just as well have been living creatures floating atop the forest floor. Letty looked up to the skies, and found them stuffed so full with clouds, she thought they might burst. She wondered if Komi were up there, watching her. She wondered why, if he was so *real,* he didn't give her more guidance.

With an irritable shake of her head, Letty set off on the path she usually took for walking, between two rows of stretching white pines that dug their roots deep into the frozen soil, evolution making them hardy enough to survive even this far north.

She hummed as she walked, tunelessly, noting the thickening fog the deeper she descended into the trees, and set each foot carefully, as though walking on thin ice. She couldn't help but think more of Komi; he was stuck frigid to her mind and she couldn't thaw him off. She just wanted to know her own power, her own strength—didn't Komi know that? Or was he not human enough to understand such fears?

Suddenly, Letty stopped her feet, and looked about curiously. The trees, though barely visible, were unfamiliar. Surely she hadn't misstepped? She knew this path like she knew her own name.

But yet, though her steps hadn't veered from their usual procession, Letty could not recognize what was around her, though she squinted through the white and the gray. She was lost, and yet she had not lost her way.

Letty refused to panic. Surely there was some mistake, or the fog was playing tricks on her mind. Had it always been this foggy? She stared blankly ahead. The drifting blanket almost seemed to glisten and shimmer, like a mirage, like magic.

Her feet picked up again, almost of their own accord, and their movements were slow and staggering, though they seemed to know where Letty was going even if the rest of her body did not. There was something lapping at the back of her mind like a murmur just out of reach, and she had to shake her head again, quite a few times, before she was freed of it.

This isn't right, she thought uneasily, as the landscape before her swayed and sparkled. She knew she should turn back, retrace her footprints through the blinding snow, but her boots marched on autonomously, and through the fog she began to see a looming dark shape that was bolder and blacker than any of the fuzzy trees that swirled her way.

There was a moment where she flinched back reflexively, startled by the sudden shape, but even with low visibility, she could easily discern that it was a cave, poking out of a large, uneven precipice. It was anything but uncommon to see high, jutting rock formations around this area, even this far from the mountains, but Letty was certain there were no formations this massive so near the house, and even more certain that none of them had giant, gaping caverns at their mouths.

She squinted. The cave towered high above her head, its entrance as jagged as an open, fanged mouth, and she knew she shouldn't approach something so unknown and foreboding, but she couldn't stop her feet. She couldn't quell the dark press of something against the far end of her thoughts, the itch she couldn't quite scratch.

Feet halted. Letty stood at the entrance. It was even taller than she had predicted, and she had to crane her neck to find the top of the cliff as it clasped the foggy sky. Inside she could see nothing but shadows and mist, a darkness so poignant and profound, it was as if the cavern existed somewhere just on the threshold of life and death—in sleep, in a slumber that if left alone would remain untouched, but if provoked, would rear its head to life.

Yet, something stirred inside Letty just by looking at it. This was something no one had discovered, a situation only she could flex her control over. And so she crept inside, feeling herself consumed by its vastness, tiptoeing as though she might wake a great beast if she stepped too loudly.

The interior of the cave was just as dark as it had appeared, and Letty had to fight through the glittery fog and the lightless rock to see the moss growing in feeble patches on the walls, the lines in the dark, monochrome rock, the high, icy roof overhead. It was shockingly warm inside, shielded from the wind, and she stumbled forward over the stone floor with a curiosity that brimmed and brewed.

There was a sudden buzzing in her ear, and Letty clapped a hand to it with a soft gasp. Then froze. Everything in her told her not to make a sound, though clearly, this cave had no current inhabitants; it was bare and black as a night sky with no stars.

She came to the end of the tunnel, and a large dome of a cavern greeted in her a circle, ceiling climbing higher than ever, the dark seeming to whisper from the walls.

A drip of water made Letty startle once more, clenching her hands, hardly daring to breathe. Her eyes were blown wide as she fought to make out the shapes of the walls, which pressed down upon her as though suggesting she bow to their majesty. The sound of plinking droplets rang on, until it made Letty lightheaded.

I think it's time to go back now, she decided, even keeping her thoughts as quiet as possible, but just as her feet before had pulled her to this very spot, they now held her captive, forced her to stare into the walls that seemed to swallow her whole.

The power of this cavern was ensnaring—it pulled her bones down to their marrow, made her small and meek and see-through, vulnerable as a flower against the wind. As her eyes pored over the black and the jagged, the room seemed to grow infinitely in size, until it was eternal and dizzying and boring into her mind so deeply, she wondered how she couldn't understand the words it was saying.

As she stood before it, a form of wily jealousy sprang up from her gut—this place was immense and strong and limitless, while she was small and weak, powerless.

Letty shuddered. Her mother would be wondering where she was, and so would Majest, when he returned from his training. She thought of his power. Had it felt like this, to stand close to her brother? Had she felt this small, this far from control?

The ceiling dripped, a dripping darkness that didn't stop, and it shook her until her feet were free. She so desperately needed to leave.

As she turned, the toe of her boot caught on a sharp claw of a rock, buried in the floor, and she began to trip, arms reeling for an attempt to save her balance. A shout ripped from her throat before she could stop it, and its echo off the rock walls was deafening.

Suddenly she couldn't see, couldn't breathe, could only scuffle away from the end of the cave with her heart pounding in her throat, hearing something rise and rumble in a warning behind her, something enough to snap her from her frozen state of blindness and force her movements into an unstable run.

Letty tore back into the fog with the reckless terror of a rabbit chased by a fox, unable to shake the sensation that something was behind her, following her, snapping its jaw at her just out of reach.

The world was hissing and glowing as she crunched down the snow, the trail of her previous footprints guiding her home, and there was nothing that could remove from her mind the image of cavernous power, of total, crushing blackness in high walls, of everything she was not.

Perhaps she had feared by stepping inside its mystery that she would awaken something hidden between its stones—but now, as her mind dilated and flared with a new, furious yearning, Letty wondered if she had also awoken something hidden deep inside the dark chasm of her own cavernous mind.

Letty thought she was still shivering the next day, long after she had stumbled into the quiet, small safety of her home, long after the fog had cleared with the morning. She rather suspected her continued tremors were a result of the fact that her body had rested, rested all through the night, while her mind had not.

When she finally pulled herself out of bed and changed into a clean pair of clothes, she found Majest at the front of the house, lacing up his boots with a determined, yet lighthearted expression.

Everything to him was an adventure, a push of positive forward momentum.

He looked up at the sound of footsteps. "Letty! Hey!" Clumsily he finished tying his boots, and stood to his feet to greet his sister with a cheery grin, uncombed hair falling halfway across his face. "I missed you yesterday."

Letty tried not to cringe at the memory of her hazy, dark discovery. "I wanted to go for a walk," she told him with a gesture to the back door. She looked around the room for the rest of her family, figuring their conversation would have an audience to some degree, but her eyes only met the bare wood of empty chairs, left cold. "Where is everyone else?"

"Hmm? Oh, they're all out, like I'm going to be in a second." Majest joined her in glancing over the house. "Father went out on another hunting trip, and Mother went to fetch fresh water to distract herself from the fact that she wants so badly to join him, but 'can't leave us without a parent', or something to that extent. I'm pretty sure Lunesta's still sleeping."

"So where are you going?" Letty asked him, figuring she already knew the answer.

"Practice," replied Majest simply, now tugging on his fur-lined gloves. "I've got to keep going, even if I have to train alone for a few days." Then he blinked at her. "I mean—if you don't want to come, that is."

Letty was about to reply, find some other excuse for why she didn't want to watch Majest fling pebbles into trees today, but she was cut off.

"I actually learned something *really* cool," Majest hedged, as though he could see his sister's disinterest. His green eyes were earnest. "I'd really like you to come and see it."

Letty hesitated, still wanting to tell him *no,* but there was something in his face that was genuine and sympathetic, and clearly he just wanted to spend time together, which had been sparse over the past week or so.

And besides, she wanted to get a certain cave off her mind.

"Okay, I'll come," said Letty slowly, and couldn't help but

smile when Majest's entire face lit like a match.

"Great!" Majest grabbed for the door, then paused. "Wait, we shouldn't invite Lunesta, shouldn't we?"

"When has inviting Lunesta with us on our adventures ever gotten us anywhere?" Letty inquired, and imagined her elder sister's sour face, eyes dark and brooding and belittling—just like the walls of that cavern, she figured, and pulled herself away from the thought as though it had burned her.

Majest shrugged. "True."

After Letty had gotten dressed for the frigid outdoors, they stepped into the front yard, the low sun among the blue already as high as it was going to get. There were few clouds today, and watching Majest's excitement as he skipped over to his practice clearing lightened Letty's spirits, too. She couldn't help but be excited for him.

"So, what great feat of natural strength are you showing me today?" she teased, crossing her arms and staring up at her brother with both eyebrows raised behind her hair.

"Just a little something that'll blow your mind," Majest crowed, and tossed her a wink. "Testing it out was my idea, after I thought about Komi's words a little more."

Letty belligerently ignored the strike of envy and fear that snapped up in her stomach, the dark shiver in her veins like a sudden *plink* of water. She smiled. "Well, show me, then, or I'll think you're all smirks and no action!"

Majest's grin intensified tenfold, a crescendo of enthusiasm. "Watch this," he said in a mysterious voice, and while Letty waited for him to slip into his state of concentration, her brother spun to the trees instead, closing his eyes and putting two fingers to his mouth.

Having known Majest for years, Letty knew better than to ask him what in the world he was doing.

From between his fingers, Majest let out a stream of loud, high chattering sounds into the forest, and Letty's eyes blew wide in incredulity, stunned by the absurdity of what was coming from her brother's mouth.

"Maji—" She started, and stepped toward him.

The chattering came again, and it was so unlike any noise Letty could recall ever hearing, even in the abundance of springtime amongst the squirrels and birds and their young. She wasn't even quite sure how Majest had learned to make such sounds—they ripped from his chest so effortlessly, and yet they sounded so much like unfamiliar wilderness, so unnatural from a boy's lips.

Letty waited for something magical to come of the ludicrous chirping, but as Majest fell silent, the trees stayed frozen; the ground remained at a leisurely stillness beneath their feet.

"Maji?" she tried again, and watched her brother rub at his neck in embarrassment.

"Um." He coughed. "Sorry. That was, uh. Supposed to work. I'll try again."

This time, Letty was prepared for the various clucks and sighs Majest emitted, and though she found them no less odd, she figured enough oddity had recently occurred that she was beginning to think nothing of it.

As if to make matters even more unusual, movement between the tree trunks made Letty turn her head, and a small snowshoe hare was shivering at the edge of the forest before them, its little nose quivering. Letty couldn't remember the last time she had seen a rabbit, as they were largely uncommon on the edge of the arctic ice, preferring to stick to safer, warmer territory with grass they could graze upon.

Majest's face lit up at the sight of the creature. "It worked," he whispered in glee.

"*What* worked?" Letty questioned, matching his soft tone, keeping one eye on the hare that quivered just a few paces from their feet. "You summoned the wildlife with noises that sound nothing like it?"

"That's exactly what I did," said Majest, eyes huge and glowing. "I haven't mastered the right sounds yet, but I can make animals curious enough to come check us out!"

"You—*huh?*" Letty felt herself gaping a little. *The forces of nature and all who dwell inside it, large and small, plant and animal.* Animal?

"Okay, let me try something else." Majest squeezed his eyes shut for a few seconds, and when he opened them, he opened his mouth, too, and let out a soft, huffing sort of grunt. He thumped his foot for good measure.

The rabbit cocked its head at the strange human before it, but responded in turn, beating its hind leg against the snow with a twitch of its ears.

"What are you telling it?" Letty asked. "Can you understand it?"

At the sound of her voice, rising in volume and incredulity, Majest snapped free of his animal trance with a visible start, and the rabbit's ears twitched in question of the situation before it decided to scamper into the trees, finishing the moment with a flourishing trail of flying snow in its wake and leaving the two Skylarks staring after it. From here, Letty couldn't see Majest's expression.

Then he spun around, and he was smiling in a very appeased manner, as though he had done the world a great favor, but there was a solemn note to his eyes Letty couldn't quite trace to a source. "Well, I can definitely understand what it's saying, though it's a *lot* harder to talk back. I'm just trying to get the greetings and friendliness down right, but animals say all sorts of things. This one outran a fox this morning—so I guess congratulations are in order!"

Letty couldn't help but laugh. "I guess you're going to be learning all sorts of new languages, then! You're the one who should be congratulated, Maji."

But instead of continuing his banter, the somberness in Majest's eyes rose up behind his eyes; Letty could see it swirling, even through his cheerful demeanor. "I wish you would be learning all of this with me," he said.

There was a sudden pang just under Letty's ribs at the words, a strange sort of anger, but she forced a smile all the same, just to mirror her brother's. "I don't think I'll be able to learn exactly what you're learning, so you'd better get used to celebrating your rabbits alone!"

Majest shook his head impatiently, and Letty could see that for once, there was none of his usual joking manner on his face. "Letty, it doesn't feel right doing this alone—where were you yesterday? I wanted you to be here with us. I want you to learn with me." His smile flipped into a small frown.

"I was just exploring," Letty hedged, uncomfortable with the direction this conversation was turning. "I, uh, found a strange cave behind the house. It nearly scared the life out of me."

"You shouldn't be scared," Majest told her, eyes nearly spilling over with concern. "Of any of this—especially our powers." He pursed his lips, wetting them against the dry air. "I've never felt more free than when I weave my way to the inside of my mind and pull this new strength out. It's indescribable, Letty; it's something that's *ours.* Maybe we don't yet know what that means, but we have something special, something for no one else—like some retribution for the northern dangers. It's like the gods are trying to give us a fighting chance at surviving out here." Their gazes met, blue and green.

But Letty could only think of her mother's words, of storms and danger that struck from the skies with no warning. She could only think of how suffocating, how belittling it had been to stand before that sort of natural power. "It's not a fighting chance if we end up just creating even more danger," she muttered, looking away and studying her boots. "It's not surviving if anyone's survival is threatened."

"If there's danger, then we'll figure it out," said Majest, almost impatiently. "*Together.* Just like we always have. I'm not going to leave you behind like this anymore, Lets."

Letty's gaze never shifted from below her, but she felt Majest approaching, felt him press one of her small hands between his own. She shuddered slightly, her chest squeezing tight with the worry she was allowing to escape it. "Even if...I can't use my powers?"

"Even then," Majest confirmed. "You're my sister, and that means your problems are my problems, too, just as your blood is my blood. And now, I guess, your mysterious elemental gifts are my mysterious elemental gifts, though that one isn't as conventional."

Sister. Letty frowned, a new thought weaseling its way into her head. "Why do you think that is? Why do you think we got power, but Lunesta didn't? She's our family, too."

Majest blinked, slowly, like he hadn't considered it. "I assume the gods didn't choose her, for whatever reason. I mean, you know she's always been the odd one out, of us three."

He didn't have to specify for Letty to know what he meant. Lunesta's quiet malice and impatience were only a small fragment of who she was, a single facet of her peculiarity. She had red, spotty scars lining her arms and shoulders that never quite matched the freckles of her siblings, and years of mystery before they had been born, and no one had ever spoken a word of those years or those scars, as though they alone held a dark power, the kind that should never have permission to fly, or even stretch out its wings. Letty had never known whether it was the story behind the scars, or something else entirely, but Lunesta had never wanted be a part of her siblings' world, before a word of element had ever been breathed.

"Letty," Majest said, and she realized she had been staring blankly into the snow. "Letty, don't *worry* about Lunesta. If she isn't with us, then we'll be with each other, alright? That's the way it's always been. This doesn't change a thing."

Letty nodded in silence, willing herself to forget Lunesta, forget about everything that clung to her thoughts like water to cold skin. She could not quite let go of the worry that drizzled over her head to toe, but for now, she let it crystallize and freeze, where it would be trapped until her internal heat would try to thaw it back out.

"When Father gets back from his trip, come and train with us again," said Majest, voice almost pleading. "It'd mean a lot to me, and to him, too."

Letty squeezed her frozen hand against his. "Alright," she agreed. "If it'll make you happy."

Majest winked. "It always makes me happy to have more people to show off to," he teased, and Letty used her free arm to elbow him in the side.

"Well, now that you can talk to animals, you can tell all of them about the oh-so-magnificent abilities you now possess!" Letty smirked. "I'm sure all the little squirrels in the trees will be *fascinated.*"

"They won't be too impressed until I tell them that both of us have the power of the heavens at our fingers," Majest protested. "Then I'll brag all about what we can do together."

For once, Letty held her doubts on her tongue and bit down on them, giving herself the right to rest, to bask in his confidence and let it take her over—at least until the panic and worry frozen in her gut climbed its way back to the surface, melted into her consciousness.

She tried not to see the poison of Lunesta's scowl on their way back inside.

III. STORMFALL

It was always difficult to trudge through the thick swamp of snow following a heavy storm, but after three days of pounding white with nothing to do but wait, Majest didn't mind the added challenge to his venturing, just let his boots sink into the powder with a satisfying *crunch,* burying him up to his knees.

Out the window, before Maxine had covered it with a wooden shield, there had been nothing to see but a frothy white blur, nothing to hear but the high whistle of the wind beating against the protective layers of logs and tundra moss that insulated the outside of the house. It felt good to finally be out among the trees again.

Especially when he might meet Dagur on his way back from hunting.

The thought of seeing his father made Majest's blood sing, and he tore through the snow with leaps and bounds like a fox, plunging his way past the front yard and into the full forest of conifers. His nose was tickled with a familiar pine scent, cheeks flushed with cold and excitement.

Majest was attempting to get a safe distance from the house—so he could practice another type of power, one that was not elemental at all.

From his pocket he pulled a small, neatly-packed ball that was a mossy green in color. It was made up of various grasses and leaves, rolled together with a highly-explosive powder Majest knew was one of his parents' old-world technologies, one of the pieces of the past they had brought back from their former home.

Thankfully, such technologies created a worthy pastime Majest had learned from his father—as the powder created a fairly-safe sort of makeshift bomb.

Majest snatched his slingshot from his belt with steady fingers, and rolled his first grass-bomb into its seal-skin pocket. His heart was thrumming with an eager freedom, and after determining he was a safe distance from the house, he pulled back on the stretchy leather strings, and launched the green bullet somewhere into the trees up ahead.

He tore after it, feeling the *whoosh* in the winter air nip playfully at his hair and his face, and when the loud thud of the explosion snapped back against the trees, the cloud of thick green smoke told Majest his bomb had been successful.

After a hoot of appreciation, Majest steadied himself with a determined inhale through his nostrils, closing his eyes and activating his element as though pushing a button, snatching up a small rock from the ground and molding his mind like clay to cover it in an abundance of freshly-fallen needles and greens. Without the need for a slingshot, he flung it with a flick of his wrists, where it crashed into the trunk of a towering spruce.

Majest laughed, and he felt so alive now—he had missed this world of green and white; it was here more than anywhere else that felt like home, and after days of nothing to do but read and roll matted grass into spheres, it was so good to be back.

And so he ran freely through the trees, unafraid of their never-ending mystery, feeling a part of their high-rise crowns and leisurely roots. He kicked up snow; he howled to the clouds; he flung his second grass-bomb in front of him, arms stretched wide as he tunneled straight through the smoke, spluttering and coughing as he laughed the gas out of his lungs.

Majest stopped running at that, hands on his knees, trembling with chortles as he slammed his eyelids shut like doors against the gray-green assault and let his body clear itself of hazy obstruction. He was still grinning when he opened his eyes to an almost-clear scene, snow just barely laced with a dusting of greenish powder.

There was something poking out of the snow, however, disrupted by the explosion, and Majest's grin froze where it sat as his eyes adjusted, taking in the form half-revealed before him, white and red and brown and blue in spatters, like something else had exploded here, something barely recognizable among its own clutter. It didn't smell like a corpse, but it had to have been something living—and something large.

Majest leaned forward, the last of his smile fading into his cheeks, and the sun caught the whiteness of the figure that lay a few paces away—it was a familiar whiteness, but it was not quite right, as though it had been bleached and pounded with black and blue like bruises.

Bile rose high in Majest's throat as he caught sight of the first identifiable piece of the mangled mess before him—it was a hand. A human hand. He was sure of it.

The hand was blue, the kind of blue Majest associated with twinkling eyes that held the night sky, the kind of blue that if you were under it, you were safe, you were covered. Its fingers were curled and swollen, as though trying to reach for something it would never find.

The hand was not connected to anything.

As Majest crept forward with a sickening, light crunch under his feet, he had to fight back breakfast as it inched up from his stomach. Whomever this body belonged to, they hadn't been allowed to rest in peace or safety—there was so much red juxtaposing the white ground, blood and sinews and entrails painting the snow in a picture that brought Majest's hands to his mouth, thankful once more for the lack of smell. Horror clutched his insides with a vice grip.

Something had torn this corpse apart. Majest suspected a flock of birds, or perhaps a wolf desperate and starved enough to scavenge. It had clearly once been a person, but now it was open like a book, spread out before Majest in frozen layers of ice and remains. He could barely make out the legs, the torso, what made up a human being. Ribs poked up from a thick, bloody soup of organs, and limbs were broken and mangled with their bones bleaching under the white sky. Everything was bent the wrong way, and everything that didn't need to be seen was showing. The sight was an unbearable shade of red, a massacre half-covered by the innocent snow that knew nothing of what it held beneath it.

Majest's eyes were fixated on the horror, like the scene might change if his gaze assailed it long enough, but he was still itching to turn away and run before he caught sight of the edge of a coat poking out beneath the carnage. A dark blanket of fur, a careful craft of the north.

Majest had seen it a thousand times.

Majest had seen this coat a thousand times.

Majest had seen this coat three days ago, headed out the door.

Now his lungs were squeezing his chest with the pressure of a mountain, and Majest felt his expression fall slack in a distant sort of dread that did not belong to him. He shook as his heart stuttered, could barely find the strength to stand as he followed the line of the coat up past torn shoulders, resting against a snow-covered face.

All Majest could feel was cold, as though he too had been opened up, split right down the middle, and the wind soaked his insides and his bones, and breathing was all but impossible. He moved closer. He brushed the snow aside.

He found a face blue and white, and remembered how it had looked when it had smiled at him, when it had laughed. When it had told him there was no storm that could ever get the best of it. That it had always seen worse. It—him—Dagur.

He was all blue now, just like the blue of his eyes had always been. Nothing had touched his face—it was as preserved as a frozen piece of meat in their family's outdoor icebox, protected from the bears and the wolves, but just barely. Just barely. And not enough.

Majest didn't know how he got to the ground, the snow seeping into his skin through a tear in the knee of his pants, didn't know how his hands lost their gloves or how they wound up at his father's frozen cheeks.

He just remembered screaming high up to the treetops, the cold that became his blood and his bones, the way his tears froze to his face before they ever had a chance to reach the ground.

It had been hours, and Letty was still crying, long after her eyes had dried. She had cried when Majest had burst through the door, face pale and ice-streaked and haunted; she had cried when her mother had sunk to the floor like her legs could no longer carry the weight of her world; her tears had flown freely when they had covered Dagur's body and set it ablaze down the nearby stream— just the way he had always joked he wanted if he "accidentally ate a poisonous rabbit or something"—watching the flames die from a high-flying yellow down to something red and crumbling, just a bloody sun crushing itself into the horizon.

And Letty cried now, silently, dryly, as she and the rest of her family packed Dagur's things into neat sacks, knowing full well these shirts and socks and spare blankets would be traded for food at the market the first chance they got to go—if their best hunter was gone, they would need the extra rations. It was such an unfeeling, cold knowledge, but it was unavoidable. Starving by clinging to memories would not bring Dagur back, and it would not keep his family alive.

Letty hated it; she knew Majest and their mother hated it, too. The two of them hadn't stopped crying, either, and just that alone was enough to make Letty's chest seize. Majest never cried. Maxine cried even less than that.

The only one whose face didn't shine red with tears was Lunesta, who sat at the edge of their mother's bed, calmly boxing a set of furry hats that slid nimbly through her slender fingers. Her expression was blank, hair falling over her eyes in a veil.

Maxine was digging through the back end of the closet, hands shaking furiously, hair flying free of its knot. She looked as unstable as a crack in the earth ready to quake and snap, and she hadn't spoken in so long, Letty was beginning to forget what it felt like to hear anything but the soft brushes of wind against the sides of the house.

She watched as her mother pulled out something small and bright hanging from a string, a little green stone on a necklace that would likely fetch a high price down at the Kartho market. But instead of placing it into her sack, Maxine slung it around her neck without a moment's hesitation, and stood up with a start.

"I'm going to get dinner ready," said Maxine quietly, and Letty could tell by the squeeze of her voice and the bowing of her head that she was embarrassed to be crying, even now, even like this, but had no intention or force of will to stop.

Majest looked up with a miserable protest on his face, as though about to insist that wasn't necessary, and Letty herself could hardly dream of eating when her stomach felt tied into unbreakable knots, but Lunesta called out to Maxine as she stumbled from the room. "Make me some squirrel, will you, please? I'm starving."

Maxine made no indication she had heard the request, and she was clutching the stone around her neck as her footsteps faded into the shadowed hallway.

Majest whirled on Lunesta once their mother was gone, face flushed with grief and fury. "How can you act like nothing's happened?" he demanded in a voice choked and raw. "Like our father didn't just freeze to death, like your stomach growling has any right to be pressing on anyone's minds?"

Lunesta didn't even look at him, just neatly folded a pair of pants that lay beside her. "Don't get all defensive. I wasn't close to him like you were."

"You aren't close to anyone," Majest spat, in a manner rather unlike himself. It was a terrible thing, what grief could unlock, Letty thought. Majest looked so utterly destroyed, he hardly cared whom he might be hurting, because his own pain was too high a mountain to see over. "He was my best friend; he taught me everything I ever needed; he was *still* teaching me, and now he'll never get to teach me again. That's no more late nights hunting through the dark, never another word of Icelandic to pass on, or stories for Letty and I when we can't fall asleep—and no more practicing our powers together." His words shook abysmally, as though realizing the truth in them, watching them fall out into the world in front of him.

There was a dangerous growl brewing in Lunesta's throat as she tightened her hands around her leather sack of belongings. "You grieve for him because he can't help you with your *powers?*"

Majest's eyes narrowed with vehemence. "You—"

"Everything's about you and your powers now, isn't it?"

41

Lunesta stood up now, and she towered over her siblings, who were crouching on the floor, forced to crane their heads to see her face. "Both of you."

"This is about our father." Majest looked nearly murderous, and refused to be talked down to, getting to his feet in a shuffle of clumsy, weakened movements. "He's *dead,* don't you *care?*" His voice rose to a yell that cracked straight through the middle.

"I care that in this family, the planets and the stars revolve around *you* and what *you* want and what *your* father meant to *you.*" Lunesta's mouth was in a thin white line that made the contrast of her eyes even darker. "And now, it's about your powers, too. Well, I won't listen to it. I'm sorry about our father, but I can't listen to you any longer."

Majest's mouth wobbled painfully, like it was trying to form words, but Letty saw them die in his throat, another round of wet drops making their way over the curves of his cheeks. He looked utterly stunned, all defenses down.

And so Lunesta turned to Letty. "Just remember," she said darkly, "it was a snowstorm that killed him, alright?"

Letty stiffened. Lunesta's eyes drilled deep into her skull as she moved around the side of the bed, and then Letty and Majest were alone in the room. He was staring at her in blank, decimated confusion, and she found the strength to shake her head, pull herself up on the balls of her feet.

"Come on, Maji," she whispered. "This is about something more than Father."

There was dread in her stomach as she turned into the hallway.

Majest tore after Letty as she tumbled away from the doorframe, both of their feet unsteady and teetering. It was already pitch black outside, and he could barely see Lunesta's silhouette, just Letty's red hair trailing after it.

She was shouting after her sister as though words alone could turn on a light to see by. "Lunesta!" she cried, bracing herself against the wall. "What have our powers got to do with any of this? You're angry because we have them and you don't, is that it?"

Letty's voice held a desperate fear that startled Majest, like she was scared her words were the truth. Majest just felt sick that this conversation was *now,* that it was *today,* that Lunesta could so easily cast their father aside as if he had never existed, only her own selfish jealousy.

They pooled together at the front of the house, where Maxine was bent intently over a steaming pot, hardly looking up from her numb line of vision as the three siblings entered the kitchen.

Lunesta whirled on her brother and sister so fast, Majest wondered how she didn't dizzy herself. "Of course I'm *angry,"* she growled. "For years, it's been you two with the attention, with the adventure, and now the power, too. Even the gods themselves think I'm second best. I'm more than angry—it feels like there's an invisible curse bound to me, one the rest of the world can see while I'm left blind."

Majest blinked, and though he had been inside for hours, he still felt frozen solid. "You've never been interested in what Letty and I do—you don't come outside with us, you don't care for our games—and you've never been close to us. If you wanted to be a part of what we are, it's not like you ever showed it! It's not like we never wanted to let you in!"

Maxine as last looked up from her cooking, and her green eyes held a watery glaze, her face bathed in steam. "Don't be cruel to each other," she told them quietly. "Not today. Please."

Everything in Majest's blood and bones agreed with his mother's words, and he saw the same in Letty's face, but if anything, Lunesta only seemed more furious.

"That's *it,"* she snapped, and her words crackled like a storm. She suddenly moved to the cupboards to her right, and from behind them she pulled a large sack stuffed to its brim. Majest had never seen it before in his life, and something about it sent another chill through his icy limbs.

Clearly, by the look on his mother's face, Maxine had never seen it, either. "Lunesta, what—what is that?" she asked, her face a ghastly shade of white.

"Supplies. Enough to last a month." Lunesta's gaze was bitter, and she wove it between her family with the slow creep of a snake. "I packed it the morning after we found out about their powers."

Something in Maxine's face was beginning to break, her lip trembling fiercely and her eyes stretching for miles. *"Why?"*

"Because these powers are unnatural, unfair, and all they're ever going to be to me is a burden. It's just getting started, and already, look what it's done to us."

Majest was too upset to protest, but Letty's lips parted in fury. "You packed a bag to what, to escape? To run away? Because you think this is *our fault?"*

"If Father hadn't been so busy training you, he would have gone hunting earlier in the week. He wouldn't have trekked out in a storm!" For the first time, Lunesta's voice rose into a shout, and Majest saw Letty flinch back as though expecting to be struck.

"Lunesta, that's *enough.*" Maxine stepped forward, her voice harsh but unsteady. She tried to grab Lunesta's arm, but it was viciously snapped away. "Put that bag away, and go back to packing. All of you."

Lunesta backed herself against the door with a wild glint in her eyes, and her hair looked like the feathers of a bird fluffed in defense of its life. *"Don't touch me!"* she howled suddenly, and in the six years he'd been alive, Majest had never heard his sister's voice at such a volume, at such ferocity. "I'll go where I want now! I've never belonged here for a second; *I'm nothing like a single one of you!"*

There was nothing anyone could do to stop what burst from the girl's mouth; it poured out in rain and snow and hail; it darkened the room with each word.

"I'm an adult now, long past the age anyone would expect me to still be cooped up here," Lunesta spat, as though the idea of this house was poison. "I'll find somewhere new; I'll tell the whole land about these powers and how wrong they are." She curled her lip, looked to Majest and Letty, her face in shadows. She looked like a monster. Their own sister, a monster. "Maybe someone will stop you before you tear apart something far worse than a family."

Majest was stunned into silence. So far, he hadn't done anything any more dangerous than flinging rocks into trees. What harm could he cause? How could he hurt anyone as badly as the skies had hurt his family today?

"Just calm down," Maxine tried again, and her tone was imploring, fingers still reaching in Lunesta's direction. She was too weary and grief-stricken to be demanding. She looked about ready to fall from her feet. "No one's going anywhere. No one else vanishes from this house today; we'll all figure this out."

"*You* will," Lunesta snarled. She opened the door, and the wind smacked against the warm kitchen air with a vengeance.

Maxine's face broke for the second time that day, pieces splintering and splintering.

Majest didn't know what he could do. He didn't know what he was supposed to do. All he knew was that the chill was soaking him, and Dagur's stone was hanging from their mother's neck, and Lunesta was stepping into the outdoors with her bag over her shoulder, clutching it tight, like it was all that she knew, all that she could trust. Majest couldn't understand; he couldn't even begin.

Their family was shattering right in front of him.

The feeling of sharp eyes on him broke Majest free of his thoughts, and Lunesta was wearing his father's eyes, the same dark blue, but hers didn't twinkle with the starlight; they put out the moon. "This is a warning," she told him, and she was telling Letty, too.

"A warning of what?" Letty demanded, and then she was the one grabbing for her sister's arm with her fingers splayed and shaking, the one pulled away from, the one left stranded and reaching, just like her mother. "Lunesta, come back—"

"You'll never bring anyone peace," Lunesta hissed, and it was like watching through a sheet of glass, slow motion and angles, as she grabbed the door, as she disappeared without bravado, without goodbyes.

The wind outside sounded like chaos without organization. It was still snowing, as night began to take hold.

It was snowing like it would never stop.

IV. FORWARD

Nearly two years passed in much the way they always did—it was dark, and then it was light, and then dark once more.

The only difference was that for the first time since Majest could remember, there were no longer five, but three, who breathed life into the cottage between the trees. It made the house seem marginally less like a home, as if its forest existence were a bit more translucent, giving an almost weightless quality to Majest's world—especially at night, when the overwhelming presence of restive sleep could make Majest feel more alone than ever. He felt more like he was floating than standing over the kitchen counter, the dark passing around him through the windows, through the cracks in the insulation, through the air and chill that could pass even through walls.

Nights like these made it almost too easy to remember—the snowstorm, and the mangled body tucked away between tree trunks, the sight of his mother shattering like ice and his elder sister tumbling away. Two years were nothing when every night was the same endless unrest as it had always been. Moving forward was inevitable, but forgetting was impossible.

A glimmer of movement in the undergrowth caught Majest's attention. He moved the edge of the curtain and peered outside the window. *Lunesta?* His elder sister's name passed through his mind for a fleeting moment, making his stomach churn with uncharacteristic anxiety. He could still see her leaving—that repulsion built up like flowing water against a dam until it had brought her to the edge and come blasting out behind her in a waterfall.

No, he decided firmly, tearing himself away from such thoughts with a spike of anger. *It's not Lunesta; it's never Lunesta.* He knew full well who it was out there, shifting on the front porch.

But all the same, the night still kept Majest awake—wary of the familiar howling wind.

"What'cha thinking about?" The voice made Majest jump a little; he turned in the dim room to see Letty's faint outline. She had grown—she had the physical demeanor of someone at least twelve or thirteen years of age, though she was merely moving past six. Her red-brown hair was matted in clumps that framed her small face like a fiery cloud, thrusting round eyes into focus.

"Letty." Majest heard his own voice crack as he closed the door and stepped back inside. "What are you doing up this late? You should be asleep."

Letty blinked at him with a sigh, exhaustion painting hollow lines on her face. "So should you, Maji," she pointed out.

Majest shrugged, turning back to the window. "I've had a hard time sleeping lately."

"Lately?"

"Well…for a while."

"I can't sleep either," Letty whispered. "Every time I close my eyes, I remember Mother's still sitting out in the cold every other night, waiting for the rest of our family to come home. I remember Komi's face, and I know he must be so disappointed that all this time has passed, and I still can't use my power."

Majest knew he should have swayed his sister from such thoughts, but there was no use; the truth in them stared the Skylarks in the face, just as it always did. Instead, he tried to smile. *"Það er allt í lagi,"* he told her, as if slipping into his father's language would allow him to be more convincing. "We still don't know for certain why Komi gave us these powers in the first place, so it's hardly something to worry about if you can't use yours yet. The future will be what the future will be."

"But what am I supposed to do *now?* It's been years!" Letty protested. Majest suppressed a sigh. It was the same set of words he heard in intervals as constant as the tide. It was always the same question, rolling in and out.

"Chipper up. Focus. Practice your knife skills, or your sewing, like you've been doing since Father died. Help Mother out—you know she's still hurting. You don't need powers to be strong."

Letty sniffed in mock hurt. "Easy for you to say; you're outside all day long chatting up squirrels and tossing trees around. Sometimes I like to think you've forgotten me."

"Despite the fact that the squirrels are usually nicer to me than you are, that'd never happen," Majest teased, in an attempt to lighten the mood. He crossed the room in two steps and bent down next to his sister, placing her head between two callused hands. "And who knows, maybe the fact that it's taking you this long to figure out what you can do means your power is a thousand times stronger than mine. Maybe once you unlock what's holed up inside your mind, nobody will look twice at what I can do."

Letty made a tiny, scoffing snort. "That'd be something—turning out to be more powerful than you and your silly leaf tricks. Then I'd be the one chiding *you* to chipper up and focus."

Majest grinned, teeth glowing in the dark. "And I would relish every word of your advice," he reassured her with a wink. But although he didn't say it out loud, he wondered if Letty would ever understand the nature of her elemental gift. Surely it wasn't meant to be this difficult.

...And Aletta, you are gifted with the greatest force known to your planet...

Majest sighed, pushing away thoughts of Komi, powers and his sister's future. It was late; they needed sleep. Majest loved sleep, loved waking up with another day to conquer. He wished he could find a way to sleep like he used to. "Letty," he said. "Letty, you should go back to bed."

"I'm not tired," Letty replied evenly. She, on the other hand, never had liked sleeping much—she preferred to lay awake, watching and absorbing the world like a thirsty sponge. "And I was serious before; I can't sleep knowing Mother's still sitting out in the cold."

"She does that every night, Letty," Majest reminded her quietly. He pictured Maxine, her nightgown and boots, poised just out of the wind with her eyes fixated on the trees. She had always waited for Dagur to come home, wherever he might have been. Now, she waited for two, and they would never come, and every night would end the same—alone. "It's her way of coping. Just let her be."

"It's her way of denial," Letty corrected, and the worry in her eyes was infinite. "At least let me have a glass of water before you shoo me out, okay? I mean—if we have enough to spare."

Majest pursed his lips. "Lucky for you, I went to the river yesterday while Mother was hunting. Now we've got water, melted and boiled. I'll get you a glass."

As he spoke, Majest eyed the vat underneath the window, half full of chilled, melted ice. He went over to it, pulling out a cup made of bone from their wooden cupboard. He opened the vat and swiped the cup through it, bringing up a puddle in its center.

"There you are. Straight from a probably-filthy river and hopefully boiled enough so that you won't be poisoned." Majest handed the cup to his sister, who immediately pressed it to her lips, which were in a hard, pensive line.

"If we lived down south, we wouldn't have to struggle like this," she murmured as she drank. "You know, like in a pack. Towards the border and the markets. Father always said they have springs running with crystal-clear water, perfect for drinking. And I bet it's warmer down there, too. They don't need to light a fire to keep the house heated."

"Well, the southerners have their own issues to worry about, you know," Majest told her firmly. "It's safer in the woods than in a large town like that. Sure, there are more bears and loners in the north, but they're less likely to find us or mind if it's just our family rather than a swarming village. We're out of harm's way in the heart of the forest. We have our own personal hiding spot."

"But it's been almost two years, and we still have barely enough food to feed ourselves without Father hunting," Letty argued. "He was better than the rest of us put together, especially when we can't afford to take long trips alone. We haven't been to the market in months. We can't make a life out here anymore."

"*Faðir* built this house here for a reason," Majest said tightly. "This is where we're safe, that's what he always told us. And Mother won't leave the place he made for us, not on her life. This home here with us is all she has left."

"I know, but what would the rest of the world say if they knew we were out here? They'd think us insane for believing we can make it." Letty licked water from her lips. "It's no wonder Lunesta left."

"Lunesta left because of us, not the house," Majest noted. "And I'm sure she joined one of the villages far away from here—Alida, maybe, or Affinia."

"Let's just hope she finds peace," Letty said, almost too quiet to hear. "She didn't belong here, not where she felt so out of place."

"She was still our sister," Majest reminded her darkly, though he remembered Lunesta's snowy skin and angular features, a stark constrast to the bright eyes and freckle-brushed smiles of her siblings. Lunesta had always been a contrast.

"I just wish she would have believed in us a little more." Letty's brow furrowed as she frowned into her cup of water, which rippled as if someone had dropped a pebble into it. She continued to drink with a strange hunger until there was nothing left, turning to her brother with tired eyes upon completion.

"Alright, that's enough of this," said Majest. "Come on. We both need sleep." Majest could see the limp movements of Letty's face and suspected his own features were a mirror image.

Before his sister could protest, a yawn erupted from her mouth, distorting whatever she was going to say into gibberish. Her eyebrows crinkled with another frown and she shook her head, drowsy. "Still...not tired."

"That's the biggest lie I've ever heard." Majest took his sister's hand, setting her cup on a nearby table and guiding her into the hallway.

Letty let herself be dragged along, the ragged hem of her cotton nightgown coiling around her ankles, teasing her feet and daring her not to fall. But she would grow into it in less than a year. She was growing fast.

As the siblings made their way to Letty's room, Majest's ears picked up the sudden hint of a noise, just out of reach. Something subdued, barely audible, and coming from outside. Something that wasn't the noise of his mother's boots scuffing against the wooden porch.

He shook it off absently all the same; there were all sorts of creatures running rampant in the night, leaving pattered prints across the snow banks under the secrecy of the moon, and he had long since learned not to let himself be bothered by them. Especially when these days, a strange noise never held the possibility of being Dagur, on his way home. And so Majest kept pulling Letty gently down the hall, their feet stumbling around the uneven wooden boards, past their parents' empty bedroom, past Lunesta's empty bedroom; every room was empty.

Then he froze. The sound was growing louder, and it didn't sound like any creature he knew—it was higher, alien, like a voice caught beneath a pane of glass, but too sharp to be quite human. "Do you hear that?" he whispered at Letty, lifting tired eyelids to widen his eyes, blinking in the dark.

"Hear what?" asked Letty sleepily.

Majest shook his head as the muffled noise came again, growing louder until he could hear it thumping like the heartbeat under his nightshirt. It sounded like someone running, charging, swinging in from a distance—

Majest motioned for Letty to stay where she was and crouched low on his knees, all his senses pricked and alert as his father had taught him. He put a hand to the knife in his belt, staring down the faceless darkness outside his window.

Letty must have heard the noise now too, because she was backing toward her room, eyes wide and blue in the dim light. "Is someone else out there, you think?" She paused, and Majest watched her try hard not to tremble. "We should warn Mother."

But before Majest could construct any sort of plan for managing a stranger at their door, a violet flash cut across the forest, illuminating the Skylarks for a brief second through their two small windows. What followed was a scream that reminded Majest of the kinds of joyous cries he had once often heard muffled by the door, when Maxine first saw Dagur returning over the snowy ground.

But there was no chance this was Dagur, and this was nothing of joy.

The candle that had been lit on the table flew out with a spark, smoke tendrils hissing in terrified protest as they vanished into the pitch-black air.

Letty bit back an exclamation of shock and panic; Majest heard her tripping over her nightgown and falling backward, panting, terrified, suspending herself up against the wall.

Majest's eyes went wide, and though his conscience was beginning to scream at him to stay inside, he leapt for the front door, pulling on his jacket as he went, heartbeat humming, hand shaking against the cold handle. When the stillness of the night struck his bare face and hands, it only took a step or two before he could distinguish the source of the sounds and the source of his throbbing heartbeat.

Another scream split the gloom, screeching the world to a halt.

Maxine was dangling in midair as if the darkness held her in place, arms seemingly bound behind her waist with invisible rope, feet kicking at the empty air. The ends of her nightgown swished furiously, waves under moonlight's tidal spell, and her face was alight with irate terror.

"Put me down," she howled, and Majest had never heard anything from his mother like the guttural cry that ripped out from her chest just then, all the ferocity of a mother bear but no power to fight; her suspension above ground held her somehow—impossibly—hostage.

"Where are the *children?"* A voice responded from a new position in the dark, high and piercing as an eagle's cry, and for a long moment, Majest could not see where the words were coming from, could only feel them in his blood as they ran it cold.

Maxine's face whipped to something below her, and then they appeared—two identical figures, long and lean as shadows, wearing dark brown uniforms and sickening yellow-white grins.

They were women, Majest could tell, but they somehow did not look human at all, from the curve of their cat's eyes, the violet aura about the fall of their long, stringy hair, the way they stared up at his mother as if she were merely a piece of meat to toy with and prod at before discarding into the forest's white fluff.

They were something from a nightmare, and Majest pinched his arm as his breath all but ceased to rattle in his chest. The women did not fade away as dreams did, but instead, grew more vivid as Majest's eyes adjusted to the night. His eyes were not wide enough to capture the scope of what was before him.

One of them held up a hand, and he could see it glowing faintly—it was pointed at Maxine, fingers splayed, nails curling. Holding her in place.

Magic? Majest's throat swelled.

"You're mistaken, like I told you the first time," Maxine spat, and her hair flying out around her had all the whipping redness of an open flame. "There are no children here for you."

There was a high, tinkling laugh, and it took Majest a moment to realize it was coming from the open mouth of one of the strangers. "But yet," it chimed, "we are here for the children. To rid the land of them."

That struck Majest out of his bewildered, horrified stupor, and at once, he leapt from the doorway, terror making his thoughts run in circles. Whatever was here, it was here for him, here for Letty. He had heard from his parents stories of rogue travelers raiding houses for food and treasures and children—but always to make servants of them, never to kill.

There was not a second to waste on deliberation or process; every thought was whittled away beneath the crushing punch of the moment, and Majest's heartbeat clung to the insides of his ears as he ran; the trees swayed before him, sky closed in on his head. Everything pounded.

Before the strangers had more than a few seconds to realize Majest's form barreling toward them, he had dug into his mind as if it were nothing more than muddy earth, drawing his element into his fingertips with a rapid but messy ease.

Rocks from the ground snapped up into the air around his hands, and he hurtled them like arrows from a bow in the direction of the women as he ran, screaming, *"Drop her!"* He could hear Letty at his side, tripping over her nightgown, could practically *feel* her tears and the stamping beat of her heart.

Two white faces snapped to Majest with expressions sewn of delight, and they sidestepped his stony assault with a quick, snakelike slither, with all the simplicity of a twitch, of a yawn or blinking eye. Their heads tilted, gazes petrifying.

"Majest and Aletta Skylark," came a voice, and Majest could not tell which woman it came from, or if they were speaking in piercing unison. "There you are."

Majest gritted his teeth and tried not to tremble, tried to instead dig deeper into his power, let it claw up the earth so that he might be able to defend his family with everything he was. There was still no focus to the walls of his mind, only blood-red panic; he could only process the night suffocating each breath, his mother's boots swinging in front of him, the earth beneath his fingertips—

And then there was Letty, her slim fingers and sharp nails grabbing at his sleeve hard enough to tear, screaming something his ears refused to make out. He understood she was trying to pull him back, away from the danger, but the world wouldn't stop rocking back and forth, and Majest rushed forward anyhow, his sister ripping from his arm with a cry.

The two women were motionless as Majest approached, just watching him through eyes of hard amber. They let him come, and they too were swirling and warping through the tunnel of Majest's vision.

"Stop," Maxine was calling from somewhere above, hands out, pleadingly, and somewhere in the chaos, her eyes found Majest's, mirrors of green meeting their match, and her voice had all the wheeze of a choked animal. "Majest, they—they *know what you are—"*

Those were the last words Majest heard before one of the women hissed and snapped her crackling lightning fingers, and his mother's voice flew from her lungs.

Her body suddenly thrashed through the air like a star scooped out of the night sky, and it hurtled into the side of the house with a somber, blind desperation that was over so quickly, Majest was half convinced he had blinked at the wrong moment, and a comet had streaked before his eyes instead—an explosion of power, a long red tangled tail.

Then he heard the crunch. The snap.

The scream.

Letty was running for the crumpled figure on the ground before it had even fallen still, the darkness unable to hold her in place. She seemed entirely unaware of the sounds that ripped straight from her chest, sobbing and tripping over imaginary twists in the ground.

Numbly Majest blinked into the air, the space his mother had been occupying, and the two ever-coiling figures grinning out from below it. He tried to remember what Dagur had told him about fighting. He tried to shout a warning to Letty. He tried to see his mother still floating before him, hear her warning voice, but the night drowned it out with its reek of death.

He fought the sudden, overbearing urge to throw up. His heartbeat commanded his body, pinned him to his own fear and inability to understand, and though he was watching Letty in an almost fetal position bent over their mother's corpse, feeling the sudden, puma-like crawl of the two strangers toward him, there was nothing but the beats and pounds inside him, pinching his processes shut, locking his legs together.

The mirrored women were raising their hands again, and Majest was dimly aware of their power, the chromatic zaps of the sparks on their fingers—he knew if he did not find a way to tear his feet from their roots and run, these intruders and their unknown purpose would have him.

And still, though his brain screamed with desperation to *do something*, his powers beating at the doors under his skull until they were concave with dents, he could not move. His peripheral vision locked on the slick red curls against the snow-and-mud insulation of the house. Each of his heartbeats seemed to ring out endlessly.

But when the women thrust their hands forward, the sparks

stuttered and died at the clawed ends of their fingernails. Their magic, somehow, was gone.

They looked at each other in a vortex of horror Majest could hardly squint to see. It was as if they had hidden under this thick veil of power, the violet sparks that commanded death, and without it, there was something naked and helpless as a child. They seemed to recoil from within themselves all at once, and they suddenly looked human, wretchedly human and deceitfully girlish. Their faces gasped and growled; their legs churned.

"Chami," one of them hissed, like they were speaking a foreign language. "Fall back!"

They disappeared all at once.

For a long moment, Majest tried to watch them go, watch their gliding marriage with the distant trees, but his head was still so heavy and horror-struck, he could hardly tell what was forest and what was just the asphyxiation of the night. All he could think was "why—*why?*"

The strangers were gone. Any hope at discovering their motive was gone. And Maxine, still as youthful and beautiful as she had been years ago when she had given her life and name to the children she'd sworn to protect, lay on the frozen ground, cold and gone just the same. One could have assumed she was sleeping if not for the dried blood that pooled persistently around her lithe, frail form and froze into scarlet crystals around her.

In the distance, Letty was still sobbing, and Majest could almost sense the tears staining the dress her mother had worn to sleep, a pale pink gown Majest had traveled southeast to the market to buy her. It was ruined now, streaked with blood and mud and little-girl tears.

And still, Majest didn't know *why.*

He stood there in this desolate, abysmal silence of unadulterated terror, until life suspended around him, and everything began to hang as if string held the landscape and not gravity. Majest began to sense the same feeling of floating he had known standing atop the nothingness of Komi's godly realm.

Then suddenly, the stars were all there literally inside his head, the infinitude of dazzling pinpricks, and they seemed to give the world some clarity.

It seemed perfectly natural among this cluster of impossible events when Komi began to speak, as if he had been there all along, not in body but in a voice as clear as water on a windless day, no rippling breeze or clamoring forest to disrupt him. Majest didn't know if Letty, sprawled several paces in front of him, was hearing this, but it flooded his ears in a gush.

"The other gods do not permit me to do this, but in light of your absent Protector, I have temporarily depleted the abilities of the Psychics in order to allow you the time to escape. There is not much time, Majest. They will hide away to recharge, but they will return, with you at their mercy."

Majest wanted to process this numinous voice he hadn't heard in over two years, now booming down from the heavens, wanted to scream and demand to know *what was going on,* but he couldn't speak; he did not belong to the clarity Komi projected.

Thankfully, the god—whether he was a hallucination or not—seemed to read his mind. *"They are proof of the evil that comes from your gifts, the kind that always festers, the darkness to fight out. And you are not yet ready for it. At costs of my own, I give you this time. Use it."*

Majest heard the words a thousand times echoed.

Our mother, he managed to think. She was saying something. Before—before the crunch.

"They know what you are."

What we are. Komi. Powers—*powers.*

This was about their powers. Those women—those catlike, bloodthirsty women—had somehow discovered them, and had killed their mother, and were coming for them. And Komi's bodiless voice had known, as if it had been prophesized.

And he had warned them. To escape.

Reality snapped back together, and Komi's voice was gone, and suddenly, Majest could see the trees again, hear his sister crying, feel the weight of loss limp and dead as it pulled his heart to its knees.

"What am I supposed to do now?" Majest whispered, half to himself.

But he knew, of course he knew. It was as clear as the empty house behind him, as Komi's impossible words lost in the folds of his mind, as the time he could only measure in the sick beat of his heart that never stopped ticking.

Time—use it.

"We have to go, don't we?" Majest could hardly hear his own voice over the swelling roar of all that lay before him. He almost felt himself beginning to cry, hearing the creak in his voice like a tree moaning in its fall. It was as if something had been sleeping inside him since his father died and Lunesta vanished, something dark and tearful and full of a silent, fearing hope, something terrified of a future with any further heartbreak and unwilling to open its eyes and face it as it blundered forward.

Majest blinked, and his eyes were dry. Only he and Letty and their powers were left. Only the flight was left. And they would have to wake up now.

Seti was running. He wasn't used to it—he hadn't needed to run this fast in many long years. Unable to age for centuries of childlike presence, years for him were both an incredibly short and an impossibly long span of time.

But that was the effect of Heaven and Hell's energy; over time, it halted the aging process, gave birth to immortality. And Seti had been purposefully stuffed so full of it when he was only a boy, he hadn't grown an inch or a year since Queen Victoria had taken the throne of England.

He tried not to pant as he ran—not only would that give away his presence, but it was a sign of tiredness, of weakness, and that was the last impression he wanted stamped to his name.

Still, despite his adolescent size and growing fatigue, Seti was fast. His slim, lithe legs moved through the undergrowth with surprising agility; his sleek black hair flew out like oil spilled behind him as he dodged the rocks and trees that made up the northwest forest—known to most as the Frozen Roots for the way the trees seemed to grow into the ice beneath a few thin layers of rocky ground.

Unlike most of the newborn, frozen population, Seti had been around during The End, when the gods and demons had stampeded across the lesser-inhabited countrysides, trailing their supernatural dust in the wake of their bloodshed, like ashes, like fallout. It was that dust, coating tundras—coating deserts and forests and long-fallen cities—breathed in and digested and passed down through generations for decades stacked together—that infected the human body like a parasite worming its way through skin, burrowing and building up in the system until mortality shut down altogether in favor of a "godlike" freezing of age and speed, of growth and recovery—or perhaps a "demonlike" resilience instead. It was all the same, in the end, a mingling of the two, of the dust.

Seti thought it rather ironic that after nearly three centuries, the rest of the world had finally caught up to his curse, but instead of holding their ageless bodies hostage, it seemed to push them forward.

Running the way he was, Seti knew he must have been an odd sight—a tiny boy tearing through the forest without more than a black tailcoat and pants to keep him warm in the freezing climate. It would have had to cost a fortune in resources to even purchase an outfit of such high class, and his was fitted to him in such a way so that as he moved, it moved with him—like an inky shell.

On normal days, Seti had no problem fitting in, hiding. He was small and normal-looking—angular features and Cognito-black hair, Cognito-milky skin. Even his name was ordinary. He hadn't been born with it, but he'd changed it so many times to fit the times that it hardly mattered anymore.

But today, blending in was the last thing on Seti's mind. He had to get away, and that meant taking his best clothes and a sack of food, praying it would be enough to carry him out of the trees.

"I'm running out of time," Seti hissed to himself, the used breath billowing out in front of him in a cloud of icy mist. He let out a bitter snort. "The one thing I thought I had too much of. And now there isn't nearly enough. Now they're onto me."

Behind him chased two shadowy figures dressed in thick brown uniforms, violet sparks flying off their fingers like malfunctioning electricity. In the breast pocket of each of their uniform jackets was engraved a black, swirling shape that twisted as they ran, teeth bared like two lionesses after a gazelle.

"You can't get away, Seti," one of them called. It was a high, female voice; the woman it belonged to was in no mood for games. "The Organization needs you. *We* need you. We need you to track and destroy the Powers; they've taken us by surprise, and by the time our magic returns to its fullest, they will be long gone."

Seti knew who they were talking about. He knew because he'd heard the whispering, spread through the villages like wildfire. The gossip, words from the mouth of a stranger with a bitter tongue. Stories of gods, of magic and treachery. Of power and danger.

Seti, of course, believed all the stories. There were many facets to a woman he had tried to forget, but he still remembered her growled tale of the spirit worlds—how gods would leave their footprints like tooth marks in the hearts of children and brew wars powerful enough to strip the earth to its core. He had seen it for himself, what kind of chaos it brought about. He'd presumed the gods didn't interfere anymore, that they had learned their lesson, but out of new village rumors arose suspicions that an old mistake was being made in attempt to reverse this land's icy destruction.

Fervently, Seti hoped it wasn't true, that this was merely a misunderstanding. The gods' experiments never played out so long as the world's fate lay in human hands. Jealousy and spite could move mountains, and this shiny newborn Organization would be the first to try.

"I told you, I have no time to get involved in something like this," Seti shouted back, becoming impatient as his stamina dwindled. His strides were growing shorter, his breath coming in gasps as he struggled to maintain composure. "If you want a little worker bee, you can search elsewhere instead of chasing me through the woods. I have no quarrel with this family."

"It's not just *those two*," the other voice responded. It had a brighter tone, high and shrill. "It'll be everyone who has the gifts. To create an equal world and build back the past as the President designed, we need to raze them all. We're only starting with the children because they're such easy targets, but we need someone who's good at sneaking around to find them. You're good at sneaking around."

"That doesn't mean I want to help you any more than I did a second ago," Seti called, coughing as cold air began to settle in his lungs. "Just because we're all older than this new world and capable of tracking each other down, Chami, Shayming—" He broke off, wheezing. "Doesn't mean—"

The twins exchanged an amused glance, green-gold cat's eyes glowing. The lighter voice's owner, Chami, was the one to reply. "You know who we are," she said in delight, not at all out of breath from the run.

"Everyone like us knows about everyone else like us," Seti snapped, catching his breath. "Don't play dumb; if you didn't know who I was, you wouldn't have been able to track me."

"True," Shayming agreed. "We know about you, and I suppose it's no surprise you know about us. And now that we're working under a new master, we're obligated to bring back the best possible candidate to wipe out this elemental nonsense and begin the restoration of the land. We know about your skills, your cunning, and the way you won't let emotion get in the way of what you do—so we picked you."

"Shay's right," Chami said, and Seti didn't need to turn around to know she was smiling, yellow and beaming like light through a musty window as she plowed through snow and dirt with knee-high boots, relentless and tireless. "You're the one. And you know what we'll do to you if you refuse."

"Don't you find it a little odd that your Organization is dedicated to destroying those who possess powers, but yet the gifts you two have are overlooked because you joined the cause? You're nothing but hypocritical cowards, aren't you?" Seti was tiring now, panting as he lurched desperately onward.

"My, my, I don't think he quite remembers the full extent of what we can do!" Shayming put on a burst of speed and flung herself in Seti's path, cutting him off with a glittering, malevolent grin. Seti hissed in frustration, trying to dart to the side, but Shayming mirrored his every move like a shadow, moving in an unnatural electric blur.

As Seti stood still, trapped like a fly in a web, Chami snatched him from behind, one hand on his shoulder and the other to her forehead. She breathed in deeply; Seti shivered as he felt a current of thoughts sucking straight out of his mind, traveling into the eyes of the women who held him tight in her claws.

"I thought—your magic was depleted," Seti choked out.

The twins grinned. "I thought we said it was on its way back," Shayming crowed, and Chami's fingers dug into Seti's scalp harder until his tongue went numb and rigid.

"As usual, his mind is impressive," Chami reported to her sister, who had—without laying a hand on Seti—pinned him against a tree where he slumped, head bowed as though praying to the gods for help, face contorted into painful gasps as he tried to retrieve his breath. "He's thinking of nothing but the escape. No emotional ties to anything or anyone."

"It's calming to absorb," Shayming agreed, gazing at Seti with an almost fondness. "He'll do great."

"Psychics," Seti managed to spit in a hoarse voice, not lifting his head. "Witches. You say the Powers are freaks of nature, and yet here you stand, creating an army of despicable supernaturals like you and I. You have no right to lay your claim to this cause."

"You're not despicable, Seti," Shayming said in a soothing tone. "Just rather…unfortunate."

"Don't try to tell me who I am," Seti growled. "You are the filthiest kind of people, you sick, twisted—"

Chami raised the hand that had been on Seti's shoulder, curling her fingers into a half-fist. Light glowed off her palms and lit the fire in her eyes. "I'm so very sorry to do this to you, Seti, but you have to learn some manners." Moving slowly, she made a gesture that might have simply been a flick of the wrist if it hadn't been for the scream of agony Seti let out in response.

The twins watched with acidic satisfaction as the boy slid down the trunk of the white pine tree to the ground, eyes closed and twitching, sweat running down his forehead. He let out a small cry of anguish. Seti, who never let anyone know when he was in pain.

"You can't defy the Organization," Chami said, icy calm encompassing the words. She ignored Seti's wounded panting and the look of pure, excruciating malice he shot her. "The Powers might be strong, but our power is stronger. And you, Seti, have no power at all without our aid."

"I'd—" Seti coughed, chest heaving as he regained what amount of strength his body could muster. "I'd rather be dead," he rasped.

"That's exactly what you will become if you don't align with the correct side," Shayming snarled into his ear, her breath reeking strongly of metal. "Your choice, Seti: you either join the Organization, do as we say, and *live*; or you refuse our offer and end up a carcass floating down a nearby river."

Chami held up a still-glowing hand as ratification.

Seti knew he was defeated, but it still hurt as he bit his lip and rasped, "With the utmost hatred, I impolitely accept your offer."

An explosion of colors greeted the Skylark siblings as they returned the next morning to the spot of their mother's murder. A normal sunrise in Cognito was an almost-blue sky, tinged by the yellows and oranges of simmering light, but today it seemed even the clouds were mourning for Majest and Letty's loss. They were a deep, dark red mingling with purples and bruised violet-blues, dappled with the occasional bloody scarlet of a sun that would appear for only meager hours before sinking beneath layers of frozen cloud cover once more.

Majest hoisted a wooden shovel over his head and swung it for the umpteenth at the icy ground, grunting with effort as the rusty blade hit the earth and filled the shovel with crumbling dirt, which he tossed into an almost-filled hole.

He proceeded to do this again and again, grit flying out and turning his hair a dark, mucky brown. The permanent brushstrokes of green in his locks were damp with sweat and hung lankly over his forehead, giving his hair the illusion of dying autumn leaves, crumpled with rain and inevitable winter.

As he worked, Letty came out to him carrying a bowl of lemming soup, which she placed on the stump of a nearby tree. "Majest Skylark," she said, and his full name on her tongue let Majest know she was serious. As if the circumstances allowed her to be anything else. "You can't stay out here all morning without eating anything."

"If I'm going to fill this grave, I'll fill it right," Majest grumbled in reply. "I owe our mother that much, at least." Another whack at the ground; dirt flew. He left out the part about how the rhythmic pound of the shovel took away the sound of a body breaking like a branch against the cottage side. "Besides, we need as much food as we can for when we set out this morning."

"This morning?"

Majest paused in his work, and bit back traces of last night on his tongue. "Yes, this morning. We can't waste any time. They know where we live; we can't stay here a moment longer than we have to."

Letty picked up the bowl of soup again and passed it between her hands, absorbing its warmth before it ran cold with the outside air. She hadn't shed a tear all morning, just shook instead, like the rain was internal now. "I know, it's just…" A sigh. "It feels wrong. To leave them."

Majest squinted through the sunlight at her. "Well, you were always the one saying you wished we lived somewhere else. Besides, you can't leave someone who's already gone."

Letty's lip trembled, and something poignant and hurt flashed in her eyes like muddy water, but she said nothing.

"Staying here means we end up dead. That's what Komi told me." Majest continued, pretended he hadn't noticed the look on her face, cringed at how insensitive his words were ringing out. He had to let his mind and voice run away from bittersweet memories and this stoic house of wood, or he would collapse in this grave along with them. "I'll be done in a minute, and then we finish our bags and set out, just like I told you. In fact…" He surveyed his work. "I think that's as much ground as I can mess up before I start being an ecological hazard."

He wiped dirt and sweat off his forehead with one hand, staring with grimness at the ruffled patch of earth that could not even begin to express the body that lay beneath it, that would always lay beneath it, in grit and solitude. He felt guilty, beyond guilty, but better this corpse rest alone than with two more small bodies on the pile.

Letty took a few steps toward him and stared, waiting. Her eyes were still sad, but she still did not cry. She seemed to forgive him his practicality, because she could see what was beneath.

Majest felt a slight pain in his chest as he looked at her, feeling her eyes graze his insides. "Well, come on," he managed. "Let's get our things."

The two of them went back inside the house, leaving dirty footprints on the old wooden floors as they made their way down the hall, seeing the lived-in marks over the walls, the scuffing in between the cracks of the ceiling. Letty's bedroom was closest, the first door to the right. She always kept her room neat and simple because she didn't spend much time in it.

After opening the door, they surveyed the familiar, cozy space. Much like the rest of the handmade house, Letty's room was wooden, walls of clean-cut cedar. The blankets on her bed were a thick seal fur that had been a gift from an elderly, passing hunter, and an elk-skin rug sprawled loosely over the floor. A few collectibles—mostly stones and owl feathers—were on a small table in the corner of the floor, and two small piles of meticulously-sorted winter clothing were packed against the bare walls. That was all.

"You have far too many belongings," Majest said lightly. "How are we ever going to be able to take them all with us?"

Letty, clearly in no mood to be livened by a joke, knelt on the floor, gathering her clothes into her arms and placing them on her bed. Along with the garments, she took the rocks and feathers she'd collected and put them in a tiny leather sack her mother had sewn when resources had been plentiful. She gathered her blanket around the pile, hoisting it over her shoulder.

"That's everything?" Majest watched her closely.

With a frown, Letty glanced over her empty room. She looked as if she needed a moment alone.

"I'll be right back." Majest patted his sister on the shoulder and left her to her thoughts, crossing the hallway to his own room. It was much less organized than his sister's, and he had to kick aside several sketches on the floor to give himself space to stand. Grabbing at the hooks behind his door, Majest shrugged on his fur coat, a pair of rabbit-skin gloves, lined boots—the most valuable pair he owned—and lastly, he took his slingshot.

Majest picked up his familiar weapon with a touch of wistful fondness, marred by the panic and grief he was suppressing. He had other options for this journey: a handmade bow and arrows from the market; a dull stone blade used for cutting up meat; a tiny knife he usually kept in his pocket or shoe—but none of them fit against his hand like they were made out of home itself.

It wasn't the finest weapon, his slingshot—carved by an adolescent, the shape wasn't perfect; the wood wasn't uniform, as though it hadn't grown into itself, and the leather in the center wasn't correctly cut and tied. Still, Majest had made it himself. It was his, and he could use it.

Majest tucked the slingshot into one of his belt loops and walked back into Letty's room, carrying nothing but a parcel of food and water he'd laid out earlier that morning. His drawings, he suspected, would always litter the floor, proof of what had once been. He would not dare disturb them.

Letty was still sitting on her own floor; she looked up when he entered and made an attempt to smile, which was rather valiant on her part, Majest thought.

"Surely you want to take more than that?" Her voice sounded smaller than usual, and tight, as if she had been holding back tears.

"I have everything I need," said Majest, shuffling his food bag onto one shoulder. "It would be unwise to take more than we could carry. Are you ready to go?"

"I think so," said Letty. "Are we leaving right now?" She wiped at her eyes with the back of her hand before picking up her sack of belongings. This time she did not sound protesting, as her home was between her arms now, like a backwards turtle shell.

"I don't see why not." Majest helped his sister to her feet. "We should probably get as much distance as we can before nightfall."

"And where exactly are we going?" Letty pulled a thick fur jacket over her arms. It enveloped her like a blanket, sheltering her thin frame with the skin and strength of wolves.

"Anywhere but here," Majest decided. "I say we head east, toward the Bay. That's only a few weeks' walk. It'll be much easier to hide near the water. What did Mother used to say the place was called? Hunter's Bay?"

"Hudson," Letty corrected, eyebrows sagging at their mother's mention. "The Hudson Bay. And yes, that would be a good place to start. We'd have water and food there, no doubt."

"We'll go there, then."

And just like that, the future was mapped. As though they weren't deciding the direction their lives might never reverse from. As though they were merely setting off on an adventure, not fleeing from a nameless enemy with an anonymous cause. As though it were as simple as the east, the sunrise, the day cracking open and shining a light ahead.

Majest and Letty walked to the front of their house, their feet leaving empty, hollow creaking sounds where they treaded. The house had a different disposition to it now, a darker impression edged with fear. It wasn't home anymore, with each step from it they took. Nothing and no one was left inside it that might make it so.

"Ready?" Majest asked as they reached the door. Pushing aside memories of the last time he'd turned the knob, the yellow grins and the darkness, he pulled the wooden gateway open and was met with a chilly winter afternoon like any other, brimming with a flurried, frozen absolution.

His sister nodded, face tight, biting her lip as she spared a glance to the house, its slanted boards and snow-crusted roof. Icicles dripped from the overhang above the door, like tears of goodbye. Letty's expression gave away nothing. They were pretending.

Majest too looked back at the wooden form behind them for a moment, though he quickly turned his gaze forward, eyes numb. It was already beginning to look like a stranger's house, just a fleeting moment of a journey. He was done seeing it, and done feeling the loss that came with it.

And so they began to walk from that tiny house and their mother's grave, nestled tightly in the forest like a cottage from a children's story.

The page turned.

V. FALL

"Are you sure we're still going east?" fretted Letty, a cloud of red-brown hair forming and precipitating around her face in the harsh wind. "I can't see *anything*, and I'm freezing."

"I have an internal compass, Letty," Majest assured her, squinting to see past the snow. "Father did manage to shake *something* into my brain. We haven't gone anything but due east since we left the house."

A storm had blown in after they'd set out in the direction of the Hudson Bay. It wasn't much compared to the earth-shaking blizzards they'd seen in the past, but it was enough to throw a few darts of doubt into their minds and hold them suspended there. Luckily, it at least hid the footprints that trailed from their cottage—as though the storm had been the gods' gift itself.

"It's a shame you didn't buy that *real* compass you saw at the market a while back," Letty mused. "Then we'd know for certain we aren't getting lost."

"They wanted an entire wolf-skin for it," Majest reminded his sister, steadying her before she could trip over a rock buried under the snow. "I've never even *seen* a wolf before."

"But we've heard them, you know." Letty started forward again on wobbly feet, unused to being outside in this kind of weather. She struggled to keep up with her brother, for whom snow and the whipping trees were second nature. "The wolves. We used to sit in the kitchen and listen to them howl." A wistful smile played on her lips.

Majest bit his lip and said nothing.

69

They trudged onward; the snow grew heavier as it struck down from the sky, more pressured and persistent. Icy gusts pummeled at them from the right, and somehow, the wind that usually ran west to east had managed to manipulate itself until the gusts were arriving straight from the south—warmer, but no less severe.

Majest and Letty walked in silence for a while, the sounds of their boots disappearing under the howling—wind, not wolves—and the swirling snowflakes Letty would have once sat inside to watch.

"This is getting messy," said Letty after a while, raising her voice to be heard. "Should we start looking for some sort of shelter before it gets dark? Do we still have daylight?"

Majest turned his gaze to the sky, shielding his eyes from the snow as he tried to judge the location of the sun. It was nearly winter, and the days were losing light, no matter how they clung to their lucid yellow guide. "It will start to get dark soon," he decided. "We left around the middle of the day, when the sun was straight up in the sky, and we've been traveling all afternoon."

"So you don't know for certain?"

Majest blew out a deep breath through his nose. "If we keep traveling and it gets too dark, we won't be able to see the ground. There's a drop-off somewhere around here, and I don't want us falling into it." He frowned. His father had taught him how to tell by the sun what hour of the day it was, but he faltered on his own without proper supervision, especially on such a stormy day.

Letty's face grew solemn, like she could follow her brother's thoughts. "It would be easier if we had Father to tell us how much time had gone by since we left," she said. "Or Mother—she was good at following her gut."

Majest stopped in his tracks. "Letty, you've got to stop doing that," he said.

Letty's eyes widened. "Doing what?"

Majest started walking again. "Feeling sorry for yourself. Wishing our parents were here. It's not helping anyone grieving for Mother and Father when we have ourselves to worry about now. We've got to keep moving."

Letty flinched back at her brother's words as if he had struck her. "How can you *say* that? Our mother died *yesterday,* less than one turn of the sun ago, and already you're so willing to pack up and leave her behind, too? Like she's just the shell of our empty house, and we can strip what's ours and walk away? We're orphans now, do you get that? Just because no one lives for long inside this wilderness doesn't make it *okay.*"

Majest felt a stinging pain slice at his heart, like a paper cut. In his mind, he saw his parents at the table over dinner, and they were laughing, deep rolls from beneath their chests, and Majest was sitting and watching and feeling the deepest form of love, and it was right in front of him—and now it was behind him. "Letty, I'm sorry," he said quickly. "That's not...I'm sorry."

Letty kept walking; Majest could almost feel the fury rising from the back of her mind in snakelike smoke tendrils as she marched through the small blizzard, boots crunching in the snow.

Majest ran to catch up, grasping his sister's shoulders in his hands the way he always did when he was trying to comfort her. "*Letty.* Stop."

Letty, eyes alight with resentment, whipped her head to the side, not looking at him. "No, *you* stop, Majest Skylark. Our parents taught us everything. They taught us to hold our roots in the ground and refuse to budge for anyone—and now look what we're doing! We're trudging through the unknown—away from everything we love—to get away from people who might not even want to kill us." As she spoke, her eyes began to water with the wind, as if she were beginning to cry, but Majest knew her better than that.

"They *do* want to kill us," Majest told her, his voice firm. "I *know* that, Lets."

"Right, because you hear the gods in your ears and I don't."

Majest bunched his fists together in his gloves, and the leather pulled taught. "Letty, we have to do this, for Mother and Father's sake as much as anyone. They'd want our safety, and this is our safest option. If we get away fast enough, the blizzard will cover our footprints and we'll be untraceable." He tried his best to meet his sister's gaze, but she wouldn't have it. "I thought you were okay with leaving!"

"I was," said Letty. "I thought we could do it. But look at us!" She threw up her gloved hands in a gesture of frustration. "We're children! We're not getting anywhere, and now we're going to freeze after half a day of blundering. The Bay is weeks away, and I don't know what we're going to do when we get there. No one will be around to help us. We'll be alone and helpless, even more vulnerable to anyone who wants to hurt us. Who's to say they aren't following us now, keeping pace with us?" Her face was contorted, cheeks flushed with cold fury. "I'm going home."

Letty tore her face from Majest's grasp and began running back the way they'd came, snow flying as she tore through it, unsteady but not falling. Majest stood staring after her in surprise for a moment before he leapt after her, supply bags whipping behind him, slowing his journey.

"Letty!" he called desperately, but her head start had made her a mere speck among worlds of white, making it impossible to find her fleeing form through the blizzard. "Letty, come back! You don't know the way! *Letty!*"

But she was gone.

Seti was dragged, blinded and gagged, through echoing hallways that vibrated with strange, blaring sounds, like that of an old-world emergency. Under any normal circumstances, he would have been listening for information to aid him in designing an escape, but these were not normal circumstances.

Once Chami and Shayming had used their psychic talents to transport him to what he presumed were the Organization headquarters, Seti was thrusted into the hands of two strangers who worked there, one male and one female.

Seti didn't pay much mind to the male worker—he was gruff and silent, and used fewer words and more force, a clear personality type that made Seti's nose wrinkle. The man grunted as he walked, one of Seti's arms in his firm, unbreakable grip. His feet made loud clanking noises on the floor as though either his shoes or the floor itself were made of something hard and metallic.

The girl—Seti presumed she was still a girl and not yet a woman—was more interesting. He could tell she wasn't much taller than him, which was atypical, and when she spoke to him, it was with the breathy tones of someone not yet sure of whom she was.

"Just a little longer," she told Seti, her breath tingling in his ear. "And I promise she won't hurt you as long as you do what she says."

Seti, unable to talk with the dry, foul-smelling rag in his mouth, said nothing.

The Organization duo continued to walk in silence, Seti dragging between them like a dead weight, a meaty carcass or war conquest, their feet the only audible noise to keep Seti's mind occupied from such distasteful self-images as they moved through hall after winding hall.

At last the male worker took a sharp turn to the right and halted. Seti heard a faint electronic noise, like the press of buttons on a machine, and was intrigued—he hadn't known technology still existed in these regions. He had presumed it dead as the modern world, faded into the frozen ground.

Then Seti realized he didn't know any more about the Organization than what Chami and Shayming had told him and the gossip that had been floating around Alida during his stay. *Perhaps I underestimated these people,* he thought to himself. *If they can work their way around technology and have enough resources to do it, they must have a few tricks up their sleeves.*

"I see you've brought the boy."

The harsh voice crashed Seti back into the present like a falling asteroid striking the atmosphere. The beep and buzz and *"ching-kick!"* of the machines had brought him into a new room—one holding a new presence, this new voice. A woman's. Her electric tone sounded persistently familiar, but Seti couldn't place it without a face. He could, however, place that the women it belonged to was hardly temperate or forthcoming, and probably more than ten birth-years old. It was rare for someone to continue aging once childhood had split between the eyes and shed from a face like snakeskin, but the immortalizing Heaven-and-Hell dust settled beneath between capillaries and vessels at a different age for everyone—sometimes eight, sometimes twelve, though for Seti, there would never be an age he needed more than one hand to count on his fingers.

"Lady President," said the girl who was holding Seti's arm. "Yes, we brought him. Seti Sinestre, just as you asked."

"Excellent," the woman—the President—responded. "He looks even younger than I'd heard. Precious, really." A pause. "Well, don't just stand there—untie the boy and let him speak."

Seti was relieved as hands moved across his face to take from him his blindfold and gag, allowing him the release of air and the reappearance of color for the first time in hours. He took in his surroundings with the thirst of something that had been blind and slumbering in hibernation.

He was standing in a tiny, stark-white room with no windows or furniture, save for three stout tables piled high with foreign devices that made Seti's blood run cold, and a motionless but firm plastic chair at the center where the President sat in all her malicious glory, a dark spot against a star. There was nothing else to define where Seti might have been or if there were any means of escape, so he examined the people of the room instead.

The two who'd brought him inside—the man and the girl—stood off to the right, their heads bowed in respect as if they were praising the promising marble effigy of some faraway deity who may or may not actually exist. The man was tall and muscular with close-cropped hair and beady gray eyes in a face of stone; the girl was shorter and slighter with messy butter-blond hair and animated eyes that darted about with clear apprehension. She caught Seti's gaze and gave him a tight nod.

Both the man and the girl were dressed in skin-tight white suits, engraved with the same symbol that had been sewn messily onto the twins' jackets. Seti decided the "O" stood for "Organization," which made his toes curl in his shoes. The bunch of jealous fools had no right to use such a pretentious name.

Then Seti realized everyone in the room was staring at him,

waiting for him to speak. They had placid expressions like blank canvases, white and cold and unknowing. Among these staring, calm-faced people was the President.

The President of the Organization had more expression than her workers, as if she knew of some deep-seated purpose they did not. Although she was sitting, Seti could tell she was tall, with slim legs crossed neatly in an almost bug-like manner. Her hair was long, too long and shining to be real, and her face was familiar, eyes crescent moons half-hidden, glinting with frozen light.

Seti felt his nerves stand on end. He knew immediately who this woman was.

He cleared his throat of a thin layer of bile. "Lady President," he began, his voice careful. He was beginning to put together the pieces: the Organization; the Powers; the President. They were connected by something stronger than ordinary prejudiced envy. "I understand you need someone to keep an eye on the Powers, which is why I was *brought* here." He said *"brought"* in a way that implied abduction.

The President smiled. It was not a nice smile. "Now, Seti, if that were why I sent for you, you should feel offended at the very least. There is so much *more* you can do. Your curse, after all, is one of a kind. Though you probably see it as unpleasant, forever in a child's body, I believe it is why you can do the things you can." She shook her head in some sort of incredulity. "You're truly remarkable."

Seti, instead of basking in the glow of praise, shrank back with repulsion. Only he knew the truth of the blood and dust that paved the roads of his veins. "How do you think you know so much about me?"

"I have eyes everywhere," the President told him. Seti's brow wrinkled in suspicion. "And those eyes led me to you. Now, I don't need someone *watching* the elemental Powers—or anyone else who may have received gifts, for that matter. I need someone to get rid of them. Particularly the Skylarks."

At that, the girl who had brought Seti to the room, the small one with the sunshine hair, pricked up in surprise. "But President," she said, "with all due respect, Seti's troubles aren't necessary; the twins are more than capable—"

"I have other uses for Chami and Shayming, Shatter, but Seti—Seti is a killer, aren't you?" The President's dark eyes moved from the girl—Shatter—to Seti, a small starburst of delight sparkling inside them. "And smart, too. He'll have them out of our minds in no time. Do you think you are up for the challenge, little boy?"

"Of removing the rest of the Skylarks?" Seti was doubtful, and quite offended. He had no desire to punish the innocent. It wasn't worth his time. Besides, this was exactly what the gods wanted—for their chosen ones to draw out evil and poison in the land like a magnet so that their heavenly power might stamp it out. The gods always brought demons out to play.

"Mostly the girl," the President specified. "Aletta. Majest is hardly a danger, although he is the elder. His heart is purer, I must admit, though his talents foul like the earth they're born from. That girl has some deep darkness knitted underneath her skin, something ungraspable and irremovable. A foul spark. She's dangerous. Her *powers* are dangerous, whatever they might be. She must be removed."

That, Seti thought, was the fault in godly logic—power was always dangerous. He knew next to nothing of the Skylark siblings, but he had known of others like them. Others with the potential darkness inked deep down. Darkness brought out by the gods' interference. He wondered if this time, things would be different.

He was about to ask the President how she knew so much about the Powers but yet had so much difficulty finding them, but before he could say anything, the woman pulled out a burnished, golden object from her pocket and held it out to him. Its presence hit Seti like a mouthful of black water, and for a moment, he had to remember how to breathe.

"This is for you and your journey," she said in a taut voice. Her mouth twitched. "It's a pocket watch infused with demon energy. You'll see for yourself what it can do, but for now, I order you to wear it at all times."

Seti hesitated—he could not shake the sense that this thing was more toxic than the Organization itself. It seemed to stare at him, even shelled up in its cool metal exterior. He did not want to touch it, to take it, to make it a part of himself.

"It's perfectly safe for the wearer," said Shatter from where she stood, not taking her eyes off Seti. "I promise, it won't hurt you. I was involved in its testing. But if you're not the one wearing it—" Her eyes flashed briefly with something like fear, but before Seti could consider her behavior, she was calm again. "Just make sure you wear it, like the President said."

"Thank you, Shatter." The President nodded, though Seti didn't miss the warning look she shot the trembling girl. "It will help you in your quest." She waved the hand with the watch in it, and it ticked with soft persistence. "Take it." It was not a suggestion.

Seti swallowed. He didn't trust it—but he had no choice. He knew when he was beat, or at least, outnumbered. Holding his breath, he reached out a pale hand and took the watch. It stung him with its bitter cold.

As Seti stared at the device in his hands, the President added, "This will also track where you are…so I know how you're doing." There was a knowing glint in her gaze that made her seem taller, let Seti know he could not flee. And since she and Shatter had deemed it crucial to wear the watch at all times…

Seti sighed. He was trapped like a lion in a cage. And the Organization was the ringmaster—hungry eyes and thirsty demands.

"Go, now." The President waved a hand at him. "Go get the girl."

"Letty! Letty! *Letty!*"

She could hear her brother's cries growing farther away as she stumbled on through the storm, shivering and furious, but her resolve did not waver or melt under the drizzling snow.

He doesn't understand, she thought with resentment. *He's too stubborn to see how much we still need our parents to help us. He doesn't miss them like I do because he's always had to do things his own way. He never wants help from anyone.* She shifted her coat. *Well, if he wants to go on an impossible mission, he can do it himself.*

The snow was picking up in speed like a chasing fox gaining momentum, white piles smacking down from the heavens in beating, unceremonious plops until it was no less than impossible for Letty to see more than an inch beyond her eyes. The trees and rocks, the sky, the ground—Letty couldn't find any of it.

Cold wind tugged at the corners of her eyes, pulling them back and teasing them until they watered. The wind-whipped tears froze, creating tiny, crusty icicles on Letty's eyes. She wiped at them in frustration.

As she continued walking—if it could have been considered walking and not staggering—Letty began to sense she had been rash. Instead of running off, she should have tried to convince Majest to come home with her, or to at least find someone to guide them through the wilderness to safety.

Now she was just a lost child, and she knew it.

"I'm so reckless," she whispered to herself, her voice drowning in the wind. "Reckless, reckless, reckless. And stupid, for that matter."

She wished she could turn back, find Majest. Even though she was furious with him, there was no hope for surviving without him. She didn't have food or water, or even a blanket. Majest had taken it all over his own back so she wouldn't have to carry the weight.

Majest, if *he* had been the one lost in a snowstorm with no resources, would have used his earth powers to start a fire using nothing but wood. *He* could have built a shelter in seconds, transporting trees and ground as if their weight was nothing. If any animals came about, he could use his fancy skills and weaponry to either hunt them or convince them to help—his choice.

Letty felt that stab of resentment in her stomach the way she always did when she thought of Majest's powers. No matter how hard she tried, she couldn't discover the nature of her own abilities or how to unlock them. Why couldn't Komi have just told her outright what her gift was?

I want my own power, she hissed inside her mind, and it didn't sound like her own voice.

Frustrated with everything—with herself, Majest, Komi, powers and the wilderness, Letty kicked at the ground in dejected anger, sending a conveniently-placed stone flying. She noted with a dull sort of interest that she didn't hear it hit the snowy ground again, cheated of its soft *plunk* as if it had disappeared into thin air. Preoccupied by the trivial rock, she walked forward, squinting at the ground with a search for the gray amongst the white.

And then there was no ground.

With a rush of déjà vu, Letty remembered the night she'd received her powers from Komi. She remembered the land of stars she had fallen inside of: dark, swirling, and utterly bottomless. That feeling of falling had now returned—returned to slink up from dreams and nightmares to wrap its claws around her feet and *yank*.

She tumbled down and down what must have been a cliff, arms thrashing about in uncontrolled circular gestures as she tried to regain a sense of direction. She rediscovered Earth when it struck her with a dull thud, toppling her into a snowdrift. Cold wetness filled the sleeves of her jacket and her face pressed into the ground with a painful squeezing jolt.

That's why the stone didn't hit the ground, Letty thought in a daze. *This is the drop-off Maji warned me about.*

She began to whimper, head throbbing and self-hatred rising. *Stupid, reckless, stupid.*

Although the drift had softened what would have been a fatal fall, it had still knocked the wind out of her and brought shooting stars across her vision, too fast to make a wish. She realized with a jolt of panic how close she was to losing consciousness.

With a grunt, Letty fought to stay awake, battling the suffocating blanket of pain and shock and forcing her way into a sitting position. She was lost, that much was certain, and unlikely to survive long in her condition, but as she looked around, she realized her situation was worse than she had feared.

She could tell this by the sight of the five-hundred-pound grizzly bear that was standing across the clearing, gazing at her with an intent, drained expression and not at all with sympathy, for she had just fallen straight into its winter home.

VI. PROTECTOR

There she is, thought Seti, peering out from behind the boulder he had chosen as his vantage point. *Aletta Skylark, six birth-years of age, powers unknown.*

He leaned forward on his knees, like a child eager to see a magic show. He had been searching the Northeastern woods at top speeds for hours with minimal evidence of the Skylarks. He had grown cold and irritated, even more so after discovering their family's woodland cottage stripped bare with nearly-covered footprints trailing tentative but steady to the east.

After pursuing the siblings for miles through unpleasant and snowy conditions, Seti had begun to hear their voices drifting with faintness over the land, just echoes that made the trees whisper, his sharp hearing picking the sounds up over the roar of the wind.

Aletta had been shouting at her brother when Seti had caught up to them. At his approach, silent and unseen, the little girl had run off into the storm. Seti had followed with reluctant interest, finding the eye of the storm to watch the girl's retreating figure through the blizzard.

The girl had led him back the way he'd come, and he'd had to duck behind a line of trees to avoid her furious sightline's red-hot burst of laser light. Luckily, she'd barged right past his shelter and dismissed any evidence of another windblown face in the forest, too preoccupied with her own problems to detect Seti's presence.

Seti had noticed with a touch of mild interest that she was heading straight for the side of a small cliff, an unpleasant rocky surprise invisible beneath snow and undetectable by fingers turned to numb stumps. At her speed, she would topple before she sensed the danger. Seti knew these cliffs by heart, of course—he wouldn't want an unpleasant surprise by falling off one himself.

Seti found the uncomfortable, frozen landscape rather distasteful. The wild animals, the constant dreadful weather, and the shortage of food—although the President *had* given him a sack filled with old-age bread, however she'd obtained it. It all made it impossible for him to see how anyone would want to live this far north, much less travel in it. The Skylarks were something special, if not mad.

As Seti had suspected, the little girl had hurled herself down the face of the precipice with a scream of surprise, landing with a *plop* on the other side, nothing but a baby bird fallen from its nest.

Seti had darted to the top of the ledge and behind a rock, where he sat now, tense as a mouse. Luck permitting, Aletta could end up dead without him moving a finger. And that perhaps would be for the best—there was no evidence the President had been mistaken in saying this girl held a wicked shadow over her heart that blocked the sun, and if Aletta or her brother did turn out to be the hazards the gods often fortuitously let fester, Seti might as well either kill them or let them die for themselves out here, pathetic victims to nothing more than a measly common snowfall.

Peering downward, Seti squinted against the pasty fluff pounding mercilessly in his face. He could just make out the fallen girl's silhouette as she sat up, eyes unfocused. As she stared around the valley she'd toppled into, her eyes widened and her mouth popped open into a tiny round shape.

"What's the matter?" Seti muttered as he followed her gaze. The pocket watch he had tucked in his belt pressed against his side as he leaned over the cliff's edge, its cold metal freezing into his hip bone hard enough to make him hiss. The *tick-tick* of the thing pulsed into his skin like a second heartbeat, and he loathed it.

It seemed, in fact, to tick to the beat of thudding footsteps, and Seti felt his intrigue amplify as a bear-face loomed out of the snow and the shabby brown mass attached to it moved in the direction of the little girl.

Well, that explains her reaction.

Seti and Letty both held their breath as the grizzly swayed forward like a mountain bobbing along an ocean surface, sniffing the air with a drowsy chapped nose. It must have been in the process of beginning hibernation, and a stranger on its doormat would be at the bottom of its wish list.

And so with a challenge, it stood up on its hind legs, unfurling like a great musty blanket or an ancient death-sentence scroll, beady eyes trained on the Skylark girl's face. Aletta seemed to still all at once, a frozen ice sculpture with snowflakes landing on her nose.

Seti, safe high up on the cliff's peak, watched with intent focus, and prepared to witness the blunt trauma of meaty paws, blood painting red vines up two yellowed incisors, gore and screams in the snow, the sculpture ripped and smashed and the stringy inside pieces pulled apart. The sight would be ghastly and the stench would be dreadful, but Seti had seen worse, smelled worse, and he would see worse in years to come. And if the girl died here and now, perhaps the Organization would set him free.

This is it, he thought with a new sense of excitement. *This is my way out.*

There's no way out.

The words circled Letty's head like moons in hyper-speed orbits as she backed herself up against the cliff as far as it would allow. Her head ached from the fall, but her heart pounded harder as she stared up at the beast before her.

Letty had never seen a bear before. Majest had told her stories of them; they were hulking terrors made of thick fur and endless bulk, with dull, serrated claws that tore, teeth that destroyed. They might be brown, black, or white, but Majest had always warned her that a livid grizzly was the worst of all.

And one was looking down on Letty like an angry god, eyes black and pitiless. It seemed to scoff at the puny girl before it.

The bear stalked closer, its eyes dark but glowing as it continued to eye the crouching figure who sat shivering in the snow, trying to stay still, as if she could disappear into the side of the rocky ledge. A rumbling snarl came from deep within the beast's gut, and Letty shuddered, the hairs on her arms sticking up to rub against the interior of her coat. The coat was wolf's fur, but she was no wolf inside it.

I'm going to die, she realized with numbness, blinking ice crystals from her eyes. *I'm going to die because I wouldn't listen to my brother. Stupid, stupid!*

"Maji," she said aloud, the familiar name the last comfort she could give herself. "Majest!"

Her voice rose in pitch as she spoke, holding onto some vain, losing-balance hope that her brother would hear, but the bear just leaned forward with a dismissive, callous grunt until she could see the drool glistening off its bared teeth.

Letty struggled to a standing position. She could not fight a bear; no one could. And there it stood, just lengths from her feet, unfeeling, merciless, only the instinct to kill to protect. Time halted and froze while the two looked at each other, blue eyes and beady black and one weighted moment.

They began running at the same time. Letty knew it would not be for long—what hope did she have of outrunning a grizzly bear, even one heading into hibernation? It was already a struggle for her to make her way through snow banks as they piled like mud and quicksand around her ankles, and her head throbbed with the buzzing dizziness of her previous fall.

Seconds passed by, painful and slow and bleak, as the mammoth form tore down the valley after Letty, its massive feet pounding like war drums over the snow as if the giant drifts were nothing but dust.

Letty fled on numb feet, willing legs to move swiftly, breaths to come easy. But she was tiring after mere moments. She had taken a hard fall, and she could feel it like blood in her mouth, nails and hammers in her skull.

Summoning the last candle-flickers of energy in her blood, Letty leapt for the ground and rolled herself into a taut ball, remembering in an instant what Majest had told her about bears months ago.

"A grizzly bear is a defensive animal," he had said. *"If you ever meet one, heavens forbid, you have to show it you're not a threat. Playing dead is usually the most effective way to do that, and will keep you safest."* He had taken her by her shoulders as he always did and looked her in the eyes, for once lacking his usual good humor. *"But Letty, whatever you do, protect yourself. Use any means necessary."*

Letty's roll carried her down a sloping valley and halfway under a drift of snow, where she lay, panting and empty, hands over her face, waiting for the attack that would shut out the lights.

My only regret is not being able to say goodbye, Letty thought desperately. *Maji, I'm so sorry. I'm sorry you've lost everyone and found nothing.*

Her frantic last words were a swarm of something that flapped and crawled its way through her head, and she wished she could think of something more than a childish apology as she heard the snarl and sensed the bear's approach. Any second now.

She didn't dare open her eyes. She wanted the last thing she saw to be the blank white snow, her brother's face filling her mind. She didn't want savage claws and teeth to wash those images away in her own blood.

But the attack never came.

The snarling stopped as if a switch had been flicked. Letty heard a *thwacking* sort of sound from the edge of her hearing, and after that, there were no more footsteps or growls or labored breathing; silence reigned except for the pound of her blood. Still pumping, still flowing.

This made Letty curious. She opened her eyes with caution, heart stuttering.

Like a ghost, another girl had appeared, brandishing a large silver blade the length of Letty's arm that curved and dipped like the hairline of the horizon. Her hair was one long black sheet, eyes the precise color of the nightgown Letty had worn on the night of her mother's death—eerie blue, like the untouchable sky. It had gone with her mother's pink one.

The girl, who looked the same size and age as Letty's mother, had somehow managed to jump out behind the attacking bear and leap high, plunge her knife deep into the knobs and twists of its spine, rupture bone and sinew and thick blubber to pierce the heart far beneath. It was an obviously trained and quite near impossible maneuver that Majest would have found impressive—it had killed the bear almost instantly.

Letty looked now at the dead monster a pace or two from her curled-up form, bleeding out crimson into the snow-struck valley, and felt Death's call slip away into the wind, falling from her skin like water, like the flakes that slid from her face as she inclined her head upwards.

The woman pulled the knife from the quivering corpse and wiped the blade on a white rabbit-fur coat, streaking red down her front. "You're lucky I got here in time," she mused in a quiet voice. It was not the voice of someone who had just slain a beast. It was… gentle. Motherly. Her bright eyes were locked on her blade, lips pursing without expression. "But I couldn't fail you again. It's so lovely to finally meet you."

Letty pushed herself into a sitting position with blistered hands, relief slowly fading to a dazed curiosity. "Excuse me," she said, clearing her throat when she learned her voice had all but abandoned her, leaving her with a croaking whisper.

The black-haired girl turned in Letty's direction, eyes considering. "Yes?"

There were many questions Letty could have asked, but the one that came out of her mouth surprised even herself. "Why did you wipe your knife on your jacket? Do you *like* it all full of blood? It's hard enough to clean clothes in the wintertime just from all the ice in the water, but blood stains."

The corner of the girl's mouth twitched upward. She gave nothing in reply except a shake of her head, kneeling down until she was at eye level with the sitting Letty. From her pocket Letty could see a rabbit's foot poking out against her thigh, white as snow not yet touched by the forest. "Are you alright?"

"Yes," Letty said automatically. "I mean…no. Maybe." Her

throat went dry. "Who are you?"

"A friend," came the indirect reply. "For these purposes you can consider me an acquaintance of your family. What are you doing so far from home, Aletta?"

Letty, despite everything, was taken aback. "You—you know my family? You know who I am?"

"None of that now, little one," the girl murmured, passing a cool, ungloved hand over Letty's face. "You took quite a fall, didn't you? And then the bear…" She shook her head, one hand going to grip her rabbit's foot and tuck it back under her coat, and Letty stared up at her without understanding, like a newborn. "A few more moments and the land would have lost you."

A rustling in the bushes distracted the woman for a moment and she turned her head in its direction, frowning. Letty followed her gaze, prepared for more danger but too numb to feel any new fear spike her veins. What now—the bear's mate come to take revenge? A wolf that had smelled the freshly-spilled blood? Something worse?

At once the woman shifted protectively over Letty, breathing loud and vigorous, and her eyes kept flickering inexplicably and expectantly to her side, as though she were expecting something. "Is someone else there?" she called, harshly. "Show yourself."

To Letty's utter disbelief, the girl's order was obeyed and a boy stepped out of the undergrowth as if by magic, a bow strapped across his back, his hands in the air and a quizzical, not-even-a-little-bit menacing look on his face. The golden-brown hair framing his angular, smooth face was flecked with snowflakes, and cornflower-blue eyes peeped out from behind long, dark lashes, a small button nose perking up between them. He was beautiful in a way that was strange and alien. Letty had never seen anyone like him in her whole life.

For the first time, Letty noticed the storm had stopped; the snow was gentle now, and seemed to tiptoe toward the ground.

"My apologies, miss," the newcomer said in a sheepish tone. His voice was foreign, lilted at the corners. He broke into a brief smile, though he shuffled his feet profusely, as if he were embarrassed simply to be there. "I was tailing a grizzly on its way into hibernation, you see, and the trail just—sort of stopped here. I'm Raizu Capricorn, by the way. Inertia Pack." When he smiled, he looked younger than he sounded, and Letty guessed he wasn't much older than her brother.

The black-haired woman's face still held suspicion, but it had relaxed. Raizu was clearly not whom she'd feared the arrival to be. "*That* bear?" she asked, indicating the dead beast.

Raizu's eyes lit despite his obvious shyness, though he jumped back at the sight of the enormous corpse before recovering to stammer, "Yes—that's the one! Did you actually *kill* it?" He leaned forward on his tiptoes to inspect the bear, though Letty noticed he didn't step closer. "Impressive!"

The dark-haired girl's eyes darted from Raizu to Letty to the forest and back again. Her expression rattled with apprehension, as if she expected something else to jump out and attack.

Raizu frowned, took a step back. "What's the matter?"

"I can't stay here," the woman blurted. "It's dangerous enough to interfere in these parts, with the eyes everywhere, but I couldn't let her die." Her wild eyes settled on Raizu's face, their color darkening with resolution, a cool shadow casted to their sky. "Can you take care of her?"

Raizu blinked in confusion and took another step back. "Take care of...her? This half-frozen girl I've never met?" He looked at Letty, shifting with evident discomfort. "Ah, look—I'm on a hunting mission for my pack here, and Kallica will have my head if I don't come back with *something*."

"I don't need to be taken care of," Letty interjected, uneasy as options passed between three perfect strangers, unspoken doubts crackling between them like lightning. "I just need to find my brother. I lost him when the storm hit; I'm sure he's frantic."

"Lost him?" Raizu frowned. "How do you lose an entire brother?"

Like a reflex, Letty glanced at the sky. The clouds were finally beginning to clear, and their thick curtain parted down the middle to revealing a setting sun. "We fought and I ran off, but I want to find him again. It was stupid of me to run. He was right, after all." She paused, then realized she had failed to introduce herself. "I'm Letty Skylark."

"I can help you find your brother, Letty," Raizu told her. It was unexpected; he himself didn't seem to know why he'd said it. His sightline swung back and forth, wary, but he spoke anyway. "I mean—there's a bear I can piece apart and take back to my friends and family—I'm part of the Inertia pack—did I say that already?— and if you say he should still be close by…"

"Definitely," Letty said with an eager nod. "He couldn't have gotten far. He's probably looking for me." A nagging guilt poked at the inside of her stomach. Majest was likely beside himself with worry.

"Then we'll find him," said Raizu. "It won't be far out of my way."

"Thank you," Letty replied, blinking at the boy with gratitude. She didn't know whether it was his awkward friendliness or the way he seemed to radiate a foreign sort of sun, but something about Raizu told her she could trust him.

"My thanks as well." The mysterious black-haired girl grimaced as she continued her nervous pacing. She turned to Letty in a flash, her eyes huge. "We will meet again, Aletta. May I always get to you in time."

Then she rose to her feet, turned tail, and away she went. The only evidence of her presence was the blood that had dropped from her sword, splattered and gleaming in the snow like an empty promise.

Raizu and Letty gazed after her, perplexed, trying to fathom the timing of their situation. After a moment of bewildered silence, the two turned to each other.

"So," said Raizu, licking dry lips and surveying their position. "Where do you want to start, Letty?"

"Impossible!" Seti spat, kicking at the unsympathetic boulder he had hidden behind. He didn't usually let emotions loose from their binding, but this was an exception. This was the worst possible unseen twist of events.

"Everything was perfect," he went on, pacing away into the trees, away from the retreating forms of Aletta Skylark and the stranger she'd taken refuge with. "She was alone. She was lost. She was injured. She fell down a *cliff*. There was a damn *grizzly bear* attacking her. And what happens?" He let out a breath in a huff of frost. "My airheaded, should-be-dead aunt Soti pops out of nowhere after decades of eluding me, and *saves her.*"

There was a long series of moments in which Seti kicked ferociously at the ground with the peaks of his boots, long enough for his toes to grow achy and then numb altogether. It had been Soti's name he had taken after when this new world had rolled over belly-up. Her disappearance had led to a convenient chance at identity. But yet here she was—still a knot in the thread of his life he couldn't quite wrangle out.

"Leave it to my mother to have the most useless vermin of a sister," Seti muttered again, barely realizing he was speaking only to himself. "Just because she decided to chase after the high life and meddle with the gods doesn't give her the right to go about ruining my life whenever she pleases."

But then, Seti thought, Soti had always been the meddling type. Seeing poltergeists between the boards of the walls and demons under the stairs in a world where witchcraft was cause for execution, she'd been in the shadows longer than Seti, dipping her toes into books on heavenly magic, dabbling in alchemy and the afterlife—taking the opposite path of her elder sister. She had always preferred to sign the world anonymously.

He had no idea when or how she had gotten this much power— enough to slink into secrecy, then fly out of hiding to slice through bears as if they were little more than ragged bits of cloth. Protecting the *Skylarks,* of all people. She had somehow bonded her protection to them, the exact children Seti's freedom depended on disposing of.

Seti's patience was thinning like a stretched length of leather.

"Let's see how long she lasts before the Organization gets a hold of her," he snarled, clenching his fists. "If they know so much about who I am, they've no doubt heard of her, too. She can't hide forever; she'll be rounded up and carted off, too."

Seti continued to stalk in anger, his long black coat whipping behind him with a gusting aftershock of the previous storm, the golden pocket watch dangling off his belt behind him, chain clanking violently. His ears and nose tip were starting to go numb, but he ignored the freezing burn.

"She's never been anything but useless to me," he continued, rambling as he glowered, aware of how juvenile he sounded and not in the mood to care. "She could have stopped Sira from learning to conjure all that demon energy. She could have stopped her from flooding her own son with it. But did she?" He flared his nostrils, centuries-old anger coursing through him with a red veil of ire that turned his vision blurry. "Of course not—she's just a runaway. A coward."

Seti stopped for a moment and told himself to think logically. So he'd failed to kill the Skylark girl the easy way. That only meant he'd have to try harder.

With an absent impatience, he rubbed at his frozen white nose, forcing feeling into numbness and hissing at the itching stabs of heat as his skin came back to life. He walked on; the pocket watch swinging at his side ticked with a soft resonance, a constant reminder he was being followed and timed.

He wasn't even sure he could take the children's lives so long as Soti was around—with her effortless magic, there were perhaps no limits to what she could do to resurrect their safety, and the thought drew a weary sigh from deep within Seti's chattering lungs. He slammed the watch down against his thigh, angrily ceasing its pendulum motion. He would have to snipe down the Skylarks from under her nose, before she knew what he was doing. His escape from the Organization depended on it.

And with no ticking time to waste, he could not afford to wait until the dawn's light to try.

~♣~

The night was blacker than black, but Letty and her newfound traveling companion were still able to make good time across the snow as it bathed in the soapy light of the moon. It had been Raizu's idea to start looking for Majest where Letty had last seen him and work backward from there, branching out in a circle. He was smart, Letty had quickly gathered. He could have worked his way out of a room with no doors or windows, building his way through the walls with his mind alone.

But despite his bright ideas, in the dark, Raizu's earlier discomposure returned and burgeoned like a fire climbing a wall of moss, uneasiness pouring off him in waves. He jumped at every twig that cracked, cringed at every rustle in the bushes. Letty felt bad for him. Poor Raizu, afraid of a little night air. Though she could hardly blame him; the dark woods were unnerving. She appreciated that Raizu was more cautious than Majest—Letty did not feel weak or childish in her careful steps; each one felt validated and appreciated.

Raizu was of leaner build than Majest as well, and a bit shorter, so he understood how Letty felt when she got stuck in the piling snow, deceived by its shallow appearance that winked under the sun, and pulled her out without a patronizing shake of his head or an ill-timed joke. He was fast and nimble and restless, allowing the travel to be quick and light, and though he didn't know Letty from any nameless stranger, he was sacrificing a day of his own travels to bring her back to the only family she had left.

"The world needs more people like you," said Letty, and immediately felt her face heat red with embarrassment. She had just said that aloud.

She attempted to save herself—"I-I mean, more people as nice as you are. It's awfully kind of you to help, considering you don't know anything about me."

Raizu laughed, a breezy, springtime sound that reminded her of Majest's usual tinkling good mood. He was flushing a little, too, obviously not used to dealing with compliments. Letty remembered how shy he was and almost regretted her words.

"It's really not a problem, Letty," Raizu managed after some time. "Where I come from, we do this all the time. You know about how vicious packs this far north usually are?" As Letty nodded, he went on, "We're not like that—not Inertia. We don't raid towns, we don't kill off those who can't hunt for themselves, and we're raised to help anyone who needs it, no matter who they are. The forest is our home, but it's not ours alone."

"Where *is* this Inertia pack?" Letty questioned. She'd never heard of anything like it.

"Down south a bit," Raizu told her, looking happy to change the subject away from himself. "A week's travel at best. They always send me north for hunting because I'm the only one who doesn't mind the cold temperatures. I usually don't come up this far, but I've been tailing this grizzly for a few days now—though heavens know what I thought I was going to do once I caught up to it. It probably would've eaten me in one bite." He smiled ruefully at the bag he was carrying, filled to the brim with frozen bear meat he had cut out of the carcass before they had set out. "Thankfully, I don't have to return empty-handed like usual. After we find your brother, I can go home."

Letty's face fell. If Raizu's pack had been closer to Majest's proposed destination, she would have asked if they could join. But it was easier to hide where there was water to float an escape. The waves left no footprints, and with Majest's powers, he could build a boat to sail right over them. The southern forests held less protection in their village-dotted slopes—a known center of civilization would attract danger like a second skin.

"So," said Raizu, eyes on his feet and voice a little unsteady, "tell me about you and your brother. Why are you traveling? Don't you have a home? Or a town?"

"We did," replied Letty, "have a place." She knew she shouldn't have been exposing herself and her life's stories, but she doubted Raizu was a threat; he could barely meet her eyes without an awkward stammer. "We lived west of here in a cottage with our mother. She was—she died in an attack last night. We're on our own."

Raizu gasped. "What—you're serious? I'm so sorry! These

92

woods don't go easy on anyone. My parents died, too, when I was a baby—poisoned rabbit meat." He blinked, as though searching for the stems of memories that had never been allowed to fully blossom. "But clearly you and your brother escaped the attack, right?"

"The murderers ran off," Letty said, face pointed at the ground. "They told Mother they knew what we are, but then they disappeared. We left before they could come back for us."

Raizu's eyebrows went up and formed quizzical peaks above long, golden-brown bangs. "They knew what you are?" he asked. "What does that mean?"

Letty took a deep breath as if to answer, but she pulled her tongue back just in time, trapping it between the chapped pink barrier of her lips. Was she really about to spill her secrets to this boy? This boy who couldn't have been older than Majest but was already chasing down grizzlies and roaming miles away from home on his own—what could she really know about someone like that?

But Letty *wanted* to tell him. No one knew about her struggle against her powerless state; not even Majest understood the pain and jealousy that spiked every time she watched him toss his element around like it was a third arm. She had to tell someone, and there was no one else but Raizu.

"Two years ago," Letty began, feeling uncertain, "I was visited in my dreams by a god calling himself Komi the Deliverer. He told me to wake my brother, and we both received powers and became what he called Messengers. He said the world needed gifts like his to help put it back together, so he gave us those gifts. We don't know what our mother's killers wanted—but somehow, they knew about it, and wanted to hurt us because of it."

Raizu stopped walking and turned to stare at her. "That's not possible."

"But it's true."

Raizu frowned, chewed on his lip. "No—the stories about gods who grant powers to ordinary people are just that, stories."

Letty shook her head, words tumbling from her mouth like pouring rain. "It's true—when we find my brother, he'll show you what he can do. His powers are extraordinary. He can move trees and earth with his mind—anything in nature is his to control—he talks to animals and speaks the languages of all the trees; he always has a plan and no matter what, he *never* gets scared or gives up, even when his own *sister* doesn't know if she'll ever be able to—"

She broke off, finding tautness between her teeth and reluctantly setting aside the jealousy in her voice. "I mean… He's my brother. He goes through a lot to protect me, powers or not."

Raizu looked impressed, casting a new glow over his previous disbelief. He didn't react to Letty's outburst or try to discredit her words, like he was purposefully avoiding the conflict. "Sounds like quite the guy," he said with a certain tentative thoughtfulness. "If that's somehow true, that's amazing. What's his name?"

Letty shook away a tinge of annoyance. Of course he'd be more interested in Majest and his powers than in any of Letty's problems. She was small and boring. "Majest," she responded with a sigh. "His name's Majest. I call him Maji."

"Majest," Raizu repeated. "I've never heard that name before."

Letty bit back an irritated reply about how nearly *any* name in this land was unique and just nodded and continued walking.

Raizu seemed to sense her discontent. "I'm sorry," he said hastily, holding out a hand in a gesture of apology. "I'm sure your powers are incredible, too. I may not believe in the gods, but I'll believe your powers if I see them, I promise. What can you do? Part the seas, control weather, light people on fire—what is it?"

Letty didn't feel any better. "I don't know."

"You don't *know?*"

Letty felt her shoulders sag. "Maji was able to figure out what he could do right away. He split a rock in two, straight out of our father's hands—nearly hit him in the face with the shards of it." It was usually a stupefying memory to recall, something straight from an impossible legend, but today, it just dragged Letty's mood down further. "That was that. He learned quickly from there. Komi never said what our powers would be—he gave us hints, but we've had to figure them out by ourselves."

Raizu tilted his head to one side. "Well, tell me your hint!

It must have been in your subconscious, because after all, your subconscious was what told you about your power in the first place. It just took the form of this…god, or whoever. It's got to be in your head somewhere. Maybe we can pull it out."

"Okay," Letty said, and didn't bother trying to understand Raizu's god-free reasoning. She had Komi's words memorized to heart. She and Majest had gone over them so many times, her tongue had tied itself up in recitation—yet the mystery remained intact.

"He told me I was gifted with the greatest force known to the planet. A force that can quench all others in a single breath." Letty's brow furrowed. "What could that possibly be?"

"You said the powers were *elemental* gifts, right?" Raizu's feet crunched in the snow, the sound of his light footsteps seeming to churn along to the thoughts in his head. Letty could almost hear gears whirring. "Do you know the elements?"

"Maji said our world's four elements are fire, earth, water, and wind," replied Letty. "That doesn't help me."

"Of course it does!" Raizu exclaimed, with a laugh that implied he thought she was joking. "That means it's already narrowed down to three options, and I doubt your dream was trying to make this difficult for you—a force that can quench all others? Letty, only water can 'quench!'"

"Water?" Letty was doubtful. Even someone as smart as Raizu couldn't solve a two-year mystery in a single breath. "You think so? You think someone could control something that…slippery?"

Raizu shrugged. "That's beyond me, but it doesn't seem too far-fetched, does it? Fire isn't the 'greatest force' because water can easily get the better of it. And wind can always be blown away; it doesn't do much of anything except cause a nuisance and a bit of noise." He grinned. "That leaves the quenching force of water."

Letty shook her head, not daring to hope, though she had to admit the argument made sense. "We never had any water around where we lived. It was all ice. The only water I ever got was to drink."

"Maybe that's why you couldn't use it, then," Raizu urged.

"You can't use something you don't have."

"But if I never find any, I'll never get to test it out."

"Then tell your brother to help you find some real water when we catch up to him," Raizu advised in a bright tone. "It won't hurt to try."

"We're going to the Hudson Bay," Letty told him. "At least, we'll try to get close to the coastline. Maji figured it would be easier to escape whoever's after us if we could sail away from them. Water powers would definitely come in handy in a place like that!" She almost smiled. "But that's getting ahead of things—how do we even know we can find Maji in the first place? He's a fast mover."

Raizu breathed out through his nose. "Well, I track animals for a living. I'm sure tracking a person isn't any different at all. Well, except for the part where it's a person." He frowned. "You, um. Just have to look for clues." A pause. "Do you think we're close to where you ran off? We should probably start looking for somewhere to stay the night soon."

"I'm not sure," Letty confessed. "Everything looks much the same. Snow, rocks, trees…more snow…" She sighed. "Though I do remember a patch of trees that had no needles on them. Maji pointed them out to me and told me he couldn't read anything off them because they were dead. That was a little while before I lost him."

"Like…those trees?" Raizu gestured a few yards from where they were standing. Letty followed his gaze. It was much darker now, the sky holding the sun hostage somewhere just below the ground, but she could still see the familiar harsh edges of the splintered wood stretching nakedly into the air.

"Yes," Letty breathed, her voice filling with excitement. "Those trees. We're getting close."

VII. MOTIVE

Seti liked the dark. In the dark, no one could find him if he did not wish to be found. Most of Cognito's inhabitants were known for terrible night vision; those were the people who preferred to spend their darkest hours safe and asleep in their cozy wooden homes, snoring blissfully, engulfed in dreams that led them to a better place than the wasteland that would return for them when they awoke. But Seti could scrutinize in utter blackness, churn his gears with little to no sleep at all—and he had no fear.

And so, under night's black veil, Seti slithered between the trees, as hasty as he could without making a sound. A tight yawn reminded him he hadn't slept since before Chami and Shayming had dragged him face-first through the Organization's white halls, but there was no time to dwell on exhaustion now. He didn't know how long he had before Soti realized what he was doing and caught onto him, caught up to him, and caught him in the act.

There was a clear bond between her and those Skylarks— something that let Soti know when danger struck. Seti could not for the life of him fathom what it could have been; he only hoped he could outrun it.

Tick-tock, sang the watch on his belt.

Going after Aletta again was not an option, not when Soti's eyes were surely to be fixed on the red of her hair to make sure it still fluttered and shone with life. The Skylark girl was not alone; she was surrounded on all sides.

Majest, on the other hand, was easy enough to track down a second time, especially as the daytime world slept alongside the

97

sun, and easier still to spot—suspended between the lower, sturdier branches of an evergreen, a makeshift hammock swaying beneath his curled form.

The boy's bags and belongings dangled down like laundry on a clothesline, carelessly flapping against the moon's breeze, and Majest himself was an unnatural cocoon-shape plastered between two sap-laden branches, which sagged and bowed under his weight. He would have been obvious even without Seti's night-proof gaze.

Idiot, Seti thought, and though this boy was a perfect stranger, he suddenly mused that he would not be too sorry for what he was about to do.

Just thinking of it, Seti's eyes crossed the horizon-line of the trees with an anxious tremor to their gaze. He had every right to assume Soti was already watching him, a personal hound to his bloodthirsty fox. He did not know the limits of what she was capable of.

In the pack the President had given him, among stale bread and rusted water canisters, was a knife. He didn't have to second-guess its purpose, and he pulled it out of his belt now, rolling its inconspicuous smallness between the joints of his fingers. It was the Organization's knife, and not his own, but it would have to do—it was an accurate sentiment, anyway; the Organization was killing the Skylarks, in the ways that mattered.

Seti noticed as he stalked forward that the wooden hilt of the blade refused to fit to his hand, sliding gawkily around in the creases of his palm, threatening splinters against the insides of his knuckles. He flicked his eyes closed in sour frustration, but did not let his movements slow, and by the time he was at the base of the tree, staring up into the bundle of furs and leather that shifted in its slumber, he felt nothing but cold conviction.

He began to climb, quickly, like a spider—feet bunched and pressed into the ribbed spine of the tree trunk, knife bared and toothy, and his thirst for freedom pounded louder the higher he climbed, and with one stroke of the blade, one stroke like an artist's paintbrush, he would *have it;* freedom would be halfway up the hill to meet him.

Seti raised the knife loosely, Majest Skylark swaying in his sightline, branches creaking, hammock rocking, and the boy's form was swelling closer in the darkness, and Seti's mouth sagged open with concentrated hunger—

He almost swung his blade forward, but then there was a hard *tink* like a small cymbal between his ears, and Seti realized he was no longer holding the knife at all. It lay slung to the ground below him, a small but decisive pebble lying dutifully at its side.

For a moment, Seti was entirely unaware of what had happened. Had the knife's clumsy form somehow tumbled from his hand? Had his concentration slipped, for all its desperation, and the knife had merely followed?

But the stone on the ground seemed to stare at him, mockingly. It clung snugly to his attention and pulled his suspicions forefront. It was as if something or someone had sniped the knife clean out of his grasp, too precise to be coincidental. Seti's breath speared sharply against his lungs as he returned cautiously to the ground and took up the hilt of the weapon once more, eyeing it up as though it had personally betrayed him.

He made the climb again, this time slowly, tracking his gaze between the knife and the stone denting the snow below, half-certain one or both of them would leap away when he wasn't looking. The climb was slow, but his intentions were not—his mind ran on ahead while his limbs inched along, and he tried to become invisible, curve his body along the inside of the trunk this time, breaths coming short and impatient by the time Majest's unconscious body was once again in arm's reach, pale neck exposed beneath the brushstrokes of his hair where his scarf had sagged to his shoulders.

There.

This time, there was no hesitation in the swing—Seti's knife jumped forward, a silver bullet glancing off starlight as it twisted for its target, so fast, it was nothing but a blur, quick and precise and just as impatient as Seti himself, and there was no possible way he could miss, no coincidental pebble that could have knocked—

Tink, chimed the woods again, and this time, Seti saw the stone flying from seemingly nowhere, meeting his knife in a challenge of brute force, and rock crushed blade, and away they sailed once more.

A growl burdened heavy in Seti's throat, and he dug his nails into the tree-bark as he whipped his head around to the direction of the assailant, all senses alert and provoked into awareness like the tap of an excruciatingly-trying finger.

He had turned around fast enough to see a sliver of white smudging against the black silhouettes of forest, and though it was nothing but a bit of fuzziness, he knew the implications.

Soti wore only white, and only Soti wore only white.

Damn it, Seti thought, and gnashed his teeth. *She's too good—she found me already.*

His gaze returned to Majest, who had begun to fill the air with soft, sleepy breathings, completely unaware of his near-death, or of his incessant salvation.

Could I smother him in his sleep? Seti wondered errantly, eyes wide enough to soak in the boy's entire form, the fur lining his boots, the grip of his hands into his homemade leather hammock as if for reassurance this new makeshift home would not leave him behind.

No, Seti decided with a quick, huffing sigh, picturing Soti launching something more perilous than a couple of broken rock fragments at him, bowling him from the tree like a squirrel's unwanted acorn. She knew every one of his movements; he was her map.

He would have to kill her first. The thought was not a pleasant one.

In one last desperate attempt, Seti scampered to the ground, scooped the knife between his fingers, and chucked it javelin-style in the direction of the sleeping boy, not a moment to spare, just letting his arrow fly, but naturally, it was intercepted cleanly by a hunk of gray falling from the sky like a meteor that landed at Seti's feet.

"Show yourself!" he hissed into the trees, and bent to savagely pick up the rock, which was small and innocent in the palm of his

hand, betraying nothing of its likely abuser. *"I know you're there!"*

Nothing but silence answered him, and a sleepy childish mumbling from above.

"Fine," Seti told the spruces and the junipers, and took up the knife for good this time. "Have it your way, then. Cowardly and babyish. Protect your Skylarks all you want, for whatever you want them for."

You may be protecting the Skylarks, but there is no one protecting you.

Dawn cracked its shell at last and spilled its eggy contents over icy alpine slopes. Golden rays of sunlight filtered through cypress and pine and lit the ground to a pale, sickly off-white color, and at the sight and feel of it, animals awoke from their slumbers and went groggily in search of purpose.

Majest, as he joined them, was uncertain of his own purpose—Letty wasn't there; she had vanished with the rage of the storm as swiftly as it had begun, leaving behind nothing but cold. There was no skyline on the horizon that could have told him which way he might find her.

It took several desolate, sober minutes for Majest to find the strength to open his near-frozen eyelids and sort the world's blurry shapes into real figures. There was a feeling like a small boulder crushing his lungs, and he fought for air. Losing Letty was like losing his breath.

Majest's vision finally focused after a great deal of squinting through the ice-crust on his lashes, and he realized he needed to move. His back ached where it pressed into the knots on the branch he was lying on, snow covering him in a lazy blanket. At least he had his hammock, its sling of elk skins and branches—meant for hunting late into the night, when you could walk no further. In the night, it was important to stay up high, where it was safe and sheltered from forest-floor harshness. That was what his father had taught him.

"*Hímin,* never you know with these woods," Dagur had told

a much younger Majest, the boy's green eyes too big for his face. "Wolves, bears, magic folk like elves. They tell you such people do not exist, but home in my land, we hear them snickering among the rocks. You want safety, you build your bubble as close to the sky as you can."

Majest hadn't wanted to take chances—then or now. In his green and white bubble was where he lay at present, staring down to the ground far below with a dejected frown. He needed to find Letty.

He set his jaw into a square line and narrowed his focus until there was a thrilling snap between his furrowed brows, a snap which told him to move his hand. He complied, and as his fingers traveled down his branch, it bent forward in a grand, sloping arc, bridging toward the snowy ground long after his arm could no longer reach. And so Majest undid his hammock, repacked his bags, and scooted toward the forest floor, supplies dangling after him, a door shutting in his mind behind him as he released his element back into its corridor.

Once at the bottom, branches no longer obscuring his vision, daylight streamed into his senses and he took in the trees around him. He and Letty had passed this point a few hours before she had run off into the dusk. There was a line of trees to his right with no branches or needles, completely dead, and to his left were a few caribou paths trampled down with footprints and a couple of small, smooth stones.

Footprints? Majest bent down to get a closer look. Some of the fresh prints were different than the others. They looked...human. Some were nearly the size of Majest's but thinner; others were petite and light and pointed. And then there was a third set, familiar and trailing decisively.

"Letty," said Majest aloud, clenching his fists at his side, daring to hope. "Are some of these our footprints?" He looked at them some more. The prints were coming from the opposite direction he and his sister had been walking. Had he gotten himself turned around? And why were there so many sets?

As he struggled to comprehend what he was seeing, a tiny red squirrel darted out between two twin conifers and scurried up the trunk of the white pine Majest had been resting in. It was chattering furiously—as though saying something.

Distracted and startled, Majest grasped quickly for his element once more, and focused on the creature until he could understand its words.

"Oh, oh, oh dear," the squirrel squeaked as Majest unfolded his brain, letting it grapple with the chattering and turn it into a language he understood. "Oh, the nuts. They're gone, every last one. Oh, dear. Oh, oh, no. No more nuts for the winter. No more food. Hunger. Oh, the *hunger*."

Majest suddenly had an idea, and set his own boots among the footprints before him. "Excuse me," he called to the squirrel, which was quivering a few yards off the ground on a low branch.

It pricked its furry ears up in astonishment, a gesture clearing stating, "Is he talking to *me?*"

Concentrating hard until sweat crept along his hairline, Majest continued, his voice slurring and rising in pitch in several degrees of difficulty until he matched the squirrel's tone. "Yes, excuse me—my name is Majest Skylark. I was wondering if you've seen a little girl pass by here."

The squirrel's nose twitched and Majest prayed to the skies it would understand and be able to answer.

After some time, the little animal twitched its rosy nose and responded, "I may have; I may have not. Oh, what does it matter whether there's a girl? What's in it for me? I cannot eat a girl! The nuts are gone, oh, they're all gone now." It began shuffling its feet and dancing along the branches, jumping from tree to tree.

Majest raced after it. "Please!" he called, desperate. "Please, if you've seen her, I need to know!" When there was no reply except distressed squeaking, he continued, "I have food! I can supply you with food!"

This got the little animal's attention. "Nuts? To eat? To eat, to spare for Amitu? Food for the winter, food for Amitu's aching stomach?" It stopped and stared through the branches at Majest with eyes made of solid black hunger, aching little pits.

"I have a few nuts I could spare," Majest told it, grimacing. "My sister and I used to collect them off the oaks in the summer. I brought along our entire supply and we won't be eating them all."

The squirrel's eyes held nothing but greed. "To eat," it repeated.

"But you have to tell me if you've seen my sister," Majest interjected. "I lost her. I've found some footprints that might belong to her, but they're all muddled, and there are so many. If you don't help me, you're getting nothing to eat."

Amitu's nose twitched in disdain, like a wrinkling flower petal. "The girl was here," it said after some time. "With a boy."

Majest sighed impatiently. "Yes, *me.* We were traveling through here last night. But have you seen her since then?"

Amitu flicked its tufted ears. "No, not the boy with the food, and not last night. Not *you.* Different boy—morning boy. Thinner, quieter—nervous as a mouse. Carrying a weapon with sharp darts. Oh, they were sharp as the hunger in my belly!" It moved down the tree trunk with fluid agility and came to sit a few feet from Majest, crawling forward on its claws in an attempt not to break through the snowfall.

"She was with someone else?" Majest's heart thudded. He could see his own desperation reflected back at him in the squirrel's eyes, hunger and hunger. "Amitu, do you know where they are now? Is Letty alright?"

"Oh, the girl and the sharp boy went happily where their footprints lead." Amitu scrabbled in the snow, up to its ears in white fluff. "On in the direction you were traveling last night, sir. In the direction every footprint travels." Its face was earnest for an animal, desperate and graying. "Now, kind boy, oh, won't you spare some nuts?"

Majest's mind pulsed hard with a rising tide of questions and relief in even spades, but all he did was nod and reach back into his food pack, pull out a handful of acorns, kneel down in the snow, and hold them out to the little red creature. "Will this do?"

"Oh, yes!" Amitu squeaked with excitement and ran forward, stuffing the acorns into its cheeks at the surprising speed a bright new morning guzzles down the night's stars. It called something of a muffled thanks, but it wasn't paying Majest attention any longer, rapidly rejoining its endless, gluttonous quest for food and survival. With a tail-wave of delight and a sequence of squeaks, it vanished.

Shaking his head, Majest went back and found the footprints, eyeing up the thin, pointed toes of the largest set. The slender boy with the bow and arrow.

Like little elf prints, he mused, curiosity brimming.

He set his feet in the same direction, sheathing the smaller toes with his booted own. Almost reflexively, he tightened the belt around his waist and secured his slingshot at his side.

The wind at his back, Majest followed two sets of weaving steps until they merged into his own, and then it was as if one great-footed traveler walked the snow, and he walked and walked.

Soti closed her eyes, head in her hands, and her hair ran between her fingers like ink pooling out of a painting. She slumped down in the cave she was residing in with a huff, and her white coat scratched in protest against the dirty ground, mingling with the bear's crusty blood.

She could not stop thinking about years long gone—years of Sira, of Skylarks, of Seti, if that were his name now. She kept remembering London, her birthplace, the secret tunnel behind the bookshelf. Two sisters, their magic hidden, feigning innocence. A game. A secret. That memory was a nuisance now, dangling in the back of her mind like a stray thread she could never reach to snap. She didn't like to think of her sister, the fork in their road to immortality, how Soti had climbed up to the heavens while Sira had sunk down into summoning books and dark energies instead.

Sunk down even upon her son in her scramble for power—the poor creature. He shouldn't have been alive, but it was not Soti's place to do anything about a cursed boy she had barely known, a sister she barely remembered.

Soti had met the End resolutely, at the side of the gods, though not without pity—the land had become as bleak and white-covered as she was.

Traveling across the northern regions of Cognito had eventually left her cold and weary, unused to the perilous landscape, but a young couple had caught her as she'd fallen and offered her their home as a safe haven and taught her the ways of this new world. Their names had been Maxine Skylark and Dagur Sigurðsson, and they had been expecting a baby girl.

Maxine and Dagur had treated Soti with all the kindness she had never known on the other side of the water—Maxine with her warm green eyes and red curls; Dagur with his quiet determination and short messy beard, mumbling in thickly-coated English.

"I come from family in a land far away," he'd told Soti. "Happy place. Calm. Many unseen *huldufólk*—elves—but few trees. Land of ice—*Ísland*. I know not of this new world. I only want our children to be at peace, to be Skylarks and fly."

Dagur had soaked up every last one of Soti's stories—gods and demons and the crossroads between—and even the not-so-convinced Maxine had rolled her eyes and played along, murmuring over the light of a warm fire. They'd shared their food, though they hardly had the means to keep their little boy and girl from going to sleep hungry.

Soti hadn't wanted to leave them, even after winter had soaked away into the dirt, but she could not have burdened them any longer. Not with a third child on their way, a third mouth to feed.

But *"you don't have to leave them"*—that was what Komi had told her, whisking her from the Skylarks' white yard into the swirling barrenness of the gods' sky, starlight in circles around her.

"I have a job for you," Komi had said, and fixed her with eyes grave and solemn and deceptively impassive. "A job that will tie you to this family for always, if you so choose to accept it."

"Anything for them," had been Soti's immediate reply. She and Komi had rarely met before, but she knew him to be of great importance, even if many gods—namely the other higher-ups—sneered away his visions of his planet's future, knew only of his past failures, of his present desperation. "The Skylarks saved my life; I am in their debt. And of course, I am in the gods' service."

Komi's wings had shaken out from his back like two great

waves, cresting and rolling back into submission. "The Skylark boy and girl are to play an incomparable role in years to come— they are needed for a service not only to me and my standing with the Highers, but to what is left of this land. And so I ask of you to protect them when their time comes, to keep them safe and make sure they arrive safely at their destination."

There had been no tremor to Soti's voice, no explanation demanded. It was her duty to obey. "You want me to protect Majest and Lunesta?"

"No, not Lunesta. The third child, the one yet unborn. Aletta. She is the one called upon."

Again, Soti had not asked, had not protested the eldest Skylark's exclusion. "I will do as you wish, but how am I to know when they will need my protection?"

At that, a white rabbit's foot had leaped into existence before her eyes, dangling in the lightless air like a question mark, little knobby toes and curved bone sheathed in matted fur.

"Take it," Komi had advised, and the painted lines on his face had stretched with the movement of his mouth, something that had occurred to Soti as oddly human, though his enormous wings had still been against his shoulders, form twice as tall as any earthly man or woman. "It will signal you when the children are in danger."

As Soti had taken the foot, which was not nearly as soft as she had expected, she had finally been prompted to ask—"Forgive me, but can't you protect Majest and his sister on your own? Why am I needed?"

There had been many unspoken things between the sapphire shades of Komi's eyes, like fish flicking their fins in the deep blue and unwilling to surface. "If I want to prove to the Highers that what I have done has not been in error, those who receive my gifts must survive on their own, without anything more than prodding. The gods, for all their glory, are not allowed to interfere with the destiny of any mortal." There had been that human look again, something scratching out from beneath the endless shells of eyes.

"Then wouldn't it be cheating to have me do a job you aren't allowed to?" Soti had dared to question, brave enough under

Komi's human—almost anxious—expression. "If I save them from danger, don't I interfere? Don't I break the rules in order to preserve whatever you seek to accomplish?"

Komi's eyes had narrowed and hardened suddenly, authority flooding back into his voice with the force to drown. Soti had nearly been afraid. "You are not a god," he had said. "You are as flesh and blood as any child of the land. But yet you are skilled; you have the power to protect. And so I am trusting you to use that power, to come to the Skylarks when their plights call. Is this too much to ask of you?"

Soti had dipped her head, submitted, dropped her questions. "I will do as you wish," she had repeated, and the words had been natural, flowing, human.

And years later, as Komi had promised, the moment had come—the age-crusted rabbit's foot had stained itself black, and Soti had torn across grit and sleet in the blind direction of the Skylarks' cottage, but she had not made it in time—the danger had gone, and the children had sobbed against a broken body pooled and twisted between the folds of its nightgown. And there had been nothing Soti could have done, but ache with them in sickened understanding.

She would never let them down again—even if it meant going through Seti, her sister's son, her own flesh and blood. But he was no more flesh and blood than the Skylarks, than any child of Komi's land, and the children were family to Dagur and Maxine, who had been better family to Soti than any of her own.

Seti, however much he might despise the witness to his mother's crimes, had never been Soti's duty to remorse over or feel for—to protect.

But the Skylarks were.

Light returned again, scorching the ground a blinding white as the trees reached thirstily for the burning rays, shivering from the darkness. Squirrels and birds chorused and harmonized from the branches; caribou ran in lines down to a wide, still-running river to wet their tongues with an icy drink. Everything shone lighter and easier; the snow was falling in wispy, thick flakes and even the wind had mellowed out to no more than a playful breeze that curled Letty's hair and tugged at the ends of Raizu's scarf.

Letty felt lighter, too. She and Raizu trotted through the snow briskly, flying past the dead row of trees and pressing eastward like wings had sprouted from their backs.

"Do you think we should start looking for footprints?" Letty questioned, shaking out her hands to remove the ice from her gloves. Even in the bright of day, Cognito was still freezing.

"Well, that's just the problem. Assuming he came this way to search for you—since we didn't see him when we returned to the spot you ran from and we haven't come across any footprints—he must be behind us." Raizu deadpanned the observation, and no matter how his voice trembled almost apologetically, his logic was a comfort to hear. Majest always tried to placate Letty even when things were hopeless, but she liked the way Raizu laid the truth out neatly for her, even as he grimaced and chewed his lip in uncertainty.

It was like being around the sun, she realized—he was a quivering, albeit constant light.

"Behind us? But aren't *we* supposed to be following *him*?" Letty stared up at Raizu, meeting his violet-blue eyes with confusion.

"Um," Raizu hedged, and scratched at his neck. "Hold on. Let me try to draw it for you." He bent to the ground and scribbled a few shapes loosely in the snow. "Here." He motioned to a small, surprisingly-even circle in the center. "This is where you lost him. Those lines above it are the dead trees." Raizu traced a line in the snow to his right. "Here's our trail, the way we've been traveling." He pointed back at the circle with one slender, leather-gloved finger. "We reached this circle just before dawn, right? Majest was most likely sleeping in a tree or some sort of cave—he wouldn't have seen us pass, and we wouldn't have seen him, so we kept walking on. When he woke up, he could have either followed our prints if he'd seen them, or gone back the other way."

A prickle of worry dug its way into Letty's heart as she struggled to understand, and they began to walk on once more, the snow sloping downward into a vale that glistened in dappled patches. "The other way?"

"Don't worry," Raizu assured her. "The way you talk about him, he seems like a smart guy. If he searches the area, he'll find our footprints and they'll lead him here."

"That's a pretty big *if*," Letty murmured. "Shouldn't we go back again? It's pointless to keep going this way if Majest isn't here."

Raizu shrugged. "We can go back if you want."

"No, that's—"

Letty broke her words with a sudden yelp, foot sinking with a bulky *crunch* beneath the snow and several layers of paper-thin ice, and something bright and cold and seeping gathered on the inside of her boot, soaking her sock, fluttering hard beneath the irises of her eyes.

Raizu was beside her immediately. "What?" he demanded. "What is it?"

"It's water," said Letty, and stared at her foot as if it were a complete stranger she was meeting for the first time. She hadn't moved it, despite the snow-crusted liquid that was staining her boot the rich dark brown of earth, and the wetness against her skin that was less unpleasant than it was perplexing.

"There must be a frozen creek underneath the snow here," Raizu noted, and glanced around the forest floor with apprehension. It glimmered at him as it sunk into its icy hideouts. "The storm must have covered the ice like a second skin—we'll have to find a way around it."

Letty still did not remove her foot, or her gaze, and she barely heard Raizu's words. All she could see was the water, and a funny feeling took over her gut as she watched the bubbles. It was a recognizable feeling, but she could not place it, could only shake her head and her thoughts aside long enough to step back from the puddle. The wetness of her foot remained, and she shivered at its clammy power, toes protesting.

Raizu began to start forward, as if to take a look, but Letty held out a hand to halt him. "Careful," she said, and didn't know why her voice was wavering. "I don't want you to end up tripping and falling into some secret stream because of me."

There was a response, some sort of agreement, but Letty could not comprehend what Raizu was saying over the roar that suddenly leapt up in both ears, and it was not as though she had never seen water, never gotten her feet wet—but it had never been like this, so full of mystery and possibility; this was the first time she was face to face with what might, however impossibly, link her to the power her fingertips had been reaching for since she was two years younger and smaller.

This was the first time she had considered the element of water—and the first time its intoxicating mystery drew her forward to it, whispering her name from beneath snow and beyond ice.

The feeling of wetness was spreading, she thought, unless it was her imagination getting the best of her, hope foolishly catalyzing a reaction. But her foot felt numb, not in terror but in more of an awestruck sort of way—numbed by marvel, by trepidation. The idea of falling and letting the shattered stream soak the tendrils of her hair and the fur on her shoulders was suddenly exhilarating. Empowering.

That's what I want, Letty thought, and the words were familiar as they echoed inside her. *Power.*

Then she placed the feeling—it was what had struck her at the mouth of a cave black and vast and ambushing in its command. It was all rising up under her skin, and she grasped at it, and she *heaved.*

The channels in her mind shot open with the kickback of a launched arrow.

Thoughts and worlds and nerve endings lit up, and for the first time, Letty could see more than darkness and uncertain void when she concentrated; she could see paths that wound about and spun and crawled around her brain, and she could see the way out, the end of the labyrinth, the twists and turns to take.

She saw what Majest was always telling her—she saw light.

Without moving, without blinking, hands out like points on a star, she traveled the path; she felt for the way and bumbled against the walls, and doors unlocked as she reached them, and she was through.

Alongside her toes, the puddle rippled.

The heavens cracked open, and Letty felt them upon her back like a great pair of wings, as though she could feel Komi's smile removing the weight from her shoulders so she instead could fly.

She watched the ripples, hands out, fingertips curled like claws and shaking like leaves, and that tiny, inconsequential puddle became her mind's art, her molded clay. It shook beneath her, and she was the cavern, and it was the scared little girl, just for a moment, just long enough.

Letty could not believe the moment as it swamped over her.

"Raizu!" she yelled, despite the fact that he was right beside her. "Raizu, look, I'm doing something!"

There was a surprised exclamation, the clap of hands, something that let her know Raizu was seeing and believing, but that lapse in concentration was all it took—she was still flying down the path in her mind, but her attention had gone elsewhere, and something thorny and barbed suddenly engulfed the walls in shadow, as if to trip her and plunge her into blackness once more. Letty gasped in surprise; she did not understand; she could not identify the murky intruder.

The thing in her mind hissed, and it was a creature that did not seem to belong; it was alien and invasive, a darkness stretching as it woke from its slumber. It filled Letty with a sudden, icy terror, and it was opening its thorn-laced mouth as if to speak, but she reeled back, off the path, and the lights went out.

The water was still. Letty's mind was dark, and reality phased back into her sight in hazy stripes of sunlight and snow. The dark thing against her thoughts had vanished as quickly as it had emerged. The thrill of her powers was for a moment overshadowed by doubt—*Majest never felt anything like that, did he?*

Then Raizu's excited chatter broke through the walls of her own bewilderment, and after a moment, Letty found she could understand what he was saying.

"You really did that? You really made the water move and dance like that, Letty?"

A fissuring grin split Letty's face at once, and everything else swept away at the bright beam across her new friend's face, the way his eyes lit up like blue lanterns. "I did, didn't I?"she asked with a breathless peal of laughter. She couldn't remember the last time a smile had come across her lips—they ached with the unfamiliar experience. "Only after two years of watching Maji have all the fun!"

"Well, you certainly made me look like an idiot," said Raizu, and if there had been shadows across Letty's face, he hadn't noticed, and Letty suddenly, stoutly believed they had not been there at all. "The whole, *'powers? No such thing!'* angle sort of goes out the window. However you got it, your element is the real deal—so congratulations."

"It's all thanks to you," Letty told him, and feeling was shaking back into her toes; the sun was striping her hair. "Without you, I never would have looked at water like it was something I could unlock. I might never have."

"What? No—no way!" Raizu protested, and his cheeks immediately flushed in embarrassed laughter. He touched Letty's shoulder. "All I did was tell you I didn't know what I was talking about!"

"You did, though," said Letty earnestly, and looked at him, the sweep of his scarf, the ruffle of his hair. "You still do—I feel like I keep owing you my life's worth over and over, and I've only known you for a day. What in the world am I going to be able to repay you with?"

Raizu was shaking his head before she had even finished. "Don't worry about me," he said. "And don't thank me so much—I haven't done the one thing I promised you; I haven't found your brother. I have a zero percent success rate."

"You can be my replacement brother for the time being," Letty told him jokingly, though the reminder of her missing family tied her heart up in knots that squeezed each pulse from her chest. "You're doing a pretty fine job of it, anyhow."

This time, Raizu rolled his eyes, though he was still blushing. "But now we *have* to find him—you've got to show him what you can do!"

"Yeah, but…" Suddenly Letty frowned. She felt closed off again, in the dark, concentration as impossible as grasping at clouds. "What if I can't even do it again?"

She expected Raizu to laugh off her concern, to give her the empty promise that *of course she'll be able to do it again,* but when their eyes met, Raizu said nothing; he just tilted his head in the smallest of shakes, and he stepped to the side of the creek beneath the snow, and he held out a hand.

Even a dark mind could not resist such a candle. Letty gripped his gloved fingers and followed him, and she was ready to find her way.

VIII. GATHER

Over the curving rise of the hill-bend, Majest saw the shadows of a familiar shape's footfalls, and though he had walked for hours along two sets of unwavering prints, over valleys, drifts, and streams, he had never imagined the owners of the prints would turn around to face him.

At the sight of the face above him, pressed against the gray sky, Majest began to run. He tore over the snow as it flew up in white-caps behind his feet; cold air flooded his senses, though his blood felt warm in its veins.

"Letty!" he called, as loud as he could. "*Systir* mín—Letty, I'm here! I'm coming!"

Furry, padded boots clanked heavily against each other, snow inside them and melting against Majest's feet, but he barely felt the sting. The only thing that mattered was Letty—Letty, closer and closer, followed by a stranger; Letty, hearing his voice and running too, all lit up and fire-red in her strides; Letty, smiling with no trace of anger.

Majest let out a breathless laugh. Letty never could stay angry with anyone.

He sped up as his sister's features defined themselves in front of them, eyes like blue moons, hair in a tangle; she wasn't more than a few paces away from him now, paces longer, steadier on her feet in the piles of snow than Majest had ever seen her. She somehow looked hardier, too, as if her trip through the wilderness had taken a great deal out of her and pumped even more back in.

The two siblings met in a flurry of arms and fur-coat jackets as

Majest lifted his sister up in the air, twirling her around in a circle before returning her feet to the ground to crush her in a tight hug. Choked, happy noises escaped from Letty's throat as she wrapped her little arms around Majest's neck and buried her face into his chest.

"I'm so sorry," she whispered, and she sounded disgusted with herself. "I did it again; I ran off without thinking. Maji, Maji, I'm so sorry. I'm sorry I'm so reckless."

"It's okay," Majest murmured into a tangle of red-brown hair. "You're alright, it's still the two of us, and nothing else matters."

"I shouldn't have left like that," Letty continued all the same. "I should have been reasonable; I should have tried to keep myself safe!"

"But you *are* safe," Majest said in a question, setting his sister upright to examine her face, searching for signs of injury.

Letty shook her head back and forth. "I would have died if it hadn't been for Raizu and another stranger. They saved me after that grizzly appeared when I fell down the cliff…"

Majest froze, gaze landing on a small red scratch on Letty's cheek. "You *what?*"

Letty nodded, lighting up rather than shrinking from the memory. "I was running when the blizzard picked up. I couldn't see *anything*. And I didn't remember your warning about the drop-off, so I wasn't expecting it—I couldn't see it—and I toppled right over it and landed next to a hibernation ground for an enormous grizzly bear. It chased me and would have gotten me for sure if I hadn't been saved by this peculiar girl with black hair—she jumped out from nowhere and killed it. And she had to leave, so she left me with Raizu, who helped me find you." Her story tumbled from her mouth in cascades.

Majest shook his head in astonishment, catching the words as they flew. "Ó *kæri*, Letty," came his breathless, bilingual reply after a second or two. "I almost lost you, didn't I?"

"Even if I had managed to save myself, I still wouldn't have made it without Raizu. He's the one who helped me find you. He's so smart—he knew exactly what to do." Letty swung her head around to where the boy was observing the scene with an awkward grimace, as if he weren't sure what to do in this time of obvious family reunion. He kicked the snowy ground with one boot in a nervous manner, hands worrying at the ends of his sleeves.

"Raizu! You're still here!" Letty exclaimed, and beamed brightly.

"I—I wouldn't leave without saying goodbye," the boy stammered, shifting his bow and arrows. He fixed light indigo eyes on Majest and blinked in embarrassment, quickly returning his gaze back to the ground. "My apologies for not getting her here sooner; it's hard to get good distance with this snow and all the food I got from that bear." He held up the sack of frozen meat. "I mean—*I* didn't kill the bear, of course—I'm not quite that good—but I kept the meat."

Majest raised his eyebrows.

The boy took a breath, and though Letty had noted his practicality, it seemed to be swept away by timidity. "My name's Raizu, but you, uh, probably already know that." He managed a weak smile. "I'm from the Inertia pack south of here; I was on a hunting mission when I ran into your sister."

Eyebrows still up, Majest stared at the stuttering boy in marvel. Here was the first boy his age he had ever met—a pack boy, no less—and yet he gave no indication of a rugged, selfish life; Raizu was clean and bright and the periwinkle wash of his eyes was as refreshing as a clear spring day, a breeze against shy sunlight.

Majest had always imagined pack members as arrogant, as living off bones and fear, skin sallow, bones hunched, hardly people at all, but he eyed Raizu and changed his mind—apparently, some pack members were thin and neatly-groomed and stammered through their words. Raizu was charming without any notion of it.

"I'm Majest Skylark," Majest said after a moment, wondering what had taken him so long to speak. A gentle smile formed on his lips as he went on, "But hey, you probably knew that, too. Thank you so much for everything you've done for Letty."

"It's no problem," Raizu replied. His voice was a little steadier, though his feet still scuffed the ground, wrapped up in his pointed boots. He dipped his head, the customary greeting between adults, though he couldn't have been older than eight birth-years. "It's, um—it's great to finally meet you; Letty's told me a lot about you, and what you can—well, what you can do. It's all very impressive."

Majest's eyes darted from Raizu to Letty and back again. What had his sister said in regards to why they were traveling the wilderness alone? Had she really shared the secret that might have killed their mother? Majest felt a pit growing in his stomach, and his smile fell into it.

"Is that so?" he asked, with a meaningful glance at Letty.

Letty cringed visibly.

It was Raizu who replied, quietly, timorously. "Yes, she, uh—told me about how much time you spend outside." He looked sheepish, and his gaze met Majest's with a slow embarrassment. "With, um, trees and animals. And how you can sort of…converse with them."

Majest's face constructed itself into a tight, irritated glare, one pointed straight at his irresponsible sister. "Letty, I know you don't have a lot of experience with strangers, but I feel like 'tell them everything about yourself on the first day' isn't something that should have so easily popped up on your to-do list."

"Sorry," Letty muttered.

"Well," Majest said, heaving a sigh and shrugging at Raizu, "I suppose there's no point in hiding anything, then. Yes, I have earth powers. I move and shape trees, I lift heavy rocks, I talk to animals. What else did my *extraordinarily* careful sister tell you?"

Letty bit her lip and said meekly, "I told him about the women who attacked our mother, how we're on the run in case they come after us, too."

Majest stared in withering blankness at her.

"Raizu's not a threat—I can promise you that" Letty exclaimed, lifting her head. "I've never met anyone nicer, or—or more honest!" She paused to breathe, and her eyes flashed with a sudden new vigor." And…well, he helped me unlock my powers."

At that, Majest thought his jaw might tumble to his feet. "He—your *powers?* What in the world are you talking about?

You unlocked them? Where? When?" His hands clamped around Letty's wrists, face boring into hers in bewildered thrill. "Tell me!"

Letty gave him a sly round of giggles. "*Well,*" she began, "Raizu and I were talking about you and your tree nonsense, so I gave him the message Komi told me, too."

"Right," Majest nodded. Nothing could have made Letty forget those words—sometimes she would mutter them in her sleep, as though the struggle to decipher them continued even into dreams.

"So, Raizu ended up figuring out what it all meant—how I might 'quench all others in a single breath.'"

Majest looked to Raizu now, eyes softening, and inclined his head toward him. "Well? What did you come up with?"

Raizu seemed startled to be asked, and suddenly his cheeks were dusted scarlet. "Oh! Um, I guess I just thought, 'what force can quench other forces?' and then remembered that water quenches fire, and it quenches the ground, and I suppose it could quench the air if it wanted—water's unruly; it destroyed half our pack a generation ago during a spring melt back when we lived up by Great Bear Lake. Water's dangerous enough to quench anything."

"You never told me that," said Letty with a gasp.

Raizu kneaded his hands. "I wasn't alive then. It—it doesn't really matter." He bit his lip, blinked up at Majest. "Anyway, it was Letty who really brought my senseless musings into the real world."

"I made water ripple!" Letty burst in, and shook Majest's hands within her own. "I did it, Maji, and it was all thanks to Raizu!"

Majest could hardly believe his ears. "It was water all along!" he laughed, and could not find it in himself to be anything but proud of his sister, the girl who had struggled so long unknowing of her true strengths, who looked at him now with such vigor and determination, even when fear flashed somewhere in the darkest parts of her eyes. "Letty, that makes so much sense! You're so—" He stopped, searched for the appropriate word. "Water-y?"

Letty snorted, and released one of his hands to thwack her glove against his ribs. "*Thanks,*" she drawled, but then returned to a face of pure sunshine, bouncing on her booted heels. "Anyway, now I can start testing it, see if I can unlock it again now that I know it's there!"

"Absolutely." Majest hugged his sister for a moment before letting her go. "Water is officially a priority! I probably shouldn't let you have at our drinking supplies, since we sort of need those to live, but any stream that comes our way—it's all yours!"

"Oh *wow*, an entire stream," Letty teased. "That's the best gift you've ever gotten me!"

"There's a big stream fairly close to here," Raizu offered, still looking to Majest tentatively; his shy gazed had not wavered, though he had grown quiet. "Back in the direction of my camp. The water there moves so quickly, it won't freeze no matter how cold it gets, so it'd be the perfect place to stop and check out. I, um. I could take you there if you'd like?" He turned redder.

Majest could see his sister was tempted by the way her eyes lit up, and he found himself, surprisingly, considering the offer as well. There was something about Raizu that drew him in; he sensed he could trust him, that this boy with words like the kind of scattered raindrops that grew flowers could make a more-than-valuable friend or ally. Traveling with him would mean direction, a constant guiding beam.

But the point of these travels was to escape the endless maze of forest and danger—he and Letty needed to disappear without a trace, and a camped-out pack in the center of the woods' attention was hardly the place to do that. A large group of people living in the crowded southern forest would be a target painted blood-red in the snow.

And so before Letty could open her mouth to agree to Raizu's offer, Majest put in with reluctant haste, "I think it's best if we keep going the way we've been going, Letty."

His sister's face fell, and Majest felt a twinge of regret at her crestfallen expression. "But *Maji*," she protested. "Raizu and his people could protect us! Why can't we live with Inertia?"

"You'd be safe from anyone who wanted to hurt you," Raizu put in softly. "We're inconspicuous, I can assure you." He looked up at Majest shyly from under long lashes; his eyes were honest and warm. "We'd keep you out of harm's way."

For a second, Majest was almost swayed by the kindness of the offer. There would be no going hungry, not when everyone provided for each other. There would be shelter, and warmth as armor against the winter, and endless companionship just as gentle and easy as what Raizu was giving them here and now. Above all, he and Letty could have a family again.

But it would be so easy for the enemy to find them.

"I'm sorry," said Majest, heart heavy. "We need to find a hiding place where no one will ever think to look. Which is a shame, because…because, well, your offer sounds really great."

Raizu and Letty both looked like they might object, but after a few seconds of silence, Raizu nodded, though Majest could read disappointment on his face. "I respect that. You'll be at an advantage staying off the map, especially if you're planning on crossing the water."

"I guess," admitted Letty, as both boys were now looking to her for a consensus. "If it's to keep us safe…"

"Which it is," Majest and Raizu said in harmonization.

Another disappointed expression flashed over Letty's face, and she sighed in defeat. "I suppose it won't do me any good to argue. Look where it got me last time."

Majest almost smiled. "At least you have the sense to make sure you never fall into the same trap twice."

"I don't think I have enough luck to worm my way out of *two* grizzly bear attacks."

"Precisely what I'm worried about."

Raizu grinned at their exchange, staring at them as if trying to soak them in before losing sight of them. "Are you two going to be off right away? I have meat to spare if you want any." He lifted his bag in one questioning hand.

"Oh, no way!" Majest shook his head furiously. "Absolutely not. I already owe you my life for bringing Letty back to me. Don't make the debt any bigger."

"I insist, though!" Raizu's brows creased in conviction, and he opened the bag to pull out a chunk of ice-crusted bear. He held it in Majest's direction like an offering. "If you're going on a long journey alone, I at least want to help keep you fed."

"But don't you need that for your pack?" Letty frowned. "I thought the food was for them."

Raizu laughed a little, sounding more confident than before. "You need it more than they do. They tend to stuff themselves before winter, anyway, so you're practically doing them a favor. Take it. Please."

The meat was tempting, fresh, and right in front of him, so to avoid any further argument, Majest reached out and took the food from Raizu's hand with a nod. "Thank you."

"Of course." Raizu smiled, turning a little pinkish.

And with that, there was no more to be said. With a sudden jolt that seemed unnatural and wrong, Majest remembered Raizu was nothing more than a stranger met by chance in a land where timing was everything, and he would regrettably never see him again. Raizu must have sensed it, too, for he cleared his throat and blinked disappointment against the ground.

"Raizu," Majest said. "If we're ever back in the area, and there isn't a possible pair of murderers after us—would it be alright if we sought out your pack?"

"That would be great," Raizu told him earnestly. "There's always room and we'd love to have you." He waved a hand in a manner of hesitant departure. His tone was easy now, comfortable enough to be direct. "It was a pleasure meeting the two of you; I consider you the first friends I've met in a long time. Good luck with your travels—and your powers, too. I'll keep an ear out for you."

"I hope you don't hear anything." Majest grinned in full now. "It seems as though we've got some disappearing to do." He turned serious for a second and added, "Raizu, you won't tell anyone about us and our powers, right? If anyone suspicious asks if you know where we've gone, you'll say you've never seen us in your life, right?"

"My lips are sealed," promised Raizu. Majest didn't think he'd ever seen someone look so sincere. "I wouldn't tell anyone."

"Wow, I really owe you." Majest shook his head in amazement. "I mean, really, if you *ever* need anything, anything at all—"

"I know where I can find you. The Bay." Raizu smiled. "It's a small world we live in, Majest, Letty. I'm sure we'll see each other again."

"Hopefully in better times, right?" Majest chuckled quietly. "That's what everyone always seems to say."

An idea bright in his mind, Majest sank his teeth into his concentration, flicking his wrist until a stone shot out of the ground, gravitating to his fingers. His hands moved in sweeping, broom-like motions, and he speedily shaped the stone into a point that flared out below like a sunray, a triangle sharp and direct. Another hand wave and a thick twig was gliding up beside it, which he fastened to the rock by pecking an elemental hole in the stone and securing the branch cozily inside of it.

It was an arrow.

Raizu watched intently during the process, blinking in bafflement when Majest held the contraption out to him without even touching it. Raizu took it in one hand, a look of wonder crossing his features as he studied it, the way it pointed, the enchantment of its sudden appearance.

"I noticed your sheath was one short," Majest said, folding his arms across his chest, and he couldn't help but grin wide from cheek to cheek at the look on Raizu's face. "Thought I might start paying my dues with fixing that."

Raizu tucked the arrow in its proper casing, speechless.

"Thanks again for saving my life and helping me find Maji," Letty piped up.

"Of—of course." Raizu shook the shock off, swallowing, and then there was laughter on his lips as he turned his pointed feet, crunching delicately in the snow, and began to carry himself away. "Goodbye!" he called back, waving with a smile.

"Goodbye," Majest and Letty chorused, and waved back as his bright steps started up the hill. There was a curious lump to Majest's throat, as though the boy walking away had been more than a simple stranger. And yet, there he went.

The Skylarks stared after his shadow until Raizu was only a glimmer between the earth and sky, something bright and untouchable and far away.

Majest turned to his sister, and smirked. "You thought he was cute, didn't you?" he teased.

"Who, me?" Letty wrinkled her nose. "Why?"

"It's just a question, Letty."

"Whatever." Letty's eyes rolled as they always did when her brother was being a typical boy. "It doesn't matter what he looked like or didn't look like; he was too old for me. I'm only five birth-years, remember? Give me a little time to be innocent and helpless before I look to settle down."

"I didn't need an answer that practical," Majest mused, stifling a laugh with a cough. "I was just joking." His eyebrows waggled mischievously. "He had pretty eyes, though. Like the blue-violet edges in a sunset, just before the night hits."

Letty elbowed him as he laughed, unable to help it. "Hey—if you think he's *that* good-looking, you can have him." She glanced out to the horizon, where Raizu was barely a dot moving over the white hills. "I just hope he doesn't get into any trouble for helping me."

"He'll be okay." Majest took Letty by her shoulder, and together they took the first reunited step of their journey. "He seemed more than capable of looking after himself and finding his way home. Besides, we've got a long way ahead of us."

"We're getting closer to the Bay, though. I know it."

Majest was taken aback. "You can sense that? Do you think it's your power?"

Letty shook her head impatiently. "No, Maji—*look.*"

Majest turned his head to the space above the trees. He thought there was a faint line of blue on the gray-white horizon that might've mirrored a shimmering expanse of water beneath, but he couldn't be sure. "I don't see what you're—"

A sharp cry echoed off the trees and they looked up with a start to see a group of four arctic gulls flying overhead, wings stretching and flexing as they soared peaceably onward, passing the siblings on a breeze, far out of reach. Their calls faded into the horizon and echoed back, like an invitation.

"Gulls go where there's water to be found," said Letty, bouncing with newfound energy. "You taught me that!"

"You're right, Letty," Majest told her, as the gulls' silhouettes gathered into one singular form in the sky. "They're on their way just like us."

Seti had always expected unpleasant surprises—but even as he walked between sunlight and moonrise, between fires lit by weakened match-sticks, distracted in the President's quest, searching for a way to search out Soti herself, he had never even for a moment expected she would come to him of her own accord.

And yet she came, with the soft treads of a nimble rabbit, out tentatively from between the trees that shielded her thin, weak frame. She was quiet and fidgeting as she moved and called out a greeting, round doe's eyes wide and blue in a way that made Seti's stomach roll. Only her jacket, streaked red with a long band of gory war paint, gave an inkling she was not as disgustingly innocent as she feigned.

Seti's thoughts were blank as the woman moved toward him, and she stared at him with a worried sort of numbness—as though she recognized the danger and turmoil that might have come with his presence, but the encounter, in the long scheme of things, meant nothing to her.

Which was to be expected—Soti did not care about her sister's son. She did not even know him.

They were standing beneath a ledge that branched out over their heads like the crest of a great oak tree, brown and buckled with a barky sort of texture. It was unstable, littered from top to floor with rock fragments, and that was where Soti nestled herself: between the shadows of its stony fragility, standing before Seti where the sun could not reach to illuminate.

One of Seti's hands immediately went to the knife in his belt at her sudden, unprecedented entrance, especially when this was the woman who had eluded him for much longer than a few risings and settings of the day.

"What, have you come here to talk?" he called, and the assertion of his voice boomed so loud, he swore he saw rocks rattle above Soti's head. "I have nothing to say to you, and no reason to listen to anything you might try to say to me. If you're going to tell me to stay away from the Skylark children, you're going to have to tell me that over my dead body."

Soti's expression pinched. Seti was not quite close enough to see the precise way her lip fought its tremble when she looked at him, took in his face, his voice, his curse. "You'd rather fight than talk?"

"I have orders to kill the Skylarks," Seti told her, and met her loaded gaze with a challenge. "And not even you can guilt me out of them. The children mean nothing to me. I protect myself, and my own interests, and my own freedoms. You have nothing to persuade me with—and no reason to care for a couple of the gods' pets. You're keeping me from doing my job."

"And you keep me from doing mine," said Soti, and a gulp bulged her throat with a nervous flicker, though her eyes remained stony. "I assume your orders come from the Organization. That they're the ones controlling you."

Seti bristled. "*Controlling* me? No one controls me."

Soti dismissed the remark. "You may have orders from them, but I have my own orders as well. Orders to protect Majest and Aletta."

"Orders from *whom?*"

At that, Soti went stiff, and her face darkened in the gloom of the ledge overhang.

A sneer broke across Seti's face, wide and cruel. "From the *gods,*" he guessed, and at the way Soti quieted like snow, he knew he had her. "And what do your dear little gods know? How to make the same mistakes with our planet, time and time again, until they destroy every last chance we have at maintaining a hale and hearty civilization?"

"The gods protect us," Soti snapped, and she was on the

defensive now, fur jacket all fluffed out, in fear and indignation, feet locking in the gritty dirt.

"The gods," Seti corrected in a jeer, "give out powers like they're rat bait, and then wait for evil things to smell it and come knocking from the shadows so they can try to take them out with the trash. With the heavenly always comes the hellish. Or don't you know that already?"

"What's happening now is exactly what's supposed to happen," said Soti, and her narrow jaw set in a level, unflattering line. "The gods know what they're doing."

"Oh, did they tell you that?" Seti's lips seemed to be locked in a permanent sneer, and something boiled beneath his jacket and skin. He was still gripping the knife. "Because you're one of their little pets, too? You're pathetic, Soti, and so are they, and so are the Organization. Can't you all just leave the world to grow and decompose and then rot as it is?"

He began to pace, glaring out high above Soti's head, at the place where rock met sky, and found a boulder sitting atop the cliff-face, perched on its throne, observing the scene unfold below with the impassive stone of a watchful bird's eye. A trail of haphazard smaller lookalikes cascaded with poised insistence for a long distance to the ground, like a match waiting to be lit; one push would send the rocks all tumbling.

Seti returned his gaze to Soti, who was unresponsive, her blank white face revealing nothing but opposition.

"I only want my freedom," Seti told her, and it was a great struggle to quiet his voice. "Which is why I cannot fail. So I don't know why you came, unless you're looking for a fight."

"I came because I also cannot fail," Soti answered evenly.

"I have to kill them."

"I have to save them."

"If I kill them, the Organization will likely lose its motive, whatever the President spews about an equal world. I know who she is; I know what she wants. This could end here, before her ambitions grow bigger than two siblings and a daydreaming god."

"They already have," Soti insisted, and the plea in her voice rang like a bell. "Because what's growing behind those walls is more than her, more than the Skylarks, more than what it looks like."

"Did the gods tell you that, too?" Seti eyed the boulder in its stone nest, and let the knife in his hand fall slack back into its proper place.

Soti ignored him. "If the Skylarks are protected, they have a fighting chance to play this out in their own hands. Which is why I'm going to warn them, Seti. I'm going to keep them safe, and I'm going to make sure they're prepared. That is my duty, and this is my warning to you. Are we clear?"

Seti's gaze swung dizzyingly to her at once, and he saw the twitch of her skin-and-bone legs, how they itched to flee, and he knew she was nothing more than a startled wild animal searching for a way to edge out of a clearing before a hunter could put a bullet between its eyes.

The boulder seemed to wink at him from above.

Seti knew he could not fight this woman—not with heavenly power packed somewhere beneath her frail surface. She could aim pebbles like missiles, slice bears clean through. She had a blade like a fifth limb.

Seti, meanwhile, had the Organization's rust-edged knife and its splintered handle.

And so without giving himself time to think about what he was doing or how he would go about doing it, Seti took a running start to where the ledge sloped down to lock arms with the land below, hopping upon it with a huffing grunt and racing up its length, one great stone in his mind and his eyes, and he found it towering before him in a great invitation, Soti rabbit-sized below his feet.

He barely had to tap the boulder. It went plunging down.

And with it came everything in its path.

Soti heard it as she saw it, felt it beneath her at the same time it touched her skin. It began with the sudden magnitude of an earthquake, a violent shudder from the sky that stopped her from running and rooted her feet to the ground with shackles of gravity. It was one push and pull after another, crash after break after pummeling blow, until the ledge was one body breaking and tumbling.

The avalanche hit her like the heavens were falling. There was nowhere to go. Seti had been too fast, too clever, strong enough to move mountains, to trigger landslides, to unlock the earth and will it to do his bidding.

If she was crushed now, who would look after the Skylarks? Who would keep Seti's knife from their throats? Who would make sure the gods' orders would be carried out, just as Seti carried out the Organization's?

The thoughts ran her over with fear before so much as a grain of rock had kissed her cheek. She fought to move her feet, to fling herself backwards, but the first impact came from seemingly nowhere. She watched it come, watched it fly from the rocky face as though it had sprouted wings.

The rock bowled her over, and she landed flat on her back. Pain ripped up her spine in a raging chain reaction as her body collapsed out from under her feet; shapes and silhouettes danced behind her eyes, blurry and bright. She screamed in agony and fear, trying to stand, but the stones kept pounding, merciless, piling on top of her in a crushing clutch until she feared her lungs would burst from her chest.

"You'll regret this, Seti!" she cried, voice muffled as death tumbled down onto her skin, stoning her against the ground. Her jacket was brown and red. "You're making your mother's mistakes!"

As she hollered, voice cracked and shattered, a large stone flew from above and struck Soti in the front of her head. Eyes rattling, skull fragmenting, she saw a single, familiar star flash across her vision like a last wish. She grasped at it desperately, clutching with everything she had.

This is time I don't have, Soti thought weakly as the world slipped from her fingers like mud, caking her from the inside out. She still held her star. *By the time it runs out, I will have failed.*

At that concession, that guilt sent straight to Komi's ears, the star took off and Soti was gone, leaving only a stony tomb that seemed to glow and shimmer in the sun. Somewhere above, laughter was ringing out over the trees, a song no one was left to hear.

IX. ENLIGHTEN

"Ah!" Majest's dismayed cry rang out over the treetops. "*Vitleysa!* I don't believe this!"

Letty sat up, startled from her sleep, finding herself in a makeshift tree bed, hair kinked and rumpled, eyes bright and worried. Her back throbbed and pulsed in protest, and she gripped the leather skin of Majest's hammock. "What's the matter?"

Majest, with a fierce, sleepy glare, extended one long finger to an unassuming branch beside them. Such a branch had been in charge of securing their food bag, where Majest had fastened it just arm-lengths from their sleeping heads before drifting off. Letty stared at it, and met its ridges and knots in dismay.

"That's not good," she whispered when she saw it.

"No, it's not." Majest grappled forward in a squirrel-like motion, and snatched the bag from its former position with hands like tiny claws. Letty could almost imagine a furious, bushy tail twitching out behind him. "*Þetta er hræðileg,*" he muttered fiercely in his father's language. Letty didn't understand what he had said, but she decided it couldn't have been anything nice.

Where a full sack of food had been placed with care the night before, there was now merely a limp, jagged-edged piece of canvas, stamped here and there with the staining remnants of red meat. The handmade sack had been ripped into worthless shreds.

Below, on the forest floor, the canister of water that had been heavy in its near-fullness lay open and cracked like a broken jaw hung open. An indent of melted snow drooled out beside it, indicating the waste and spill of what had once been enough water to last weeks.

"Must have been a raccoon." Majest ran his hands vainly through the ruined pack, as though planning on scraping away the few meaty smears their assailant had left behind. "That's what these scratches look like. I should have been more careful. How did I not *hear* it?"

"You've always been a deep sleeper; it's not your fault," said Letty in a small voice.

Majest let out a noncommittal grunt, hands still moving around the destroyed food pack. "There's nothing left," he muttered. "Not even a crumb."

He chucked the leather tatters aside and they fluttered down to the ground like ashes, settling brown and gray into the snow and tugging slightly with the breeze.

"What are we going to do?" Letty fretted. "We're completely out of food and water, right?"

"Yeah. We'll have to go hunting." Majest heaved himself out of the branches, displeasure in every creak of his movement. "There's nothing else we *can* do, unless you happen to know of a food source around these parts."

Letty groaned, a pit of apprehension forming in her stomach. "All that meat Raizu gave us…"

"Wasted," her brother agreed. His green eyes looked more annoyed than concerned. "At the very least, Raizu could have fed that to his pack. Now no one gets it."

"Well, no one but the raccoon." Letty watched with curious eyes as Majest neatly unpacked and unfolded his power to weave branches into a ladder that curled down the trunk as natural as climbing vines. His disgruntlement seemed momentarily faded into determination, and he broke into a slight sweat as he wove branch after creaking branch into knots and turns, hands twisting about like the wind.

"Alright," Majest muttered upon completion, and worked his way down the makeshift rungs with surprising agility for his lanky size, hips swaying for balance, knuckles white in the moment before he dropped his feet to the forest floor. "It's pretty late in the season for elk hunting and it'll be hard to find anything decent so far north, but there's nothing else we can do, and we might as well start looking now, before we get too hungry." His voice held weary conviction.

Letty made a face, staring down at her brother. He looked tiny from so high up, and it made her stomach flutter with dizziness. He'd made the drop seem so easy.

"Letty," Majest called back up the tree, snapping her into focus. "Are you coming?"

"Oh, um—yes!"

Letty gathered her furry pack in her arms and tied the ends around her waist, and when she clambered down the tree after her brother, she nearly tumbled for lack of grace, nothing compared to Majest's effortless dexterity. Her legs scuffed hard against the rough bark in her attempts to slide, and she winced as she felt the tear of skin. In defeated frustration, she leapt the last few lengths in a clumsy flourish, arms reeling, and landed with a thud beside Majest.

Once steadied, she grimaced in embarrassment, shaking off her boots. "Are you sure you want me to come with you?"

"Would you rather stay in the tree?" Majest raised his eyebrows.

Letty was uncertain. "I don't know anything about hunting—"

"I'll teach you," Majest told her, and waved the slingshot that was already snug in the curves of his fingers. "But come on, we've got to start now or we'll starve for certain. It can take days to bring down a decent piece of game."

"Alright," said Letty, making a face, and the thought of *days* feeling useless and hungry made her stomach sag like a wilted flower. "But won't I just slow you down?"

"Not if we're already going too fast," Majest said, lifting his head to scan the trees. With no warning, he snatched up Letty's wrist in a cuff of strong fingers, and then they were sprinting, Letty towed along at her brother's side.

"What—? Hey!" Letty spluttered, barely managing not to trip. She regained her balance and huffed, "Maji, this is hopeless. You can't just run around and expect things to jump into your hands."

"I'm not!"

"Then where are you going?"

"Here." Majest stopped running and examined what had all along been in their line of sight: a tall fir tree growing impossibly through the ice of the ground. Letty had never been able to quite grasp the concept of evolution Majest had once explained to her—how the world's natives had once lived with an hourglass of age ticking down their days and the branches of trees had craved warmth to thrive.

Letty tugged her hand free and watched as Majest plunged his arm between a forest of green needles that shivered and pricked, running his fingers along the bark at the tree's heart, eyes falling limp and shut.

More powers, Letty figured, and hugged her arms against her chest.

"According to this guy, we just missed a herd of caribou." Majest's eyes opened, and there was a bright glee circling their green. "One buck, four cows, and a calf. They weren't moving that fast when they were in the tree's range. We can catch up if we hurry."

Letty's nose wrinkled. "You're sure? All the little pine needles agree? They whispered to you?"

Majest faintly pouted. "*No.* I see things in my head, things the tree saw. Things it heard, or smelled, or felt. I don't know how, because trees aren't alive the way we are, but that's what happens. Can't explain it. It just is." He blinked, clearing his throat of the dry, cold air.

"So there are caribou just north of where we're standing?" Letty prompted, her stomach growling in impatience. "Just like that?"

Majest brightened. "Apparently they're traveling west and they're to our north, so we'll have to head northwest if we want to find them. But not too fast, or we might scare them off." He shifted his feet on the ground in anticipation. "It'll set us back a bit, since they're in the opposite direction of the Bay, but it'll be worth it if we can replace our food supply."

Without waiting for a response, he trotted off and began through the line of trees, feet crunching over his former footprints, blotting out heel and toe with toe and heel, reversing their course with nothing more than a step at a time.

Doing her best to match her brother's pace without complaint, Letty followed. "What about water, Maji? We have to find water, too."

"There'll be moisture in the meat, if we can get any," Majest responded. "If all else fails, we have that." Glancing at Letty to find her face sullen, he quickly added, "Of course, we're on the lookout for drinking water *and* power-testing water."

"Alright," Letty said, relief in her voice. Every day that passed with no further clues to what could set all her thoughts and channels ablaze in cosmic understanding was a day she was growing increasingly restless—restless and *thirsty*.

The Skylarks walked along in a comfortable silence, and Letty was reminded of the easy traveling of their first steps from their vacant cottage, all pale clouds and grief and uncertainty. The sun was snooping around a blue-gray sky and the weather was pleasant, but Letty could feel her mouth running dry, bones aching for sustenance.

But she bit her lip and marched on.

After nearly an hour of trekking broken only by the occasional bird-chatter or Majest-chatter, Letty's mouth was parched and her stomach was rumbling so loud, she wondered how the whole world couldn't hear it. She thought of the red bear meat Raizu had given them the day before and her head swayed with hunger and dizziness imagining the taste, the smell, the *relief.*

"Are we getting closer?" Letty croaked, clearing her throat over and over again in an attempt to soothe her dry mouth, which blazed excruciatingly in protest. "Can't you ask another tree?"

Majest's eyes remained fixed stoic and unwavering on the path ahead, and at first Letty thought he may not have heard her. She was about to repeat her questions when he turned to her over his shoulder and smiled. "Letty, stare at the ground for a minute and tell me what you see."

Letty dragged her gaze to the blinding snow, head throbbing at each sunlit crystal glimmer of it, and noticed after a few squinting seconds it wasn't all the same depth. Fleets of round, hoof-shaped prints roamed in wavering lines that stitched in and out of each other in an animal carelessness.

Letty's eyes shot up to her brother's. "How long have we—?"

"Shh." Majest put a finger to his lips, motioning for her to be silent. With his other hand, he gestured in front of him. "The prints just crossed ours back at the last clearing. They're fresh, which means the caribou are close. We have to be quiet." His voice was only a harsh whisper registering in Letty's ears.

She nodded. "Okay."

Majest crept forward in a slow seizing of limbs, bending his knees until his tall form was folded into a compact crouch, head no higher than Letty's. He pulled the slingshot from his belt once more and Letty saw what was inside of it: a tiny, green-gray ball about the size of her fist.

"Grass-bomb," Majest told her in hushed tones, noticing her stare. "You've seen Father make these for me, haven't you? I use them to hunt; they're smaller than arrows, more expendable, and just as accurate."

Letty was hesitant. "Are you sure I should come with you?"

"You should see how it's done in case you're ever on your own again," her brother responded. His gaze was still locked straight ahead, and there was something in his eyes that glowed brighter than green glass against sunlight. Letty wondered if he always got this excited when he hunted.

"Oh, Letty, look!" Majest whispered, pointing to something in front of him.

Letty looked.

Several paces ahead, the caribou stood, like something from a dream, dropped in against the wash of the winter background. One bull, four cows and one calf—just as Majest had said. Or rather, just as the *tree* had sensed. Their size was stunning, even at this distance, towering high above Letty's head on long, bony legs and tapered faces with eyes that bulged. They were graceful yet ugly, enchanting yet fearsome in their ruggedness. The bull had a head of antlers like the bare skeleton of a dead tree, earthy and gnarled. Letty was mesmerized, though their slow movements made her uneasy.

"Watch this," Majest said with an effortless smile, picking up a dark rock from the ground and tossing it roughly into the center of the caribou cluster.

At once, the animals' heads bobbed to a startled upright position, and they unbent themselves from the snow in a panicked haste. Their muzzles buzzed with the grunts and snorts of warning, and in rapid, uniform succession, they began to divide, the herd branching in half and in half again as they sprang out like an exploding star.

"Now we go!"

Majest was on his feet and running before Letty had time to question his obscure hunting methods, slingshot in hand. She blinked after him for a long, burdened moment, and then joined him, struggling to catch him at his quick hunter's pace.

The click of the caribou's ankles, steady and ticking as a metronome, rose above the flurry of commotion as Majest flew through the trees, long legs giving him a blurry strength of speed as he tore after the clicks and snorts. There was no hope of catching a healthy herd, but these caribou were scrawny with winter hunger and lethargic under the gloom of the slow-moving season, and Majest managed to get close enough to their fleeing forms to take a shot.

Majest's arms went up, practiced and polished, pulling the leather-corded strings of his weapon back, feet not missing a beat. The grass bomb was intact and in place, ready to fire. He aimed with a careful, albeit jostled precision, pointing his sling to the bull as the creature wove among the trees, racing swift but slowing, bones quaking in panic. Its only hope was to swerve, and it did, back and forth with the swaying motions of a bird on the wing.

Majest visibly grimaced in response, struggling to reposition his aim.

How is he going to hit it when it's moving like that? Letty, trailing behind the chase on shorter legs with a touch of jealousy, had never seen anything like it.

"Come on, Letty!" Majest called, his voice echoing back through the tall trees in a series of cracks. Letty didn't have to see him to know he was still laughing, a metamorphosis transforming him into something of endless energy and instinct where hunger pains and stamina limits did not exist. "I've almost got it now!"

With great incredulity, the girl saw her brother fire the slingshot as if she were watching him in slow motion. His arm pulled back and released with a snap, body recoiling in ripples. The grass-bomb flew through the woods like a diving bird of prey, a high-pitched whistle screaming out behind it, and it glanced off the tails of the fleeing caribou before it, gaining on the bull with an agonizing precision. Letty heard Majest cry out in preemptive victory.

But then the caribou broke out of the line of danger, whipping legs clicking, veering to the left, narrowly swerving past a jutting tree limb as it hurtled south. It disappeared over the buckling crest of a small hill, antlers waving in goodbye.

A detonating crash sounded as the grass-bomb overshot its absent target, collapsing gauchely into the trees instead. Letty covered her ears in shock at the sound that seemed both to blind and deafen, a squeak of surprise passing from between wide lips as she stumbled to her knees. The ground shook so hard, she thought it might give out and tumble down with her.

There was a cloud of green smoke blowing up from the hilltop, one sickly fir creaking and swaying in agony from where it had been struck. It threatened to topple, a bullet hole ripped into its shell. The gas flooding from the impact was fast-moving and thick as soup, and soon, Letty could not see the tree at all.

"Maji!" she cried, and the word became a throbbing cough in her chest. "*Maji,* where are you?"

There was the pounding of feet, and then arms were lifting her up from under her shoulders. She gasped and choked for clean air, and when she found it, coughs whooshed out of her body in windy gusts.

"Letty," Majest said, and set her down in the snow. "Are you okay? The gas isn't poisonous, I promise, or by now I'd be dead a hundred times over." His eyes darted to the former silhouette of the vanished bull caribou with a hint of agitation, but he pointedly looked away, kneeling next to Letty.

Letty couldn't reply at first; her lungs were still convulsing as they expelled their sickly-green intruder. Her nose was filled with the rancidness of rot, and her breaths were jagged, edged with pangs like glass.

"Cough it out," Majest advised, and patted her on the back. They were on the hillcrest some ways away, and the ravine below swirled in front of Letty's eyes as she fought for her vision. "You'll be okay in a minute or so. As for our next meal…" The caribou swung into view somewhere below, slowing its pace to nonchalance as it neared a wide, lapping stream that seemed to appear out of nowhere, and waded into the water.

"Water," Letty croaked, and she forced dizzy nausea from her senses; even from here, the stream was thunderous; its roar pulsed right under her skin, hitting her with an impact like a landslide. Water. *Water.*

"Huh?" Majest turned his head, eyes scanning the distant trees. His eyes met the line of the stream, the animal bowing its head to drink, and he stood to his feet at once. Every nerve ending in his body seemed to snap back into focus. He stared back at Letty, a question in his eyes.

Letty nodded as the last of the foul smoke emptied from her lungs in one long cough. "Go," she said, though she could hardly hear for the sudden thrill steeping in her ears, in her aching fingertips and parched throat. "I'll be right there."

Majest's face broke into relief, and then he was pacing away down the slope with a creep in feet that itched to move faster, but the hoofed creature below still had no inclination of his return, moisture gathering in glassy beads at its muzzle, ears flicked in dismissal—Majest's vigilance was imperative.

Letty dragged herself into a standing position and limped after him, and she could already feel the rush of water over her skin, the cool against her throat, the blue song in her veins, the chance at open doors between the creases of her mind once more—it was thirst.

They approached the stream together, and the caribou was wading now, hooves casting rippling shimmers of cerulean against the lazy sunlit flow. It seemed to have forgotten the danger, and yet it slid out from between the siblings' grasp without knowing.

"I can't go in there," Majest whispered. "My boots aren't waterproof, and I don't want to have to chop all my toes off. We're going to have to let him go."

"You don't have any more grass-bombs?" Letty asked. She didn't want to feel smoke press into her lungs again, but it was far better than starvation.

Majest shook his head. "I only had two at home, and I'm saving the second one in case of emergency. I don't know when I'll ever have the chance to make more." He glared after the animal in frustration. Catching a bull that size could feed them for weeks if carried properly.

"Oh," said Letty, looking past him at the stream. It was a deep blue, rippling and cold. It seemed to beckon her, and her head grew foggy. She found that her attention for caribou and grass-bombs was dripping and pouring out from inside her. All she knew, all she sought, was the chance at the water.

"I suppose we'll have to find something else to eat," Majest was muttering. "Are there berries around here? Do you think we could we eat tree bark? Maybe if we drizzled melted snow on it first. For extra flavor. Though I suppose if the snow had a flavor to begin with, that would be concerning."

Letty barely registered his words. She stepped forward. A nervous excitement bubbled up within her, and she felt as if she were being pulled by a string, by a chance, by that elusive power she was beginning to realize flowed through her. The water was beautiful, vast; it was gentle waves and an icy shore; it was a swooping downhill flow and a threadlike winding of life against the frozen earth, wide and unrepentant.

She grinned, and she was tingling. With a strange suddenness, Komi's words rang in her ears.

"While thought to be uncontrollable, you will have its strength at your beck and call whenever it presents itself to you."

I'm here now, Letty thought, and the rest of the world blurred. *No one can control the water. It does what it wants, goes where it wishes. But I can control it, can't I? I can bring our meal back to us.*

"Can't I?" she asked out loud, making the caribou's ears prick up and Majest turn his head.

She slid off her glove and dipped her hand between the lines and ripples of the stream. There was a small shudder against her heart as her fingers went numb with cold, but she could feel the locks on her mind trembling against their doors, hear the spitting of matches as they dared to light a candle down her darkest paths. She closed her eyes, the water leaving a ring between her ears like a trembling voice, an echo of a presence.

There you go, a voice whispered in Letty's mind, and she gasped as her mind's chambers lit, but there it was, that shadow again, that clawing of darkness that tripped her on her way out. *That's it,* the dark said. *You've got it now.*

Letty trembled in marvel and fright and a concentration thicker than stone, and she could feel Majest's eyes on her as she lifted her bare hand from the water. It clung to her hand without streaming, stuck to her by a force boring into her skull. With a thrill, she plunged her arms back into the stream, ignoring the ache of her skin or her drowning fur coat, and she felt the water grip her in a frigid, steadfast vice. It was her own.

I can still do it, she sang to herself, and everything seemed to unlock before her, and she had already forgotten the voice of shadows; it had sunk somewhere inside her, climbing her walls, nestling in her veins. Perhaps it was gone.

She was pulling on her waterlogged arms, and the stream was following in a submissive trance, and she was breathing deep, and she could concentrate, and she was Majest, with the bend and bravery of something beyond understanding.

Wicked glee clouded her mind, perhaps in a warning, but she ignored it.

"Now, fly up," she muttered, not daring to break focus, not like the last time. She would hold onto her command for as long as she still had the breath left to. She might never let it go.

At her words, nothing happened, and a snarl grasped her teeth. She dug fingers like claws beneath the soft waves.

Behind her, Majest made a noise, the birth of a word, of a caveat, but she didn't let him start.

"*Fly up,*" Letty repeated, tone harsh and darkened, lifting her arms above her head. *Why won't it work?* After all this suspense, all this success. Something still held her captive at the gates of her own consciousness, not daring to let her dip her toes in her full potential. Majest made it look so easy. He was so practiced.

"*Up, up, up! Come on! Now!*" Letty shrieked, and a shadow snapped to attention behind her eyes. There it was *again,* that creature. It had never left. Something was wrong. She felt her body teeter.

Majest never struggles. Majest never falls halfway short. Majest always succeeds.

"Letty," her brother said now, warningly, and the caribou was whipping its head in distress. "What are you—?"

Letty didn't hear the rest of his sentence. A mad roaring pushed forward from the back of her mind, back where the strange black presence began, and she was engulfed in a tidal wave.

Ride it out, won't you? Isn't this what you want? asked the shadow's voice. *To be like your brother? To be...in control? Even over him?*

Letty gasped at the thoughts. She could not control them; they came from somewhere just outside her reach. She sensed the final release of her element—the fuzzy light that would let it all out. The last gate holding back the flood. Power.

And yes—she wanted it.

"*Up!*" Letty howled, one last time, and she burst through the gate.

The water went up with a *whoosh.* It flew backward, knocking Letty flat to the ground and all thoughts of element or shadows from her head in one loaded blow.

Immediately she was soaked and shivering, and she could no longer forget the dark voice that lay somewhere within her. She was like the stream, frothing and churning where it had enveloped her sleeves, struggling to flow one way with a force yanking in the opposite direction.

Amidst the roar and the pounding, Letty opened her eyes, and all she saw was water. It was everywhere—it seemed as if the stream had been dragged up on shore, beached in a tidal wave and left grappling against the rock and mud. In its wake was a barren, drained bed of blanched stone left naked to the eyes of the clouds, and on top of it, the caribou was knocked stunned on its side, limbs in a lifeless tangle that jutted out this way and that. This segment of the stream was decimated.

Letty's body trembled as the ire and clout drained from her skin, and she hissed at the pain that reared up to replace it. Her head ached; she was frozen and dizzy.

For the first time in what had seemed an eternity, she turned to Majest. "That was a disaster."

Majest was at her side before their eyes had even met, helping her sit up, his hair and clothes damp but not drenched, like he had jumped away from the blast in the nick of time. With a trembling hand, he brushed hair back from Letty's forehead. "No it wasn't, Letty, you did it," he told her, and his breaths heaved in disbelief. "You found your power again, just like Raizu said."

Letty rubbed her aching temples with the sides of her red hands. "Well, it *hurts.*"

A little laugh escaped her brother's chest. "That's what practice is for." He winked, as though this were all a matter of fun, of a game. "Honestly, imagine what you could do once you've trained a while! You could create *storms* of water—you could give it to the villages, warm a world of it up, build castles of ice high over even the mountains..." His eyes sank into hers. "I told you not to doubt yourself."

But Letty remembered the voice of some invisible creature, the uncontrollable rage, water rising and crashing over the rocks, and shivered with unease. "I wouldn't get your hopes up."

Majest didn't know about any of that. He never felt any of that.

Sighing, she continued wearily, "I can't harness the water power.

I can't even control it enough to catch you a blasted caribou."

"Oh—the caribou!" Majest leapt to his feet at the offhand reminder, leaving a dismayed Letty behind him. He jogged easily through the emptied basin, even as it began to refill from what was further upstream. His boots sloshed gently against the beaten stones, bubbles shooting to life between them.

The prey before him was lying on one side, flanks heaving, limbs mangled. It was in no position to move.

Letty watched, still a bit dazed from her exertion, while her brother bent over the animal and took its great patchy head gently in his arms, as though comforting it in an embrace. But then a crack rang out high into the woods like a great log splitting, and the caribou did not even have the time to struggle as its neck snapped.

"Congratulations, Letty," Majest called, and Letty jolted, nearly forgetting she was here with him, in this moment. "Thanks to you, we eat tonight. And the night after that, and quite possibly a good few many nights after that. Oh—and we found water, too!" He bent over and slurped a handful of the stream into his mouth. "Delicious water!"

Letty grinned weakly. "Too bad you're out of luck if you ever want me to do anything besides nearly drown myself and everyone around me."

"You're the only one willing to get your feet wet, so like it or not, you're going to have to try to add a few things to your résumé. No complaining, Letty—you're more than up for the job." Majest's words were firm, though his eyes glinted in jest. He indicated the dead caribou at his feet. "Now come help me with this guy. The dead eyes are creeping me out."

Letty rolled her eyes, annoyance finally softening into affection. Majest's smile was a familial comfort even this much unease could not sweep aside. "Sure."

And so they worked as the sun sloped in its curve through the clouds, sitting cross-legged against the rocky dirt and slicing the meat into strips with knives Majest fashioned from the weathered stream stone. The points of them reminded Letty of Raizu's arrows.

They cloaked the meat in dressings of ice and returned to their sleeping tree just before sunset struck the earth in orange darts. The pack was repaired, their water refilled, and there was enough food stuffed against the leather sheets that Majest joked he would be complaining about a backache before dawn. Letty could not explain why worry still paralyzed her gut.

Many long hours of dusk later, they set their sights due east once more, their hearts as full as their stomachs.

And yet still, Letty worried.

Raizu Capricorn treaded back into the steady, unchanging clarity of Inertia's camp with a spring boosting his step and a bag of rich food strewn across his shoulders. He hadn't stopped smiling from the second his eyes had caught hold of the cliff-faces and protective hedges that meant home.

"I'm back!" he called, and parted the branches of the outside world. "I brought food!"

Raizu was met with a flurry of excited squeals as two dark-haired children, hardly the size of newborn bear cubs, flew from a hidden cave mouth to barrel forward in glee, wrapping warm little tendrils of arms around him. "Raizy!" they squeaked. "Raizy's back!"

"Is he really?" Another face appeared from one of Inertia's three smaller tucked-away caves, and the slender figure attached to it was swaying with laughter as it approached. "I thought you'd fallen down a rabbit hole."

"Kallica," Raizu grinned, enveloping his closest friend in a hug that squished her against him. There was no discomfort here. This was home; this was family. "How has everyone been?"

"Great," Kallica replied, eyes amused as Raizu released her and stepped back. "Arathiel was back a day or so ago with a few fish. The kids are annoying as ever. There's plenty of water from the stream, as always. Everyone's fine, Rye, don't worry so much." She laughed.

"Then why am I still worried?" Raizu muttered, but forced his features into a tentative grin that noted but dismissed Kallica's tapping foot, the way her gaze never settled. "Where *is* Rath, anyway? You'd think he'd at least have the courtesy to welcome me back himself, leader or not."

"Talking with Coda and Sylver in the sleeping cave." Kallica gestured to the largest cavern at the base of camp's rocky slope. Her hair flicked her cheekbones as she turned, short and black and coarse. Typical Cognito hair. "He'll be delighted to see you."

"Thanks, Kallica." Raizu patted his friend's shoulder and made his way across the sheltered expanse of clearing, nodding greetings to the two children—Arathiel's son and daughter, Mayrin and Chee—who sat on a floor cleared of snow and rock alike, the seats of their pants gritty with bare earth.

"Hi again, Raizy!" They chorused, and collapsed into an ecstatic fit of giggles, to which Raizu barely refrained from rolling his eyes.

The sleeping cave was dark in its vastness, stretching back under the broad-shouldered arms of the hill that coated its roof. Packed wall-to-wall, it had the space to fit Raizu's full three-dozen packmates—so long as they were comfortable breathing in each other instead of air—and as he poked his head into the entrance, the darkness of its distant corners was alive with a murmuring that let him know this obscurity held nothing to fear. These caves were different than the crawling nightmares of the forest beyond twilight; they invited him in, spoke his name.

"Arathiel!" Raizu called, and edged his boots against brown stone, freshly-swept and giving off a milky smoothness. "Rath, I'm back! You in here?"

In response, he received several murmured greetings, by packmates and family and friends in an indistinguishable blur of sound. There was no telling whether or not the voice he sought had called back, and so Raizu stepped under the low-hanging roof, and began to make his way through the shadows that glanced and played against the walls.

"Hi, Raizu," said another friend as he passed. Impril, one of Kallica's sisters. "Good hunting?"

"Fantastic, thank you," Raizu answered, and remembered the

146

twirl of Letty's hair, the freckles dotting Majest's face like points on a map. "I, uh, brought bear meat for you all!"

"You took down a *bear*?"

The echo came running down the long cave wall, and Raizu blinked until his eyes adjusted to Coda and her twin, Sylver, tucked against the farthest back corner, rustling in their nest of furs and feathers. Coda's big brown eyes shown in the dark; Raizu could almost see the puff of her russet hair dancing around her shoulders. They were sitting with Arathiel, and Raizu advanced with the breath of a smile's ghost.

"No, but I met a woman who could—in one blow." Raizu reached them and sat down, feeling the warmth of bodies stuffing up the cave as though it roasted above an open flame. "She was rescuing a little girl from the bear, and when she disappeared, she let me have the meat; I was just in the right place at the right time."

"Well, timing is everything, I suppose." Arathiel stood up, and Raizu's wide pupils absorbed the compact, lean form that was a mirror image of his own. The same gold-brown hair, same round eyes of hyacinth. "It sounds like you have an adventure worth sharing, brother."

Raizu exhaled with a meek shrug, and met Arathiel's taller stance, even sitting. His elder brother had arranged his features to look welcoming, though there was something that faltered about them, just as Kallica's had—and there was a bend to his ankle that looked swollen and purpled.

"It looks like you all had some excitement, too," Raizu said, and crouched before him. "Your foot looks terrible, and you're all staring at me like I'm the first ray of sunlight you've seen in years. What in the world is going on around here?"

Arathiel lifted his chin with a grimace, gaze powerful but dull with a violet pulse Raizu did not understand. "You talk to your pack leader like that?"

"I talk to my family like that—I'm worried. Tell me," Raizu said, and he tried to put force through the words, but his voice came out rocking and weedy. He was terrible at being direct. Quieter, he added, "I'll tell you my story if you tell me yours."

"Alright, then," Arathiel muttered, and he looked away, everything about him hoarse. He picked at his shoe. "You first; that's an order."

"Fine." Raizu finally sat down, between Arathiel and an anxious Sylver, and his shoulder brushed his brother's. The touch was chilly despite the bath of searing air around them. He wondered how much he should say about Majest and Letty—he wasn't about to break his promise to them, even to family.

Arathiel's gaze still fell to the floor, to his bloated lower leg, to the dust settled on fur blankets, and Raizu felt safe to speak without eyes boring pressure against his skull.

"I was trailing a grizzly," he began with haste. "But I lost the prints when a storm hit. I stumbled into it eventually, but it was already dead, and two girls were already there—a woman with black hair and a sword the size of a branch, and this little girl, Letty, the one she saved."

"What was some little girl doing out in a blizzard on her own? Was she *crazy?*" Raizu turned to see Kallica striding toward them in knee-high fur boots, and she plopped down next to the group with fervor. "Sorry," she said. "I wanted to hear the story, too. I didn't miss anything, did I? Before the grizzly?"

Raizu tried to smile. "No, you're right on time." He cleared his throat, finding it arid and parched. "Anyway, like I was saying, the older girl saved Letty—she was lost, looking for her brother, Majest. They were traveling together, and when the black-haired woman left, I helped her look for him."

"Did you find him?" asked Coda.

"Yes." Raizu thought longingly of the siblings, affable and determined. He wished they could have returned to camp with him, that all their power and mystery hadn't vanished over the slopes and left him hungry for more. He wished he could have convinced them Inertia meant safety. "Yes, we found Majest. I gave them a slice of meat and we parted ways. That's all there is to tell."

"That's *it?*" Sylver protested.

"That's it," Raizu confirmed. He cringed at the disappointed faces of his friends, but his lips would remain sealed. He'd

148

promised.

"Sounds like a bunch of bogus, Raizy, no stranger in the woods is going to wreck a bear like that and then give it all away," Kallica commented, and plucked a frozen chunk of meat from over Raizu's shoulder. Her delicate teeth tore off a strip, and she chewed impenitently. Raizu almost rolled his eyes—only Kallica preferred her food raw rather than cooked crisp over a fire.

"I believe him," said Arathiel, and his nose turned up toward the bumps in the ceiling. "How else would he have found all that meat? Raizu's never caught a bear in his life—it's too difficult for him. He was stupid to have been tailing it in the first place." He sat up straight, and the curls in his hair seemed to jeer in half-moon smiles. "Someone else obviously killed the bear for him. And there's no point in making up a story about two lost siblings, though it is strange they were traveling by themselves. Didn't they have parents?"

Raizu felt a prickle of annoyance on his tongue at the condescending words, but he responded in an even voice, "No, they're orphans like us."

"Rath, have you told your brother about the Organization conundrum yet?" Kallica cut in, seeing Raizu's unease.

Arathiel's gaze grew stony. "I was going to build up to it," he snapped. "You didn't have to butt in, Kallica. Pack secrets are not your place."

Raizu's eyebrows slipped down to form heavy slopes that brushed his lashes. "What's the Organization?" he demanded. "The deal was, I tell you my story, you tell me this one. Whatever's going on, this is my pack, too. I can handle it."

Arathiel looked about ready to light something ablaze, kindled by the hazy warmth of the air and Kallica's big, babbling mouth. "I suppose," he said through gritted teeth. "You do have the right to know. You would have known anyway, had you been a bit speedier in your return." He paused in lengthy displeasure.

"Get on with it," Kallica said, rolling her eyes to the cave ceiling. She seemed completely unfazed by her leader's irritation. "It was just a couple of strangers; you don't have to be such a melodramatic grump about it—"

"Yesterday, just after dawn," Arathiel began loudly, ignoring her, "two strange men came into our camp, all dressed in white. They had these symbols on their jackets—round like circles. They told us they were from some rising group called the Organization, led by this *Lady President* they wouldn't stop spouting off about. Apparently they're on a quest to wipe out whoever isn't 'powerless,' whatever that means. They want to restart the old world." Arathiel's voice held disgust. "They told us to join them or become the enemy. We told them to get lost. They kicked my leg in before they agreed."

Raizu's head spun. "Did they say where they were from? Who their President is, what she wants? What kind of people they were after? Who that might be?" He thought of Majest, of Letty—their powers weren't powerless, of course.

Arathiel looked up for the first time, and sighed. "Not *you*, Raizu, don't worry. Not us. We're about as ordinary as the next pack, save for the fact that we live like bats in a cave."

Raizu sighed, impatience making his fingers clench. "But what else did they say?"

"They didn't say where they were from—only something about 'the place of the Redwoods, the ones the President's parents knew.' They didn't seem to know themselves what exactly they wanted, or who they were." Arathiel was sneering. "Sounds like a phony clan to me."

The words meant nothing to Raizu, and he was about to continue his barrage of questions, but his brother seemed to think of something else, and cut his open-mouthed concern off in its tracks.

"There was one other thing the bumbling idiot mentioned, if you're really that curious," he said. "One of the men, he told us if we heard anything about someone called *Skylark*, we should find one of the Organization's people and tell them everything we know. He said members of the Organization are…" Arathiel held up two fingers on each hand in mocking quotes like cowardly rabbit's ears, and they shook and twitched with cold jest. *"Always watching."*

150

Raizu's heart seized up in a painful stutter that knocked his breath aside to make room for the pounding and skipping of beats. *The Organization—they must be the people Majest thought were after he and Letty, the ones who killed their mother. He was right. They're in danger.*

"Those two were so full of it," Kallica snorted. "All the same, it's been tense around here—who knows if those lunatics will be back. We can't be too careful."

"No," Raizu breathed, ignoring his friend. All he could think of was Letty and her little-girl smile, Majest and his cheerful courage. His hand tightened over the strap that held his sheath of arrows. "No, no, I've got to get back to them."

"Get back to *whom?* Raizu, where do you think you're going? You just sat down!" Arathiel's eyes blazed.

Raizu, for once, didn't think, not of the consequences, not of his own absurdity, only what a warning could prevent, what words breathed and timing mastered could do. The lives he could save. The difference he could make—for *once.* "Would you mind covering for me for another few weeks?" he asked cautiously.

Arathiel's face was a twisted landscape of thorns. *"What?"*

"I have to help Majest and Letty," Raizu replied, already calculating how much food and water he would need, what would carry him to the Hudson Bay. His bags would be heavy as solid stone, but Inertia would manage the loss. They would have to.

"Help them?" Arathiel wrinkled his nose. "Those strangers? Didn't you already help them?"

Raizu pulled his jacket tighter around him. "They're the Skylarks," he deadpanned, and his friend and brother blinked in astonishment. "And they need me."

X. HORIZON

Tap-tap.

Shatter held her breath as she heard the knock of knuckles on her chamber door. She got up hastily, untying her legs from the knot they had been crossed in. Strands of light-bleached hair crossed over her sightline, and she tucked them behind her ear, turning to distinguish the sound.

As she stood from her Organization-plastic chair—a privilege for those as trusted as she was—she set her book charily to one side, creasing the corner of one page over with a quick fold so she could return to her spot. She could not read the words, as she had never been taught, but she enjoyed her books with a fascinated observation, characters and symbols flitting by in endless clues of mysteries she could contemplate but never solve.

Shatter knew she was lucky to be privy to such books, but she couldn't help wishing they held more for her than just scribbles in ancient parchment. Still, she thought of her sister Sedona, what she would say if she knew Shatter had *books* in her new home—and *pictures,* and *maps,* the old-world treasures their family had sought for their collection. Shatter was lucky.

She would've come with me if she'd known, Shatter thought, remembering her two sisters' uneasy glances to the stranger at the door, their refusal to follow him. They had smelled of fear.

The knock came again, more persistent, and Shatter shook herself. "Coming!"

She crossed the room and sighed. *Probably just Caiter,* she thought as the door loomed into focus. *Perhaps he has a new experiment he'd like me to see.*

Shatter liked Caiter. With a charming half-smile on a face smooth and mild as honey, he was a near-blessing in the science labs—some of the others were foreign and strange, no company to anyone but themselves. But Caiter, Caiter was good. He had been her recruiter—he'd shown up at Shatter's door in Affinia and promised her adventure, the future—*purpose.* Shatter had been curious of this new Organization, but had been first on board.

Before Caiter, Affinia had not been known for visitors—except for Lunesta Skylark, who had appeared as a sudden storm, thunder on her tongue, spreading word of her siblings, poisoned by power from an out-of-line god. She had vanished just the same as she had arrived: vaporous, indiscernible, short hair spiking up in the wind—and Shatter had never seen one called Lunesta Skylark again.

When Caiter had come calling, Shatter knew the world had awoken to Lunesta's warning. The third Skylark had done her job.

Now, as Shatter moved to the door, preparing to answer, she found that it *wasn't* Caiter, Nona, or any other scientist who met her eyes across the doorframe. It was the President.

"Afternoon, Miss Seacourt." The President's face was calm, the picture of deception. "May I have a word?"

Shatter was perplexed. The President rarely left her room, and when she did, it was not to request from a worker—even a trusted one. "Of course," she managed, and gestured to the room's singular chair. "If you please, Lady President, take a seat."

The President's mouth twitched. "No, thank you. This should be brief."

Shatter dipped her head, though she felt herself jitter. "Very well. Is there an issue?"

"It's not so much of an *issue,* per se." The President took a few slow steps, and then she was above Shatter's eye level; Shatter had to look up to meet the dark of her eyes. Her boots, made of a metal that clanked on the hard floors, glimmered a burnt orange-gold in the light of Shatter's lamp. It made them look rusty.

"Then what is it?"

The President stopped her pacing. "An inconvenience." She took a strand of long hair and wound it around one spidery finger. "It's the boy. Seti."

Shatter brought her lower lip between worrying teeth, remembering the boy she'd led into the building, delicate as porcelain, equal parts sinister and stunning. A toy soldier in a little-boy's suit, an antique in mint condition.

"I'll cut straight to the point—our unfortunate friend has failed in his mission thus far," the President went on, startling Shatter out of her thoughts. "It's a shame—I expected him to do so well. According to the data I received from the watch, he's been moving, but he hasn't been *hunting*."

Shatter flinched. The *watch*.

Always hold onto it; put yourself in control. You do not want to be at time's mercy.

Shaking her head as bile rose in her throat, Shatter responded, "You're saying he's run out of time to complete his mission?" Unease crept over her. She did not know why, but the thought of Seti in trouble made her heart swell up to her throat—she was drawn to him. Perhaps she thought under those unreadable smoky-gold eyes and stiff expression was something more, something locked away for bone-aching years. Perhaps she thought Seti was like a machine, but she wondered if machines could be unmade.

"He's out of time; I'm out of patience." The President's tone was even.

Still gnawing on her cheek, Shatter continued, "Isn't that a bit unreasonable? He's only been out there for a week or so."

"With his skills, success should have come long ago," the President snapped, making Shatter's eyes narrow. "There isn't any more time to waste waiting around for him to get the job done. We need someone to replace him."

"Where would you ever find someone else like him? You sent for him specially!"

"I have already sent recruiters out, and they are heading north." The cold voice held no second thoughts. "They are to search the packs this time."

Shatter swallowed hard. "What's going to happen to Seti, then?"

The President shrugged delicately, bony shoulders rising and falling with a passive disinterest. "I suppose we'll have to kill him. We can't have him running free; what if he exposed our secrets?"

Shatter felt her heart skip a beat. "Let's not be rash," she stammered. "Can't we see what he does next? He's still going after the Skylarks, isn't he? Any moment now, he could find them."

"Shatter." The President's tone was measured. "Though I do admire your heart, we can't take a chance. Failure dwindles time." She turned as if to walk out of the room. "We can't afford to risk anything. The mission must remain intact."

"You could bring him back!" Shatter wouldn't let herself give up, although she was not quite sure why she was fighting for a stranger. "You could keep him here, in the building. He could stay with me; I'd make sure he didn't cause any trouble. He wouldn't have to die. No one innocent should die."

The President didn't look back. "Why don't you visit the scientists down in the laboratory, Shatter? See if they have any ideas. If Seti couldn't kill the Skylarks, we'll need someone stronger, someone less distracted, and that can't happen unless we recreate the effects of his curse—with more demon energy, like what we put in the watch. I'll consider your words, though I make no promises on either his or your behalf. The future of the Organization comes first, and this is our first mission."

Shatter opened her mouth to reply, but no words came out. The President's metallic footsteps faded fast down the hall with all the impact of a closing door.

A shuddering breath catching painfully at her tongue, Shatter stared down at her feet. She had no choice but to obey orders, forget Seti for the moment. He was in other hands now; she could not touch him, not even with the tips of fluttering fingers. She stepped out of her room after the President.

Shatter took apart the hallway's distance briskly, methodically, feet sliding over the shine of the white floor in lengthy strides. She had to blink several times in rapid-fire succession to adjust to the blinding starkness of the halls, the way they seemed to light up with a colorless prowess. White and more white.

As she walked, Shatter decided on optimism and pinned it to her thoughts like a butterfly to a corkboard—the President hadn't placed Seti's certain death into stone. Not yet, at least. But Shatter knew if the scientists could fathom a greater plan, one that didn't need the boy, his chances of being left alive and well would be vacuumed at once away.

I'll have to play dumb and see what they're up to.

The laboratory wasn't a far walk; the white door loomed over her head after only a few steps. She knocked on the door. It always seemed so strange to her, this slab of metal, flimsy as a sheet, yet the lone barrier between the outside world and the unpredictability of what festered beyond.

The door, which had been locked as a worrisome precaution, shied open, and a familiar face peered out. Caiter. His dark blond hair was streaked with the sweat of a hard day's work, and his brown eyes were framed with the tacky plastic of goggles.

Caiter smiled when he saw her, but it was a weary smile, weathered at the curves. "Hi, Shatter. We're kind of busy right now. What do you need?"

"Lady President sent me here to talk to the scientists. It's about Seti. Well—that is—*sort of* about Seti."

Caiter shrugged. "Alright. If it's on her orders, I guess you might as well come in."

Inside, the Organization laboratory glowed with the effervescence of an artificial sun and sky—as if everything was underwater. The walls, the floor, even the pinched-tight faces of the scientists seemed to shine with and iridescent blue, and it echoed in a dome-shape that followed the architecture in concentric circles. A constant whizzing seemed to emulate the buzzing about of the workers, gadgets and gizmos whirring, and that was all circular, too, bouncing on every tabletop and test tube.

Shatter felt dizzy just trying to take it all in.

Caiter led her fluently through a labyrinth of littered tables, wall to wall in rank potions and glass vials Shatter could watch her distorted, wide-eyed reflection in. There was a man or woman at each table, and they were all frowning, eyes all lit up with the finery of their work, pupils huge on dull faces.

One, a small boy with a mop of red hair, saw them walking and looked up from a pile of marked-up maps. "Caiter, I think I was onto something earlier," he called. "About the Hudson?"

Shatter creased her brows together, but Caiter simply sighed in clear dismissal. "Well, make sure you're still carrying out your assigned work, Ohanzi, or she'll take all your maps away."

Ohanzi made a face and went back to his work, fading among the countless strangers, the buzz like bees that swerved left and right to avoid anything but their own purpose.

Shatter wondered what the scientists were working on. Enchanted objects, like Seti's pocket watch? Potions? Fiddling with the left-behind technology scrapped high against the walls of back rooms? She shuddered to think of darker possibilities. This was why she worked in the information department.

At last they reached Caiter's lab table. It was plastered with strange devices that drew blank after blank upon Shatter's mind, and one of them had a screen that blinked and spat out beeps with the vigor of a bird guarding its nest. A lone plastic chair accompanied the ensemble, looking uncomfortable and stiff.

Caiter sat down, spinning in a loose circle and propping his feet up on the underside bar of the table. "So," he said, suddenly sounding unsure, though he was in the epicenter of his own environment. "What does the President want us to do about Seti? Isn't he the little guy with the demon juice?"

Shatter nodded, leaning her elbows against the table. "She's starting to doubt his capabilities, seeing as he hasn't yet managed to take down Aletta and Majest Skylark, so she wants to see if the scientists can come up with something to take his place."

Caiter seemed to ponder this. "You mean, *someone?* Someone else filled with demon energy?"

Shatter's heart sank. He had caught on to the President's idea without prompt. The scientists would create a new, powerful demon that would be able to wipe out the Powers without delay, without defiance. Seti wouldn't be needed, and the President would kill

157

him.

Then there was another voice, from Caiter's right, and black eyes bugged out from under the lenses of two rounded glasses, swiping the attention of Shatter's periphery. "I've been working on something that might just be on your grocery list."

Shatter knew that voice, those eyes, the unruly russet hair glossing down over his shoulders—it was another scientist, a man named Malory, with the gangly maturity of someone around thirteen birth-years old. There was an odd lilt to his vowels that seemed to ring back and forth in Shatter's ears and make them itch. She realized she had never heard Malory speak before. He was the madness behind the metal laboratory door Shatter feared; he practically radiated unpredictability, though he was supposedly brilliant—he had been in charge of teaching every face that had followed Caiter from their wilderness towns, shaping ordinary men and women into blue-lit scientists.

Caiter took Malory in with eyes that flickered hazel. "Really? You've been working on an independent project?" He seemed to put quite an effort into keeping his voice steady. "You know she doesn't like when you do that."

Malory sniggered, and his hair jostled with his smile. "Our dear President likes when I try new things! She likes that I can make a potion that's a level *ten* exciting instead of a level *five* exciting, so she's been giving me little medicinal projects and energy boosters, but what she doesn't realize is that I've done more impressive feats than that in my sleep, so I took her advice a step or twelve further and called a few old friends up from the underworld—and added a pinch of salt." His gloved hand held up a bottle of deep crimson. Shatter's skin crawled. "*Voila*—demon serum, only fifty calories per bottle. Makes your blood like diesel fuel, gives you all the power you could want."

Caiter's nose wrinkled, though his eyes remained transfixed on Malory with a strange force Shatter could not have described if given all the world's languages. "Not saying I'm doubting you, but I can't think of one reason why having the power to stuff a human full of demon goo is a good idea."

158

"Oh, I don't know—do *you* have a reason why sitting in a desk all day, up to your nose in silly papers and doing a productive amount of *nothing* is a good idea, Caiter?" Malory snapped, and Caiter flinched with a sad jerk of his eyes. Malory didn't seem to notice, and he set the vial down with an abrupt laugh like the bark of an animal. "Use your head; imagine the possibilities! We could create a whole fleet of demon soldiers in any shape or color our hearts desire—take care of those pesky Powers, then show up at the feet of the gods and demand their obedience, too, and maybe—"

"Except that's not the mission," Caiter cut in nervously. "We're creating a fresh future by building old-world technology and making sure there are no dangerous dark powers in the land. We're not taking anything over, much less the *gods.*"

Malory gritted his teeth with a gnashing that scraped in the air between them, and Caiter bit his lip.

Shatter's mouth stayed shut in a thin pink stripe.

"There's unfinished business in other places, Caiter," Malory growled, and Shatter could have sworn she saw teeth flash in his dark mouth like shooting stars. "There always is, for me. I'm not here for your world; I'm here for mine."

Caiter seemed to shrink back at that, a mouse in submission to the claws catching at its tail, and he turned to Shatter with a wide, apologetic stare, as if to say, "What can you do?" As if he were responsible for Malory's behavior. It was not the Caiter Shatter thought she knew.

Out loud, Caiter said, in a mechanic, vacant sort of way, "Thanks for delivering the President's message, Shatter. If she asks, tell her we're on her case. Okay?"

"Alright." Shatter nodded, but she couldn't manage a smile as she turned and stalked from the buzz and the whir of the laboratory's momentum. Her thoughts churned, and Seti's face pressed heavy and warm against the recesses of her mind, right where she did not want it, where it did not even make sense.

Seti's thoughts did not matter; Seti's fate was as inconsequential as a passing blink of a second or a rustle of wind stirring grains of sand. He flowed away with the breeze. These scientists, even

Malory—they were on Shatter's side. They knew what led to a new world, the world of the Organization, the equal one. Seti knew only the past, didn't he?

Shatter straightened the collar of her shirt, setting her gaze straight ahead. Seti would become the past. She would forget the smallness of his pale face, the eyes alight like fire.

Forget.

Weeks passed. Majest and Letty's travels pressed on, two shadows inching closer and closer to the Bay with steps that suffocated and faltered and pounded on in turn, raging red-hot with blisters until they went numb altogether. They didn't find themselves among the threats of predators or storms to bar their way any longer—it was just walking, endless walking, the repetition of footfall and snowfall, hunting and sliding from trees, then more walking, always walking.

The only release from the pounding of four feet across was when there was water. Majest watched his sister's water powers swim to her surface like a tiny fish fighting a feverish current, and though she struggled and twisted in the waves, fear in her eyes, she could concentrate, and she could hold water firm and deferential in her hands, grasping the tide with fingers like the moon's gravity.

"It's not just concentration that fuels the power," Majest had told her. "When you've truly mastered it, you can see it, hear it in your mind, smell and taste it in front of you. It's about feeling it, owning it, claiming it as your own."

"I *can* feel it," Letty had told him, frustrated as she crouched over another river flowing toward its vast infinity. "I know it's there. I can reach it now. But I can't control it. I can't." Her eyes had grown dark then, and she'd turned away.

"You're meant to control it, I promise," Majest had said, firm and loyal. "Do you remember when I almost killed myself trying to pick up a tree half as tall as a mountain? Just keep working at it."

"Almost killed *yourself.* I could kill everyone around me."

"Don't talk like that, Letty—keep trying."

And she had, and she'd pushed back that dark spark behind her eyes, moving her arms fiercely, mouth clenched in the concentration of someone fighting the bounds of everything she knew.

But even in all her desperation, she was shying away; Majest could see it—she feared whatever had taken her over at the river with the caribou. Every now and then, she'd find herself lifting drops into the air, painting timid ripples into the edge of a lake—but nothing more. She would not flex her muscle, even while Majest dreamed of shaping valleys, moving mountains. She was—for a new, vivid reason—afraid.

In the woods, they fed on the pink stringiness of caribou leftovers and the occasional small prey. There was always food on their backs, water sloshing against their canisters. After three long weeks, there was an edginess to every step that made Majest's toes curl and lashes flutter against falling snow. The cold was beginning to harden their routine, freeze it to solid pieces of morning and night that did not thaw with discovery, with a destination in sight. Nothing but ice, footsteps, the fading in and out of trees.

"Maji," said Letty, and it interrupted what had been a protracted silence. They'd left the forest of their birth far behind and were tumbling across plains and mountains that shone with a bald capping of ice, as far as the eye could see—giving them more momentum, but less protection. Less hope that something might be waiting just beyond the next line of trees. The skyline was empty.

"What's the matter?" Majest glanced over his shoulder at her. "Do you have more snow in your boots? Don't worry—we'll be over this peak soon, and I can help you. It's not much higher."

"That's not it," Letty shook her head. "My feet are fine. I wanted to ask if you know how long we have left to go."

"Oh." Of course. The looming uncertainty, the regular question. "Well, the sun has come and gone two dozen or so times, and Mother always said it was a few weeks' walk, so it could be any day now." He frowned at the sun then, which had already sunk below the clouds, though it seemed as if it had just risen. It was dark again. The days were getting shorter; winter stalked toward them in the lengthened nights and waited to pounce.

"I think we're almost to the Bay," Letty said. "You know how I told you the way I felt when we found that first stream, when we were chasing the caribou? How there was this pit of *something* in my chest? How it had been the water, drawing me in?"

"Sure," replied Majest, nodding. "I remember. Are you feeling that now?" Hope blossomed in his chest.

"I am," Letty said, breathless and vivid. "There's a rush, like I'm tumbling face-first down a waterfall, and it's pulling me under. I know there's something big just around the corner—bigger than a stream. I can feel it all the way from here."

As if to ratify her words, the cry of gulls rang over the lazy peaks.

"Around the corner? How about over this mountain?" Majest gestured to their current slope, which was fading to a final peak before them.

"We won't know until we get there," replied Letty. "Come on!" She grabbed Majest's hand and meshed her fingers between his, and then they were charging up the hill, snow flying. They ran hand in hand until the cold air turned their breaths to wheezes, and they reached the summit where the snow met the sky, the world before them on a windswept plate. Majest's eyes feasted as they clambered the last few steps.

The top of the small crest was high and cold; a breeze whipped in Majest's face with relentless authority as he dropped Letty's hand, squinting out at what he still could see under the last ashes of sunlight. Silvers and whites jittered into each other in the squiggles of blowing snow, and earth and sky were one, blurred into blue in the distance.

Except it wasn't the earth, and it wasn't the sky—the blue was something greater than them both, echoing with the sound of thunder, the screech of birds, the slap of shoreline. The wind drew its foamy curtain back from the view, and Majest found the Hudson Bay.

Miles and miles of rich, waving power pierced through the cloud cover, and it was the sky inverted, the clouds reflected; it was water, rising up from below, swelling and breaking over the earth's edge.

It seemed to stretch on beyond bounds, beyond comprehensible space. It was everything he could see, hear, smell—he could taste salt on the breeze, feel its haunted whispers in his bones, and it all was beautiful, the kind of beauty that drowned all things before it.

Letty quivered beside him, and Majest could not imagine what she must have been feeling, watching her world fall together. "It's *huge,*" was all she seemed to be able to whisper.

"What did you expect?" Majest asked, and he found that he couldn't stop grinning. "A puddle? There are *legends* about this place, endless legends—and here we are, right above it." He swallowed. Even in the dark, the bay was striking in its power. It made him feel small, swallowed and safe in its presence. No one could find them. He dared them to try.

"What now?" asked Letty, still shivering, and in her eyes was that same presence, the reflection of the rolls and white-caps, the foam and the blue. The darkness at the center, the mingle of sea and sky. The question that pounded and kept on coming, curling against the rocky shore.

Majest knew there was only one answer. "Let's head down."

Careful not to trip on their own thrilled feet, Letty and Majest half-ran, half-skidded down the foothill's slope, and the fading light of the sun showed them how to keep from slipping.

The way before them was a straight, treeless stretch of rock and whiteness, hovered over by a ticking clock on the rising moon's face. In desperation, it took less than an hour to reach the shore from where they were.

Up close, the Hudson Bay was overwhelming; it took Majest's tongue and swam away with it. There was no visible land, no other side; the horizon was all trembling lines, the dark blue of his father's long-gone eyes, and icebergs—empty, lonely power. The call of the incessant gulls rang high and long and searching, and Majest's spine clacked with chill.

Letty ran right up to the water's edge with a sudden bravery, fingers wiggling against the lap of low tide before she brought them to her mouth, licked the salt from underneath her fingernails. "This feels like home," she announced.

Majest smiled. "Not unless you feel like building a houseboat. We're not done yet; we're going to need shelter."

Letty looked up, rubbing her frozen hands against her coat. "There's not going to be anything along the shore, is there? It's all rocks. And out there…" She gestured to the expanse of the Bay, scrutinizing its shape, its bounds, but then froze to lean forward, so far Majest thought she might tumble in. "Wait a second. Maji, what's that?"

"What's what?" Majest followed her gaze, though he doubted anything could pierce such a decisive horizon. But there was a bump in the blue, nudging the clouds, spilling into the water and making itself comfortable.

Letty bounced up on her toes. "You think it's an island?"

Majest shook his head. "There aren't any islands this far north, are there? Father never said—"

He stopped himself. His parents had never made a journey like this. Their words could not guide him beyond the trees.

"Well, that's what I see," Letty declared. "Those are trees out there, and trees don't grow in the middle of water. Although if you've heard otherwise, you're welcome to object." She turned to her brother, and her gaze held sudden conviction. "We should go."

"Go *there?*" Majest reeled at her conclusion. "Letty, there's probably nothing over there!"

"Then we come back," Letty reasoned. "Come on, Maji, you said you'd make us a boat, that we'd sail in search of a home. It can't be that far offshore, or we wouldn't be able to see it from here. And there's no chance anyone could find us out there without making a boat of their own."

Making a boat. Majest had hardly considered what that might be like. He thought dizzily of his father's old stories, when he had traveled ocean spray from his homeland in search of an end to the End. That boat had housed dozens, had climbed tree-heights, had whipped the wind on sails and split the seas with impossible lengths of wood. "You're kidding," he said, throat suddenly dry.

"A small boat," Letty persisted. "Just for the two of us, and just enough to get us out there. Couldn't you do that with a few trees?"

"I…guess." Majest pursed his lips. He had promised an escape over water. He just hadn't realized all it would entail, the endless, frigid waves they were up against.

"Don't look like that; we've got to try," Letty said, and nudged her brother. "And if this is because you're too lazy to row us out there, I could help us paddle with my powers!"

Majest made a pained face. As hard as Letty might work, she could barely budge a stream, much less propel a boat across unpredictable depths. But he could make paddles, and they could move with the motion of the waves.

As if carried on the wind, skepticism teased his thoughts, fluffed them up in high alert. Was it wise to have come this far just to throw it away into the blue? Majest had lived his life amongst the trees and the green forest, branches weaving a roof over his head and setting food at his feet. That was behind him. He knew nothing of this Bay, save for its obvious hazards—if they lost their supplies, there would be no food. If a storm hit, there would be no shelter. There was no hope of rescue out there, no protection.

But such doubts would not get them anywhere, and certainly would not take them home.

"Fine," Majest agreed after a long pause, and felt all his doubts exhale on that one word. "We can *try*. But I'm not promising this is a good idea. And if we get stranded out there and die, it's no fault of mine, alright?" He fixed stern green eyes on Letty, who nodded solemnly.

"You can tell me 'I told you so' in the afterlife."

Majest took a deep breath through his nose. "Fair enough," he sighed. "Now let's find a tree."

Seti looked on from the mountainside in disgust, standing where the Skylarks had left their impish prints above the ice. A gull cried out from its perch on a rock below, and he jumped despite himself, a growl in his throat. He should have known better than to spend so long seeking out Soti—losing the Skylarks was unforgiveable. He could see the President's furious face in his mind at his futile weeks, feel the pocket watch measure the waste.

Of course—by the time he reached them, they were preparing to set sail somewhere even further out of reach.

The Bay did not fascinate Seti as it may once have. It had lost its magic; he'd been at its feet too often for the endless, icy waters to lull him into bowed wonder. Now it only made him feel small, made conflict seem trivial. Made stupid children seem even stupider.

He was watching Majest Skylark, eyes trained on his stupidity with a dull gold interest. He was approaching a pair of tall pines— the only trees for miles, the guardians of the Bay's shore. The boy kept lifting his hands as though praising the skies, and then one of the trees was falling with an unceremonious thud Seti could not hear over the roar of the waves.

Seti should have swooped in right then, killed them where they stood. Perhaps this would be his last chance—but he could no longer bring himself to do it. And he did not know why. He simply stood, crawled closer, watched the boy's baby hands do their elemental work with a spreading uneasiness like frostbite that bit at his skin.

The Skylark boy, as his sister looked on, set to work over his fallen wooden victim. His hands weaved the air; his feet scuffed the earth. He did not so much as touch the tree, and yet it carved and mangled itself at his command. For the first time, Seti saw the danger of the Powers, and yet, he did not move to stop it.

Soon the tree was hollowed out like a picked-apart carcass, like a wooden coffin, with sturdy sides and enough space for a child. It was a boat, Seti saw. A boat that could fight the waves.

"That's not going to fit both of us." Aletta's voice drifted over to Seti as she spoke up in displeasure, almost lost in the wind. Her little-girl hands were on her hips, the shape of her hair fluttering.

"You're right," her brother responded. "Well, we'll have to use the bigger tree, then. Come on." Majest, still using his powers, picked up his too-small wooden boat with a grunt of effort and threw it behind a large rock with a dismissive swoop of his arms.

Just like that?! Seti felt his nostrils flare in disbelief. They really thought they could do what they liked, didn't they? They had wasted the life of a perfectly good tree! What else were they willing to waste for their own gain?

Aletta and Majest walked back up the bank, and they reached the second conifer, which greeted them with callous indifference, high rings of needles gathering in crowns. It towered high over the rocks and its bark creaked and moaned with the Bay's salty gusts. The Skylarks should have used this tree in the first place.

Another scene of power-controlled carving ensued. Majest had to work slower now; he was tired from his earlier efforts. *Serves you right,* Seti thought. The girl just stared at her brother with eyes of glass, weaving strands of her hair through her fingers.

They're going to drown, Seti told himself, watching them drag their heavy creation against the rocks, gouging lines against the grain of the wood. *One storm and that boat's flipped upside down, and they're mauled by a whale, or a polar bear—they won't make it to that island. They'll die.*

Seti paused, breath halfway up his throat. They were setting off, and would soon be out of reach. Could he run after them, kill them now before they took a step from the shore? Perhaps he should wait—it was unlikely they would make it even a few lengths into the Bay before becoming victims of the icy tidal pull, eaten alive under biting waves. They would never make it out to sea.

Unfortunately, Aletta Skylark had other ideas. Although Seti knew the siblings had discovered the watery answer to the mystery of Aletta's element, he didn't think the President was right to believe she could become a threat. She couldn't move raindrops, much less the untamable tide.

But the girl dipped one hand in the icy water without hesitation, and breathed in deeply. Her movements were uncertain, but nevertheless, her hand traveled in a slow pendulum rhythm that lulled the ripples passing out between her fingers. Even at a distance, Seti could see her lip trembling.

And then, much to Seti's surprise—and to the girl's as well, by the shocked look on her face—the boat began to move. And this was no simple rocking along in the right direction; the boat drifted clumsily out to sea.

"She learned how to control currents?" Seti spat out loud. "In just two weeks? No!"

But then he realized that Aletta wasn't controlling the current at all—she was doing nothing but simply trailing her hand in the water. Behind her, Majest plunged a paddle ferociously into the waves, taut with effort, and rowed forward. The girl did not acknowledge the boat's true power, though eventually she drew her hand away and clutched it against her chest as though it were injured.

But no matter how the Skylarks were moving, they were still moving, and their shapes were shrinking and shriveling before Seti's eyes like wet salt dissolving. Seti clambered out of his hiding spot with tremendous haste and charged along the bank, curses swamping his mind in a sudden shattering of his dammed composure. He was losing them.

There was that smaller boat, fit for one, and for one fractured second, Seti thought of slipping after them after them—but he had no paddles, no power; he would be swept away. He would be stranded; he would be dead.

I'll probably be dead all the same once the President gets her claws on me now.

Failures cumulating in a rush, Seti kicked the boat in frustration, leaving one sharp dent. At the jerky movement, the pocket watch flew from his belt and landed on the sand below, ticking furiously. Seti could see the thin weave of its hands as they stroked the clockwork face, the gold Roman numerals, the brassy bad omen.

Reluctantly, and feeling rather childish, Seti bent to pick it up. Its hands were hardly moving—but then, they never were. Days would pass, but the clock's hands would only worm along through minutes, despite their clicking heartbeat. They were too slow. Seti had been too slow as well.

The children were beginning to fade away into the foggy blue. Seti put his watch back in his belt, and he knew as much about its purpose and future as he did his own—after all this time.

XI. DIRECTION

"Malory, are you sure it's such a good idea to be waving that around?" Caiter cringed backward in his plastic chair, skid marks striking black against the floor as the other scientist cackled with relish.

"Nonsense," Malory replied, tone lighthearted, though he set the vial down anyway. "It's perfectly harmless unless you touch it. Or ingest it. Or have it injected into your bloodstream. Or breathe it in."

Caiter frowned. "Have you even moved since last night?"

Malory seemed to consider this, much in the way a cat might consider springing on a toy mouse. "I haven't moved in *weeks,*" he clarified. "Ever since the President decided I could go ahead on my project, I did as any well-rounded man of science would and vowed not to stop working until it was completed. It's a pride thing."

"When was the last time you…slept?"

"Seventy-six hours ago."

That explains a lot, Caiter thought worriedly, seeing in his mind a vision of a future Malory, a hunchback shape like a distorted hill over a desk of acid and human blood, reeking of delirium, obsessive and mad. Well, more mad than usual.

"Caiter," Malory snapped, and he jumped from his thoughts.

"What is it?"

"I want another cat."

"For what? Don't you remember what happened last time?"

"Not particularly."

But Caiter remembered. He remembered he had been worried deeply, yet intrigued—like he always was, with Malory. After several feline test-subject injections of the serum, one last cat had been brought in, a pretty silver tabby, untouched by dirt or grime. But Malory had plunged his filthy needle in without remorse, and the cat had shook like a baby's rattle, eyes rolling into dullness, mouth foaming and throat roaring hoarsely while blood oozed out from under its claws. Red flecks had dotted silky fur.

The animal had grown and swelled up like a balloon. It had been too much when the beast had sprouted talons, fangs, horns— Caiter's fingers had slapped across his eyes like spattering blood.

By the time Caiter had opened his eyes, the cat had returned to its ordinary state, as if nothing had happened. Its eyes, however— those were still lifeless. The animal had been promptly thrown out in the snow to die.

And as he sat shaking now from the memory with bile in his throat, Caiter decided, as he quite often did, to leave Malory to his work and visit Charan instead. Malory was too much, like a star that burned too brightly, something you loved to watch, but something that blinded you when you did.

"I'll…see what I can do about getting you another cat," he told Malory, silently cursing himself for being so compliant, and edged away. "First, I'm going to go take a walk."

Charan, perhaps the gentlest of the Organization's home-taught scientists, had been one of the first to follow Caiter between white walls, interested in learning potions and magic, in sparking the old world back to life. He was young-looking, hair in thick dark curves framing bright eyes.

"Caiter, hey, come here for a second!" Caiter's quick journey was punctured by the sudden songbird's call of a pretty dark-skinned woman with gleaming gold loops in her ears. Her name was Nafuna; she worked with the restoration of the President's historical artifacts. She was always busy.

"Yes?" Caiter halted, and heard Malory chortle somewhere behind him.

"Look what the President told me to fix." Nafuna's voice was urgent. She held out her hand, and in it was a long board riddled with bumps and sliced through with long, even cuts. At closer glance, Caiter saw when Nafuna applied pressure to one of the bumps, it pressed down into the device with a satisfactory click.

"What is it?" Caiter asked, scrutinizing the apparatus with a frown. "Looks rather useless, if you ask me. What do those buttons do?"

"That's what I don't understand," Nafuna said, placing the board back on her table with mild worry. "It's some kind of keypad, but it looks like it's supposed to be attached to something else. It makes no sense. But she needs it by tomorrow, for some new project."

"Nothing she ever finds makes any sense," Caiter reminded his friend. "Don't worry about it. Just do your best, Nafuna. Clean it up—perhaps you can distract our President from its uselessness by making it sparkle."

Without waiting for a response, Caiter carried on to the back end of the laboratory where Charan was working, dark head bent over scraps of metal and a short cut-out of parchment, reading with the kind of concentration that could bore holes into paper. He looked up with a start when Caiter approached him.

"Hey, Charan." Caiter pulled up a chair.

Charan gave a startled expression, the corners of his mouth tugging upward. "Don't you have work to do?"

"I needed...a break."

"A break? From what—?" He seemed to remember Malory. "*Oh.* Right. Understandable." He nodded, fidgeted with his papers. "I don't know why you bother talking to him. As soon as he was finished instructing us, I was ready to never see that disquieting smirk again. Anyway, how is your project going?"

"Oh. Um." Caiter had nearly forgotten, and he burned with embarrassment. "Alright, I guess. I don't really know where to start."

"Well, she wants a sleeping chamber, doesn't she?"

"Whatever in the world that means. She just said to create a machine to keep one 'suspended indefinitely in dreams', but alive. I don't know how she plans on using it, or how anyone could stay alive trapped unconscious in a box."

"How long ago were you given the assignment?"

"Um." Caiter scratched the back of his neck. "Last week?"

"Did Lady President give you the sleeping powder?" Charan asked, trying to be helpful.

"Yeah. In a vial."

"You could design the chamber with the powder circulating through the air. And you could install tubes using some more of that weird, hard stuff Malory kept showing us. What's it called? Plastic?"

"Plastic," Caiter confirmed. "What for?"

"If you got the tubes hooked up to someone's bloodstream, you could supply them with nutrients to keep them alive while they sleep. You know—like the old-world hospitals."

Caiter frowned. "I never knew that. Would that really work?"

"It should."

With a shrug, Caiter took mental notes. "Alright. Thanks. I haven't, uh"—he broke off to laugh nervously—"haven't really gotten too far yet."

"What *do* you have done?" Charan's question was calm.

"None of it," Caiter admitted with a sheepish face. Straightening up, he declared, "I'll get it done eventually. It's not like she'll notice for a few months—she hardly comes down here."

"I don't?" A dry voice sounded behind Caiter's head and he spun around in the chair he was sitting in to see with a shock, the President herself.

"Lady President," he stammered, and felt himself turn crimson; he knew there was no way out of his blunder of disrespect. "I wasn't—"

"I know you weren't." The President looked amused, mouth turning up at the edges, the overhead lights like stars in her night-sky eyes. "Caiter, you're a good scientist. You usually do so well with your work. What's gotten into you?"

Caiter could still remember in the Organization's beginning, when the responsibility was simply to soak in the knowledge you could, when his leader never had the tendency of a watching hawk, gaze cutting you down, swooping into all the wrong places. The unnerve of it all nearly provoked him to snap, to hurl some snarky sort of Malory-esque comment at the woman—a notion that surprised him, that surely must have been a testament to his high-strung nerves.

But Caiter was pledged into obedience—and didn't particularly want to consider Malory a good role model—and so he curled in on himself, and replied, "I'm sorry, my lady. I just can't, um, seem to work properly in my current environment. I keep getting distracted."

"He means Malory," Charan pointed out usefully, and Caiter flushed an embarrassed scarlet all over again.

"*Malory.*" The President formed the name with a careful tongue, a small smile playing with her lips. Her eyes seemed far away, like she was recalling a distant thought. "I find it funny you should say that, Caiter. I came down here to check in on his project—that's when I noticed you weren't where you're supposed to be."

"His project?" Caiter's frown was queasy. As intriguing as Malory was, as brilliant as he was with his work—he did not seem like someone who should be trusted experimenting for the President; no one knew the first thing about him, why he was here, what he *wanted.*

Apparently, the President thought otherwise. "As he's told me, Malory has completed a potion that will turn a volunteer from an ordinary human into something powerful enough to obliterate any wretched gift-holder we come across—which will make our job infinitely easier."

Caiter was appalled. Some*thing*, not some*one*? "But President," he protested, "don't you remember what happened to that cat? Do you want that to happen to one of us?"

"Yes," the President said with delicacy. "To an extent. We need a mutant. Something potent. Any normal demon infusions—such as Seti's dosage of other-realm dust—will fail as well. We don't need another mistake like him. We need someone who will thrive and bring the new world to our mercy, to our healing. And Malory's new and improved substance will do this."

Caiter's stomach twitched with an uneasy roll of nausea. Lunesta trusted Malory, trusted this unknown stranger—why? He wanted to know; he wanted a reason to trust Malory, too, to grasp onto hope of something beyond mad black eyes, to be convinced there was no jeopardy, that he would not be eaten alive.

"I know you don't understand, Caiter," the President continued. "Not everyone does. Shatter doesn't, either. And it's quite alright. All I need you to do is get started on that sleeping chamber." She folded thin arms across her chest in a gesture that should not have been as commanding as it was. "I will have use for it soon."

Caiter pursed his lips. No matter what he wanted to know, he was a servant of the Organization; he did not get to choose what he wanted.

"Yes, Lady President."

Letty and Majest paddled until the froth of night was lit up by the sun once more—a welcomed sight after hours of uneasy quiet and the slosh and burble of waves that crept up and away. By means of this new light, the siblings were able to notice with an eager desperation how the island seemed to float closer, more than just a stroke against clouds; it was treetops and rugged shoreline; it was looming toward them with a dawn-lit, anonymous shadow.

"But Maji, it still hardly looks like more than a green-black blob and we've been out here for hours," Letty noted, dipping unfeeling, stumpy fingers back into the water. Her powers had never been the propelling force of the boat, and Majest knew she knew it, but yet she kept forcing aching hands to drown against the Bay, kept beating and stretching her mind until Majest feared the cords inside it might snap and send her reeling.

"Are you even listening to me?" Letty protested, clapping her hand against the side of the boat. It was redder than her hair.

"This was your idea," Majest reminded her, a bit sharper than he'd intended. He was worn-out from his paddling's ceaselessness, and his arms felt like soggy tree trunks "We're already idiots for trying to cross the largest body of water in our world, not to mention doing so on a tiny boat made out of a rather small and weary tree from along a deserted beach without *any way* to protect ourselves if something were to go wrong."

Letty frowned in a way that made Majest think she hadn't really heard him. "Our world," she mused, eyes cast downward to the boat's edge, and they still reflected the churning blue of what lay beneath them, pupils rinsed silver. "What else do you think is out there besides Cognito? Where Mother and Father came from, what sort of places they knew?"

"I don't see why anyone would care," Majest said matter-of-factly. "No matter the stories our parents told us, the outside world is buried in the past. Maybe the answers you're looking for are buried in the past as well."

"Oh," said Letty in a small voice, shrugging outwardly, though curiosity continued to skip stones in her eyes.

Majest left her to her imagination, paddled on even as his wooden board splashed in protest of the friction, of the wind and wave that towed backwards. He could not imagine hours longer of this, the heavy ache in his arms, exhaustion in a veil that blurred his vision.

A slight nudge rocked the boat. It was subtle—barely a tap on the shoulder—but it was enough to send their food bag gliding and seize Majest's balance for a split second of turbulence.

"Did you feel that?" He frowned, inspecting the water. Nothing but Bay.

"Yeah." Letty slid over to her brother, peered in beside him. The boat lurched in disapproval of her added weight, and then the bags were back at Majest's feet.

"Get back on the other side," Majest told her. "You're going to flip us over."

Letty scoffed. "Fine. It was probably nothing, anyway," she said of the bump, and sat back down in her place. "A fish, maybe. What other kinds of animals could be out here?"

Majest shrugged. He hadn't thought about it before, but now thoughts of polar bears and deadly whales were beginning to make him nervous. "Whatever can tolerate the cold, I guess."

"I wonder if this water ever used to freeze," Letty pondered. "A long time ago, you know? We have all these stories of how different life used to be, but we never know anything about what there actually *was* long ago. Maybe there was even a time when there was no snow at all!"

Majest clenched his teeth, exhaling sharply through his nose. "Letty, focus—"

But before he could finish the reprimand, the knock came again, more adamantly this time, jolting both Letty and Majest from their perches and sending them sprawling into the middle of the boat. Majest landed with his foot twisted and Letty's hair in his mouth, and he untangled himself with a grimace, knuckles bone-white against the wooden floor for balance.

"Alright, that wasn't a fish," he said in annoyance, finally managing to sit steady as the aftershocks died out in the water. "Seems there's somebody under there who doesn't like us."

"You can talk to animals, right?" Letty pulled herself upright, sounding vaguely agitated, and she was rubbing at her temple. "See what it wants!"

"Letty, I've never spoken to anything that wasn't from the same forest as us. How am I supposed to communicate with something I can't even see, much less understand? I'm going to sound like a squawking idiot!"

"Well, if you don't try, we might end up swallowed whole, which in my opinion, is worse than you making a fool of yourself," Letty observed dryly. "Besides, you make a fool of yourself all the time; it's not like this would really be so embarrassing. Squawk away—just don't get us killed."

And so Majest sighed with a shake to his chest, and crept against the walls of his mind, quickly procuring what light lay just out of reach and snagging it out as though he were a fishing line and this was his prize. His power rolling on his tongue, Majest could taste them, bitter but soft in his mouth: the languages of squirrels, of lemmings, of rabbits and birds.

And it tasted something nearby, something of the salt and fury of the Bay, and then he was snapped to its attention, fumbling to decipher what he did not yet know. Everything was fuzzy shapes and uncertainty; Majest felt as though he were grasping at shadows, clouds, something formless and slippery as the water it was hidden in.

"Letty, I don't think—"

Then his eyes cracked open and fixated over the side of the boat—and there was a fuzzy white head poking up from under the surface.

"Hello there!" it said, and its voice was mangled by distressed grunts, by the unfamiliarity of an alien tongue. Majest could barely piece together the words.

He fought to anchor his tone down to this animal's level. "Hello indeed," he tried, and his throat felt thick and muddy. "Who are you and why are you rocking our boat?"

"My name is Donec," the strange thing answered. "I'm lost."

"What is it? What is it?" Letty stretched her neck out in an attempt to see, though she did not dare move, all-too-conscious of the boat's instability.

Majest did not dare break focus, and his gaze bolted itself to the creature. "You're lost?"

"Yes," Donec replied, and the whiskers cloaking its muzzle dripped beads of water like tears. "Seals like me aren't usually in these waters. It's too cold, too much salt." Its face twitched with its soft barks, eyes big and mournful. "I don't remember how I got here."

"And you think *we* know how to help you?" Majest eyed the creature with disdain. "The only seals I know of are the ones whose fur became blankets on my family's beds. We're on a journey of our own, my sister and I. We don't have time to give a strange animal directions. Especially one who tries to tip our boat over just to get our attention."

"But I'm *hungry*," Donec moaned. "Your boat is all I've seen in these waters for *days*. I needed to get your attention so you would give me something to eat!" His eyes seemed to spark with malice, his words nearly human in their guile. "Feed me, or I'll tip your boat over."

Majest folded his arms across his fur-coated chest and sighed. "You're kidding. First, the squirrel won't tell me where my sister is until I give him my only good nuts. Then, a raccoon breaks into our bag and takes all the food we had without ever even bothering to have the manners to ask for it. And now, you're telling me if I don't give you something to eat, you'll try and *drown* us?" He snorted. "And to think, I sometimes wonder why humans are the dominant species."

"Maji," Letty protested. "What's going on?"

"It's a baby seal," Majest said, finally shifting into human tones with the awkwardness of shedding a second skin. "He's lost, however he managed that, and he's going to try and tip us over if we don't feed him something. And quickly," he added, wrinkling his nose at the impatient creature.

"Give him a little piece of meat," Letty said. "We've got to keep moving."

"Oh, I'll just start paddling again," said Majest, tone coated with derision "*Donec*, I'm sure, can keep up."

The seal blinked, and in fury, Majest wondered how something so diminutive and cute could be so ineffably bothersome. "I'm hungry," it said again.

"Not my problem." Majest, despite himself, questioned the effort it would take to spear the little animal with a block of wood and haul it into the boat. Did seals make for good eating, too, besides their soft fur? He was tempted to find out.

Although Letty couldn't understand what the creature was saying or what her brother had replied, she seemed to grasp Majest's exasperation. "Don't kill him," she warned. "He's just a baby." With an apparent lack of memory for her previous mistake, she hobbled to Majest's side of the boat and grinned down at the little animal. The boat slanted perilously to one side.

"Letty." Majest glanced at his sister with disapproval.

"Don't *Letty* me," she interrupted. She rocked back on one foot to keep her balance. "I think he's adorable. How did he get so far away from home?"

"He *doesn't remember*," Majest mocked, silently cursing

the seal for being just the kind of creature his sister would find endearing. "I suppose now that you're attached, we can't just eat the thing and move on?"

"Don't be gross." Letty wrinkled her nose. "No, I'm feeding him."

Before Majest could stop her, Letty picked out a section of caribou meat from the bag between her toes and tossed it haphazardly into the water. Donec's head bobbed beneath the surface and came up with the food in his jaws.

"Much obliged!" the animal chirped, and disappeared with a splash.

"See, was that so hard?" Letty rolled her eyes and returned to her side of the boat, dipping her hand back into its usual drowning position, as red and gleaming as a ruby. "Now we can go."

The boat lurched forward as if shoved by a god's hand. Letty let out a yelp of shock and fell to her knees, and the wind roared up in a sudden streaking cry. It was as though the boat had come to life, and now it was an eagle, a wolf, an elk gliding along the Bay's surface. Majest was blown back against the wood floor, eyelids whipped back in the force.

"What's happening? Are you doing that?" he cried over the roar, struggling to stay upright, and he grappled for his packs, for the side of the boat, for any security to hold onto. The spray of water struck his face.

"No!" Letty protested, and held up innocent hands, feet grappling against wet wood. She spat a strand of hair from her mouth. "I couldn't do anything like this if I tried!"

"Then what—?" Majest's incredulous exclamation was interrupted by a soft, inhuman laughter. He peered into the water behind the boat to see Donec, of all things, shoving the boat along with his great white head, tail worming in the water like a fish's.

"The *seal?!*" Majest cried. "Seals aren't that strong! Seals can't—they don't—" He cast an incredulous eye to the skies and spluttered, as if Komi himself had sent and super-powered their furry savior. "I don't believe this. We're dreaming. Somebody pinch me, please; the gods are playing practical jokes, and I'm terrified."

Letty began laughing then, her voice blown away on the wind, and within seconds, she had Majest laughing, too. "Who cares? We're going to make it to the island in no time now!"

XII. ARRIVAL

The sun evaporated once more. It was not as if there were anything else to be expected of the sun, but even so, each time the light was swallowed, days morphing into weeks, Raizu felt crushed with dismay.

"Of course, the one time I'm brave enough to go on a dangerous mission, I end up picking the darkest hours of the year." Raizu laughed nervously to himself, his eyes darting back and forth into the trees as a sensation of terror crept around his skin like a cold wind.

Don't panic, he kept telling himself. *Don't panic, don't panic.*

Raizu hated the dark more than anything else he knew. It petrified his bones into glass, frozen and fragile, leaving his muscles weak and his thoughts in a frenzy. In the dark, he couldn't see, and his sense of the world was out like a candle. At any moment, some great savage beast could spring from the bushes and rip him to meat-and-cloth strips without giving a warning.

As a hunter and traveler by nature, Raizu knew it wasn't convenient to be scared of the dark—and his packmates didn't let him forget it. It was a burden that usually resulted in lanterns propped up during sleep, and a grateful fondness for the stars. It was a burden that could not follow him here, if he were to succeed.

Tailing the Skylarks, Raizu had plenty of ground to make up, and stowing himself away at the first sight of a sunset was not an option. Majest and Letty weren't afraid of anything; they stalked through the dark woods like it was nothing, like they enjoyed the kick of the black unknown. They were built of tougher fiber than Raizu ever could be, which meant if there were any hope of catching them, he would have to travel twice as fast, sleep half as much, and journey on even when the sun fell face-first.

The night before Raizu was a still one. Usually, the wind puckered its lips and whistled through the trees with an eerie rattle, making it painfully hard for him to be anything *but* scared senseless—but this night was calm, subdued as though under a spell. No wind, no owls hooting from gnarled perches—*silence*. That was almost worse.

As he crept on, pointed shoes brushing in light darts over the ground, his stomach unsettled in the silence, it was only *too* easy to pick apart the quiet, to cast his hearing outward by an accidental instinct, to hear the sounds that made him want to roll into a ball and pretend he was dreaming until sleep granted him his wish. Those sounds of crackling undergrowth, murmuring animals, the hinge-creaks of branches, the click-clack footsteps of elk in the distance—sounds that, to Raizu, held wordless threats.

"I have to get a hold of myself," Raizu muttered, breaking the loud silence of night life. He blinked in surprise at how loudly his voice had discharged. A nervous glance backwards made sure nothing and no one had heard.

"Logically, there are slim chances something would want to kill or eat me," Raizu went on. He was whispering now, treading through the snow with painstaking care. Kallica had always told him talking out loud to himself would help shake off anxiety. "I'm too scrawny for a carnivore to want a piece of, and I have the exact opposite of coveted magic powers." He huffed. "What is the matter with me? I never get this worked up when I hunt."

But this isn't animal hunting, he knew. *This is life or death for people, real people.* For them, he had to move in the dark even once safety took its leave over hills and horizon.

Raizu snatched up an enormous breath, a futile attempt at calming his frayed nerves. Talking aloud hadn't helped. The mist from his breath shone in the pallor of the moonlight, though there were no stars to light it ablaze.

To distract himself from the way the trees were creaking and flickering under the moon, Raizu went through his plan in his head. His plan was tracking, and tracking was his expertise. He could not be scared in the dead-center of his comfort zone.

He had returned, as any tracker would, to the spot where he had parted with the siblings. The footprints left by Majest and Letty were drastically faded, but still visible under critical scrutiny. They led east, as Raizu had known they would, and thus, he followed.

A few detours became unavoidable, of course. Even with careful packing, Raizu had only so much strength, and only so much willpower to rob his packmates of their next meals, so he had only taken enough nourishment for a week's travel. Because of that, there was the occasional drift from his path to hunt a few squirrels or refill his water canister—but he always came back.

What is it about these Skylarks? Raizu still didn't understand himself. *I barely know them, but I'm risking my life just to tell them they're in danger. And not just that—they already* know *they're in danger; I'm only giving them names: Organization. President.*

Just one or two scanty words could not have brought Raizu into the dark of his own accord. No, this was a new compulsion that beckoned him beyond the sun's reaches. A feeling that somehow, he belonged to this story. But it wasn't that, no—he *wanted* to be involved.

A gust of wind took off from between trees, and a branch above Raizu's head rustled in rickety grievance. Raizu jumped forward with a start, hearing his heartbeat in his ears, and his foot brushed across an unseen rock, sending him teetering.

Regaining his balance with a shudder, Raizu forced his lungs to inhale, exhale, and fear sickened him, fear that even if he found the Skylarks, his cowardice would prove worthless in their fight.

For a moment, Raizu's uneasiness got the best of him and he stopped dead in his tracks.

The world around him cranked louder. Somewhere, an owl hooted with an ominous brand of scorn, and Raizu moved to clutch instinctively at the sheath strapped to his shoulder, feeling for an arrow and wrestling his fingers around its shaft. It was Majest's stone arrow, and Raizu whipped it out, prepared to use it as a weapon if necessary.

The wind erupted again, and it buffeted Raizu's jacket around him, flipping his hair, creeping into his sleeves and pressing its cold pulse to the veins in his arms. Branches squeaked as a squirrel—at least, Raizu hoped it was a squirrel—shot from tree to tree, perhaps frightened out of its slumber by the owl.

Night's veil seemed to come down upon Raizu all at once, and his eyes popped wide, hyperaware of each beat of his heart, each moving whisper on the breeze. Panic clawed its way at his mind from the inside, stripping him first of reason, then bravery, replacing it all with a fog of impenetrable hysteria.

Raizu slammed his eyes shut, lashes twining together. He wanted to disappear from the trees, to climb somewhere far away until the morning returned to him.

No. Raizu fought the dread back from his mind, panic spraying everywhere. *No, I'm already behind on time.* His fingers shook as he drew a tiny hunting knife from a handmade pocket on the inside of his long coat. He felt like a child, clumsy weapons in each hand. *There, you'll be fine.*

One foot at a time, he began to walk. *Everything is alright. Everything's fine, you're fine.*

He had almost managed to convince himself when out of the black, the hooting owl swooped down in languid precision to snag a squirrel just rabbit-lengths from where Raizu was standing, a flurry of feathers and eyes that burned. The bird's talons dug into soft flesh and the squirrel's screeching swan song rang out high and strident into the night, enveloping Raizu in its terror.

He began running faster and faster, two owl eyes in his mind. They might have watched him, even here, in his blind fumble over the ground. Branches seemed to loom from trees like clawed hands, catching at his clothes, snagging his hair and skin in their fingers, coaxing him in the direction he had come with a bitter, creaky laugh, trying to send him tumbling backwards.

"No!" Raizu screamed, no longer able to make out individual shapes. "Leave me alone!"

But the night held its victim fast, and its grasp did not weaken, did not falter, and sent Raizu hurtling toward the Skylarks along his tortured way.

"Stop pacing," Shatter told herself, and not for the first time that day. "It's not helping."

As a matter of fact, stalking back and forth across her plastic chamber instead of working was detrimental, even—and she'd been at it with such tense fervor for the last hours, the President had sent her a further pile of work to crush her nervous energy.

Though she tried to deny it, Shatter knew Seti held the key to the lock of worry binding her thoughts. Though she told herself over and over to *forget* him, visions of his face kept her held hostage, in chains, in captivity. Visions of him lost, alone, dead, defeated—destroyed by an enemy not his own.

And all the while, Malory drew closer to his delirious fever-dream of potions and monsters, and the President was on his heels with an eager smile, as though she could possibly know who he was, what he might do.

Before long, Seti would have no purpose in these halls.

Shatter's mind felt as wound up as a clock. She forced herself to sit down before more thoughts could spill out of her, and the cold vice grip of plastic on her legs was almost calming. The envelope the President had sent was still motionless on the desk, and Shatter picked it up, began to sift through it, seeking something trivial enough to distract her from her worries.

She found with dismay that the papers in the envelope were all in the same jumbled writing as her books. She couldn't understand them.

The President had sent her the wrong files. She would have to return them and get new ones.

Cursing illiteracy, Shatter put the papers back in order and closed the envelope with a fold and a crease. She stood up again and opened the door to her living quarters, finding white hallways that were colored like emptiness but brighter than the sun.

Shatter moved through the corridors she'd learned by heart with quick, brisk steps that seemed to fall with the sounds of metallic rain. She passed the laboratory entrance, the scientist dormitory, endless closets, endless clutter.

When at last she reached the gadget and resource room where the President spent most of her time, she discovered with dismay that the door was locked, an electronic keypad blinking mockingly out from the wall.

She's probably busy, Shatter decided, and bit her lip. Should she knock?

The sudden murmur of low voices gave Shatter a sort of half-hearted answer. It was the President's voice that permeated all others, drifting through the wall like a formless spirit. The voice was pressing, guarded—she was in a meeting, and an important one, by the sound of it.

Intrigued, Shatter pressed one ear to the door, no second thoughts.

"…time to remove him," the President was saying. "He's got the watch; we can't just let him go. He knows too much."

"What do you want us to do, President?" A high-pitched voice answered—Shayming.

"Yes, we can't just kill him like he's some bug on the floor." Chami seemed to agree with her sister, and it might have just been Shatter, but her voice sounded strained. "He's far too valuable, isn't he?"

They're talking about Seti, Shatter realized with a lump in her throat.

"I thought his value depended on his success—therefore, he is not quite the rarity he used to be. He's a common jewel. Anyone could do his job." The President sounded sharp as blades; Shatter could almost see the woman's eyes narrowing into dark stripes.

"President, he's one of a kind! You said so yourself!" Chami protested shrilly. "He's spectacular. Absolutely lethal. This has to be some kind of mistake."

"You saw the data from the watch yourself, didn't you?" The President's tone was dry. "He was moving splendidly—after the Skylarks, no doubt. But did he ever approach them? It doesn't seem so. Has he killed them?" A bang sounded as if the woman had slammed a hand down. *"It doesn't. Seem. So."*

"Maybe he has a plan," Shayming tried. "Maybe he's waiting for the right time."

"He's sitting at the edge of the Hudson Bay, Shayming!" The President snapped, losing patience. "It says so right on that shiny new screen in front of you! What, you think they're all enjoying the view together? Who knows where the Skylarks are by now? He's *lost them*. He blew his chance."

Shatter felt bile rise in the back of her throat. They were going to kill Seti after all. She would never learn his story, see that porcelain face again—gold ingot eyes or black lashes or tight scowls. The thought made her irrationally faint.

For one brief moment, Shatter considered knocking on the door or shouting her disapproval through it, but that was a surefire road to punishment—she was supposed to be working in her room, not eavesdropping.

"So you want us to kill him, then?" Chami's tone was taut. Shatter remembered how the twins had always showered Seti with praise, even before his initial consideration; it had been their woven words that had gotten the President to consider him to begin with.

"No," the President replied, much to Shatter's astonishment.

"No?" Shayming echoed, sounding just as stunned as Shatter felt. "But you just said—"

"I know what I said," the President said in an even tone, her voice a sheet of thin ice. "I also understand your concern. There may come a time when the boy is needed after all. When that happens, I don't want him dead."

"Then what shall we do, President?" repeated Chami.

"Capture him," replied the President. "Catch him as you did before, and bring him back. I will take him from there."

"Very well," Shayming and Chami said, in the harmonized synchronization of grating metal.

"We'll leave immediately," Shayming added.

The door to the President's chamber swung open then, nearly bowling Shatter over as she staggered back, making an attempt to look as if she had just arrived and had not heard even a word.

"Shatter." Chami nodded to the girl. Shayming nodded in turn, and the twins walked off down the hallway—though it was in truth more of a *flow* than a walk; they cast an illusion of feet that did not even touch the ground. They paid Shatter no mind, and certainly no suspicion, and so with a sigh of reprieve, Shatter strolled through the now-open door, crushing her papers to her chest like a shield.

The room inside was cold as always, and the President sat in her usual chair, but her hands kneaded in her lap and a troubled expression stained her pale face.

"President?" Shatter began, hearing her voice project weak and tentative. The woman didn't seem to notice her at first, so Shatter repeated herself, louder. "Lady President?"

Midnight eyes glanced up from the floor to stare Shatter down, and something inside them seemed to snap away, broken off like a twig. "Shatter. Yes." The President smoothed down her spotless coat. "What is it?"

"These papers." Shatter held the brown folder out in her hands. "I—I think you sent the wrong ones. I can't read, so I can't work with them."

"Oh." The President's lip puckered, like she hadn't expected an issue so trivial. "Yes, of course. Let me get you something else to work on, alright?"

On metal heels, the woman made her way to the wall of shelves, running spidery fingers over the drawers with a touch like the tickle of feathers. They found their mark, and she snagged the handle of one drawer and pulled out a few sheets of off-white paper, which she handed to Shatter.

"These are maps of Cognito, with a mark for each city. The red marks are the cities and packs we haven't recruited members from, and the black ones we have. I need you to count how many red marks there are and find Organization workers willing to travel out to them. Give each recruiter three different marks to go to, and organize the travel routes in a way that makes sense, alright?"

"Certainly, President," Shatter replied, dipping her head.

"Excellent. Off you go, now." The woman waved her hand

in Shatter's direction and she nodded, one yellow strand of hair catching in her eye, and found herself back in the hallway. The door closed behind her with a click.

With anything *but* the new assignment brushing through her thoughts, Shatter paced back to her room, Seti clouding her mind until she could hardly see. He would not be killed. He still had a chance.

Shatter smiled. There was a flickering candle of hope after all, however feebly the flame burned. Now she could only wait as the present melted away in the drip of burning wax, leaving only the drizzling fire inside, and the ashes it would become.

Against all odds, their runt of a wooden boat had defeated the bounty of the Hudson and grasped a strange new island shore, which rose high with unfamiliar trees and seemed to perch within the waves itself, gravity anchoring it down.

"This is so strange, don't you think?" Letty whispered, and she was kneeling against the ground with sea legs that still wobbled, the sun at her heels as she watched the undulation of the water's edge. "How big this place is, like it's a whole new land slowly growing up out of the water—it's even got animals!" She motioned to a quizzical rabbit's form, which ducked away shyly at the attention. "It's like we took a boat into space and we're on some other planet."

"Don't get too excited," Majest warned, though the shine in his eyes was unmistakable. "This place could still be barren and dangerous—we've got to head inland, where it's less exposed. We can look for shelter there."

"But if it might be dangerous, shouldn't we be careful about traveling inland?" Letty frowned.

"The danger wouldn't go away if we waited longer around here," Majest protested. "We're just wasting time and getting hungry, and when night hits, it'd be open season on us."

"You're so stubborn," Letty told him, eyes rolling. "Relax for a bit, would you? You always have to charge right into things without second thoughts. Patience is a virtue—isn't that what

Mother would say if she were here?" Letty ignored the clench of her heart, maintained her frown. "Why can't we enjoy our victory for longer than four seconds?"

"Because you've been sitting there babbling to yourself the entire sunrise."

"*So?*" Letty felt incredulous laughter bubble in her chest. "This is exciting! This is the best thing to happen since we left home. Look around!" She stood with her hands on her hips, staring her taller brother down with her best stern face.

Majest, a sigh on his lips and a roll in his eyes, grudgingly glanced about. Tall evergreens blocked the view of anything beyond the shoreline, standing guard to the forest kingdom it held tight. A few rocks littered the stony coastline, enveloped in frozen beach frost until the much deeper water made its homecoming at a drop-off farther out. Small animals shot through the trees as they did on the mainland, and birds chirped with cheer.

"Alright," Majest said after a minute. "I looked. I saw birds. Also, trees. Plenty of dirt. Let's go."

Letty glared at him. "Doesn't it look like home?"

"If home is here, we haven't found it yet. Come on. Through the trees."

"Fine." Letty shrugged, sparing one more glance at the blue they were leaving behind, the lonely boat tied up to the rocks. She could have sat on the shore forever, but Majest needed to *move* to feel satisfied, and she would not rob him of his discoveries, not when they had come so far.

Following Majest's lead, Letty approached the skyscraper pines, green needles glistening up into snowy peaks like mountains. Past a layer of prickly branches, a small forest ensued. Only a dusting of snow brushed the frozen dirt from where it had fallen through the ceiling of trees. Letty thought it felt almost foreign to walk over ground she didn't sink into.

Despite the distinct lack of a familiar white blanket, Majest was clearly at ease among the strange forest, and Letty felt it, too. She'd missed the bristle of evergreens, the sharp smells she'd grown up with. The trees were a roof over her head where there was not one built for her, and a return to them was long overdue.

Before long, fully submerged in coniferous bliss, Majest was skipping as he walked, relishing in almost comical happiness now that he was into the woods, picking his pace up high as if he enjoyed the exhaustion. It made Letty want to laugh out loud.

Although they walked until the shore took its exit behind them, there was still no sign that anything or anyone larger than a seagull inhabited the island. It was peculiar—Letty had assumed *something* would have crossed the water with the temptation of a home that would never be found. Was there not something comforting about a hidden new world across the blue?

"How big do you think this place is?" Letty questioned, hearing her own voice split the rustling of the woods.

"Bigger than the tiny little black star it seemed on the other side," Majest replied with a grin. "It's like these trees go on forever. I thought we'd end up on some overgrown iceberg, but this place looks like it can sustain itself."

"So I was right," Letty deadpanned, a wry smile on chapped lips.

Majest pretended to sigh. "You were right. This wasn't a colossal waste of time; this was your greatest idea—*whatever.* We're not safe yet. We don't know what's out here."

"Hopefully there's somewhere to live, not just this endless forest," said Letty. "I'm getting the feeling that soon we'll just come out on the other side with another shoreline, and that'll be the end of it."

"If the island is as long as it seemed when we washed up on the coast, it won't be that simple," Majest reasoned, the trees seeming to clear his thoughts. "My guess is there are probably some cliffs and rock formations near the water. The entire coast was rocky, remember? Perhaps along the shore a different way is a cave. That would be a good home, don't you think?"

Letty nodded, though she felt her face wrinkle itself into a grimace. Something her brother had said set off a flicker of concern in her mind. "Won't all the water around here be all salty? We can't drink that—we'd get sick! And that canister won't last more than

191

another couple of days."

Majest frowned. "You're right," he murmured, though he didn't seem concerned. He never did. "Well, I guess we're going to have to find a way to get the salt out of the water."

Letty snorted. "Yeah, *great*. Why don't we go back and try that right now? What are you going to do, Maji, talk to the salt and ask it nicely to separate from the rest of the water? It's not a squirrel."

"Hardly." Majest didn't turn back. His attention was on the trees, the land, the new and untainted discovery. Knowing him, he would expect drinking water to simply fabricate itself at some point without trouble.

"Sometimes your optimism worries me." Letty sighed. "So, what *are* we going to do?"

"Wait and see," her brother told her. "We didn't come all this way just to die because of a little salt. Besides, if you keep working at them, your powers might be able to separate the clean water out of the Bay—who knows?"

"But *Maji*," Letty protested, "that's not fair. The last time I thought I could do something with my powers, we ended up taking help from a *seal* instead. I got bested by *a magical lost baby seal*."

"You'll figure it out," said Majest with nonchalance. "It just takes time. It took me time."

"I'm not you!" Letty growled, loud enough that Majest looked back at her in surprise. She immediately regretted her outburst.

Majest stared at her. "Why are you getting so upset? All that matters right now is finding somewhere to live. Once that happens, you'll have all the time in the world to work yourself out. We'll be perfectly safe, too. Nobody can find us here."

"There are footprints leading up to the shore, back on the mainland," Letty noted in a dull voice, still embarrassed. "If someone were following us and saw them, they'd know we went this way."

"But they'd never suspect we crossed the water," Majest pointed out. "Over here, we're all by ourselves. We'll eat birds and live by the Bay in peace. Isn't that the dream?"

Dreams aren't real life, Letty thought, though she didn't say anything to spoil her brother's good mood. They kept walking.

Their steps held the same easy rhythm of their former long weeks among strange trees, but now that they were so close to a definite triumph or letdown, a success or failure set into stone, Letty's anticipation peaked until her head ached with an eager desperation.

Then she began to see something beyond the trunks of the woods. A white, snowy absence of trees, empty purity tinged with browns and—most surprisingly—*other* colors. Reds, yellows, oranges, purples—colors Letty hadn't seen in what seemed like a lifetime.

"What *is* that?" Beside her, Majest was squinting into the distant background, face a mirror of the confusion Letty felt. Turning to his sister now, he grinned in excitement. "Looks like we found something. Come on!"

Letty followed as her brother swerved through the last few rows of trees, feet brushing over the brown-white ground that rustled like wind beneath them. Pine needles and snowflakes crunched underneath tired boots, seeking color like the earth sought the sun.

Before long, there was only one row of trees separating them from whatever lay beyond. Majest pushed back the branches obstructing his view and stepped into an open clearing, Letty right at his heels.

A startling lack of wilderness hit Letty's eyes like the pierce of an arrow, and in synchronization, the Skylark siblings gasped aloud at the sight beyond the blanket of trees. It was so unexpected, so impossible—and yet there it was, with towering buildings made of stone, pebbly paths entwining them like speckled, gray rivers. Large tables perched in the cracks between the buildings, each with baskets of brightly-colored cloth and wooden boxes, stacked high and smelling brightly of foodstuff. In the center of it all was one large circular rock structure flooded with crystal-clear water that spilled in abundance, burbling endlessly over the edges.

"What in the world...?" Letty felt her heart skip a beat.

"A town," Majest whispered, his eyes large and green. They reflected the hues off the snow in shimmering prisms of color.

"Like the marketplaces back in Kartho. In the middle of the Bay. A town. Like, an *entire town.*"

Before Letty could stammer a reply, the sharp sound of someone clearing their throat jolted the siblings' attention to their right. A girl about Majest's age was standing off to one side, dressed in a fluffy white jacket. Her hands, covered in rabbit-fur gloves, were on her hips. A bag was tied to her belt, and the scent of meat wafting from it was enough to make Letty's stomach churn with hunger.

But that was not what made Letty and Majest step back at the sight of the girl. She was slim and of average height, with sky-blue eyes, calmer than Letty's. But what was so intriguing about the stranger was her *hair*—this girl's locks were white as a snowstorm pounding out of the clouds. Letty had never seen anything so strange.

Majest put a hand on Letty's shoulder. He was staring at the girl without any discretion, mouth open and eyes blinking once, twice, three times in astonished succession. He made a noise as if he were about to speak, but no words came out.

"Well, well," the girl chimed, not taking any notice to the siblings' incredulity, her voice breezy and musical. Her eyes raked Letty and Majest up and down. "What do we have here?"

XIII. LOSING

"I don't understand!" Raizu exclaimed miserably. "They couldn't have just *vanished!* I did what I was supposed to—I went back to *exactly* where Majest and Letty were and then went east! I ended up at the Bay, just like they said they would!"

He stopped for a moment, breaths bursting in and out of his lungs. A part of him had known coming into this that it would be a long-shot. "They should be here," Raizu finished weakly.

But the shoreline stretched on for what seemed like light-years, without so much as the brush of a footprint, the echo of a laugh. They should have been here, but they could have been anywhere.

Ever since the rising sun had prompted Raizu back into full spirits and fearlessness, he had been pacing the water's edge, the Bay looming like the great blue heavens before him, and he had been scouring that snow-and-rocks beach with eagerness.

After minutes of searching, he had lost that eagerness.

After hours of fruitless endeavors, he was beginning to lose hope.

"I should have never lost the trail—when that owl scared me off, did I start running the wrong way?" Raizu ran his hands through his hair, dislodging ice crystals and shaking them to the ground. "How could I be so *stupid?*"

The exclamations dragged the anchor of his thoughts into murky depths. Weeks had gone by at the expense of Inertia's resources—the people of his family, his life's only duty—and he had failed at the one fleeting chance he had dared to take.

"There has to be a reasonable explanation," Raizu told himself.

Talking out loud helps relieve stress. Helps solve problems. Right. "I was going the right way. I was careful. My calculations were aligned with the footprints and I was going fast enough to be able to catch Majest and Letty as long as they continued the pace they left the clearing at. It's not my fault, is it?"

Continuing his pacing, Raizu felt the words leaving his head in a rush, gathering worriedly into the air around him so that they swirled about, each possibility stretching its legs on the breeze.

"Maybe their hiding place is just really well thought out," Raizu muttered, trying optimism out on his tongue. It tasted foreign. "Maybe they took refuge farther along the Bay than they thought. Or they could have changed their minds and never come to the Bay at all."

Then a newer, darker prospect arose from the corners of his mind and he froze where he stood.

"What if the Organization caught them already?" Raizu's words came out in a hoarse, petrified whisper. As dread clutched at his bones and drained the blood from his face, he felt his eyes grow wide with a sort of fear he had not known since his mother's poisoning—the fear not for his own foolish life, but for someone else's.

Raizu began running now, running down the shoreline, not even caring if someone were to hear or see him. "Majest!" he called, stomach twisting, voice shaking and shaking, "Letty! Where are you? Can you hear me?"

As he suspected, there was no reply, just a lonely echo of sea birds and the lap of salty water.

They never would have seen it coming, Raizu thought with bitterness. *I wasn't there to warn them about the Organization. All they knew was that something was after them. They didn't know the true danger. They never—*

Raizu hastily shook his head as the thoughts threatened to drown his mind and suffocate him. That was always his problem, the thoughts. There were too many, and none of them were what he wanted to believe.

"Alright, time for *positive* thinking." Raizu forced himself to slow down. "There are two of them, and only Letty is vulnerable without proper use of her power. But Majest would keep her safe, and then they'd both be safe together."

Raizu took another deep breath, and it trickled in a slow stream from his nose. Perhaps Kallica's advice had some substance. "So, what do I know?" Raizu kicked at the hard, snow-covered ground thoughtfully. "There aren't any footprints, which means either Majest and Letty were never here, or they *were* here and their footprints have just been covered. It snowed earlier this night, after all."

Breathing easier now, heart no longer hammering through his coat, Raizu wove his gaze around the beach once more. Tall rocks formed a barrier that enclosed sections of the Bay as though they were restricted areas; caves or hideouts might have crept between them, sheltered from the salty spray. There were no trees, but two stumps were visible from a distance, little woody nubs against the endless shore.

"Tree stumps?" Raizu frowned. "What could have happened to the trees?" A light flickered on in his brain. Majest could move trees. Would he have had a reason to knock a couple down to make a shelter?

In minutes, Raizu had pounced excitedly on the stumps, finding their surfaces rough and broken, as though some great giant had come along and snapped their necks. This was no even lumberjack's slice. This could have been element.

Maybe Majest built a wooden house for the both of them, nestled between the stone walls. That seems logical. Majest seems logical.

The nearest rock formation was a boulder laid out in jagged lumps, enclosed by smaller stones that bumped along beside it. Raizu did not suspect it was the ideal placement for a home, but he wanted to check everywhere.

As he approached the boulder formation, Raizu saw a fragment of something peeking out from behind it, vivid brown within the gray. *Wood?* He walked quicker now, thrilled at his first real clue.

But it was not a house—not even a piece of a house, not even a door, or a floorboard, or a chunk of roof. It was a curved bottom like a hill upside-down, four short walls bowed like the tide. A boat.

But why a boat, and why so carelessly abandoned? Raizu touched the wooden surface with hesitance, as if it were somehow dangerous. It looked new, the wood beaming like the grains might burst from their seams and become trees once more. Had Majest made it? Why would he have left it?

Raizu took a moment to stare.

Maybe they're coming back for it—maybe it's not their boat at all—but who else could make a boat from scratch like this? Was there another boat? There was another tree—did they head out to sea? Raizu turned his questions to the endless waters of the Bay.

At first glance, the blue horizon told him of nothing but emptiness, no land or shore hinting where the other side might have been. If Majest and Letty *had* gone out on another boat, they wouldn't have gone straight out. There was nothing there except water—treacherous, fatal water.

Then a spot appeared over Raizu's vision. At first he thought it was his eyes playing a foul trick on him, but it would not budge, even after a series of persistent blinks. Something was there.

An island? Raizu frowned, standing up from where he had been kneeling in the snow. *A floating house? A really,* really *big bear?* Whatever it was, it was there in front of him, plain as the sun in the sky. Which—he noticed with an upset stomach—was slowly sinking again. His daylight was running out.

The boat behind the rocks seemed to call to him, posing a question. But it was beyond reckless, beyond *reason* to jump into its wooden curve with sporadic intent, flying into the blue with attempts to reach a distant shoreline.

Raizu would never do it. He was not spontaneous. He was not brave.

"Except Letty and Majest are," Raizu decided. "If they saw a sign that might get them across the water, they'd jump at the chance. If they saw that island, they would want its sands under their feet—no matter the risks. Letty never stopped our journey to find her brother, even when she was injured and terrified. Majest never stopped looking for her. There's no way they'd stop now."

But would Raizu?

Seti did not resurface from his troubled, half-conscious slumber until the Skylarks were long-gone into the water. He did not even bother to lift his head until the sun had come and gone and come again. The last thing he wanted to do was rise and rediscover what he already knew.

What at last prompted Seti out of his gloom was a noise. It wasn't a particularly loud noise, though to Seti's sensitive hearing, it was an audible nuisance, drifting over the rocky beach like a siren. It was the cry of another boy—not Majest Skylark, but someone calling his name.

Seti forced himself into a kneeling position, rocking forward on his hands and knees until the black spots released their pressure on his vision and he could stare out to the coast between boulders and snow.

Sure enough, it was another boy. This boy seemed older than the Skylarks, and of much different structure. Where the Skylarks were lean-muscled and tall, this boy was slender and nimble, a bow and sheath of arrows strapped safely on his back and a halo of golden-brown locks falling around a charming, angular face.

The boy was running across the rocks, hair flying, desperation in every step. Salt water dampened the lining of his boots, and even from this distance, Seti could see the sweat on his temples as he galloped forward.

As Seti watched, intrigued, the bronze-haired boy called out again—for the girl this time.

"Letty!"

Curiosity brewing, Seti crouched still in his place between the rocks, a bird of prey in waiting, pulling his last hunk of bread from his pack. It was frozen solid, but he bit into it anyway, sending waves of energy back into his aching body.

Well, this is something I can tell the President, Seti thought eagerly, latching onto any hope he could. *A clue, at least, a stranger who knows the children and is looking for them, too.* A boy, who was likely a friend of the Skylarks and had lost them just as Seti had.

Briefly Seti wondered if he should kill him. The President would have wanted him to.

Seti eyed the distraught stranger with scrutiny, still wandering about like a lost spirit. He didn't look like much of a threat. It would be a surprise if he could even lift a knife, much less use it.

With an internal shrug, Seti turned his head from the boy and forced himself back into his own reality. His long and troubled sleep hadn't changed the fact that he was stuck on a beach with no Skylarks and no escape.

Not that he would have killed the Skylarks, had they been here—he had learned his lesson by now. For whatever reason, he did not hate them. And this was not his war, not this time. It was not in his heart to pick sides.

Another noise shot Seti out of such thoughts. A high-pitched noise, the grate of metal on metal, blown in on a wind that seemed to come in from all directions, from above, from below. The boy with the arrows was a long way down the beach by now, just a bug scuttling across ice and stone. He had not made the noise. The noise had not been human.

But it had been familiar.

Teleportation, Seti realized, his heart thumping twice the normal rate. *That's the sound I heard when Chami and Shayming whisked me away to the base of the Organization.*

He lifted his head with a rapid snap of movement, and though he peered around, no one was there. "Where are they?" he hissed, his voice a furious whisper. "What are they doing here?"

Thinking fast, Seti bent his knees and leapt to his feet, skidding as he darted across rock, over points and dips, teetering along the structure's rooftop until he approached the snowy edge of the cliff that loomed over the beach. Grunting, he gripped the ground above his head and prepared to lift himself onto the base of the foothill.

But he never got the chance. His second hand reached for solid snow, a blind grasp above his head, and a booted foot kicked that hand with a harsh crack that sent him reeling, the ground swaying dangerously below.

"Shayming!" Seti regained his balance just in time, arms out like birds' wings, and he was just barely gliding, right into the wind, but it was not enough to fly. He perched on his rock, swinging.

Above him on the ledge, a woman's chuckle sounded.

"I've got him, Chami," Shayming cried, leaning over to grin at Seti, cat's eyes green and noxious. The stringy tangle of her hair fell to dangle downward in front of her face, tickling the space above Seti's head.

Seti's eyes narrowed, and he bent into a crouch on the hard rock. "What do you want?" he hissed. "I'm *working*."

Chami's face, a mirror of her sister's, poked up over the cliff's edge, making Seti feel dizzy, as if he were seeing double. "Seti," she crowed. "We've *missed* you! It's a good thing you did such a terrible job with your task, or we might never have gotten to see you again. What a fortunate misfortune."

"I didn't do a *terrible job*," Seti snapped, disgusted. "I've been tailing the Skylarks for weeks without letup. They never knew I was there, and I didn't lose sight of them until yesterday, when they took off over the water and I was unable to follow them. But I'm working on that."

"That right there is the problem," Shayming told him, shaking her head in mock sorrow. "Over the past few weeks, you must have had many opportunities to dispose of the siblings—you *must have*—and yet what did you do? *Nothing*. You played it safe, refused to get your paws wet. Now not only have *you* lost the Skylarks, but the Organization has. And you can be sure that the President is not happy about this."

Before Seti could protest, Chami piped up. "You know, Seti," she said, sounding thoughtful, "no one expected you to fail. Everyone was waiting for your great triumph. The President, the scientists, the research workers—everyone! We were going to have a celebration for you once the Skylarks were dead. A party, with food and decorations! You'd go back out into the world and take care of other Powers, and you'd be a hero." She pursed her lips.

"Such a shame you failed your one simple task."

"If it's such a *simple task*, why don't you fly over the water and kill them yourselves?" Seti retorted, though he knew defending his actions was little more than useless.

Shayming and Chami laughed as if Seti had just told a particularly amusing joke, and their voices mingled together like shattering glass. Seti's skin prickled in fury.

At last, the roaring subsided long enough for Shayming to address Seti's question. "Fly?" she asked, letting out a tiny giggle. "You think we can *fly?* Oh, Seti, you're too precious. You know we can't teleport anywhere we haven't been before. And we don't quite care to get our feet wet either—I suppose we have that in common."

Seti gritted his teeth to keep from leaping up above his head and smacking the twins senseless. Any momentary satisfaction he would get from getting the sisters to shut up would be outdone by whatever he would suffer for it—he had not forgotten he was dealing with Psychics.

"Fine," he snapped, the red haze over his vision cooling. "But what do you two *want?*"

"Is that any way to talk to two people who care about you, Seti?" Chami tilted her head to one side, eyes glimmering with faux hurt. "We only want to help you."

"Help me *how?*"

"We're taking you back to the Organization," Shayming clarified. "The President feels you would be better off there, since you can't seem to be of any use in the forests."

Seti's heart sank. He could not go back to that building. It was achingly pristine in its horror, it smelled of a foreign clarity that made his ears itch and his throat swell with bile, and it was so *white.* Seti hated white; it was so empty; there was no substance. And in the Organization, there was nothing else. He would go mad.

He was not prepared when Shayming hurtled down the ledge before him and slapped a hand to his shoulder, but he did not have the chance to move, and then he was frozen in time and space, helpless against the crush of her fingers, the glint in her eyes.

After only seconds of Shayming's psychic work, all Seti could feel was the cold rub of the pocket watch against his side, and it ticked along to his humiliation jadedly. An energy-draining spell. Classic.

The twins laughed as Seti swayed on his feet—tired, like he'd walked the earth until his feet had bled and his muscles had become dust. He used the last of his strength to peer under the edge of his coat. The watch had changed: one hand on XI and the other on XII. The eleventh hour.

Shayming seemed to notice the travel of his gaze and snatched the watch from Seti's belt. A sudden protective spark flared up in Seti's gut, but his arm could not move fast enough to stop her. She frowned into its face, but said nothing, just wound the watch back through Seti's belt and managed a grin.

Seti tried to conjure enough energy to spit at her feet, but it was all he could do to keep from falling.

"Are we heading back now?" Chami asked, still perched over the ledge.

Seti could not open his mouth, and so he said nothing, leaving Shayming to respond:

"Yes, we'll be leaving."

Seti could do nothing to stop them as the twins carried him down his rock structure like one might cradle a baby, and when the world began to blur and glow, he was powerless.

With a puff of icy breath into salty air, Raizu cast what must have been his thousandth glance into the murky water before thrusting his wooden paddles forward, back, forward, back again—the rocky rhythm lulled him into valor, despite the thrum of his heart.

Here he was—being rash, chasing danger, unchained from safety. Everything he hated. But his gut told him there had been a second boat from the second stumpy tree, and the Skylarks had sought the island in the blue.

The boat, mercifully, had waited for him behind its shelter when morning had come, posing a question. Raizu had pushed away every instinct screaming at him to stop and answered by climbing aboard, salt water splashing into his eyes as he shoved across the rocks, into the Bay, against the tide.

He'd needed to pry two scraps of wood from the boat's frame to use as paddles, and he was still afraid they wouldn't hold, but hours of struggle later, he was paddling to the island, slow but sure.

Now, too far to think of turning back, it was everything Raizu could do to keep from panicking.

"Everything's going to be okay," Raizu told himself mechanically, though he felt fragile and rigid, like his insides were glass. "The wind is going the right way; it will push me right to the island. Even if Majest and Letty aren't there, there should be enough food to sustain myself until I can find my way back to land."

Even at his own reassurance, Raizu still gnawed on the inside of his cheek with absent apprehension, tasting the metallic tang of blood in his mouth. A soft snowfall seemed to start from nowhere, and he shivered as he glanced mournfully out to the brooding distant shape—still hours of fierce rowing away.

"These paddles could've been better made," muttered Raizu, spitting blood into the water, a hole torn into his lip that ached and fretted. "They barely push this boat at all. What if I dropped one in the water? Then I'd have no way to keep going."

The snow continued to fall ceaselessly around him, painting his clothes and hair powdery-white and filling the bottom of Majest's boat.

"Any more of this and the boat will rot right out," Raizu continued, even as everything in him told him to just *shut up already*. "Does wood rot in water? No, no it doesn't. Does it? Oh… what if water gets through the bottom and I sink? Or an animal smells me and tries to tip over the boat?"

He thought ruefully of Arathiel and Kallica, the way they would taunt him if they could see him now. But he could not help the *thoughts,* the endless streams of possibilities—the good, the bad, the in-between. He feared that which he could not control— like this water that raged on around him, trapped him between chapped, arctic waves, like the dark that stole his paths. There was no formula for darkness, no formula for water, and—as Raizu was beginning to realize—no formula to being stuck on this boat other than to hold on tight and hope he wouldn't get stranded.

"But I'm not *going* to get stranded," said Raizu, and forced his voice loud and decisive. "Come on. *Row.*" He thrusted the paddles back into the water, pulling them forward with as much force as his weak arms could muster. The boat creaked as it lurched forward, and Raizu grinned in satisfaction. "There we go."

But before he had a chance to row again, the wind crossed over as though making a purposeful gesture of cruelty, switching from its former eastward stride into a spiral, sending the boat reeling to the right.

"No!" Raizu cried, panicking, and his paddles pushed opposite the wind in desperate, sloshing thrusts. Coldness splashed up into his face, soaking his clothes, and his arms shook. "No, go back! Cursed wind!"

After several agonizing long minutes of fighting the fierce gust, it let up, leaving the air unnaturally still, only the falling snow a remnant of the sudden storm. Raizu breathed a sigh of relief as the resistance faded, blushing at his panic though he knew no one else had seen.

Eventually the lazy breeze picked back up in its proper direction, and Raizu carried on in little strides and strokes, the boat crawling along the water's crest as if it were as tentative as its rider.

He noticed the sun had peaked, too, in another personal gift of misery—it plummeted like rain. The edges of the trees on the shoreline ahead were dimming as light grew absent, evolving to silhouettes, and the water's reflection danced an angry deep indigo.

"I hate this," Raizu muttered in response, the cold dampness of his clothes making him shiver all over. He was paddling faster than ever despite the ache in his arms. "First the wind, now the darkness. What's next, a storm? A tidal wave? Earthquake?"

Tentative, he glanced at the sky. Unluckily enough, the clouds were dark and brooding, about to burst from their seams. A low growl rumbled from the distance.

Raizu turned back to his paddling with a suppressed whimper of panic. He wanted to quit, to crawl under a rock and leave this sopping mess behind. He would catch his death in a storm if his wet clothes froze, and he could do nothing about it.

He could not sleep, could not stop. He had to keep going, and he knew it.

Raizu shivered, and it was all he could do to shake any and all thoughts from his head as best he could. They clung to the insides of his mind like wet clothes to cold skin—a familiar, tangible feeling now—and they refused to let go.

And so he gave them one last shove, dislodging them enough to paddle in peace.

Overhead, frozen rain began to pour.

XIV. INTRODUCTION

Showing the island villagers they meant no threat was a short process for Majest and Letty, but it was, apparently, a process needed to be done. Majest could not imagine how two children—cold and tired from weeks of journeying, at that—could possibly have been seen as a problem in the first place, but the townspeople were cautious.

"We live in a tight circle," the white-haired girl had explained, only after the Skylarks had given their names and their intentions this far from land. "We don't trust anyone. There are all sorts of evils on the other side of this water, and by living here, it's our hope we can stay out of its path." She had nodded in a firm bob of her chin. "I'm Sedona Seacourt."

She was seven birth-years old like Majest; she and her sister Sunni had stumbled—and paddled—upon the island a year ago, fleeing their previous home in the south. Because of what, Majest hadn't asked. The island they had all found, by whatever chance of fate, was affectionately dubbed "Hi Ding" by its people—a place to keep hidden.

"You never know who might want you dead, who might know your secrets," Sedona had warned. Majest and Letty had exchanged a startled, uneasy glance. "This place tries to make sure they never find you."

Majest had tried to laugh, but it had come out all strangled and wrong. "That's good. I suppose…that's the reason we're here."

Want you dead. Know your secrets.

As Majest rewound the words through his brain like fraying

threads, Sedona led him and Letty into the center of the town, a circling plaza wrapped around its fountain. It was like stepping through a mirror to a parallel world. Letty had never set foot in a village, and all Majest could remember of Kartho were crumbling buildings and the mouthwatering, desperate scent of meat. This was nothing like that.

Now that Majest was up close, he could see the worrying lines in the stone buildings, the squeaking wheels of the carts rolled into the streets, people jostling the painted scene with movement and eyes like eagles'. They peered from holes in the wall, pinched faces adorned with suspicion. They were all staring at Majest and Letty.

Majest frowned. He was not used to being distrusted.

"I'm going to take you to see Vosile," Sedona told the Skylarks, and Majest tried to tear his gaze from vigilant strangers. "Legend has it he discovered this place a long time ago, and he's named himself our leader."

"So what, he's been here so long, he just decided he owned the place?" Majest snorted, and the thought of meeting one of those hawk-stares head on had his gut in tied-up loops.

Sedona shrugged. "He's been here longer than any of us can remember. Apparently he vanished for quite a few years, but he's back now, and ever since then, he's truly led us—he came back with all sorts of new knowledge, sent down to him by the gods. It's not about how long he's been here—he's just our leader, and that's that."

"Where does everyone think he vanished to?" Letty piped up, leaning nervously into her brother's shadow.

"To another village across the land, I presume," said Sedona. "I wouldn't know. I'm fairly new here myself." Her voice dropped. "But I do know that after he got back, he wasn't quite the same."

Majest and Letty exchanged a glance of disquiet.

Sedona immediately changed her voice. "Oh, no, don't look like that! Vosile is lovely. He's the one who fixed up the village, treated the ground to grow our food, brought the plants we make our clothes from—he recovered that fountain, too!" She gestured to the stone structure still spilling in translucent curves. "There's a freshwater stream that runs through here, odd as it seems, and he got it to run under the village."

"That's not possible," Majest said immediately.

Sedona gave him a hard look through narrowed blue eyes, and Majest almost felt nervous. "I think you'll find that here, everything is possible."

"But it's like you're from another time," Majest insisted. "No one can grow food in this climate, or find fresh water in the middle of a Bay made of salt. Next you'll be telling me little birds weave your clothes and foxes brush your hair. Things aren't this easy."

"Not in the woods, they're not—but Vosile knows so much about the old world, and he's brought it here to us," Sedona responded evenly, and the words sounded programmed into her. "Or so I've been told."

"Old world?" Letty sounded intrigued. "You mean…the *really* old world?"

"Sure," Sedona responded in lighter tones, and dropped one hand to Letty's shoulder, guiding her toward one of the buildings and jerking her head at Majest to follow. "Have you heard the stories?"

Majest couldn't help but grimace. "We live in the present, not the past."

"We use the past to make the present. And Vosile knows much about both. That's why he's so respected—well, that's what everyone else says." Sedona was frowning, and Majest wondered briefly if he had just upset their new tour guide, but then she shrugged, and her eyes were bright on Majest's face. "You'll have to talk to him, otherwise no one will let you stay. That is what you want, right?"

"Yes," answered Majest, spirit lifting. "At least for now. Thank you." He blinked at Sedona in the daylight, and the sun seemed to jump through her hair in slanted leaps and bounds, throwing reflections into the snow that glared and sparkled. It almost hurt to look at.

Sedona caught his eye and smiled. "I'm sure it'll be alright if you stay. If you've really traveled as far as you say, Vosile will have to keep you. And, well, if he ends up not trusting you, you might be at least lucky enough to get an escort back." They reached the door of a quaint wooden house, and Sedona pushed the door open without knocking. Majest was tempted to exchange another perturbed glance with Letty, but she seemed to breathe easy at his side.

"Sedona!" As the door swung free in the whoosh of a passing cloud, a small boy appeared in the space left behind. Probably Letty's age, he had the open, refreshing face of childhood innocence—big blue eyes like Sedona, but his face was yielding and round, his hair an inky black that reminded Majest of Letty's story: the black-haired girl who had saved her life.

"Vari, hello." Sedona greeted the boy with another brimming smile—a knowing smile. Majest wondered what they knew. "Look what I found."

"Hi," said Letty, and her smile was tentative, familiar, a new stem budding up from the earth. The boy's eyes traveled to her face with a burst of interest as she went on, "I'm Aletta Skylark—Letty—and that's my brother, Maji."

Majest almost gave her a disapproving look for revealing herself like that, but then he remembered—this place was far from the mainland. No one would know them here.

"Well, I'm Vari Nyght, and it's great to meet you! Where did you come from?" Vari grinned, and his eyes trained themselves to Letty's face, lashes batting with intrigue. Majest tried to relax—clearly not everyone was going to be uncanny and unwelcoming.

"A long ways away," Sedona answered for Letty, not bothering to elaborate. "We're here to see Vosile. Is he fit to talk?" Glancing at Majest, she added, "Vari is Vosile's caregiver. Although our leader's mind is strong, his body is growing frail, I'm afraid."

"He's fine," Vari said, almost defensively, and Majest could read in his face the respect he carried for this man. "He was just finishing eating."

"Of course," Sedona said with an immediate gentleness. "Thanks, Vari."

The black-haired boy gave a nod, and there was color to his

cheeks as Letty stepped past.

Sedona led Majest and Letty to the back of the house. There was a certain coziness to it, and Majest thought it gave an impression like their old cottage back home. The walls were a sharp-scented cedar that closed the outside world away, and Majest felt safe in its grasp, at home among trees, among warmth—among the wood chairs draped in caribou furs, the rusting water vat, the dishes against the shelves. He had not felt safe in many long weeks.

"Sedona?" a rusty voice called.

Majest turned to see a man sitting in one of the chairs. His hair was only wisps, sparse feathers dwindling down to gray tendrils, and his eyes were the surrounding wood, an aging brown, wrinkled and smudged. A face in this land could not be old; it was impossible, and yet his was sunken and hollow. Cheekbones protruded in punches around his eyes, and he seemed haunted by the sag of his beak-like nose, the creases of his chin. Majest could not tell when he had stopped aging.

"But I do know that after he got back, he wasn't quite the same."

Majest refrained from making a horrified face as the unsightly man went on, "Is that you, Sedona? Did Vari let you in here?"

"Yes," replied Vari. Majest hadn't seen him come in. He was peering into the room from behind Letty's shoulder. "Sedona found two more children outside."

"What?" Animation came into Vosile's face at once, eyes coming to life against the bland tug of his skin. "Children? Let me see."

Majest tried not to feel uncomfortable as the man's eyes fell to his sister, a brood to their beady shine. He seemed to gather her in all at once, collect her in the basket of his mind.

"I'm Letty," said Letty. Her eyes darted to and fro as her name slipped from her lips. Each time she gave her identity away, something new seemed to come to light. "This is my brother, Ma—"

"Majest Skylark, son of Maxine of the Larks and Dagur of Ísland, brother to Aletta and Lunesta." Vosile folded bony arms across his chest. "This is a strange coincidence."

"How do you know that?" Majest automatically took a step forward, knees rocking. How would anyone know—unless they were the ones who had killed their mother? Had they stumbled into a trap?

"Your names are all over the land," said Vosile, chuckling. "Good heavens, you two. Everyone knows who you are. You're modern-day celebrities, how about that. Majest and Aletta Skylark, famous children of element."

"I didn't know who they were," Sedona said, to no one in particular.

"Because you don't hear things like I do," Vosile told her. "I am told of the words in the wind, through the trees, in the water and the ground we walk on. Word is spreading! The two Skylark siblings are famous across Cognito, and you have your elder sister to thank for that."

"*Lunesta?*" Letty queried. "She told people about us?" Majest didn't like the sound of that.

Vosile waved a hand in her direction. "None of that is important, dear Aletta. The point is that you're alive, and you're here now. This is such a wonderful surprise! Many had presumed, perhaps even hoped the two of you to be dead. I was so interested in your story when I heard it. In fact, I know so much about you and your powers already!"

"You know about our powers?" Majest heard his own heart thudding in his chest, threatening to burst out and run away. "Who—who told you?"

"Powers?" Sedona interrupted, and her voice was thunder, no longer her previously-ignored drizzle. Her eyes were wide, and she was staring at the Skylarks with a startled intensity, half unbelieving, like they had just announced plans to raise an army of rabbits. "Like...Komi's?"

Majest was taken aback at the name. To hear their Deliverer's name from another's mouth was odd—no, it was *wrong*—and it sent a shiver of clammy cold down his spine. It was all he could do to keep from gasping aloud.

"The three of you have Komi in common," Vosile said, unfazed

212

by their incredulity. "You were gifted with two of the elements, were you not? Sedona and her wind powers are third. Three Messengers, finally all here."

"Sedona has *wind* powers?" Letty burst out, and her eyes bulged. "Komi visited her, too? I thought we were the only ones!"

"It was only about a month ago," Sedona said, looking a bit flustered. "Komi visited me in my dreams and told me I have a duty to the gods—to be a Messenger. Supposedly, I have wind powers, according to what he told me—though I haven't mastered much yet." Her voice was unruffled, though her gaze still drifted wide and wary. "You have powers, too?"

"I have water powers and Maji has earth powers," said Letty. "I can't do much with mine yet, but Maji's amazing! He moves trees and earth and talks to animals, too!"

"Really?" Sedona's gaze shot up to Majest's, impressed.

Majest felt suddenly self-conscious, alienated. "It's nothing," he muttered, staring at his boots. "Just a lot of practice and stuff."

"Alright, that's enough of this in my house." Vosile sat back in his chair with a creak and turned a stern expression on Majest, Letty, Sedona, and Vari. "I already know about everything you can do and I don't need to hear it again. If you need something useful to do, why don't you get to know the town? Since the infamous Skylarks will be staying with us, I presume."

Majest couldn't help but frown. The man made him uneasy, all his knowledge with no proper explanation, and there was nothing Majest could do about it, because he did not understand it.

"Well, I'd be happy to give a tour," Sedona said, and she was still staring at Majest with a light expression. "Vari, want to help me show these two around?"

"Okay," Vari agreed, and seemed unable to help an excited beam in Letty's direction. Turning to Vosile, he asked, "Will you be alright here if I go with them? I won't be gone long."

"What do I look like, an old man?" Vosile's eyes flashed. "I haven't aged since the world was a much younger place, and I've been keeping myself up fine long before you were born. *Go.*"

Saying their thanks and goodbyes, the four of them turned and shuffled their way back through the warm little house, and the town outdoors greeted them with a wary, glaring brightness, as though the sun had narrowed its eyes. Villagers milled about, and their glances were heavy, pinning Majest and Letty with their arrows.

"Don't pay them any mind," Sedona said. "I'll introduce you."

She turned to the crowd. "Rapple!" she called, and beckoned to a tall man standing next to a pretty woman with red-blond curls.

As the man approached, his eyes narrowed. "Sedona, who are these people, and why hasn't anyone said anything about them? You can't just invite strangers in here—strangers are usually *murderers.*" The words were forceful enough to make Letty flinch, but Sedona seemed to pay them no mind.

"Rapple, this is Majest and Letty Skylark," she announced. "They're runaways from the mainland. They need a place to stay, and Vosile approved them himself." In a quieter voice, she added, "They have *powers.*"

"Oh." Rapple straightened up, eyes losing their suspicion like a sudden change of direction in the wind. He popped a smile, dipping his head to Majest. "My apologies. Welcome to Hi Ding. I'm Rapple Ardyn."

Majest, a little bewildered, nodded in turn. "Thanks?"

Rapple nodded, and held up one finger. "Wait just a minute." He swung around to fix his gaze between the crowd of hostile townsfolk, and addressed them with long waving arms. "Hey, everyone!" he called, and the villagers ceased their restless chatter to face him. "There's just been news—these two aren't threats! So will you please stop lurking around here like you're waiting for blood to come spilling out of the sky? Go home; I know you all have knitting to do, or sandwiches to make."

Majest almost laughed as the villagers tossed sour faces in Rapple's direction, but disappeared from their suspicious perches with a slow, slinking defeat all the same. "Thanks, but you don't have to worry about that," he said. "I don't expect them to like us. I wouldn't trust us, either."

"Why not?" Rapple snorted. "They're the nicest people you'll ever meet; they just need a little softening up sometimes—like frozen meat! They're great once you thaw 'em out." He pulled something red and smooth from his jacket pocket, and crunched his teeth into it.

"Are you wasting all of Jay's apples again?" Sedona fixed Rapple with a condescending glare. "You *know* the Souleias grow those especially for him." An impatient sigh. "He'll skin you alive if he finds out you keep sneaking them out of his storage like that."

Majest quirked an eyebrow. "Who?"

"Jay. He lives down the street," put in Vari from where he stood dutifully at Letty's side. "Sometimes he helps out around here, and sometimes he doesn't. He has a very interesting assortment of potions, concoctions, and tea—and he generally knows everything about *everything*—but he's hardly someone you want to meet."

"Why not?" asked Letty, tucking a lock of hair behind her ears with a gloved hand.

"Because he's a crazy blind freak," put in a new voice. The group whirled around to see yet another young girl standing beside them, chin-length waves of brown hair curling around her face. She seemed to realize her bizarre interruption and shrugged self-consciously. "You know it's true."

"Sunni." Sedona sighed. Majest instantly knew this girl must have been Sedona's sister—though Sunni's hair was hardly cloud-white, their faded blue eyes and the swooping jaw-lines of their faces were identical.

"You shouldn't talk about Jay like that," Sedona continued, staring her sister down. Majest couldn't tell if Sunni was the younger sister, or if Sedona just acted like everyone's mother. "Just because he's a little inhospitable doesn't change the fact that he's saved more than one of us with all he knows and can do. The fact that he's willing to help anyone at all after what he's been through should be more than enough to excuse a few oddities and a bad temper."

"One time I asked him if he had any tea for a sore throat, and he nearly threw me out the window." Vari sniffed.

"Well, you try being blinded and tortured by your own father," Sedona snapped.

"You don't know that's what happened!"

"It's not like anyone gets close enough to ask. Besides, you know what Vosile always says, and it's no wonder the kid doesn't trust anyone."

"But he lives in *Raylea's* house," Sunni protested, as if that explained everything. "She was always so happy, and even happier to take care of everyone—with all her little pine-needle potions. It's because of her Jay's even alive in the first place after he was brought here half-dead. She was a *doctor,* for skies' sakes! You'd think she would've rubbed off on him—she was brilliant! Jay's just *weird.*"

"What about the rest of the town?" asked Majest hastily, growing impatient with nosy stories he didn't understand. "So you've got an old man who spreads stories of impossibilities, a crazy blind guy who hates everyone—what else? Merchants with inferiority complexes? A band of angry adolescents bent on stealing food from polar bears?"

"Well, *I'm* the teacher," Sunni boasted, her eyes gleaming. She turned to Letty with an impish grin. Majest was shocked, unused to such mischief in such a small package.

"You? The teacher?" Letty looked at the other girl in doubt. "You're hardly older than I am!"

"In a few years, I'll know everything in the whole wide world," continued Sunni, as her sister rolled her eyes again, a more pronounced gesture this time. "More than Jay and Vosile *combined!* Then I'll have to teach the rest of the town what I know. For instance!" Sunni grinned. "Did you know if you stick your tongue to a block of ice for too long, it'll get stuck there?"

"You only know because you were foolish enough to try," Sedona retorted, though not without affection. "Enough, Sunni. You don't have to be the center of attention all the time."

Sunni sighed in exaggeration, looking pointedly at Letty, who giggled.

"Anyway," Sedona continued in a wry tone, shifting her gaze back to Majest, "I suppose it won't do you any good to start shouting out names of villagers—you'll have to meet us for yourselves."

She gestured to Rapple, who had drifted away across the pebbled road. "You already know Rapple. The girl with the strawberry-blond hair is his partner, Acillia. She's expecting his child."

"What about those two?" Letty motioned to a small house on the right, and two heads of brown hair flickered visibly through a gaping window. "They keep looking over here."

"Quell and Idyllice," replied Vari. "The Souleia twins. They grow most of our food. When I was little, they'd always come visit my parents and give us fresh fruits and vegetables. They're the hardest workers in the whole village and the nicest people you'll ever meet." His eyes shone with a sort of little-boy infatuation. "They're *amazing*."

Majest didn't know what fruits and vegetables were—he had never even heard the words before—but he didn't ask, either. He was beginning to feel rather out of place.

"Like the words, quell and idyllic?" asked Letty—more words that rang in unfamiliar tones against Majest's ears. "Those are pretty names."

"Aletta's a pretty name, too," Vari told her.

Letty blinked, caught off guard, and said nothing. Her face turned a slow, obvious red, unhindered by a pale face and freckles.

Majest gave a weak cough to keep from laughing, and Letty caught his eye in a glare. Maybe she thought herself too young to start thinking about partnership, but clearly, Vari had other ideas.

"Vari," said Sedona, not missing the exchange, "will you please go find Cydinne for me? I'm sure she'd be happy to find someplace for Letty and Majest to stay in."

Vari glanced from Letty to Sedona and back again, and his eyebrows went high above his hair in quizzical peaks. Then he shrugged, gave a wave, and pattered off in a new direction.

"Sorry about him." Sedona turned to Letty "Was he bothering you?"

"No, no," replied Letty quickly, giving her brother a sharp glance as he began to chuckle again. Her face deepened in color until it was redder than the stolen apple. "It's quite alright."

Before Majest had time to comment, Vari was back, and with

217

him was a tall woman with the longest hair Majest had ever seen, and almond-shaped eyes against elegant bones. She dipped her head.

"Cydinne Floodleaf," she said, and Majest knew it would only be seconds before he forgot her name—he had learned too many today, and he felt waterlogged with strangers. "I'm responsible for settling in newcomers. It's been a long time since anyone has found their way into Hi Ding with intents to stay. I'd nearly forgotten my job entirely."

"We have intents to stay," said Letty decisively, and Majest made no move to stop her.

"Then we will have to find you a house." Cydinne's voice was even.

"Thank you very much," Majest told her, making sure to remember his manners, though he was beginning to feel a bit dizzy. Names and faces seemed to flash before him. "I'm sure…we'll love it here."

"Good." Cydinne's response was like a rustle of leaves. She was so at ease—this entire island seemed coated in a sticky sense of peace.

"Majest and Letty can live with Cilli and I in our house if they'd like, Cydinne," Rapple offered. Majest hadn't realized he had returned.

"You don't have enough space," Cydinne told him before Majest could respond. "Acillia is due any day now, and the spare room will be needed for your new son or daughter." She fixed her stare on Majest. "I'm sure there's someone who has an extra room or two. I know Minka's family is one short since her brother passed away, and Linus and Sharlytte's son just moved into his own home."

Majest remembered the stares of the villagers, their suspicion, their alienation. He didn't like the idea of staying with one of them, of being thrust into a stranger's life without warning.

Letty seemed to sense his disinclination. "Aren't there any empty houses we could use?" she asked.

Cydinne's eyes flicked downward to her. "Of course. You'll

have to fix one up a bit, but there should be a few with proper beds and tables and things of the sort, if you would prefer."

Majest was about to concur when an irritated voice sounded from behind. "What are all of you idiots doing out here? Don't you know there's a storm coming?"

Everyone turned, startled, and found a short, scrawny boy clad in a dark jacket standing before them, arms crossed and eyebrows up.

Majest fixed a startled squint on him. The boy looked normal enough—somewhere around eight birth-years, face just barely grasping the last scraps of childhood, though his demeanor implied someone much older than the sixteen years in his features. His hair was a dark mess of dull blue-black slate that framed his face in feathers, and the expression on his face, though cross, was ordinary—perhaps even miserably endearing. Yet Majest felt put off by something he could not grasp.

"Jay," said Sedona quietly. In fact, everyone had dimmed down, and in the silence, Majest could hear the faintest rumblings of thunder, like someone's growling stomach.

"There's no storm," said Sunni loftily, the only one not put off by the sudden appearance. "If there *were* a storm, there would be storm clouds in the sky. I don't see any storm clouds, do you?"

Jay's lip curled like her words had personally offended him, and his scowl furthered until his forehead started to wrinkle. He already reminded Majest of Lunesta, so much aggression on such a young face. "I don't *see* anything," came his response to the girl's careless outburst, such a forceful statement that Majest felt the urge to step back. "I *know* things. This village has relied on my abilities to tell of far less trivial things than storms."

"Hardly," Sunni grumbled, making a point of looking down to straighten her jacket.

"Now here's where the craziness steps up a notch," Majest heard Vari mutter into Letty's ear. "He thinks he's some sort of prophet, that he sees things in dreams before they happen. Like, actually *sees* things. Nobody believes him except old Masotote."

Majest thought of his father's stories—prophecies and

predictive dreams, spirits and psychic visions. His father would have believed Jay. Dagur had believed in everything, everyone.

"Listen, do you want to be blown away?" Jay snapped. He didn't make any indication he had heard Vari's words. "If you'd prefer attempting to redirect the wind as a sort of talent show for your apparent new pet guests, Seacourt, you may do as you like, but if you're in the mood for a more reasonable approach, it would be a capital idea to retreat into your homes and *not* get pummeled by an onslaught of freezing rain."

Majest watched Jay's face with interest. Pinched and tight, cold as snow. Majest could easily see how anyone would feel uncomfortable with him around; he was as stormy as the approaching rain clouds themselves. Majest was soon lost in thoughts of snow, in Lunesta's departure into hail and thunder.

Then he realized with a start what had chilled him to the bone at his first sight of Jay.

Maxine had always said eyes were the path to the soul, that in them, you discovered who someone was and what they were living for. If that were the case, then Jay was hardly anything or anyone at all. His two pale films held no light, no life, not even a shimmer of something beneath dark pupils. It was like two milky blue clouds were permanently hanging down from his lashes, keeping out the warmth, forbidding the filtering of sunlight. Even as Jay spoke, his eyes remained still as the sky, unmoving, focused straight ahead to something that did not exist.

He's blind, Majest remembered, averting his gaze though he knew it was silly—Jay couldn't tell he was looking at him, right?

What must it be like to live in a world where you can't see what's in front of you? You can't move forward because you'll never know when something unexpected might jump out to throw you off of a path you think you have memorized by heart. What can you ever truly trust?

"Would you quit your staring?" Jay directed his next snap at Majest, who almost jumped out of his skin as the sightless eyes grazed over him like needles.

For once, Majest was speechless. "I—I wasn't—" he faltered.

"Just because I can't see doesn't mean I can't feel your clueless eyes on me," Jay drawled, irritation clear in his voice. A peal of thunder clapped somewhere in the distance and shadows were thrown off the sun as it took cover. "Now, if you'll excuse me, I have tea brewing, which is probably getting cold by this time, and if the lot of you would prefer to be stormed upon like a bunch of unlucky treetops while my drink freezes, then consider yourselves warned."

Spinning on one heel, Jay turned and marched himself back across the town's center with surprising accuracy, and stalked up the path of what must have been his house. He slammed the door behind him with a bang that mingled in familiarity against the thunder.

After some time of awkward staring after his retreat, Vari broke the silence. "As you can see," he said, "you shouldn't bother Jay the grouchy, creepy blind kid with the potions and tea. Don't talk to him, don't look at him, or he'll make sure you regret it."

"So I see." Letty snorted, flashing her brother a reproachful look—the same look she always gave him when he ate the last rabbit leg or accidentally got mud in her hair.

"But Jay was right about the storm coming," Sedona said. "We'd better get inside."

Jay was right. Majest frowned, and he heard his father's rumbling voice in his mind like wind in the mountains—"*Sometimes dreams have the power to take us places we cannot find on our own. And there are some people, prophets, who have the curse of dreams that take them so far from reality that they no longer see the world at all, only the future in their nightmares. The gift of the prophet is the worst of all. It is nothing but blackness.*"

He rather thought his father and his stories were right.

As Sedona began leading the way indoors, she turned to Majest, a peculiar expression crossing her face. "You're lucky, Majest. Looks like your arrival was just in time before the storm hit."

"Yes," replied Majest, frowning at the sky as it burbled, a frightening mass of swirling obscurity. He had only known two skies that had been blacker, two nights of darker terror. "Looks like it was."

221

XV. EXPOSURE

Bang!

A noise like the loudest clap of thunder shot across the interlocked buildings of the Organization, swarming like insects down the hallways, into the deepest rooms and corners. It jolted Shatter from her research and caused a momentary clench of the heart; moving fingers fumbled, and a yellowed map went waving to the floor. An aftershock of rumbling followed in conclusion, shaking the table and sending a few last pages to the ground.

Shatter let out a cry, breaths coming in gasps as she bent over hastily to pick up the fallen work. Her head pulsed, heart restarting. Questions bursting into the air before her, she got to her feet and crossed the room in a few quick steps, throwing open the door to peer into the hallway.

As she stared out into empty white space, silence ringing, Shatter's first thought was that she had imagined the noise. She didn't know of anything that could create such a racket save for an explosion, and the science labs never got that out of hand.

Did they?

Shatter decided—perhaps against better judgment that had long since flown out the window—to investigate.

If anyone could clue her in to the origin of the noise, it would be the scientists. She wasn't exactly permitted to leave her room as she pleased—especially since she was supposed to be working—but curiosity always proved to be the overriding factor.

It's not as if Lady President doesn't trust me. I always do my work on time, and never cause trouble. Surely I'm allowed to investigate.

A brisk walk down the colorless smears of the hallways and she was turning into the laboratory. With a flaring surprise, Shatter realized the door was left dangling out into the open, bent backward like a broken limb, exposing loud, anxious voices and bright lights that blared into the hallway.

Not needing to knock, Shatter poked her head into the room nervously from around the corner.

"Malory!" A voice was calling—Caiter's. "Malory, *stop!*"

"It's perfectly harmless!" came the jovial reply. Malory was standing in the center of the laboratory, holding an unsealed vial of foul-looking substance above his head. Gray smoke poured out from its rim and hung around his face in ghostly clouds, fogging his glasses so that black eyes looked to be nothing more than pits. "I promise, Caiter—no need to worry about me!"

"You're breathing your own demonic fumes!" Caiter yelled back, his already flustered face burning crimson. "You have to put the cover back on!"

Shatter watched in a sort of horrified amazement as Malory ignored the warning, snatching up a syringe from a nearby table and filling it with his toxin. He was snickering with an utmost glee that pooled saliva around the corners of his lips, gleaming before it was swallowed away. He and Caiter hadn't seen Shatter watching from the doorway yet.

"Malory," said Caiter again, worry cracking his voice. "Malory! Are you listening to me?"

Malory waved a hand vaguely in Caiter's direction, thrusting the last of his vial aside and holding up a full syringe to the light. It shone a deep, dark red against the lights—like poisoned blood. "Danger is the primary ingredient, my friend! This is the perfect mixture! This is the one!"

"If it's that good, why don't you put it down and fetch Lady President?" asked Caiter, taking a pace back. His tone was defensive and careful, a stone not wishing to drop and throw ripples into boiling water. "Perhaps she can get you another cat to test it on."

"*Cat?*" Malory guffawed, a voice like smashed glass echoing across the laboratory, earning him the first of many frightened and baffled glances from the other scientists. Before long, everyone was staring at Malory, though no one dared to move.

"Cats are *boring,*" Malory went on, long, white fingers waving in the air in a gesture clearly implying he thought Caiter was the one being ludicrous. His skin glowed an ethereal pastel in the dull blue fluorescents, pallid as the halls. "Even the talking ones. The deal was, if I help our little President build this Organization, I get the *full benefits* of this technology to do with whatever I please."

"We have to follow the mission—"

"*I have my own mission,*" Malory growled. The ends of his words stuck into the air like pointed knives. "And it requires more than a couple of cats—I need a real person to test this on!"

Shatter's mind on red-alert, she felt her feet shuffle backward, and fought to keep her legs from wheeling her straight out of the room.

A stunned lull in time allowed the smoky room to simmer. Malory began waving his syringe in the air, as if he were contemplating who to inject with it.

Unfortunately, that was just the case.

"*Caiter,*" said Malory in a low voice, waggling his eyebrows. "Caiter, you're always good to me. Do you want to help the cause of *revenge?*"

Caiter edged away, farther and farther away, until he was backed up against the wall, breaths coming in petrified gasps. "Well—I mean—it depends what you're asking—"

Malory took a careless step forward as someone might step to embrace a child, and he was smiling with all the sharp teeth and gruesome glory that could ever chill Shatter's bones, syringe up and poised, needle gleaming.

"Malory, stop," Caiter stammered, hands out, pleading. "The President wouldn't allow you to—"

"No!" Shatter's voice rang out into the laboratory before she could stop it; the echo bounced across the dome of the room with ease, repeating the cry in a series of short bursts. She immediately clamped a hand to her mouth as not only Malory and Caiter but the entire room turned to gape at her with mouths dropping to the hard, dustless floor.

"Shatter Seacourt," said Malory, shifting large black eyes from Caiter in a worm's crawl. He retreated from the sweating blond mess of a scientist with one short step, leaning back casually. Something about the sound of her name on this madman's tongue make Shatter sick to her stomach.

She remembered in vain the weeks long gone, when Malory had been nothing more than an unpleasant disturbance in the atmosphere; now, he seemed to be another planet that dragged the Organization into his gravitational pull, spinning them into a new direction, his own direction, something he had described as *vengeful* direction—a direction the President believed god-sent, though it filled Shatter with dread.

Realizing the entire laboratory was intending her to speak, Shatter cleared her throat, feeling her face grow hot under the glare of the lights. Her voice rang out across the laboratory clearer and louder than she had expected. "You were all just going to sit by and let him do this? Don't tell me you're *okay* with letting Malory turn Caiter into a mutant!"

"Malory's plans are phenomenal," answered a voice from the back. The crowd before the speaker parted to reveal coiled cherry hair and gray eyes much too large for the bones of his face. Ohanzi?

"Because of his potions, we finally have a better advantage over the Powers," the boy went on. Everyone's eyes were on him. "They won't be able to lose against a force with the energy of demons on its side. And that's the first big step to a new world like the old world." He stepped forward until he was standing next to Malory, who turned to the younger scientist with a charmed smile.

"That's right, Ohanzi," said Malory, putting a hand to his supporter's shoulder, voice as velvety as a cat's purr. "We'll be unstoppable with this potion, won't we? Like hellfire, only…more *me.* Don't you like that, Caiter?"

"Not if the potion doesn't work," pointed out Caiter in a small voice, gaining back enough of his composure to step forward from the wall, straightening out his back with a creak that sounded like it hurt. "All but one of the cats you've tested so far have died. Any human you try this new formula on is likely to end up the same."

"Shut up," snapped Malory, his moment of good nature vanishing, and Caiter's face sunk into despair. "It *will* work; I'm sure of it. I thought at least *you* would wag your tail and support me. All I need is for someone to step up and volunteer."

He looked out expectantly over a silent crowd, which flickered with the uneasiness of a lone candle, one that seemed rather inclined to melt into the walls and disappear.

"I *said, I need someone to volunteer,*" Malory snarled, and his lips mashed into a pout, fire leaping from the glass over his eyes. "Do I need to hold up a bloody cue card?"

"I'll do it," said Ohanzi. Shatter's stomach clenched.

Caiter stepped forward. "Don't—"

But Malory's eyes were already set aglow to a wicked black light, and without another word, he raised his arm high, syringe needle going up like a flag, and then it was diving down into Ohanzi's arm. Soundlessly. As though it had not happened at all.

At once, any murmurs turned to stone. Even the whir of the machines dropped under the floor, and the empty silence of a usually-buzzing room fogged Shatter's ears. A blank miasma froze the world systematically to a stop, like a blanket of snow had turned each scientist to ice.

Ohanzi was the most frozen of them all, mouth falling open with a pop. He must not have thought of the consequences. He must have only wanted to please his twisted idol.

But it was too late to wind the clock back around. The boy was still, still as death; the gray of his eyes, the color of dust and sunless skies, had faded, and they blanched white as the walls.

Next to him, Malory hooted.

"Ohanzi," whispered Caiter, breaking the crowd's silence with the quietest of exclamations. His eyes held defeat, a ghastly foreboding. He knew what would follow. "Oh, no, Ohanzi. *No.*"

The last *no* rang out like a sorrowful echo, and then Ohanzi was on fire.

Not literally on fire, of course—although the Organization and its employees were capable of many extraordinary feats, human beings bursting artlessly into flames was not one of them. But *fire* was the word for what made Shatter clutch her arms to her chest and suppress a wail.

Ohanzi's fire was all inside him, and he sank to his knees as if his legs could no longer hold the flames. His body seemed to arc forward, violently curling in on itself with the charred air of something defeated and gone. And he *screamed,* screamed a chorus of howls straight from Hell, spasms shaking his body like a volcano about to erupt. The sound was anything but human, and Shatter gritted her teeth to keep from whimpering.

Somewhere between screams, Ohanzi's body began to change, burning under sizzling, invisible white tongues of pain. His skin burned crimson, hair falling from his scalp to the floor in curls of blood. And then he was charcoal and crisped as two white orbs consumed his face, became unseeing eyes. There were horns and claws growing out from all over his skin in a thousand diseases, and what was left of his mouth was foaming, blood gurgling from deep in his throat. He was a broken machine.

Malory's laughter had risen to a full-blown scream, the screech of an owl tearing prey into bloody strips, guts flying. His eyes were not visible through their lenses, which reflected Ohanzi's poisoned demise in miniature twin mirrors.

Shatter fell like a limp doll to the blue-white ground and opened her mouth, expecting to throw up the bread she had eaten hours ago, but nothing came out, just tremors and gasps.

At once, Ohanzi's destruction ceased and the boy's mangled, distorted body lay on the laboratory floor, unmoving as it sank into its own ashes.

Shatter held her breath tight in her throat, bile rising but never coming to a boil. Was he dead? Had Caiter been right?

But no, in Ohanzi's place was a black cloud that rose up from the floor in a spitting tornado. It was if a shadow had opened its mouth and swallowed the boy whole. There was only a mass of darkness that flew up into the air like a mad raven, the quintessence of a nightmare.

As the shadow rose, it let out a hiss, and though Shatter could not comprehend, there did seem to be two words among the razing whisper—"Island. *Destroy.*"

Shatter quaked. Every evidence of the incident seemed to fade and evaporate all at once as though it had been summoned, and she realized the *thing*—Ohanzi or not—was gone. It was over, and there was nothing left.

For a long time, there was an uncomfortable, shell-shocked silence. Until—

"What have you done?" spat Caiter in a surprising, stable tone. His usual flustered appearance had disappeared through the roof with Ohanzi. The look on his face now was a dangerous sea of calm.

Malory's eyes were visible again, and they were gleaming. "I did it; I put a demon spirit into a human being," he said, voice distant, as if he were speaking through a foggy dream. "That shadow—that was the force. It took Ohanzi and just… floated him away. He'll be out in the world now, doing who knows what. Stealing souls, possessing minds—oh, the *possibilities.*"

Horror-struck faces greeted him from all corners of the room. Shatter heard someone vomit.

Oblivious, Malory eyed his half-full syringe with appreciation. "Alright, who's next?"

And then, with a cry of some emotion Shatter was not equipped to grasp with her own two hands, Caiter was springing forward, his hands slamming into Malory's shoulders; they tumbled to the ground in a flurry of wheeling arms, open mouths. "You can't do this anymore!" Caiter howled, a desperate, mournful cry. "You *can't!*"

The words seemed to ring home to Shatter's chest. Caiter was right—she could not bear this. And so she turned tail and fled without the urge for more, the need for a finale. She slammed the door behind her, and streaked through the hall.

As she ran, her stomach threatened to pump her heart up and out of her throat, and she had to stop several times, hands on her knees, breathing hard with her hair tangling down her back. This was the burden of gratified curiosity, and it weighed her down until she thought she might be crushed. How could she simply return to her room now?

But she didn't have to. Two familiar twins took the laden pause to materialize in the center of the hall, their violet-brown hair a splash of welcome contrast to walls of white oblivion.

With them was Seti, slumped between them like a corpse, struggling to keep himself standing as he was dragged through the hallways.

Seti.

Forgetting Ohanzi, forgetting Caiter and Malory and the turmoil she had shut behind the laboratory door, Shatter pushed herself to the center of the hallway as if stepping in front of a barreling avalanche, as though she meant to stop something that could bury her alive.

"Shatter," said Chami casually, and even without flavor, her voice was still bitter music. "What's the matter—shouldn't you be in your room?"

Shatter took a deep breath, heart still battering. She still saw the fire, heard the screams. But no one could know where she had been.

She watched Seti out of the corner of one eye—exhausted, depleted, stripped of his defiance and spark. It felt as if he took over her senses, made her forget shadows and demons and poison.

"I was helping out in the resource room," Shatter fibbed.

"Good for you," said Shayming with a lifeless absence. She and her sister were pulling the half-conscious Seti toward the President's chamber.

Shatter's face molded into a wobbly frown. "Where are you going with him?"

Shayming grinned, crooked teeth peering out of thin lips. "To see the President," she replied.

Seti grunted in an indistinguishable response.

"Are you going to kill him?" Shatter burst out, shocked not for the first time that afternoon at what was capable of escaping her mouth.

"We don't know yet," said Chami, her strident voice like pins and needles. "We hope not." A rare look of vulnerability came across her face, and Shatter blinked in astonishment.

"What Chami means is that the President is going to see him before his fate is certain," cut in Shayming; her mouth was tight as she glanced at her sister. "You aren't really permitted to know any more, Shatter, despite the soft spot the President has for you."

"I understand," said Shatter, and dipped her head, though her mind reeled.

"I do believe no matter what happens, this could be the last time you ever see our precious Seti Sinestre," Chami added, voice sloping downward into a low tone, a somber bell that foretold nothing good. "So you'd better get a long last look."

Shatter's breath caught. Even the twins pitied Seti.

Despite the way she knew she shouldn't, her eyes caught on Seti. Seti didn't seem to have heard any of the conversation; his head was bent over, gold eyes invisible under the mop of dark hair that hung over his small face. It was as if he did not exist.

Not waiting for Shatter to say anything more, Chami and Shayming gathered Seti in their arms and hoisted him up, and down he went to the door that would decide whether he lived or died. Shatter still could not see his face, and she could not follow him.

That's how I'll always have to remember him, she thought as they neared the President's room. *Broken and defeated—everything he used to be swallowed up by defeat, by a failure he should not have suffered. He never wanted to be part of the Organization like us, did he? He didn't want to kill the Skylarks.*

"I'm not getting caught up in this any longer," Shatter whispered. She refused to start crying, although her head and heart felt heavy, threatening to drag her through the floor. "Not Seti, not the scientists—I'm done. No more distractions, no more curiosity."

Without her permission, a single tear like a star caught in her eye and streaked to the floor, silence in its fall. And she hated it.

"It's not my place to do anything else."

There were subtle clues to where Chami and Shayming were taking Seti—like the hard click of linoleum under the twins' feet, the strain of Shatter's voice like a lighthouse in the fog—but apart from the weight of his failures pressing his shoulders forward, Seti felt nothing, no sense of apprehension, just numbness as he was dragged away.

He was aware of a knock and a whirring, of a new set of harsh footsteps, coming from a distance. A metallic whoosh sounded as a door was opened, and Seti was thrust into the familiar chamber of the Organization's President.

Light and sense flooded him as the fog of the halls rolled away, and Seti fought back a hiss as his eyes burned under the whiteness of what was before him.

"And so the toy soldier returns," came a soft voice. The President seemed to appear as if by magic, swinging Seti's gaze around as the stench of chemicals caught in the air. She was not sitting in her chair as Seti had seen her before, but standing, her thin, bony arms at her sides, her white buttoned coat pristine. Not a speck of dust graced her black, cotton trousers, and her metal boots gleamed.

"Of course," replied Shayming. "We did as you asked, because you asked for it, Lady President."

"Thank you, Shayming, Chami." Dark eyes traveled to Seti with a gradual care, their midnight color seeming to see right through him. "You two may go now," she told the twins.

"Go?" Chami sounded disappointed. "But what—?"

"I give you my word that the fate of Seti Sinestre will travel quickly to your ears, but for now, I must be left alone with our guest." The President's words were as rigid as the harsh white of the walls; they mingled with the beeps and whirs of the gadgets lining the room. Everything was ringing.

Allowing Chami to give one final thwarted sigh, Shayming touched her sister's shoulder and the two of them turned and walked out of the room, their feet seeming to just graze the ground, making no sound. Seti began to wonder if anything in this building truly existed, or if it was all a mirage.

Chami threw a glance at Seti over her shoulder. Her expression looked much like a goodbye.

Seti lifted his head, fighting against the weakness in his neck to see the President clearly. He staggered off to one side and leaned up against a glass case, unable to stand on his own.

"So," he said after a moment, not bothering to clear the rasp from his throat, "I presume you brought me here to yell at me?" He found no point in courtesy, not when he was bound to be executed on the spot. That girl, Shatter, had sounded worried enough to make Seti wonder if the President actually had the backbone to kill him for what he'd done—or rather, what he hadn't done.

It makes no difference to me, thought Seti, feeling weary. *It's not as if I'd be dying young and naïve. If she wants to end my life over a few trivial children, that's her faulty move, not mine.*

"I did bring you here for harsh words, yes." The President answered the initial question in a cold deadpan. "I was counting on you, Seti, and you let me down. You're such an incredible talent; I can't understand what could *possibly* have kept you from doing as I asked."

"Many things," Seti growled, trying to keep his eyes open. "One of them being that you asked murder of me, and I only kill those who have done wrong."

The President's lip curled. "This was *important*. It was not murder. It was the first step to everything."

"If it's so important, why don't *you* kill Aletta and Majest?" Seti forced his eyes wider, wanting to gauge the President's reaction.

The woman flinched, and Seti made a noise between a growl and a sigh. "You're scared. You don't want blood on your own hands, duty crawling through your own skin. Have you ever been in my position before? How do you know what it feels like to destroy the innocent? I've hurt many people in my life, you know. I've killed, I've murdered, I've slaughtered."

"Then why couldn't you do it again? One more time?" Her voice pled with him. "It was such a simple thing to plan—sneak up behind them and knock them out, then leave them in the snow to freeze. That's all it would have taken. Then you could have found the other Powers—and at least on the surface, this land would have become equal."

"You don't think I *believe* all this about an 'equal world', do you?" Seti pressed his lips together. "This isn't about the good of the world. You're just jealous of the powers given to the other Skylarks. You couldn't *stand* how they were chosen without you, so you created a phony army of psychopaths and misfits with old-fashioned gadgets to help you remove the siblings under the disguise of some larger purpose because you're too much of a coward to kill them yourself."

The President seemed to gasp for breath. The malicious spark in her eyes died and her skin went whiter than the walls. "You— you said *other* Skylarks," she stammered, apparently not concerned with anything else Seti had said. "You didn't just say Skylarks. Why did you say that?"

Seti crossed his arms; his head ached, like oxygen had all but abandoned him. "I know who you are," he said softly. "I suspected it from the moment I saw you. Everyone knows about you just as everyone knows about the Organization—they just don't connect the two together. But I saw right through you, Lunesta Skylark."

The President's eyes flew open into two moons, face no longer in slumber, full and broad with borrowed light. A flicker of uncertainty flashed across her pale face.

Weeks of tailing Aletta and Majest plundered Seti's mind, and he could see the same angle of their noses, the shapes of their eyes, all reflected back in the face before him, mouth opening without a sound, stunned into silence.

"You thought you were so clever, Lunesta," continued Seti, scorn bleeding through his words. "You thought you could grow out your hair and run away into the arms of murderers, take out your little brother and sister without lifting a finger. You thought all this was worth it, for two stupid kids."

"I did what I had to do," growled the President—Lunesta—in a dark voice. "Their powers aren't *natural*! I had to get rid of them, don't you see? They could have destroyed everything!"

"Not really," said Seti, unsympathetic and dry. "You're nothing but a coward and a fake, not to mention a flaming hypocrite. Using psychic twin sisters and planning to let one of your scientists inject human beings with demon energies to make a more dangerous version of me?" Fire raged in Seti's mind, ire rising up his throat and coating his words with molten fury. "Chami told me about Malory."

Lunesta blinked, the broken look still on her face, like Seti had thrust a knife into her side. "I didn't take any chances," she whispered. "Chami and Shayming found me crossing the forest alone, and told me they understood me. They wanted to help me, and so they helped me find Malory—I knew him beforehand, I'll admit. He told me of a place far away, where the past lived on behind an ancient waterfall. The laboratories, the technology, everything. He had the demon energy, the plans for a greenhouse, for weaponry, for wrangling this place into his own hands—and I had to accept. It was the perfect opportunity to do away with my brother and sister.

"But all that was too much just to kill two children, you're right—so, I broadened my claim. I decided to use this place to jumpstart a modern new world. And people liked that. People came to me."

"Because they think killing the Powers will somehow make this world the way it used to be?"

"Maybe they're right," said Lunesta. "Maybe I can lead a bettered world. It's all fallen into my hands so far. And I rather like where it is going."

"You're disgusting," Seti told her. "You're selfish, and you're incompetent, you lie about every last motive up your sleeve, and yet you still have the audacity to wonder why I refused to help you. If it weren't for this *damned* pocket watch, you never would have seen my face again."

"The watch," repeated Lunesta feverishly. "Of course. You never got to see how it worked, did you? I'm sorry for that, Seti. At the very least, it might have brightened your dark travels with a bit of entertainment. But don't worry. Someday—perhaps a long time from now, but someday all the same—you will see its power."

Seti felt no better at the small and insincere apology. What did the watch even matter? Everything was over. "What are you going to do now?" he asked, not looking forward to the answer. He glanced around the room for a possible way out, but there was none.

Lunesta fixed a long, hard stare on Seti, who stared back, unafraid, trying to hold a challenge in his tired eyes.

"I'd like to kill you," Lunesta said after some time. "I'd like to, but it would be unwise of me."

Seti wasn't sure whether to feel relieved or not. "Why is that?"

"I may need you later." Lunesta put a finger to lips and eyed Seti with consideration. "Though you obviously don't wish to be a part of the Organization, and you're rather bitter despite your devious charms…somehow, I feel as if we need you. You're of the old world. Perhaps you will become part of our new one."

"*Really?*" Seti asked the question as if he were spitting into the dirt. "I'm of no importance to you, or to anyone! Why don't you just let me out of this god-forsaken place, save yourself all this negativity?"

"Shut up," said Lunesta, though she said it mildly. "You're more than you realize, although no good for the mission I sent you on. Later, when the Powers are gone, you might decide you can take the next step with us."

"So you expect me to wait around in this cursed place until the other Skylarks are dead and you come up with something you'd like me to do in absence of any bravery on your part?" Seti felt his voice take on something dull and weighted between its inflections.

Lunesta's mouth twitched. "I imagine you'd grow quite mad by then, and turn me quite mad in the process. Perhaps you'd even escape, and I can't have that. No, Seti, I have just the place for you." She gestured to a boxlike structure in Seti's direction, and at first he didn't know what she was doing.

"What?" he snapped, leaning and turning to look at the thing. It was like a bulky glass coffin, tubes and wires running like veins all across it, buttons beaming like berries on its outer rim. "What in all Hell is that?"

Lunesta's smile evolved into a full grin of pearly scheme, one part contemptuous and one part amused. "It's an infinite sleep chamber," she said with a slow resonance, like the words themselves could cast a spell. "A few seconds inside of it and you're sleeping like a baby mouse. I had my dear Caiter make it for me—he's such a fantastic asset to my team, and *such* the great recruiter."

"Sleep chamber?" Seti didn't like the sound of that. He stared down the kinking tubes, and a flashing memory appeared in his mind of his aunt Soti and the teeming white hallways she had worked in a century ago; he shook it away. "Looks like some sick hospital trick."

Lunesta almost rolled her eyes. "Oh, you're no fun—you know all about these sorts of things already, don't you? The technology, the strategies—you've probably seen a sleep chamber before, am I right? I got the idea from a book I found in one of the drawers. Whoever lived here last must have written it, though the initial plan involved some electrical nonsense I couldn't understand. Here, we use magic."

Seti shook his head with a touch of impatience. "I'm not concerned with intricacies of the past. What are you planning on doing with that sleep chamber?"

At this Lunesta laughed—a thing so casual, Seti wondered how such an ordinary woman had ended up where she was. From ordinary forest girl to spineless mastermind.

"Spit it out," Seti snapped.

Lunesta was still laughing. "Seti, Seti," she said between chuckles, "why would I show you my masterpiece and then conceal it away without giving you a chance to test it out? I'm quite proud of the work Caiter has done the past few weeks—I wouldn't want to put it to waste, would you?"

Seti's stomach churned. He was fully awake now. This was far worse than the thought of being held prisoner—put to sleep, he would be locked in unbreakable binds, unable to do anything but dream. And he knew his dreams would only be nightmares.

"Well, what are you waiting for?" Lunesta scoffed, taking a pace forward on steely heels. They clicked against the hard floors like a timepiece, counting down like the watch he was trying to forget. "Get in the chamber, Seti, or I *will* make you."

"What do you think you can do?" asked Seti, edging away from the sleep chamber with his hands up defensively, preparing for a fight. He would not let himself be made a fool of—not again. "You're no warrior, Lunesta Skylark. I know this because you're a coward and a fool. You'd sooner die crawling than die fighting. Do you honestly think you can beat me face-to-face?"

"No," Lunesta said with disdain, "I know of your skill in battle. By myself, I would not be able to contest. But you seem to be forgetting that just beyond these walls is a force plenty men and woman strong. They are trained. They will come rushing to defend me at moment's notice."

Seti narrowed his eyes until all he could see was her face, tight and angry. She was in his aim. Energy was rushing back into his veins with adrenaline and resolve, and he knew he could kill her if he just had a chance to face her one-on-one.

But she was right, Seti reflected with reluctance. One scream and the entire Organization would be on top of him; Seti would be killed within minutes, and he didn't want that.

But still...

"I'm not getting into that chamber unless you agree to my terms." Seti dodged Lunesta as she took another step toward him, dipping under her arm with ease and twirling gracefully to the center of the room.

Lunesta looked irritated at the deflection of her authority, but she just snorted and replied, "And what might those terms be?"

"You have to promise to wake me up quickly," Seti demanded, crossing his arms. "Even unconscious, I doubt I'll take kindly to being cooped up in a stuffy box for long. You have to swear on your life you'll set me free once the Organization has run its course. And it *will* run its course," he added as Lunesta was about to protest. "Lastly, I want your word that you'll let me be the one to stand my ground and declare your pitiful life's worth over. Is that clear?"

Lunesta wrinkled her nose in the picture of disgust. "I have to hand it to you, Sinestre," she said, shaking her head. "I never thought you'd turn on us like this. I thought the Organization would grow to be like a family to you. We could have had all the glory together, Seti. Now you've lost."

"Is that a yes or no?" Seti spat out from between his teeth.

"Fine," snapped Lunesta right back, looking the vaguest bit hurt. "I'll promise you the first, at least. You'll be out before long, despite how much I'd like to leave you rotting for a couple lifetimes. Get in the sleeping chamber before I change my mind."

Seti gritted his teeth, crossed the room and swung open the chamber door much harder than needed, flashing Lunesta a scornful glance. He found with strange surprise that he believed her words—she would wake him up, wouldn't she? She thought he might yet be *"useful."*

Between walls of spotless glass, a sweet smell wafted into Seti's nose, a sickly aroma like soap and chemicals. A thin layer of gas seemed to float about the chamber at its own leisure, soft and somehow welcoming as a bed full of blankets. And he wanted none of it, wanted to turn around and break the doors down, to burn white walls to the ground and never return.

"I'm doing this with pride," Seti told Lunesta as he flared his nostrils to clear such thought. The President was smiling in a mocking sort of way, clearly pleased with her power. "I wouldn't be laughing, *Skylark*. When I get out of here—like you promised—I'll be your worst enemy. You'll find yourself wishing to be sent to the depths of Hell rather than face the wrath I will put upon you."

"Big words for one so helpless and small," jeered Lunesta, puffing herself up. "You'll be lucky if I feel like letting you out at all."

"You're such a *child,*" Seti snapped. "I mean what I say." He climbed between the walls, let the door sweep shut before him. "Someday you'll learn that envy burns hotter than flame."

The sleeping medicine began to pull him down into the depths, and he fought to keep his eyes open, muttering, "You're wrong about me, about the Powers—about everything, you are."

With that, everything turned a fuzzy shade of gray-black behind Seti's eyes, and he swayed backwards, though invisible hands reached up at once, caught him before he could hit the glass and shatter. His senses melted like butter.

Seti almost welcomed the sensation. This was not the end; it was the beginning.

XVI. LURKING

The storm did not pass quickly.

After retreating indoors, there were only a few moments of patient silence before the rainy snow began dribbling down between the cracks in the heavens, drenching the ground in a slushy white paste that filled every one of Earth's dips and valleys. Thunder rolled its wheels on ahead, and lightning flashed as it scorched the trees, ripping roots and branches until Letty could hear the whole forest creaking.

Majest kept cringing with each new flash, each new fallen tree, as if he could sense their anguish. His eyes flashed to the swaying, helpless leaves screaming outside the window with a dejected frown.

And Letty watched, standing at the window of her new wooden home, shivering as wind and rainy snow blew through the see-through window curtain. She thought with a certain selfishness that for a village so caught up in the impossible, they should have been able to build more efficient windows than covered gaps.

As the storm pressed on in loud ferocity, Letty shuddered—normally, she loved watching thunderstorms erupt while she stayed warm and dry inside, but since her mother's death and the strange violet lightning that had come with it, her former love for the rumble of the sky as it poured out its heart had vanished.

Vari had followed the Skylark siblings uninvited through their new front door and rummaged to and fro, bringing chairs and food and extra clothes from across town despite the way the storm soaked his skin. He sat close to Letty now, in the place Majest would have otherwise been—his presence was something different than the comfort of her brother.

"You don't have to get yourself all wet just to make sure we have enough furniture," Letty told him. "We just got here—we don't need three lamps per room, you know."

"Don't worry about it," Vari chirped, interrupting his own speech to jump up with eyes that shone like the rush of the fountain outside, sorting plates and cups into the cabinets. Damp black locks curled around the nape of his neck as he worked. "No one's expecting me back home—and you can *never* have too many lamps."

Letty frowned as he returned to her side, a little hesitant of this boy butting in on their budding life here, despite the bright-blue friendliness of his eyes and the warmth of his smile. Out the window, the storm seemed to have decided to give up its attempts at drowning the island; it was slouching begrudgingly to the west, in search of another place to spill. Letty could see only blue and green as Vari brushed close, close enough that their shoulders touched. Letty's skin prickled.

"We have these storms all the time," Vari soothed, and Letty could feel his eyes on her face. "You don't have to be afraid."

From the corner of the room, Majest made a noise somewhere in between a cough and a sneeze, which Letty recognized as his conspicuous form of covered-up laughter.

Feeling her face flush red, Letty scowled and shifted herself pointedly to the right, saying in a harsher voice than she intended, and not with complete honesty, "I'm not afraid. I rather like thunderstorms. The more lightning, the better. You don't have to try and comfort me."

Vari's smile didn't even twitch. "I like the rain, too, when it comes down in the summer. That is, until it floods half the village. The fountain's probably overflowing as we speak—though, of course, that only means more water for us to drink."

Letty bit back a sigh. It was hard to refuse the kindness of a boy as forthcoming as Vari. Just because she wasn't used to this kind of attention didn't mean she had to be callous about it. "That's a good thing," she said with reluctance, placing her hands in her lap and resisting the urge to sit on them.

A knock sounded at the wooden door, and Vari immediately leapt up to answer it. Behind it, they found the troubled face of Sedona staring across the threshold, white hair sticking out around her face in wind-blown tufts. Her eyes glowed with sunset, half-hidden by retreating storm clouds.

"What's the matter?" asked Vari, as if he were in charge, as if this were his house. Letty saw her brother's jaw stiffen, eyes cast in irritation to the ceiling.

But Sedona seemed to want to speak only with Majest. She stepped past Vari, boots leaving mud-spattered prints on the hardwood floor, and came to a stop in front of Letty's brother, tilting her face upward to look at him.

"We found another boy outside," she burst. "He was all battered by the storm; he'd clearly been out all afternoon. Rapple found him wandering out in the woods, half-collapsed into the dirt—we took him to Jay's, because I figured he might be sick, and Jay would have medicine or at least something warm to drink—and it's not every day some stranger shows up on a hidden island like this, especially after you and Letty did the same thing not even half a day earlier."

Majest's eyebrows went up behind the brown and green mass of his hair, suspicion printed all over his face. "Who is it?" he demanded. Then he corrected himself—"I mean, why fetch me instead of someone else? Is something the matter?" He flashed a worried glance at Letty, which she returned.

Sedona swallowed. "He didn't look dangerous or anything, just disheveled—we were going to question him once he warmed up." She fiddled with her jacket. "But then he started talking. It was a little hard to understand; it mostly just sounded like gibberish—Jay said he was disturbing the peace—but he repeated himself enough that I eventually understood."

"What did he say?" Letty asked, and finally, stood to her feet.

Sedona made a strange face, expression stirring misgiving with marvel. "He said he came here looking for you two, actually. He was cold and probably hypothermic—but he kept muttering your names, like they were the only words he knew." Sedona bit her lip. "If I were you, I'd have a look at him yourselves. He's in Jay's house, like I said."

"Of course," replied Majest, already making his way to the door. Letty couldn't imagine what the dizzying whirlwind inside his head must have felt like. "Coming, Letty?"

"Yes, coming!" Letty followed her brother's swift feet out of the tiny house and into the dripping streets, Sedona and Vari trailing behind them. Boots sloshed against stone; the sky sent its last wet regards. "Jay's is the one to the right of ours, isn't it?"

There was no need for an answer, because Majest's long legs had already arrived and halted atop the slope that held the neighboring door, ignoring the drops plinking onto his bare face. In an unafraid, Majest-like manner, he rapped on the door.

As Letty caught up, breath rattling in her throat, the door whipped back with hinges that squealed in surprise, and an annoyed face framed in dark hair peeped out. Blind blue eyes regarded Majest with distaste, as if they could know without seeing that whoever was at the door was bad news.

"Who is it now?" Jay snapped, harsh enough to make Letty flinch.

"Majest Skylark," her brother said, with the to-be-expected discomfort of someone come face-to-face with a stranger he had already offended. "I'm here to see the boy Sedona found—the one who was looking for me and Letty...?"

Sightless eyes narrowed before Jay opened his mouth to reply. "Oh," he said unpleasantly. "You're the new resident again, aren't you? With the earth powers? I had a dream you would come here, you know. It was more of a nightmare."

Majest stared at him. "I—"

"Well, don't just stand there," growled Jay, turning away from the door. "Get inside."

There was nothing to do but oblige.

The house was less of a haunted mess than Letty would have assumed. Jay was rude and gloomy, but he kept his place clean—

cozy, even. Fuzzy chairs were strewn across the front room in neat little pockets; there were miniature tables keeping them company, and one that held an engraved metal box.

Jay pushed through the house without a moment to waste, his fingers feeling their hurried way into the warm back end of the cottage, giving Letty no time to stop and sightsee. "I can't quite fathom what it is that makes you people storm into my house with your problems like I'm some sort of voodoo tribal medicine man," he muttered as he went, and Majest made a face.

They were led into a stuffy room with no windows or lamps—the only light drizzled in from down the corridor, and the dimness seemed to flicker as Letty stepped into it. This seemed to be the only room in the house without an air of comfort; it was tables draped in a thick, itchy cloth, lined up and around with bottles, plants, powders, all stifled between shards of glass. A heavy herbal scent dripped everywhere, and some of the bottles had tipped to stain and smash against the fabric. Letty was instantly overwhelmed, and found that her senses all at once seemed to fail her.

"Your boy's over there," muttered Jay suddenly, and gave a loose, approximate gesture to Letty's left. "And quit sniffing about; you'll make me sneeze."

Letty turned, peering around potions and concentrating through the rage of scents to find the sole empty corner of the room beyond the clutter, where something like a bed had been fashioned out of a few wooden planks—and someone was laying there, curled on his side, lashes twitching in an uncomfortable, feverish sleep. Though water had soaked his hair to a dark bronze and Letty could not see his face, she immediately recognized the jacket, the laced boots, the sheath of arrows tipped over on the dirty floor.

"Raizu!" Letty and Majest exclaimed at once, rushing to the boy's side in a flurry of legs and fur clothing.

Jay leaned back against the doorframe to the room, sightlessly regarding the scene in front of him. He seemed to be more concerned with his supplies being jostled than any sort of reunion.

Majest reached Raizu first; he knelt to on the floor next to him and put a gentle hand to his forehead, brushing the damp hair out of

Raizu's eyes until they fluttered still. *"Hímin,"* he muttered, eyes huge and greener than ever. "How did he get all the way out here?"

Letty, not sure of anything besides her own stun and worry, put one hand on Majest's shoulder and the other to Raizu's cheek. It was like ice. "He must have had a reason. He must have tracked us here." She frowned, shook her head. "But how could he have known...?"

"The island is hardly visible at all from the shore," Majest said, scrutinizing Raizu's face. "And crossing the Bay is nearly impossible without a seal helping you steer. He must've had to—" He broke off, bewilderment seeming to rustle the freckles on his cheeks.

Behind him, Sedona and Vari fidgeted with confusion. Sedona was the one to step forward. "Majest, who in the world—?"

"M-Majest?" At the sound of the voices above him, Raizu blinked groggily, peeling long lashes apart and squinting against the dim, unforgiving light. His violet eyes could not seem to gather focus as he stared up at Letty's brother, who had his hands back at his sides and was eyeing Raizu carefully in turn, as if he expected him to slip and tumble back into unconsciousness.

It took a bit of throat clearing, but after a moment, Raizu was able to speak. "You're here? Really here?" He tried to smile, weak excitement flooding his features. "I was so afraid you wouldn't—"

"Finally, you're awake." Sedona pushed past Majest, leaned over the stirring boy with crossed arms. "You said your name was Raizu, right? You tried to tell us, but I could hardly understand you through your shivers." She paused. "Anyway, so you *do* know Letty and Majest? You're friends with them?" Her expression wasn't inhospitable, but it wasn't all too warm, either. "Tell them what you told Jay and I."

Somewhere in the room, Jay made an impatient noise.

Raizu frowned at the pummeling of questions, and Letty could almost see them building up a nervous wall of pressure before him. His face turned a pinkish color as he stammered out, "Oh. Um, well—I came here to this, uh, island thing—whatever you folks want to call it—and, well, I was looking for Letty and Majest and

I saw their boat—at least, I think it was their boat—if not, I think I probably stole someone else's, which was quite rude of me—and it was on the beach, and, well—"

"If you objectionable lot are done kissing awake your prince here, would you kindly take him away so I can stop listening to that *noise?*" Jay's dry, derisive tone cut through Raizu's senseless story. "He can't even get a sentence out! I've given him tea to help the hypothermia he got by *sailing across the Hudson Bay during a storm,* and because that's all I'm good for, I think we can be done here. After all, what I'm *not* good for is standing around listening to you babble about this boy's rather boring travels while I am forced to listen to what I already know."

Letty, Majest and Sedona stood upright at once. Behind them, Vari took a step back into the shadows, as though avoiding the spraying onslaught of words.

Letty glanced at Jay with the uneasy regard she might have once given her sister. "You already knew?"

"Of course I *knew.*" Jay's voice was like knives. He glowered in Letty's general direction. "That dream was *days* ago. It was dry, so I ignored it." His arms folded across a gray cotton nightshirt.

Everyone blinked. Vari rolled his eyes in a scoff of disbelief. Letty saw Majest purse his lips.

"I—I don't mean to be a problem," Raizu put in, voice frail. His eyes were glazing over, and Letty could feel waves of heat radiating off of him as if she were sitting near a fire. He coughed hoarsely, rubbing his head with one shaky hand.

"You're not a problem," Majest told him gently, face creased with worry. His eyes stayed on Raizu, but his voice traveled to Jay. "You have to give him some real medicine—he probably caught his death out in that storm, more than just chills. You can't send him off, not when he's clearly got a fever and cough and can barely speak straight."

Jay's eyes were cold and stony. "I'm not a doctor, you know," he snapped. "I don't just have custom-made remedies and medicines lying around. And even if I did—which I don't—I wouldn't waste them on a perfect stranger."

"He's not a stranger," Letty said in a meek voice, cringing as everyone turned at once to stare at her. "He's our friend." Self-consciously, she looked at the ground.

"No friend of mine," Jay grumbled, but something about Letty's voice must have softened his shell because a moment later, he crossed the room; thin fingers danced over the center table until they closed around a bottle of green-brown liquid. He held it out to Majest. "That should work well enough."

"This means a lot to me," Majest said fervently, taking the bottle. "We owe you—"

"Whatever, whatever, now *get out,*" growled Jay, his moment of sociability cast away and replaced with a storm of anger once more. "I'm quite done dealing with you petulant, whiny travelers. It's not my job to take care of every new stranger who decides to wind up on my shore in the middle of the night—nor do I actually *want* to." His sightless gaze cut into everyone in the room. "You Skylarks brought this burden on my village—now get it out of my house."

Letty felt a stab of resentment pierce between her ribs. Hotly she protested, "We didn't *bring* anyone into your village; Raizu came on his own! He came all this way to find us—he could have died! We never asked him to do that for us, whatever the reason. He's *not* a burden."

Behind Letty, Majest was working at lifting Raizu from the makeshift bed. Raizu was no longer awake or mumbling apologies; he was limp as a dead animal as Majest cradled him awkwardly in his arms. Letty stepped over to help, taking as much of Raizu's weight as she could, though unconscious and with clothes soaked through, he was heavier than expected.

Jay regarded the scene unfolding before him with a sigh. At last he responded to Letty's outburst, and his voice was calm like the eye of a storm: "I'm not talking about the boy."

Raizu could not find himself for a long time. It was if his mind had been taken from him and thrown against rocks in a stream, each thought drowning in churning, blackened waters. Every now and then, a thought would leap from the pool like a fish and jolt him from his distorted dreams, pummeling him with a force of panic that he could not comprehend.

Storm. Boat. Hudson Bay, boat, water. Wind, storm. Majest. Letty. Organization, President, Skylarks. Skylarks, Organization, Skylarks, Skylarks.

Each thought filled Raizu with a new sense of delusional terror; he tried to lash out as if he were being attacked, but he could not feel his arms or even sense them at his sides. He was lost.

Raizu had never been sick before. Not a chill, not a cough—not anything. He put as much caution into his health as he did anything else. He stayed away from pack members who were sick no matter their relation to him, didn't lay a finger on any suspicious-looking food no matter his hunger, and kept his hygiene no less than pristine no matter how Kallica teased him for it. He always dressed for the weather and—up until recently—*never* went out in a storm. No matter what.

Since he'd never been ill before, the shock only heightened his feverish state now. His body wasn't used to the foreign invaders and lacked the proper experience and arsenal to fend them off.

After what seemed like an eternity, the pain and feverish haze subsided enough to let Raizu know he was being carried. Carried where or by whom were two other questions entirely, but he found feeling beginning to creep back into his skin. Not good feeling, though—flashes of extreme sensations, of boiling cold and icy warmth—they raged through his body with a fire that made him nearly wish he were fully submerged in unconsciousness.

Nearly.

I have to wake up, he thought, panicked. His senses were screaming, his veins pulsing with fever and fire like a web of dry branches catching flame. And yet he could not force his mind to surface above the flaming black pools that drowned him. In desperation he threw his arms out without realizing it, and they hit something hard, something wooden. Starbursts of red pain erupted behind his eyelids, and they split open.

Raizu gasped, waking with a start.

"*Þakka skýin*," came a relieved voice. It sounded distorted, like Raizu's ears weren't functioning properly, but somehow he could tell the voice with the strange, crisp-sounding language belonged to Majest.

"I was scared to death you'd never wake up," Majest continued amidst Raizu's thoughts. "Letty's been asleep for a while now, but she was terrified, too."

Raizu couldn't see him—he couldn't see anything but darkness, which tightened his already-aching chest into knots. A sound came from his throat, words trying to form, but he erupted into a coughing fit before they could become coherent syllables. His throat ached, his head pounded, and his chest felt constricted, each breath ragged and painful. Throwing the lack of light on top of all that was enough to make him want to curl into a ball and die.

"Don't try to talk," Majest told him from somewhere in the darkness. "You'll just make it worse. Jay gave me some medicine you can take—even if he was much less than pleasant about it. Where did I put that bottle, anyway? Let me get a lantern."

Moments later, a dull yellow-green light flooded Raizu's surroundings and he saw from bleary eyes he was in a small bedroom framed with wooden walls and a wide, curtained window. He'd been placed on a soft bed lined with fur, seal blankets snuggled up around him.

Majest was rummaging in the corner of the room, pulling something from a white bag, the handle of an ancient-looking lantern gripped in his teeth. Rays of candlelight bounced around him as he moved, casting strange shadows to the walls that swooped and intertwined. Letty must have been in a different room; she was nowhere to be seen.

"Aha! Got it." Majest turned and faced Raizu with a half-hearted grin, lantern in one hand, bottle and cloth rag in the other.

Majest crossed the room in two quick steps and knelt down next to the bed, setting the lantern on a side table. He pressed the wet rag to Raizu's burning forehead, cooling its fire, though it did little to help the sopping mess of his hair that soaked the pillow.

"Do you think you can swallow a bit of this?" Majest asked, twisting the cap off of the medicine bottle with a pop. A harsh, bitter smell emitted from the inside of it, pungent enough to cut through Raizu's weakened senses and make both he and Majest wrinkle their noses.

"Hopefully it's not poison," muttered Majest. His eyes sparkled mischievously with the glow of the lantern. "Here, sit up."

Raizu did as he was told, pushing his aching body upward on the wooden bed frame. His head swarmed with the slight movement and he had to blink in pain a few times before he could see through the black pool again.

"Heavens, what have you been up to these last few weeks?" Majest's tone was light, but it had an undercurrent of worry as he handed Raizu the bottle, which he tilted into his mouth after only a second's hesitation.

Swallowing the foul stuff—which tasted like mud and the sharpness of wintergreen tree sap—enough strength came back to Raizu's gagging body for him to hand back the bottle and reply, "I've been…looking for you two. You and Letty."

"Yeah, I gathered that," said Majest, rolling his eyes, setting the medicine on the table, and picking up the lantern again. He went in an easy circle around the room, pulling himself up onto the other side of the bed, where he sat with his legs crossed, hands wrapped around the glowing lamp between his knees. "Why, exactly? I mean, certainly we have our charms, especially Letty and her world-class arguments, but you didn't have to *drown* yourself if you wanted to—"

"I know something," Raizu interrupted, his voice hoarse, his face warm.

"You know something," Majest repeated. "What could you possibly know that would make you come out this far?"

Raizu turned his head to find Majest perched on top of the blankets, looking intent. "As soon as I got home, my older brother—Arathiel—told me about a group of people. A group calling themselves the Organization."

Majest looked interested, tilting his head to the side like a quizzical squirrel. The lantern in his hands set off the green streaks in his hair and lit the planes of his face, making him look as if he were Element Earth itself, not just its Messenger. "Organization?"

Since Raizu couldn't nod without a rush of pain, he responded, half-croaking, "Y-yes. According to Arathiel, these people want to create an equal world, a world sort of like the old one. A world without…supernatural powers."

Majest's eyes widened into huge, luminescent orbs. *"What?"*

"They've been recruiting members. Members determined to wipe people like you and Letty off the face of Cognito. It's led by some woman calling herself the President. One of her associates specifically told Arathiel they were after you—the Skylarks."

Majest's face crashed like a fallen tree, and there was fear, actual fear crashing through his expression. *"That's* what's after Letty and I?" His voice trembled with a strange vulnerability that didn't seem to belong there. "There's an entire organization—*the* Organization—that wants us dead? Because of our elements? How—how could they know? Letty didn't even know what her powers were until—" He broke off, probably realizing how hysterical he sounded. "Who—who is this President? Did your brother say?"

Raizu frowned. He was usually the hysterical one. He didn't like having to be the voice of reason. "N-no, nobody seems to know her name." He coughed weakly. "Do you think anyone else could have known about you and Letty?"

Majest shook his head slowly, casting a glance out the dark doorway, down the hallway to wherever Letty was. "Of course not. We kept it a secret in our family. That's five of us, and our parents are dead, and our elder sister Lunesta left shortly after we received our powers. She was upset she never got any of her own. We haven't heard from her in years—she could be dead by now."

There was a long silence. Almost absently, Majest reached over to pull the rag back up to Raizu's forehead where it had been slipping down his face.

Raizu blinked, forcing his feverish brain to think, to come up with something. "This…other sister of yours. Lunesta. She left because she was…jealous of you?"

Majest nodded, eyes blank where they stared at the empty space of the hallway, flickering with lantern light. "Yeah, but she'd always been like that—she never wanted anything to do with us. She hated us. She felt left out." He rolled his eyes again. "As if these powers are much to brag about. Lately they just seem like more trouble than they're worth."

Raizu knew there was something there, some pieces to connect, but his brain was growing muddled again, the fiery waters rising. "Jealous enough to want you gone," was all he managed.

All at once, Majest's face froze, and he turned to Raizu with a start, eyes snapping wide open. His voice was a dead monotone as he whispered, "You don't think it's *her*, do you?"

Delirium climbing up the tendrils of his mind, Raizu could hardly register the words. "What's her?"

Majest uncrossed his legs and leaned forward on the bed until he was hovering over Raizu, his eyes forming huge, distraught orbs like moons out of orbit. "Lunesta! What if she's leading the Organization? Quick, Raizu—what else did your brother say? Anything at all?"

Raizu fought to remember, fought with everything he was. "Something about…the place of red…?" No, that wasn't right. "Red trees, or the wooden red, or—"

"Redwoods," Majest finished, and he sounded numb. "That's where my parents came from. The place of the Redwoods. They used to live there, before they fled out to the forest."

"That's what my brother said," Raizu realized in a rush. "The ones the President's parents knew—the Redwoods."

"*Þetta er ekki gott,*" said Majest in a voice like crackling ice, slumping back into his sitting position. His hands were shaking as he swept back hair from his forehead. "Lunesta—it's *Lunesta*. She did this. My own sister murdered her mother and gathered a group of *more* murderers, and now they want us. They want Letty, my Letty—and the *world*, too? What kind of joke is this?"

"Don't worry," said Raizu, though he knew how lame his words must have rung. "Maybe her people have better things to do than chase you down. And anyway, she won't find you here, not on a hidden island."

"*You* found us," Majest said dryly.

"I almost didn't," Raizu pointed out, remembering his beach-bound panic with a cringe. "And I knew where you had gone. Even despite that, it was a one in a million chance you ended up being exactly where I wanted to find you." He coughed, blinking in succession as his eyes watered with the jolt. "I, ah, usually don't take those kinds of chances."

Majest stared at him with crinkled features, sunken in and blown wide all at the same time. "That's what I don't understand. You came out here all this way by yourself just to warn my sister and I about the Organization. You almost *died,* Raizu. And that's not to mention the time you saved Letty's life, the meat you gave us, all the mysteries you've solved on our behalves—I barely even know you and I already owe you more than a lifetime of service could ever pay back."

Before Raizu could respond, a burst of agony shot through his head in one long needle, and he pinched his eyes shut, the rag falling down to cover them. Majest dutifully moved it back to its place without a word, just with big green eyes that smoldered concern.

"I—" Raizu took a shaky breath through lips cracked like eggshells. "There's just—something about the two of you. You—you and Letty, out here all alone. When I heard about the Organization, I had to warn you of the danger. More than that, I—"

He had to break off once more to cough; this time a bout of foul-tasting mucus rose up in his throat, which he swallowed with a gagging sound, nearly losing his stomach.

"You what?" Majest reached over Raizu's head to retrieve a water canister from the table next to the half-empty medicine bottle. He twisted it open and held it out. "Here, drink this."

Raizu took the canister and sipped at the cold water gratefully; it quelled the rage of his throat. "I…wanted to help you. Help you escape the Organization and fight if it need be." That pull was nagging at him again, that pull toward the unknown, toward adventure even at the cost of danger.

Majest blinked. Raizu couldn't gauge the feeling in his expression. "Help us," he said, the words sounding like a question. "After you already saved my sister, brought her back to me, gave us food, and traveled across the entire land of Cognito just to have this conversation, nearly freezing to death in the process." He shook his head again. "*Himin.*"

"I wouldn't be a bother," Raizu protested in between tiny bouts of coughing. "I swear, I'll do anything. Just tell me what you want me to do and I'll do it. I mean, I barely know you, but—"

"*Raizu.*" Majest was laughing now, full and lustrous. "*Himin, himin.* That means *heavens,* did you know? It's my gesture of incredulity. You're sick, probably delusional. You don't know what you're saying. You don't want in on this, believe me. You'd be better off back in your pack."

"I want to help," Raizu repeated, hearing himself as if from a distance.

"And force me to owe you my life even *more* times?" Majest sighed, though the corners of his mouth were still turned upward. "I suppose I can't stop you, but *honestly,* it's hardly fair. When do I get to be the hero for a change?"

Raizu couldn't decide whether or not Majest was joking, and whether or not a reciprocal smile was appropriate, so he merely averted his eyes, cheeks warm.

Majest took up the lantern in his hand and made a motion as if to turn it off. "Well, I'm glad to have a friend out here, anyhow," he whispered, easing some of Raizu's nerves. "I suppose we should get to sleep. I don't want to have one more thought about Lunesta or any Organization until I'm awake enough to give the matter the appropriate amount of freaking out. Are you going to be alright?"

"I…" All at once, the thought of being alone and ill in the pitch-black darkness made Raizu's chest seize. "Wait. Majest?"

"Yes?" Majest slid under the fur blanket, turning over on a puffy pillow to look across the bed at Raizu with eyes full of sleep. His hand was still over the lantern.

Raizu felt his cheeks burn, and not only from the fever. It was almost humiliating as he asked, "Can you leave the lantern on for me? The darkness and I…we don't quite get along."

To Raizu's relief, Majest nodded, only a tiny flicker of surprise in his eyes betraying the disbelief he must have felt hearing an almost full-grown boy was afraid of the dark. "Sure." He pushed the light over to Raizu, and he smiled the kind of quiet grin that meant security, even if it was penetrated thickly with worry. "Not a problem."

Raizu propped Majest's lantern up on the table, and it seemed to shine down on him with a warmth brighter than a weeping candle—it was something new, something safe, something that took away his fears. "Thank you," he said, and he meant it.

XVII. SUSPENSION

To Shatter, the Organization's halls were barren, empty. Even emptier than usual—the bareness leaned heavy against the walls, and it seemed to repel all who threatened to venture inside them, as though they too might be sucked bare and dry.

Shatter found no desire to roam, not since Ohanzi's burning death and Seti's disappearance—the outside of her room was a subzero, ice-wrapped package of landscape, too dangerous to forego alone. She could still hear Ohanzi's howling as the shadows devoured his bones, still see Seti's limp and lifeless form dragged away to near-certain execution.

Only one day had passed since, but already, everything had changed. The laboratory had been washed clean of blood and grime. Ohanzi's duties had been covered by Nafuna. Chami and Shayming had disappeared back into the forest, out on another top-secret order.

Shatter never heard of Seti's fate. There had been none of the Organization's usual grapevine, no faces wandering the hallways. Everyone seemed content to their own isolation—Shatter's silent, desperate cry for answers went unheard. The only answers she had found had been of her own accord, and they were not quite the answers she desired.

Some long hours after Seti had disappeared from her line of sight, Shatter had gathered her wits about her and decided to speak with the President. Someone needed to spread the news—that Malory had released a shadow spirit onto the world born from one of their own scientists.

The sudden silence of the halls had come in chills that dripped like the pointed ends of icicles. The President had opened her door, and Shatter had told her everything—of Malory's poison, of Ohanzi's burning, of Caiter's bravery.

And the President had listened with no change of expression, eyes seeming to pass right through Shatter like water through the cracks of glass. And even when Shatter had finished, had laid it all on the table, the Organization's leader had merely muttered something like a reply—

"Yes, Shatter, thank you. Perhaps Ohanzi's spirit will find itself a suitable purpose. Malory, of course, will need to be punished. What a shame." A frown. "Well, lock him up downstairs until he decides he wants to obey me again, then, and post a guard. We can't have our best scientists frazzled enough to tackle each other to the ground."

Shatter remembered her mouth falling open. The President had sounded so detached, lifeless—not aghast at the incident, not engineering a new plan. Something else must have been on her mind. A different terror.

Lunesta Skylark, Shatter had thought, curious, remembering when the dark-haired woman had burst into her hometown, spilling tales of horror, of dangerous power and two siblings who wielded it like swords. She had seemed so helpless then, so lost—with short hair and big eyes like a doe's, young and terrified.

Shatter had thought such weakness disappeared when you gave your life to a cause, to a shiny new Organization and shiny new plans, plans that stretched far beyond the Skylarks. But she'd seen the desperation in that younger Lunesta's eyes, the lifeless terror in her face even now. The past did not truly leave. It was numbing.

That feeling of numbness had not vanished in the hours that followed. Even now, staring blankly at the walls in her own room, Shatter could not seem to gather the will to determine what to do. Her leader had no plan of action. Caiter, when she had passed along the orders to put away Malory, had looked about to fall straight to his knees, some kind of miserable desperation caking his face.

There was no Seti, whatever his fate, and no twins watching the halls with cat's eyes aglow. The President was distant, a demon was on the loose, and the scientists were tumbling about in their own tortured heads, Malory's plans scratched, no new ones ordered.

The Organization was at a standstill, caught in suspense thick enough to slice.

I wish there were something I could do, Shatter thought tiredly, tearing her eyes away from the patch of wall she had been drilling with her eyes and forcing herself to look back down at the new set of paperwork she had been sent the previous day.

Her paper was a map from Ohanzi, the last evidence of his contribution. Red lines ran through the towns where recruiters had been, their populations dotting the land with blotches of ink, and Ohanzi's own sketches marked the path of Seti.

Narrowing her eyes, Shatter traced Seti's path with one finger, the parchment leading her across the northern forest, to the edge of the Bay.

"If the recruiters have been to so many towns without a Power in their path, then the Skylarks must have woven their way east in a way that evaded every marked place on the map."

She tapped the map, the jagged coastline. "Seti was found by the twins right here. The Bay. If he was supposed to be tailing the Skylarks, they would have been there, too. That must have been the last place he saw them before they disappeared. He's hardly an idiot—he wouldn't have just *lost* them. Not unless...unless..."

A memory flew into Shatter's brain, one she had been trying to avoid. "Ohanzi said *island,*" she realized aloud, finger drifting over the Bay. Sure enough, a mark was scratched against its emptiness, a circle, a question. "Destroy, *island.* That's what he said. And if Seti was sitting helpless on the edge of the Bay..."

Her eyes flew wide. "What if the Skylarks found an island?" Her thoughts raced. That explained shipwrecked plans on the coast. Ohanzi's outbursts. His work on the map. The Skylarks' easy disappearance.

But she shook her head, slamming the map face down on the desk. This was not her task. It was not her place to wonder in such foolery, to make inferences that did not belong to her.

She put the map at the back of her pile and turned to her next page, a diagram of some sort of programmed machine. This was straightforward. This held no doubt.

And yet still her mind wandered, and she could hear Ohanzi's striving voice again, as if calling to her. He had been on the brink of a discovery that could have changed everything. And demon or not, somewhere inside was that same knowledge, that same discovery.

Some faint feeling danced inside her, and it stirred up the ashes in her thoughts, cleared the dust, brought her back to day one of the Organization, back to pounding mystery and exhilaration that ran through her blood and made her thirsty, made her crave more.

If Ohanzi found the Skylarks, the shadows would take them, too.

For the first time in what seemed like an eternity, Majest woke up without his sister beside him. For weeks he had awoken with hair matted against his coat, with pointy elbows dug into his ribcage, with a tiny body that sought warmth and comfort and safety in a forest that held none.

For the first time since he and Letty had left home, he found that he did not have to individually defrost each wiggling finger and toe and find the strength to open the sack of food that would soothe two aching stomachs. His hands felt fine. His feet felt fine. His eyelashes weren't even *trying* to frost together.

And for the first time in many long, dangerous weeks, he woke up feeling refreshed, comfortable, warm and full, and—this was a novelty—*safe.*

He knew that safety was not the right word, not with Lunesta out there somewhere and her apparent plans to take their lives, but it was hard for him not to feel relieved at the journey's end.

Somehow, this is all because of Raizu, Majest noted, stretching. The sunlight filtering through the curtains of the window felt heavenly on his face, and he sat with his legs dangling off the bed for a moment, musing. The pack boy who couldn't even sit under a dark storm without crumbling to pieces—he was the hero, no matter his fragility.

Raizu, realized Majest with an abruptness that jolted his bones. He was still sick. Had he gotten worse overnight? Majest had fallen asleep to the sounds of wheezy breathing, but now, the air was still and silent; the only noise was the gulls calling from the shore.

Shifting himself around, Majest realized with a jolt of panic Raizu was not there on the other side of the bed. The seal blanket was left rumpled and cold in his absence.

Frowning, Majest rose to his feet, rubbing sleep from his eyes and shoving his feet into a furry pair of socks before they could hit the cold wood floor. He walked into the cottage hallway, shivering against the arctic breeze coming from the windows. He stopped to glance in his sister's room, but Letty wasn't in her bed, either. Majest was alone.

A bewildered worry shaking up his joints, Majest broke into a near-run, his feet making the floorboards creak in protest, and skidded to a halt in his new kitchen.

"G'morning," said a cheerful voice.

Majest whirled to see Raizu seated comfortably at the faded wooden table, covered in a thin blanket, his slender hands wrapped around a steaming cup. He grinned at Majest, blue-violet eyes bright. "I was sure the sun was going to have time to set and come back again before you got out here. Do you always sleep this much?"

Majest exhaled, realizing he had been holding his breath. His heart was pounding. "Good morning to you, too," he managed, sitting down next to Raizu and eyeing the other boy reproachfully. "Do you always disappear this much?"

"Sorry," replied a different, higher-pitched voice. Letty came in from a room in the opposite direction, hair fluttering down her shoulders in curling layers like crunchy leaves. She was carrying a basket loaded with colorful, rounded objects that looked almost like playthings, which she set in front of a delighted Raizu. "We woke up early to make tea."

"Tea?" Majest repeated, wrinkling his nose and eyeing the

basket. "That's not tea."

"That's the fruit basket," answered Letty. "Vari gave it to me; he got it from Quell. The *tea* is on the table." She nodded to a pot across from Raizu. "It's really amazing what they can grow out here, you know. Vari's been telling me all sorts of stories, and now I've gotten to try some of the fruits for myself—they're just as amazing as Vari said!"

Majest, still confused and a bit bothered, just stared at her. "Sure," he said, hearing his voice sound more like a question than a statement of concurrence.

"Sorry," said Letty again, sitting down in the chair to Majest's left, catching his eye in guilt. "I went out without telling you, I know, but I had Vari with me and we were fine, I promise."

"Vari was over this early in the morning?" Majest asked, frowning. *He'd* planned to take Letty to the market. They had been going to discover the secrets of the village *together*.

"We've been out since before dawn," replied Letty, pulling out what Majest remembered to be an apple and taking a delicate bite. Its inside was a pale, exposed white against her matching teeth. "He brought us some bread, too, and a few rabbits."

Majest's mouth twitched in annoyance. "He didn't have to do that, Letty," he muttered. "Really, he didn't. I could have gone out and gotten you something to eat."

Letty shrugged. "It was awfully nice of him, I think. He said he would be back in a little while to make sure we were doing okay." She smiled. "Isn't it fantastic we have a friend like that?"

Majest was about to retort that Vari's intentions were hardly those of someone wanting to be Letty's *friend*, when Raizu cleared his throat in a composed little sound, startling both siblings, who had nearly forgotten he was there.

"Letty, aren't you going to tell your brother about my phenomenally speedy recovery?" Raizu glanced nervously at Letty, then at Majest, who was more than grateful for the subject change.

"Of course," Letty said, looking surprised to be asked. Turning to Majest, she noted, "Whatever you did, Maji, it must have worked, because he's hardly coughed once all morning and his fever is almost nonexistent." She paused for a moment, eyeing Raizu curiously. "You'd think someone that sick would take *days,* even *weeks* to completely recover, but he seems to have done it overnight."

Majest smiled. "That's fantastic," he said. "It must have been Jay's medicine." *I suppose now I owe him my gratitude as well.* "I'm glad you're feeling well, Raizu."

"Thanks," Raizu murmured, staring down into his tea, red-faced. Sipping at it slowly, he said in a quieter, more serious tone, "By the way, I told Letty about the Organization."

"Yes, I'd almost forgotten!" Letty jumped up from her seat, eyes round and broadening. "Is it true, do you think? About Lunesta?"

Majest flashed a glance to Raizu, then back to his sister. He thought he tasted something foul on his tongue as he answered, "I believe it. Raizu said Redwoods—those were Mother's people. That's no coincidence. Lunesta might have been able to track their home down, wherever they are."

Letty, still standing, creased her face into tight lines like wrinkles. "How could you think she would do something like that? She was always a little dreary, sure, but she was our *sister.*"

"Jealousy is a bitter thing," said Majest plainly, and both Letty and Raizu looked toward him in surprise. He shrugged. "You can't say it isn't true. How would you feel if she and I had been Komi's chosen without you? I know it would have driven you mad with envy and self-doubt. Lunesta just took it a few steps further."

Letty's eyes narrowed, something dark flashing behind them. "You don't find this even a little bit disheartening? Our own sister wants us *dead.*" She stared down at her feet. "It's my fault, anyway. When Komi first came to me, I told him there were only two of us. He asked me to bring my siblings to him, and I just brought you."

Majest blinked. She'd never told him that before.

"There's no way it works like that," Raizu said with an immediate flick of his hands. For once, he sounded sure of himself. "I'm sure there was more of a reason why Lunesta wasn't...chosen."

"Chosen," repeated Letty, still looking dejected. Her eyes flicked to Raizu. "If you don't believe in Komi, then how do you even explain our powers at all?"

Raizu shrugged, shifting and readjusting his blanket so it was tucked around his arms like one might tuck in a baby. "There are many possible answers," he dodged, lifting his cup to his lips. "You could have been born with them, for one thing. You know, like a birth defect. It would be the same sort of thing as how some people have different hair." He gestured to Majest, who patted his green streaks absently. "Perhaps the dream you had was just your brain's creative way of letting you know what you could do—that you were ready."

Letty rolled her eyes with exaggeration. "Yeah, right," she scoffed, pulling another fruit out of her basket, one that looked to Majest like a long, yellow nose. "Like any mind could conjure *that* up. Well, you believe what you like, then." She bit into her fruit, making a face of disgust when she was greeted with a mouthful of tough shell.

"That's a banana, Letty—you have to take the peel off." Vari's cheery voice rang through the room and seconds later, the boy strode into the kitchen wearing an expression like a tiny warrior returning from battle, his hair a dark halo of static perking up from the hood of his coat.

Majest suppressed a groan at the intrusion, while Raizu just arched an eyebrow.

"Oh." Letty frowned at the banana, peeling the top off to reveal a paler fruit underneath, which she began to munch on. "Thanks, Vari. I didn't see you there. Back so soon?"

"Sedona and Sunni wanted to check in on you all," said Vari, still grinning like he had just single-handedly saved the world from demise. "I came with them." Behind him, Majest could see he was right; the Seacourt sisters were standing in the entryway of the kitchen, both with small smiles on their lips.

"Oh," Majest said, hearing his voice waver.

"How've you been doing?" asked Sedona with an urgent peck to her voice, a bird tearing up its meal. "Anything wrong?"

Raizu stared down at the floor, red-facedly pursing his lips. "Majest, should we tell them about the Organization?"

"What Organization?" Vari demanded.

Majest shrugged, eyeing Vari with a hint of distaste he knew was unwarranted. "We probably should. After all, Sedona may be targeted as well if she has the powers she says she does." He met Sedona's gaze across the room and gave her a nod.

As their eyes met, Sedona frowned. "Targeted?"

Sunni looked defensive. "What's this about?"

"You know how Maji and I came to this island to escape the people who killed our mother?" Letty started, standing up and shoving the rest of the banana into her mouth. "Ith thi goop callth Ognivashn," she tried, mouth full and teeming yellow-white.

"*What?*" said Vari, Sedona and Sunni in synchronization.

"She means there's this group called the Organization," Raizu's eyes flickered with self-consciousness. "I heard about it from my pack; it's the reason I came here, actually." He cleared his throat to cough. "Their mission is to supposedly create an equal world—partially by removing anyone with supernatural abilities." He took a deep breath. "Like your powers."

Sedona's skin turned white as her hair, giving her a ghostlike appearance. "*Us?*" Her voice held bursting astonishment. "How—how would anyone even know about our powers to begin with, much less think they're so horrific?"

"I have an answer to that," Majest told her. "You all may want to sit down for this one."

One by one, Sedona, Sunni and Vari filled in the remaining chairs at the kitchen table, unsettlement sparking in the air. Sedona was biting her lip while Sunni stared at the floor, kicking the wood with a booted foot. Even Vari had fallen silent.

Together, Majest and Raizu told them about Lunesta—with the occasional interjection from Letty, somewhere between her mouthfuls of fruit. Somehow, the truth seemed less overwhelming when it was shared.

Sedona was the first to speak up when they were finished. "Your own sister put together a whole band of recruits just to destroy you and Letty?"

"She must have serious issues," Sunni added, pursing her lips.

"If she wanted you dead, she could have just thrown you off a cliff or something before she left home."

"It's not just us," Majest insisted. "Maybe it started off that way, but from what Raizu's brother said, it's definitely become something more. We might be targeted now, but we won't be the only ones, not if she wants a whole land rid of power and replaced with old-world technology."

"Don't worry," said Vari, moving closer to Letty and wrapping an arm around her shoulders. "We're not going to let anyone near you. Right, Sedona?"

Letty froze rigid, eyes going with incredulity to the hand against her collarbone, but Sedona just sighed and pretended not to notice the scene before her. "Of course not. Just as long as they don't let anyone near us."

"We're all on the same team now," Majest concurred.

"Great! Well, that's done with," said Sunni, standing up and brushing imaginary dust from her pants. "Now we just sit back and wait for the Organization to *never* find us." She grinned. "Come on, guys—you don't actually believe they'll spot out this island, do you? Besides these three—" she gestured to the Skylarks and Raizu, "—no one's come here on purpose since before we were born. Everyone here is a happy little accident." She puffed out her chest, grinning. "We'll be fine."

Sedona gave her sister a curious stare. "Why are you always the only one who's never worried?"

"Because there's nothing to worry about," answered Sunni with supreme confidence. "In fact, I'm *so* positive of our safety, I say tomorrow we take these three out and show them the ropes of the town. They're completely out of place here—they need to learn how to live like we do."

"We're learning," Letty protested.

Sunni smirked, nodding to the bitten banana peel on the table. "Of course you are."

Majest couldn't help but smile. Sunni was right—most of what the villagers talked about sounded like a third language to his ears, just nonsense like the language of dreams.

"Fine." Sedona shrugged in a manner of agreement. "I suppose it couldn't hurt to give them a tour." She turned her gaze back to Majest, her eyebrows raised in a questioning manner. "If you think your…sick friend is up for it." She glanced at Raizu like a chain might eye its weak link.

Majest opened his mouth to reply, but Raizu cut him off. "I'm feeling a lot better," he said quietly. "I want to see the town. And I want to stay here on the island and help Maji and Letty, even for just a little while. It takes weeks to get back to my pack—a few days here isn't going to hurt."

Majest smiled at him and the familiar nickname, feeling a glow budding up in his chest, something sprouting against his heartbeat. He wasn't quite sure if he trusted the villagers and their startling unfamiliarity—they were, at the very least, something he would need to get used to—but Raizu already felt like family, like he was the final piece to something no one had ever known was incomplete to begin with.

And for the time being, he was staying right here.

"Fantastic," Majest said after some time, clearing his head. He glanced back at Sedona, who was staring at him oddly. "We'd love to learn more about our new home."

"Tomorrow, then," Sedona promised. She got to her feet and pushed her chair back under the table, taking her sister by one arm and Vari by the other. "We'll leave you three alone now." She shot a meaningful glance at Vari.

Majest nodded in agreement as the door clicked shut behind them. "Tomorrow."

XVIII. AROUND

The next day seemed to race forward with the unbridled persistence of a lost animal nosing at the door—it wanted in, wanted that next thrust into what lay beyond the present. Raizu and Majest spent their cottage afternoon swapping childhood stories, while Letty's curiosity stole her back to Hi Ding's markets to trade some of Majest's squirrel meat for shirts and supplies.

Night fell, and was filled with drowsiness and trivial chatter, a meal of bread and fish—a feeling between the three of them Letty described as "like a little family." A beam swept across her cheeks in a thick pink stroke. Raizu was inclined to agree, and he slept easy, tangled in warmth and furs.

"Today's our tour day," Majest was saying now through a yawn, the next morning flickering steadily down upon them. His hair was charmingly tousled, eyes drowsy-lidded but enthusiastic. "Maybe now we'll finally get to uncover some of the mysteries of this place. *Fruits. Tea.* Whatever else they've got hiding under their perfectly-sewn sleeves."

"You and Letty really didn't have much back in the forest, did you?" Raizu asked, watching with bemusement as Majest scuttled around the room, trying to find a clean shirt.

Majest laughed, a short, loud sound. "Did *you?*"

"No, but—"

"We lived off of acorns and fatty, half-cooked meats. It's a wonder we're still alive and all turned out to be the proper size. I don't know anything about villages and their villagers and their *fruit baskets.*"

Raizu shrugged. "I guess our pack just lived closer to the market than you. I've seen a lot of this stuff before. The clothes and tea, at least. The food, on the other hand—that's new."

"Letty seems to be obsessed with trying every piece of it herself." Majest snorted, at last locating a shirt and pulling it over his head while at the same time yanking his nightshirt out from underneath. It was a practiced and efficient movement, but also a ridiculous one that had Raizu stifling a laugh. "Her stomach's going to burst and it's all going to come pouring back out."

"I'm not obsessed," protested Letty, appearing in an instant in the doorway and leaning against the wooden frame. Her hair was pulled back from her face with a thin rope-like cord, bringing out the soft angles of her cheeks. Raizu thought she looked suddenly older and somehow more regal, like a miniature goddess—one who stuck her tongue out at her brother. "I happen to like trying new things. If we're going to make this our home, I'm going to find out what I like and don't like to eat. Yesterday, for instance, I discovered I like bananas but can't stand celery."

"I liked the strawberries," Raizu put in, getting to his feet. "I mean, those were the only ones I was brave enough to try, but I liked them."

"They were delicious," Letty agreed, looking pleased at the agreement. "I've never tasted anything that sweet before." Her eyes were almost dreamy, their blue color flickering with delight.

"Yeah, yeah, *hvað sem*, Letty." Majest rolled his eyes. "I'm sure they taste like the heavens having a dance party in your mouth, or whatever. Now let's head on over to Sedona's house, alright? She and Sunni are probably waiting for us already—these town people are surprisingly early risers."

It was Letty's turn to roll her eyes. "Actually, I think it's just *you* who sleeps like a log half past sunrise." She ducked as Majest swiped a hand in her direction. "Do you think Vari will come with us?"

Majest paused, hand still in the air. "Oh, so now you *want* him around all the time?"

Letty blushed between her freckles, looking at the floor. "*No—*

I was just wondering."

Majest snorted once more. "Well, I doubt you'll have anything to worry about. That boy can't seem to stay away from you, can he? It's pretty hilarious—maybe even *adorable.* In fact, if he's not there waiting for you at the Seacourt house right now, I'll be positively astounded." His voice was coated with enough mockery to peel off in layers.

Raizu stared at him with a slow grin riding up the corners of his mouth.

"Vari's really nice," Letty protested, pulling at the shirt she was wearing under her jacket, a pale blue one made of village fabrics. There was nothing of her forest home that touched her skin, none of the woodsy smell that seemed to cling to Majest like the sun to the sky. It was as if the entirety of her previous life had been swept away the instant she'd washed onshore.

Letty stood upright as if she could sense Raizu's train of thought, taking her arm hastily off the door frame and narrowing her eyes. "Either way, you're right—we should be leaving now. We wouldn't want to keep Sunni and Sedona waiting."

Majest gave his sister a peculiar look, one stacked upon itself with perplexity. But after only a moment, he broke into another smile. He seemed to smile a lot, which was odd for the burdens that lay on his shoulders. Raizu found it curious but somehow reassuring—a steady constant.

"Alright, then. Let's go," Majest said after some time, crossing the room to stand next to his sister. Raizu followed suit and the three of them were out the door at once and into the fresh, chilly air.

The Seacourt house was quiet and tidy—not quite like the cozy cottage Letty now shared with her brother and Raizu, but neither like Jay's dim space of bottles and herbal claustrophobia. The Seacourts held their own sense of space.

As Letty followed her brother through the tall wooden door, she was aware of a sweet fragrance and walls of gray stone, not weathered wood. Pots of flowers boasting high shades of red and violet with long, luscious petals were arranged in pleasant swirls on every open surface, coating stone cracks in the walls and wooden tables that stood proudly in every possible corner. A challenge was posed to simply get through the door.

Sunni greeted them with a mischievous grin, gently designing a path for walking. The waves of her hair stuck up at odd angles, generating a cloud of static around her face. "Good morning, newbies," she said with her hands on her hips, peering around Majest's shoulder. "Ready to go?"

Sedona appeared behind her sister, eyes bright. "Well, I am!"

Vari was there too, poking his head out from behind Sedona's white coat and fixing Letty with his typical boyish grin. Majest was smirking from the second he appeared. "I already decided what we're going to do today, Letty," he told her. "Well, what we're *all* going to do today," he amended as Sedona flashed him a condescending look.

"We thought we'd split up into two groups," Sedona said, hands on her hips. "Since you, Letty, already know enough from your meandering yesterday, I thought—well, Vari thought—he could take you to Quell and Idyllice's house to see how they grow fruit and vegetables." Her gaze went from Letty to Majest and lit with a beam. "You can stay here with Sunni and I. I have something amazing I want to show you."

Raizu frowned. "Where do I go?" he asked, tentative.

Sedona blinked at him, taken aback. Letty got the feeling she hadn't remembered the village's third newcomer, and for some reason, she didn't look too happy about his presence.

"You can come with me," Majest told Raizu. "It's probably best you don't go out in the cold for a while, anyway." He smirked at Letty. "My sister gets Vari all to herself. Hope they can manage."

Letty's jaw set into a hard line, and she willed herself to keep calm and not slap her brother across his stupid, meddling face. "Sounds good," she said coolly.

"We're off, then," chirped Vari, not seeming to notice Majest's jeering. He was all irreversible excitement, spread across his face in a map, as though visiting the twins in their garden was the most exhilarating adventure he could think of. He took Letty's arm and pulled her toward the front door.

Letty nearly tripped over her own feet as she was half-dragged once more into the morning air, barely refraining from *accidentally* knocking into Majest on the way out.

"Bye, Letty!" Majest called as he shut Sedona's door, and he was making kissy faces at her until she was out of sight. Letty could see Raizu behind him, sighing to the ceiling with a forced-back smile.

Once outside, Vari let go of Letty's arm and turned to face her, eyes dancing even though the morning sky held more chilly clouds than sunlight. "This way," he said, beckoning toward a stone path.

They started off at a quick walk, and Letty realized her skin was prickling, and not just from the cold.

"Quell and his sister, they really grow fruit? As in—fruit from plants, the way acorns grow on trees?" She forced conversation, trying not to shiver.

"How else do you figure the fruit gets in the market? It doesn't come in with the tide!" Vari laughed, breath billowing out in front of him. "I know—you've probably heard plants can't grow this far north, and you're usually right. But Quell and Idyllice heat all of theirs with lanterns that act as the sun. I would know. I visit all the time."

"Don't plants need *real* sunlight?"

Vari shrugged. "When you're missing something, you've got to make do without it, right?"

He came to an abrupt halt next to a large stone house Letty recognized—she could see the open window through which two brown-haired siblings with curious stares had peered. The Souleias.

"This is it," said Letty before Vari had a chance to announce their arrival.

"You remembered," Vari said with a smile. He sounded pleased. "I wouldn't have, not as cold and hungry and bewildered as you must have been when you got here."

Letty shrugged, following Vari up to the door and standing

behind him as he knocked thrice. "I have a good memory," she said, trying to sound indifferent and not as though another blush was creeping up her face.

Footsteps sounded from inside, muffled noises on hard stone.

Letty's heart began to pound, something about the unseen source of noise making her skin crawl in itching waves. Perhaps years among forest creatures that shifted through the nights with baleful groans and sighs had tuned her ears to hear danger in all foreign sounds.

Fortunately, the person who opened the door was not a deadly woodland creature and in fact was a rather short woman who looked somewhere in her twenties by old-world standards, with pale brown hair wound into a rose-like twist atop her head, a few strands trickling in escaped tendrils around her face. Her eyes were the gray of a winter sky, and just as calm. She did not seem fazed by the sudden appearance of Letty and Vari on her doorstep.

"Hi again, Idyllice." Vari greeted the woman with a polite nod.

Idyllice returned the nod. Her gaze was soft, doting, and with a jolt, Letty was reminded of her mother. "Vari," she said in a voice like smooth pebbles. "You brought a guest today?"

"This is Letty," Vari told her, bouncing on his heels like an excited rabbit. "You know about the Skylark siblings who arrived two days ago, right? With the powers? She's one of them. She has the water element."

Letty fidgeted as Idyllice looked at her in wonder. "I can't work them too well yet," she corrected, her voice coming out as a shallow mutter.

"Well, either way, it's pleasant to meet you," said Idyllice. "To what do I owe the unexpected pleasure?" Letty noted with interest that although her eyes were the unflattering gray of stone, they seemed to soak up and reflect other hues around them.

"I told Letty I would show her around the town, and she wanted to see your gardens," said Vari. "May we come in to look around?"

"Oh." Idyllice looked surprised at the inquiry. "Weren't you just here last night?"

Vari almost looked abashed. "Well—Quell always says he

doesn't mind having me here. He even made me a fruit basket to give to Letty."

"I'm not saying it's a problem," Idyllice said with a laugh. "You're welcome here whenever you want. Quell could use the company, and I could use a break from watching him spill potted soil all over himself. As for giving Letty a tour..." She eyed the both of them thoughtfully. "Follow me."

Letty followed Vari as he eagerly stepped into the house. It was warm and plant-laden like the Seacourts', though the walls were also adorned with loose, whimsical sketches that made Letty smile with memories of Majest's own amateur doodles hung around his bedroom and drifting over the floor.

"Is Quell here?" Vari piped up from Letty's side.

Idyllice looked at him a little bemusedly. "He's in the garden. Probably making a mess."

Vari visibly brightened. "I wonder if he'd make me another fruit basket while he's at it."

"You'll have to ask him when we get downstairs."

Downstairs? Letty wrinkled her brow.

Idyllice led Letty and Vari into the first door on the right, and to Letty's utmost surprise, there was nothing inside the room save for an empty hole in the floor that seemed to gape at them like an open mouth in perpetual surprise.

Letty frowned at it. "*That's* the garden?"

Vari laughed, and Idyllice replied in an amused but patient voice, "No, but it is down that way. Look into it."

"*Into* it?"

"The garden is below us," Vari told her. "It's underground!"

Letty stared into the blackness with quizzical intrigue, and before long, individual shapes seemed to rise from the gloom far below as though through clearing fog. The dim light of candles cast a grayness of shadows that echoed through one hollow space—a corridor, dark and snug, a jacket for the darkness. The sweet smell of flora and fruit filled Letty's nose and she made a noise of delight. "I see it!"

"Go on in," Idyllice advised. When Letty whipped her head

around to give a bewildered exclamation of disbelief, she went on, "I know, it looks like it's a long way down, but it's not too much of a drop. And keeping the plants isolated with the lamps down there wards off the cold better than anything up here ever could."

"There's nothing to be afraid of," Vari added. "I've been down here a million times before, and I promise, it's not scary at all. Here—I'll even go first."

Without waiting for a reply, Vari lowered his legs into the hole and slid off into it with a short whoop and a push, landing below with a soft thud. Letty could see the top of his head glowing by the lantern's light, and he turned his face up to her with a grin, feet scuffing on the dirty floor. "See? Just like jumping out of bed!"

Taking a deep breath and not allowing herself to hesitate, Letty sat down and scooted in after him, fluttering her eyes shut and trusting the fall into empty space, body going slack and windswept. *And I'm tumbling down again,* she thought as the world whipped around her. *First Komi's starry land, then the cliff, and now this. It's as if I'm doomed to simply fall over and over again.*

But the feeling of falling was familiar now, like a rush of tumbling water that came and went and left life lingering behind it, and Letty hardly minded the short drop down. She landed with knees bent to absorb the impact, feeling her pupils dilate at the dimness, nose flaring at the sudden sweetness.

After a second or two of blindness, Letty's eyes adjusted and she saw the hallway stretched in front of her in a winding curve that gestured ahead, mirroring the low arch of the dirt ceiling. A soft yellowness floated in spores between the dust of the lanterns, and there was a cave at the end of it all, high and wide and winking out to her. Letty could not help but step forward, mesmerized.

Vari appeared in front of her, making her start, but she relaxed at the friendly glint to his expression. The distant brightness blossomed his irises into a verdant green-gold, and his smile glowed in the dark. "Pretty amazing, right?"

"Idyllice, is that you?" inquired a new voice before Letty could agree. The voice was muffled, its owner somewhere in the cave ahead. "Is there someone else with you?"

"I brought Vari and one of the Skylark children," Idyllice replied, landing next to Letty on the dirt floor and stepping forward. "Letty—Letty Skylark, that is—wanted to see the garden."

"Did she now?" Finally, a face peered out—pleasant and framed with Idyllice's pale woodsy locks, dotted with familiar eyes of deep gray. "Sure she didn't come to see my prize-winning smile?"

"Quell!" Vari's eyes lit like wildfire, and Letty followed as he leapt ahead.

"Hey, Vari," replied Quell, and his expression was fond. "Always good to see you! And welcome, Letty." He stepped further into view, and Letty could see the knees of his pants as well as his fingers were blackened with soot and soil. "Idyllice, you didn't tell me we were expecting visitors! I'm a mess!" He wiped a hand across a sweaty brow, smearing dirt, which he seemed to regret immediately. "Ah, nuts."

None of that seemed to deter Vari. "Sorry for barging in! Letty really liked the fruit basket you made her, so I thought I'd show her all the other amazing things you do down here."

Quell raised an eyebrow. "Less *amazing,* more *time-consuming.*"

"Amazing," Vari clarified, though he dipped his head with a sudden shyness. "How are the bananas? Better than yesterday?"

Quell shrugged. "Not much. They're not supposed to be in temperatures this cold, but we're trying. We're doing everything short of knitting them little sweaters."

Letty was intrigued. "I don't mind the dirt," she said, stepping forward until the garden threatened to engulf her. "May I see the bananas?"

Quell shrugged again, wiping the rest of the dirt from his hands onto his already-filthy pants. "Go right ahead. Just don't knock anything over, okay? It's a bit crowded."

Letty nodded, and Vari beamed.

With just one more step, the lighting changed, and Letty could see everything as if she were standing in the sun. The garden was as beautiful as she'd imagined; rows upon rows of lush trees held on tight to winding trellises, while tiny berries of black and blue rested over leafy bushes, tiny boats with fruity crews on a ruffled soil sea. Lanterns laced the room in mesmerizing lines, radiating white heat against the warm, earthy halls and painting silhouettes of leaves and stems into the dirt. Letty was in a nighttime forest, and yet she was indoors, and there was nothing evergreen or crawling with danger. Everything made her eyes water with a freshness that seemed almost tangible.

"This is absolutely incredible," she breathed, reaching out to one of the plants tentatively, as if afraid its mirage would shatter at her touch. But then her hand was brushing against smoothness dappled with the veins and lines of something mortal and true, and its vitality among such black underground depths brought Letty a strange happiness, as if this garden held proof that beautiful things could indeed grow in dark places.

"Letty, come look at this!" called Vari, skipping around between rows of low-sweeping trees and breaking Letty out of her reverie. "Oranges!"

"Oranges?" Letty found him through the blurry green in a few curious steps. Sure enough, bright fruit the color of early dawn was nestled into a fragile tree with leaves like pointed animal ears. Letty marveled in wonder, seeing the sun in a place where the sun could not reach.

"Those are my favorites," Quell said, coming up behind them and eyeing the tree with fond appreciation. "In Masotote's tales of the past, fruit like this only grew in places so warm, you could sweat from your ears without needing a jacket."

"Wow," said Letty, hearing her voice echo. "And here I thought a summer day without a hat was a victory."

"Hey, Quell! What's in here?" Vari was on the move again, darting about with all the jittery curiosity of a baby bunny. Perhaps Letty's enthusiasm was contagious, or perhaps Vari simply never ran out of energy.

Letty watched as Vari poked his head inside a thick crack in the wall, back in the farthest corner of the garden. His voice was muffled as he exclaimed, "How come I never noticed this place before? What kind of things do you keep back this way?"

"I wouldn't go in there!" called Idyllice as Vari's tiny form breached the gap, squeezing himself into darkness. "We don't know what's inside. Quell's been meaning to check it out, but—"

"Heavens, it's tiny in here," Vari said, ignoring the advice and slipping further behind the garden. He was obscured from view, and it was as if it were the wall speaking to them and not a boy. "Hey, did it just get colder in here?"

All was quiet for a moment.

"Vari," Quell said warningly, worry all over his face. There was no response.

"Vari—" Letty broke off her own caution as an exclamation of shock and then a terrible, boiling gurgle sounded from where the boy had vanished. "*Vari!*"

There was a screech like the darkness had come to life, and something very inhuman was crying, wailing from beneath the ground. Shards of rock were crumbling off the back wall, as if something shook and rattled them, and chunks like teeth went flying. Everything seemed to scream out all at once with a ferocity unprecedented, an explosion set off by something unseen and unheard.

Before Letty had time to think or even breathe, Quell had crossed the room and snatched Vari from the shuddering crevice in the wall, dragging him out into the open. The abandoned darkness hissed out after them in rage, and Letty's heartbeat beat her stomach into flattened knots.

Vari's face hit the light as Quell pulled him backwards, and Letty nearly cried out. His eyes were open and black, pupils feasting on every morsel of their light, eclipsing the whites and irises until there was nothing but the dark. His face was a hungry pit; his lips were peeled wide and bloody. His arms and legs twitched in a stricken frenzy, tongue lolling as a line of foam trickled down from his shining mouth and pooled in the crook of his neck. Skin ashen, sweat beading across his brow, Vari screeched and writhed—he was rabid, infected, broken, somewhere beyond himself.

Quell was trying to hold onto him with a frantic jerky succession of movements, arms locked around Vari as if they could shield him from whatever had taken him hostage. But Vari merely squirmed with the vigor of a caged beast, eyes like ebony beads, and he screamed, and he *screamed*.

Letty forced herself to look away, tried to close her eyes, to cover her ears so she wouldn't see that face, hear that *sound*. Something like a broken gasp came up from her throat, and there was no way to close herself from it; it was everywhere, Quell struggling with Vari in his grasp, calling for help, Vari somehow both lifeless and undying in what had him in its claws.

Behind them all, Idyllice had petrified. "Run," she hissed, breath cold and itchy against Letty's cheek. "Fetch Sedona and Jay. *Now*."

And Letty, terrified and without explanation, turned and clambered from the hole in the earth, hoisting herself onto solid ground even as it pinched and tore under her nails. A rush pumped through her as doors slammed and winter air struck her shaking face, and she ran, feet pounding the snowy powder down to the rhythm of her racing heart.

"I have to hand it to you, Sedona," Majest was saying, shaking his head with a chuckle. "You sure do know a lot more about this land than my parents ever did, and they've practically covered every last corner of it."

"Well, it's different here on the island," said Sedona, smiling at the praise. "We learn so much about the old world from Vosile that there's hardly a point in living in the new one."

The four of them—Majest, Sedona, Raizu, and Sunni—were squished together on a large couch in the Seacourt house, cushions riding up between them with plush little ripples. From Sedona's mouth spilled Masotote's most famous stories—of faraway lands across oceans and continents, of boats and gadgets that whirred to life in places too far out of reach to even imagine.

"I thought Cognito was the only land anyone ever knew," Raizu said from where he sat to Majest's left, their shoulders brushing. His head rested in his hands. "I thought the world started and ended with us. Now I feel like I've been living under a rock my entire life."

"Do you want to see what the world really looks like?" Sunni asked from across the couch. "Or at least, *used* to look like?" She stood up and the cushions buckled forward and back at the jostled weight. "Sedona, I'm showing them the map!"

"Of course," replied Sedona, joining her sister at a nearby shelf to shuffle through books and papers, pulling one gently from between hard covers. She held it up to the faint window light, undoing layers and sheets until she could unfold a parchment like a pair of new butterfly wings, lined in black ink and scrawled lettering.

"What is that, exactly?" inquired Majest, curious.

"It's a drawing of the world," said Sedona. "Where the land meets the water, and everything in between."

Majest wrinkled his nose in disbelief. How could there be a way to know what the world looked like when you only lived it a piece at a time? He looked to Raizu as though he might have held the answer, but there was even more doubt in the eyes that met his gaze.

Without giving either of them the chance to question, Sedona and Sunni plopped back onto the jostled couch, sprawling the map across their laps. Majest peered at it from the side, wary as though it might jump up and attack him. Strange words leapt up off the paper, for starters—they jutted in arrows, in directions Majest could read but not comprehend. They were titles of a world that was a mystery, full of meaning beyond his understanding.

"I see Canada," said Raizu, leaning in front of Majest to point at a large, water-dappled shape. Sure enough, Majest recognized the spelling. *C-a-n-a-d-a.*

"Yup," said Sunni, nodding in agreement. She poked a spot inside of Canada's shape. "We're here, just off the coast in the Hudson Bay."

"The rest of the map is mostly ancient cities," Sedona continued, her voice a persistent lecture. "For instance, this one is Vienna." She pointed to one in a thousand tiny dots. Raizu's eyes lit. "And over here, Shanghai." Her finger moved again, farther from the world Majest knew. "Lastly—and this one is my favorite—this is Sparta." One last time, Sedona's hand jumped to rest on an island in a sea of even more islands. Infinite Hi Dings. "According to Masotote, a great people ruled there and fought their enemies with strength and sword." Her eyes were foggy, as if she were over the ocean and far away. "I mean, the stories may or not be true, but it's so wonderful to think of what could have been, right?"

Majest said nothing. She sounded like Letty with her dreamer's talk, visions of a world that held more than it could ever return to be—fantasies that would bring only disappointment. He made a face.

"I'm sure Sparta was a lovely, brave place," Raizu said to Sedona, but Sedona ignored him, watching Majest over the bridge of her nose, as though his opinion were the only one that mattered. In fact, she had not spoken a word to Raizu all morning, Majest noted.

"Well? Majest?" she pressed.

Raizu blinked with a confused hurt, and flashed Majest a disconcerted glance that clearly asked if something was the matter with him.

Majest just shook his head, gave them both an apologetic grimace.

Sunni seemed to sense the deterioration in atmosphere and stood to her feet. "I'm going to go get us something to drink. Everyone okay with apple juice?"

Sedona looked down at her map. Majest pursed his lips. Raizu's legs shifted uncomfortably.

"Whatever." Sunni exhaled a sigh, shrugging and exiting the room with a tuneless hum.

Sedona folded her map with a slow, deliberate precision, avoiding Majest's eyes and still avoiding Raizu altogether, displeasure in every one of her movements.

"I'm sorry, Sedona," said Majest, in the fervent hope this awkward moment would pass. "The map is brilliant; it's just not my type of thing."

"I know," Sedona said with a tight nod, hands kneading the

folded map between them. "You're all about moving forward." She gave a wry smile. "I can understand that, I suppose. What's the point of the old world when it doesn't change what's happening in this one?"

Relief flooded Majest's mind. So she did understand, in whatever way she could. "Exactly. I guess I don't concern myself with something that's long gone. The past isn't going to do me any good unless it knows something that takes me where I need to be."

"But if the past takes you where you need to be, you'd be nowhere without it...which sort of makes it important," Raizu teased with a small smile, visibly relieved at the averted discomfort.

"Shut up," Majest muttered, and elbowed him.

Sedona smiled reluctantly, and even managed an uncertain glance in Raizu's direction as she got up to put her map away, tuck it back into the recesses of dusty shelves and books long unread.

Majest was about to open his mouth, attempt another winding route at conversation, but then the noise of pounding feet sounded from the kitchen and in ran Sunni, not at all holding the promised cups of apple juice, but instead with her hands pumping at her sides. The waves of her hair fluffed around her face like a bristling fox tail, her usual playful humor swallowed whole by the terrified moons of her eyes. Her mouth opened, but nothing came out.

Letty was right behind her, face stone-cold with terror. "You have to come quick, all of you!" she gasped, lips trembling.

Majest rose to his feet. "Letty, what is it?"

"It's Vari," cried Letty, rivulets of tears building up around her eyes. "He's been possessed!"

XIX. RESPONSE

"Normally I'd claim *'possession'* to be a considerable overreaction, but I'll have to go with the Skylark girl on this one," said Jay, in the voice of someone rather bored. He was leaning up against the wall in his house, as far away from his company as he could get. "Nothing else explains *that*." He gestured to Vari, whose eyes were wide open and pitch-black, staring into nothing.

Letty closed her eyes and swallowed hard against a foul taste in her mouth, remembering this room hours earlier, Vari snakelike and writhing hard in Quell's arms, the Souleias tying him to the makeshift bed in a sickening whirlwind of voices and hands that snapped like thunder in a twister.

Somewhere in that whirlwind had been Jay, petulance lost in a series of hazy moments, and he had ushered everyone inside, making no move to stop the flow of sudden guests as he stood back against his walls, blind eyes wide with some glazed form of deep-seated horror. That horror had lasted for no more than a moment, but it had been enough to land upon Letty's skin with a chill like freezing rain.

"Shadows!" Vari had cried, voice distorted as if he were held underwater. His voice was no longer Vari's. He had struggled against the ropes with which he was bound, gouging bloody gashes into his wrists and ankles that stained the table in red leaves. His back had arched upward, fingers curling inward like gnarled branches, claws scraping.

Letty remembered her trembling hands gripping the wood of the doorframe, fingers aching and white. She had not found the strength to enter the room, had stood back while Idyllice had propped Vari's head up on a feather pillow and Quell had murmured soothing words to unhearing ears, stroked Vari's hair until he had stopped screaming and fallen to unconsciousness.

Eventually Jay had snapped out of his stupor and to attention instead, moving about the house with surprising fluidity to retrieve bottle after bottle of liquids and dried plants in so many colors and shapes, it had made Letty's head spin.

Now Vari lay on the table, empty eyes open but unseeing, breaths coming in shaggy gasps that sounded like monsters in the night, somewhere between nightmares and reality. Quell and Idyllice still stood worriedly at his side.

"Possession?" repeated Majest in disbelief. "That's not even possible."

"Do I have to spell it out for you?" Jay barked. He prodded one of Vari's limp arms. "The world can't just be gods and powers and all the skies singing in reckless abandon—there's another side. Hell's side. Obviously, some sort of demonic force got a hold of Vari when he was down in the garden. The symptoms are clear, though it's never happened here before."

"Then how do you know it's true?" challenged Majest. "I know the gods are real—I've met Komi myself—but there are no demons in this land!" He faltered. "My dad—he would've told me."

"I'm with Maji on this," Raizu agreed. He was watching the scene before him with his breath held tight between his lips. His face, usually flooded with color and sun, had gone whiter than Sedona's hair.

"Thank you," Majest said, with a glare in Jay's direction.

"I don't believe in any of this stuff," Raizu continued, staring at his feet as though he thought he would be screamed at if he met anyone's eyes. "Gods, demons—nothing. There has to be a reasonable explanation that doesn't involve supernatural activity."

"If you can understand the four elements of the earth, you can understand the elements of the dark," Jay said with a sigh, less harsh than he had been with Majest, like he didn't want to make Raizu any more uncomfortable than he already was. "There *is* no other explanation. And I would know because I've seen it before, awake and present." His eyes went dark. "As for your friend's possession, I saw *that* in a dream. Or rather—I saw shadows and darkness and storms, and I knew they were coming for us."

Majest opened his mouth to say something, then let the words go with a frown. Jay ignored him and in fact ignored the numerous looks of perplexity tossed his way, stalking over to a table to snatch a canister from it, taking a drink like the conversation had parched him.

"And you don't know where this force came from?" asked Quell, frowning, looking between Vari and Jay with a face molded from concern. "Because I need to be down in my garden, demons or not. The plants will die if I don't give them special care. There's never been a problem before."

Jay sighed, his breath coming out in an impatient growl. "No, I don't know where it's *coming from*. I'm not stupid enough to seek answers from the realms of demons. I know what darkness that brings." He took another quick drink of water. "My best guess? Someone summoned this force. Demons don't usually stray to Earth without coaxing or threat; the fact this one is here means *someone* has been playing around with dark power." He scowled. "Which requires a certain kind of idiot. Demons aren't to be messed with."

Letty wondered why Jay knew so much about demons and how to summon one, but she did not ask. "Do you really think this demon energy is focused in Quell and Idyllice's garden?"

"I didn't do it," said Quell immediately.

Jay wrinkled his nose, looking insulted. "No, of course it's not. Don't be ridiculous. Demons have no souls; they can never find a home or stability. That's one thing you can be certain of: demonic forces are always on the move, until they find a way to feign a human form, or until they slink back to their abyss."

"How do you know that?" Majest demanded, clearly more nosy than Letty.

"I was raised in a place that taught its children these things." Jay's voice was sharp enough to cut stone. "Because for us, it was not fantasy."

Majest did not dare say anything more.

"Then we owe that knowledge for Vari's well-being," said Sedona, voice strained, though somehow laced with a careful softness, like a mother trying to comfort a child. "Thank you."

Letty stared at her. While Sedona didn't have Raizu's gentle compassion or Jay's mind packed with bitter truth, she seemed driven to please, to be her world's anchor. Letty didn't know why, but the thought made her a little sad.

Jay, obviously not feeling the warmth either, flinched back at the kind words like he had been struck with them. "If you hadn't noticed, not much of Vari's well-being is left," he said curtly. "And there isn't anything I could have done except tie him down to keep him from writhing about, then drug him full of potions until he sleeps."

"But *you* had the potions," Sedona pressed. "Without you, he'd still be screaming and thrashing and potentially hurting himself."

"Knocking him out would have worked just as nicely."

At that, a rather disgruntled-looking Sedona clenched her jaw and stared at the floor. Sunni patted her arm, muttering something about Jay in her sister's ear too low for anyone else to hear. Letty imagined it was nothing all too pleasant.

"So what does all this mean for the town?" Idyllice cut in. "And my garden?"

"Right. The town." Jay folded his arms, taking a step back from the conversation. "The garden of yours, Souleias, is safe—though I can hardly say the same for the rest of the town." He shrugged. "Heavens know where the demon has gotten off to. It could be long gone or right around the corner. Perhaps it's taking a swim in the Bay as we speak. Perhaps it's right in front of me, but no one's bothered to mention it. Who knows?" He shrugged, like he didn't care either way.

"Isn't it important that we find it and get rid of it?" Majest demanded.

"And will getting rid of it make Vari better again?" Quell added.

"I don't *know*. If you have any idea how to find an invisible demon and either kill it or ask it nicely to heal your little friend, then go right ahead. Or you could always ask those gods of yours, since apparently they care enough about you to start a war over your powers. Otherwise, you seem to be out of luck. Not that you had much to begin with."

All at once, Jay froze, seeming to remember he was never this sociable. "Well, that's all the information I can offer you," he said stiffly, walking over to hover at Vari's side.

Vari was motionless and pale gray in color, but his breathing was a steady metronome, and there was no clawing twitch to his fingertips, no mutters from bleeding lips. He looked like any other sleeping boy—eyelids fluttering, mouth slightly ajar, hair strewn over his face.

"And there's nothing else I can do for him," Jay went on. "Knowledge alone can't save anyone."

"Then now what?" asked Majest. He looked impatient.

"We wait."

"Wait for *what?*" Letty protested. "Is Vari going to be okay?"

Jay closed his eyes, probably more for dramatic effect than anything else. "I'll keep him in here for the next few days, though I doubt he'll be getting better."

Letty inhaled in surprise. "You *doubt* he'll be getting better?"

"That's what I said," said Jay in an unfriendly tone. "As long as the demonic energy that attacked and possessed him still runs rampant, he won't be able to overcome it."

Majest glared at Jay. Letty had never pictured him as Vari's defender, but perhaps he was more willing to advocate for a boy who cared about Letty than a significantly grouchier boy who already disliked him. "You know about this demon magic," Majest protested, matching Jay's growling tone. "*Do* something."

Jay's eyes grew even darker, and then they were no longer clear skies, but storm clouds brooding dark and wrathful. "I've done all I can," he retorted.

Majest opened his mouth to reply, but after a warning head shake from Raizu, closed it with a sigh.

"Now get out of my house before I collapse from claustrophobia and the smell of you lot put together," Jay continued, gesturing in the direction of the front door. He was pretending to examine his nails, the picture of apathy. If Letty hadn't known he was blind, she never would have guessed.

"If you can smell well enough to get a whiff of us, wouldn't your nose give out from the reek of this place of yours? It smells like a berry bush exploded in here." Majest stalked toward the door.

"You're only about half as funny as you think you are, you know," responded Jay.

Majest wrinkled his nose at Jay but said nothing, yanking on the knob and exiting with deliberate flippancy. Letty followed, and caught a glimpse of Jay rolling his eyes before the door shut behind her.

Please, she thought, a silent plea in his direction. *Please keep Vari safe. Keep him out of the shadows, whatever it takes.*

Shadows.

Vari's screech rang in Letty's ears with a shattering resonance, and she gritted her teeth, drowned the shrillness of it in the crunch of her boots. *That's what it's been ever since we left home— shadows and doubt. I thought Hi Ding was different. I thought it was safe, a perfect escape from the rest of the world. I thought we'd be protected from harm here.*

As Letty looked up into the sky, she found a setting sun, twilight casting dark lines across the ground. Her eyes watered as they adjusted to the light stolen from right under her nose.

Nowhere is perfect, is it?

"I still can't believe I'm doing this," muttered Caiter, and his feet gripped the hall's floor tight.

This was not one of the Organization's ordinary white halls; it was the dingy gray of soiled snow, and it gave a brittle crunch against Caiter's boots. In fact, where Caiter walked was hardly a hallway at all—more of a narrow passage, back in the farthest, deepest corner of the building, shunned and lonely. It stank of metal and fear.

At the end of the hallway was a metal door rusted around its edges; Caiter pushed on its great, heaving lever without second thoughts, which was rather unlike him. But then, there was nothing of the flushed, careless scientist here now—perhaps he should have been afraid, coming down here, but his agreement to make this visit left him with more fear for his mental health than any physical consequences.

Only a fool would come here willingly. And show sympathy *of all things,* Caiter's thoughts jeered. He ignored them.

The open door led him into a dim square room, buzzing with the absence of light. It was just like the hallway—a dungeon of faded walls, holes like animal burrows in the ceiling. A guard sat at a tall rickety desk in the center; he had mahogany skin and a shining bald head, eyes the same shade as the walls and not any friendlier. He looked up at the sound of the door.

"Can I help you?" The man's voice was threaded with surprise, and Caiter couldn't blame him.

"Ah, yes," replied Caiter, biting his lip. Despite attempts to deny his fears and foolishness, this place gave him the chills. "I'm here to see someone."

"See someone?"

"Like a visit," Caiter tried again, swallowing hard. "I'm a visitor."

The guard looked amused, as if Caiter were a fly he had just watched land in his web. "You're Caiter Mandle, aren't you? The one who invented the sleep chamber? There's no reason you should ever be walking this hall—or attending to our one and only *someone* held prisoner."

"I was the one who brought him down here," Caiter announced, clenching his jaw. "Charan and I did. Well—I mean—we brought him to the door." He wished he could have smacked himself.

The man's mouth curled. "Charan. Yes, I remember him. The little boy with the curly hair and the big brown eyes. I remember you both." He looked at Caiter with a new light, gaze now considerate instead of condescending. "And you're serious about a visit?"

"I am," Caiter said, willing himself to remain composed. He could not show fear in this place. "I got special permission from the President to come down here. She wanted his side of the story, and I thought a little company might do him some good."

At this the man at the desk laughed. "I don't think anyone could even *begin* to put the pieces of *that* man back together again—not even you!"

Why. Why am I doing this.

Trying not to let his face redden in color, Caiter waited nervously while the man continued to howl, skin blotching a flushed purple that hung bruises on his cheeks, breaths coming in wheezes.

"I'll tell you what, Caiter," the guard said after some time. "You go right ahead and see him. Just stay on your own side of the glass, alright?" He reached into a deep desk drawer and pulled from it a ring of keys, jerking his thumb into a dark corridor that broke off from his right. "First door on the left."

"Thank you very much, sir," said Caiter, dipping his head and scuttling off into the hallway. There was no light between its high-rising borders, only a grimness and the tang of copper in the air. It almost made Caiter want to turn back, but he would not let himself. This was a façade; he would not be in danger.

Caiter found the first door on the left side with fumbling fingers, squinting down at his keys in a blind attempt to discern which one was which. He pulled them out one-by-one, jamming them against the lock with a tidal beat until a click presented him with victory. Upon twisting, the door swung open and Caiter was thrust into a sea of white light.

The room that greeted him was so vivid in its bright intensity, Caiter felt the urge to look away—though there was nowhere else to rest his eyes except on the man who sat across the room, knees pulled to his chest, raven's eyes contemplating the ceiling. His hair, ruffled and unkempt as always, was the only real color in the room. Even his clothes were whiter than white.

The man looked up at the sound of footsteps, eyes widening and teeth surfacing in a lopsided grin. *"Caiter!"* he cried, getting up to cross the room. His voice was muffled. "I *knew* I liked you best, I *knew* you'd show up, I *knew* you wouldn't leave me here to rot here!"

Caiter flinched back without really meaning to, and then a familiar face was pressed up against the glass barrier that split the room in two, hands gripping for purchase, eyes blinking out at Caiter as if he were an old friend.

"Malory," said Caiter, voice catching on something he didn't quite understand. All he knew was that Malory had never hurt him, whatever his plans for vengeance and deceit. He was not afraid of this man, and did not hate him, even now. "I didn't come to let you out. The President wanted someone to come and talk to you."

"Oh." Malory's face fell into a childish pout. "Well, that's no fun." He slid his hands down the glass, the wall squeaking with a frequency that made Caiter squirm.

"Everything you say and do will be reported immediately back to Lady President," Caiter added, as if the words were an extra seal of protection. "Tread carefully."

Malory rolled his eyes. "Oh, I'm *terrified.* You've always been so terrifying, Caiter, you know that? I suppose I'd better be on my best behavior, then, if I ever want to get out of here." He adjusted his circular glasses; they surrounded the black holes of his eyes in orbits. "Did Lunesta give you a script of questions to ask me? I would imagine she did. Shall I recite the alphabet backwards?"

Caiter folded his arms across his chest, feeling his muscles tighten and cramp. No one ever addressed the President by her real name. "She didn't give me a script," he said after a moment's hesitation. "But she did want to know as much as possible about the demon energy you used on Ohanzi. She wants to know where he might be, and what he might be doing."

"Oh," Malory said again, though this time his eyes lit with a dark glow. He clasped his hands together, grinning, his teeth yet another splash of white in the colorless room. "Spectacular! I'd love to explain it to you, my dear Caiter." He smirked. "Clearly, it's one of your favorite topics—got you all excited back in the lab, huh?"

Caiter tensed and felt his hands clench, skin tingle. "I'm not here to play games with you."

"Well, that certainly ruins the session of charades I was planning for us later."

Caiter sighed, and found himself with gritted teeth. "Tell me what you think happened after you turned Ohanzi into a walking Hell. Tell me where he is."

Malory raised dark eyebrows. "Touchy, aren't we?" He chuckled, and Caiter felt a chill run up and down his spine, though he tried not to let it show. "Let me think, let me think." He pressed a finger to his lips in an exaggerated show of concentration. "Well, underneath all that demon razzle-dazzle, he's still Ohanzi on the inside. Still knows what Ohanzi knows, feels what he feels."

"Right," Caiter agreed, relieved to be back to business. "So how do you think that might affect where his...*spirit* would travel?"

"Don't be silly. It's impossible to try guessing where he is without a demon tracker—a needle in a haystack, they say. Too bad we can't just burn the hay."

"Then what—?"

"He's a demon shadow, isn't he?" Malory cut him off. "He's controlled by darker forces now. In that injection was all the demon energy I've been able to summon for the past few months. Enough to be unpredictable."

"You *summon* the energy?" Caiter wrinkled his nose.

Malory smiled, as if he thought the words held admiration. "Of course. Demon energy and fancy chemicals are the family business. I can summon any demon from any realm I please—want to watch?" He waggled his fingers.

Caiter refused to take a step backward. "No—tell me how to track him, how to predict where he is. Do you know?"

"Do I know how to make a demon tracker?" Malory scoffed. "Of course I do. It's just magic, not rocket science."

Caiter swallowed hard against a strange taste in his mouth. "So...?"

"*So,*" Malory said, and winked, "I'll tell you what you should do: go see those nasty twins of yours, and tell them to start up their demon watch tracker again—should lead them right to it, since it's designed to track demon energy. Simple enough?"

"You're—you're helping me?" Caiter's chest swelled. He

almost couldn't believe it.

"Why not?" Malory shrugged bony shoulders. "Is it so wrong for me to be curious about my own creation? Besides, Ohanzi always believed that Sinestre boy got lost following the Skylarks because they jumped across the coast to some unknown island. Perhaps the demon energy wrapped its claws around that thought and drove him out to find the truth, and if he does, I want to know what that truth might be. Believe it or not, Lunesta and I want many of the same things."

Caiter blinked, eyes watching Malory's face carefully. "And do you think Ohanzi has a chance to find the Skylarks?"

Malory splayed his palms in the air in starbursts of frivolity. "Who's to say?" His glasses slid down his nose and he pushed them back up the swoop of his nose. "Tell my dear old friend Lunesta there's no hope in predicting the future, and no luck for those who do. She'll just have to wait and see."

"Fine," said Caiter, and with reluctance, realized his allotted time was running short. "I'll tell Lady President what you've said." He tried for a smile, distorting his face with some great effort. "Thanks for, well, talking to me."

Caiter turned to leave, heart thrumming like a mouse's as he realized the door was just steps away, an escape to *where he should be* just down the hall—

"Wait! Caiter!"

"Yes?" Caiter whirled around with an immediate obedience, cringing in a cold sweat at the knee-jerk reaction.

Malory's face was open, eyes big and importunate. A hand was outstretched in a sort of demented appeal. "I'm really not going to get out of here?" he asked, voice creeping upward in pitch. "You're not taking me with you?"

Caiter sucked in a breath. He was not supposed to show pity for the man who had nearly destroyed dozens of lives in his unyielding havoc. Not even as his heart teased into a clench, resolve weakened by the plea he tried desperately to ignore. "I was given strict orders to leave you here until you decide you want to fight for our mission again, and not your own."

Malory made a noise of protest. "Did I not just tell you Lunesta and I both want similar things? I have debts to settle, Skylarks to run down, same as she does—and this place has always had the technology I need!"

"How do we know if we let you out, you won't go right back to poisons and potions?" Caiter's feet inched toward the door. He would not falter. He would not show compassion. Malory was hardly human; Caiter had to remember that. He had to.

Malory opened his mouth like he was trying to say something, but no sound came out. He sank to his feet, palms crushed into fists. "I've done nothing wrong," he said in a low voice Caiter almost didn't catch. "I've given the Organization a valuable pawn for their board." He lifted his head, eyes blazing. "Caiter, you *have* to let me out!"

Biting his lip again, Caiter shook his head, avoiding Malory's eyes, remembering the syringe pointed like an arrow toward his heart. "I can't," he said. "I'm sorry."

"Caiter, *please!*" cried Malory, voice shrill with starved desperation that nearly had Caiter turning again, succumbing to weakness.

But he forced himself to push through the door with a clumsy deliberation, teeth clacking in his skull as he slammed it shut. His fingers were like trembling leaves as they redid the lock.

Cries erupted from the other side, wails of pure, desolated betrayal, and though Caiter's skin crawled and heart twisted at the sound, he did not unlock the door, did not make a move to turn around. His task was done.

Caiter did not let anything stop him as he marched himself to the ugly front room, set the keys on the red-skinned man's desk with a brisk nod, and strode out of the prison.

He did not look back.

XX. THREAT

Their cottage was pitch-black by the time Majest, Raizu, and Letty returned. The day still held hours more in its grasp, but with the limited light, there was hardly a thing to do but sit in the dark—unable to move, unable to see.

Majest thought he almost envied Jay's lack of sight—at least Jay had adapted to it, was comfortable enough with no light and no direction, only the familiar layout of the world as it lurked around where no one else could see. Darkness would not change Jay's perspective.

On the other hand, I rely on my sight, meaning I can't find anything. Majest made a noise of disgruntlement, hands fumbling over the counter like blundering bear paws in a boredom-driven attempt to locate something to eat.

"The fruit basket's on your left," said Raizu, voice drifting over from the table where he sat in the dark next to Letty. "You put it on the end of the counter." His words were shaky in the blackness.

Frowning as he moved his hands to the left, Majest located the basket and dug through it blindly, pulling out what he hoped was an apple. "Got it. Want anything?"

"I'm fine." Raizu sounded strained.

"Suit yourself." Majest took a bite, relieved as the sweet taste of apple juice dribbled into his mouth—as well as all down his chin in sticky little rivers. He wiped it off with his sleeve.

"Well, this is no fun," remarked Letty. "Even in the dark, we can usually sit around and tell stories by the lantern-light; it's not so bad. Everything's different with that demon on the loose. All I can think about is Vari."

"Then his mission is accomplished," muttered Majest, though he was sure his sister didn't hear. Louder he said, "We could at least try to have some fun—there's got to be a book or two around here. Do either of you want to learn how to read?"

"There's no point," said Raizu. "Since you can't find our lantern, we're stuck in the dark." His voice continued to tremble.

"I swear, it was right on top of the table where I put it!" Majest protested, feeling a bit guilty.

"Must have fallen over," Raizu mumbled. "Just our luck."

"Cheer up, Raizy," Majest told him with another bite of apple. "The dark's just the same as the light. You've got the same world out there—just a bit harder to see."

At that, the apple was gone; Majest tossed the core over in the direction of the counter, hearing it skitter next to the basket and then falter, tumbling onto the floor with a noise like a wet stone.

Raizu sighed. "Yeah—you can't *see* what's lurking in the dark. That's exactly the problem."

"I really hope you pick that apple up," muttered Letty absently.

Majest thought for a moment, then directed a question at Raizu. "Hey, do you know what we should do?"

"Get a new lantern?"

Majest snorted. "That too." He walked awkwardly over to the table, managing to find a chair without injuring himself and sink into it. "No—I just had a great idea. We'll get to snoop around the village, feed ourselves, and cure your fear all at the same time."

"That's a tall order to fill," Raizu's voice said, though he did sound curious, and after a moment he asked begrudgingly, "Alright, what is it?"

"We're going to go out," said Majest, grinning and combing through his hair with cold fingers.

"Out *where?*" Majest could hear the doubt in Raizu's query.

"To the forest," Majest clarified. "The two of us are going to go out into the forest and have an adventure—night hunting. I used to do it all the time back at our old cottage."

"That sounds…like it involves a dark forest in unfamiliar

territory. Two things that don't really sit well with me."

Majest leaned up against the counter. "It's fun, I promise."

Raizu sighed, and Majest pictured him with his hands kneading in his lap, eyes cast to the floor as he gnawed on his cheek. "Whatever hurt Vari is still out there somewhere. Vari got attacked in the darkness, right? I don't think it's the best idea to go out when it's so *dark*—"

"Do you honestly think I'd let anything happen to you?" Majest scoffed. "Nothing ever happened to me back in the forest, not even when Lunesta was supposedly forming some murderous assembly. Tell him, Letty."

Majest could almost *hear* his sister rolling her eyes. "You both make a good point," she said. "But back in the forest, there weren't demon spirits running loose. Not to mention, you sort of knew where you were going."

"We can't get lost," Majest protested. "The island is a circle; it goes on forever."

Letty made a noise. "But with Vari the way he is—I don't know if you two should get to go have fun and leave me sitting here a quivering ball of worry."

"I could always do that for you," offered Raizu.

Majest let out an impatient breath. "What happened to Vari was awful, but there's *nothing we can do about it.* Is there anything wrong with forgetting the bad things for just a little while?"

"Not when the *bad things* could be anywhere, including currently possessing a friend of mine," said Letty. Majest couldn't see her face, couldn't see the eyes that would give her heart away, but he thought she sounded heated.

"You can't move on to the future if you're stuck dwelling on the past," Majest recited, hearing his father's gravelly voice in his mind, and the thick string of Icelandic that had followed—*"Þú getur ekki farið til framtíðar ef þú ert fastur í fortíðinni."*

Letty let out a breath from in between her teeth. "Fine," she said at last. "Do as you like." With the noise of creaking wood, she stood up from the table, footsteps carrying off into the direction of her room.

Majest waited until the steps disappeared, trying to gauge the extent of Letty's anger. The fire in her words was usually doused quickly. It was best to leave her alone until the flames died down on their own. She would be alright.

Raizu seemed to sense this too, because he made no motion to follow, only exhaling harshly through his nose before saying, voice laced with diffidence, "Perhaps…we should give her some time to herself. And if we're going to leave her be…" A pause. "Maybe the forest isn't such a bad idea."

Majest's eyes widened. Raizu, *voluntarily* agreeing to engulf himself in his worst fears?

"Great," he replied before Raizu had time to change his mind. "You still have your coat on, right?"

Raizu made a nervous noise, which Majest took as a yes.

"Then let's go!"

Raizu did not know what delirious lapse of insight had led him to agree to this. Each new step into the cold, empty darkness was like a plunge into ice water, drowning his thoughts with a familiar bath of terror, twisting each nerve until it frayed and threatened to snap. He was shaking all over.

He took a deep breath, finding the light of the moon, which blinked gently down through rows of clouds determined to never quite let its shine reach the ground. Silently, he fought to find an internal voice of reason, and he asked himself *why* he was doing this, again and again, but deep in his tangled stomach, he already knew—he wanted to prove himself to the Skylarks, no matter what they claimed they owed him. He wanted to prove he could be more than a coward.

"Hey, Raizy, you still alive over there?" Majest's voice cut through Raizu's worries. "You're awfully quiet. Don't tell me you've died of fright *already.* We're not even into the woods! That's when the fun starts."

"What fun?" Raizu tried to keep his voice just as light, but a twig cracked under his foot and the sound sent a cold stream of nerves down his spine, creating a voice small and croaky.

Majest just laughed, and loud enough for Raizu to wonder how the whole world didn't hear. "I think you need a new definition of fun, then," he chortled. He grabbed Raizu's wrist and gestured to something in front of him, his hand a pale flash in the dusk. "There are the trees! Let's go!"

Raizu wasn't given a chance to protest; Majest was already dragging him forward, and it was all he could do to keep from toppling over as his feet came to life, skittering over the ground—a soft, snowy earth. After some time, the sound of Majest's thumping footfalls became a reassurance in the silent darkness, slowing the flurry of panicky thoughts, and Raizu found himself smiling breathlessly, feeling much like a child.

They ran for what seemed like a few forevers, but after some time, when Raizu gained some balance and confidence, Majest let him go. The footsteps stopped.

Raizu skidded to an awkward halt, breaths coming in pants. He put his hands on his knees, faint forest shapes moving back and forth in front of his dizzy vision.

"Fun," Majest repeated.

Raizu pressed his lips together. "How do you know where the trees are so you don't hit them?"

Majest had started walking again. "Which way is which?" he called back, laughter in his voice. "*Hímin,* I don't know! They're awfully chatty tonight, but that's hardly any help when you can't see them." He chuckled once more, then seemed to realize Raizu was no longer following. "What's the matter?"

Raizu was frozen rigid. "You don't *know?*"

The footsteps returned, drawing closer, and Raizu found Majest's faint outline in the moon's shadow. "It's not like we can get lost. It's an island—everything comes back to the coast."

"I'm going to run into the trees."

"No, you're not. I won't let you. Trust me." Majest picked up again, and Raizu had no choice but to follow on shaking legs, gritting his teeth to keep the worried wrinkle from creasing his brow.

Still, he couldn't help the nagging apprehension that bumbled, invisible, in his mind. *Does he even know how big the island is? What if it's bigger than we think? What if we get attacked? What if we can't find our way back and have to sleep outside? We'll freeze! Oh, or what if—*

"Hey! Raizu!" Again, Majest's voice cut through the panicked succession of thoughts, stopping them short until he nearly forgot them entirely. "I think I see the coast! Look!"

Trying not to shiver from the cold, Raizu squinted ahead, trying to distinguish shapes. "We can't be at the shore already," he said. "It took me hours to get from the beach to the village—we haven't been out here that long." *Long enough, though.*

"It took you hours because you were soaking wet, exhausted, and frozen half to death," said Majest matter-of-factly. "Maybe the island dips in over here, has a coast closer to the village. I don't know." He paused for a moment. "Do you hear that?"

Raizu listened, and sure enough, he could hear the gentle lapping of the Hudson's waves, kissing the shore with soft splashes. "I hear it," he agreed. "Guess you're right."

"Of course I am."

Raizu nearly smiled before he remembered the surrounding darkness. "It's probably a nice view in the daytime."

"Or just a lot of water," Majest noted. "Letty would be all over this place. She'd sit here staring at it for hours if she could. Now that she's got her powers, all she wants is what's wet. She's going to turn into a fish, and then someone's going to accidentally catch her for dinner."

"Well, her love for water *does* seem a lot like your addiction to the forest," Raizu countered in a teasing hedge. "You know—even when you *can't see your own hands in front of your face.*"

Majest made a sheepish noise. "I suppose that's true," he admitted.

"It's probably because of your powers," Raizu pointed out.

"What *isn't* to do with our powers?" Majest muttered. "They're hardly worth Lunesta's fuss."

Raizu didn't know what to say to that, so he asked, "Are you ever going to help Letty practice hers? And Sedona?"

"What do you mean?"

"If they were trained like you, they'd be a lot safer with heavens know whatever's out there."

"You think *I'd* be able to teach them something?" Majest sounded amused. "Letty nearly started crying and strangling me the last time she tried using her power. We had to get the help of a baby seal just to get here." He sighed. "You're right, though," he said with more sincerity, "I don't know about Sedona, but Letty needs training. And Sedona says her powers are brand new."

"Sedona would love it, I'm sure. She seems to like you well enough." Raizu blinked cold air out of watering eyes.

"Really," said Majest, less of a question and more of a statement. He sounded indifferent, and somehow, that was relieving. "I hadn't noticed. It seems like she takes everyone under her wing, though, doesn't she?"

Raizu shrugged and made a noise of agreement. *Everyone but me, maybe.* He couldn't explain why Sedona put him on edge, but at the very least, she didn't seem too fond of him. Turning his gaze out over the water, he noticed a tiny speck of light glowing soft and faint in the distance. He glanced up at the sky, but the moon wasn't there any longer.

"That's odd," he muttered aloud. "How can the moon be reflecting off the water if it's hidden behind the clouds?"

"What do you mean?" Majest leaned close over Raizu's shoulder, tilting his head to the stars.

"The moon," Raizu said again. "It's not in the sky, but it's reflecting off the water over there." He gestured to the speck of off-white above the horizon.

Beside him, Majest had gone still. "Oh, no," he whispered. "That—that's not the moon."

Raizu's heart began to pound as he squinted at the whiteness ahead, realizing with a jolt that it was floating closer, losing its lifeless mask with each passing second, becoming something mortal, something breathing and sending the water roiling away in tiny rows of ripples. Something with beady eyes set in an elongated face, teeth with the sharp precision of ice, fur the color of the snow where they lay in waiting, hunting to catch their prey unaware—

Majest was edging away from the coast now, slow and still. "Polar bear," he hissed.

Raizu began to tremble, and all at once, forgot every word of survival advice he had ever been told; it was sucked straight out of him, along with his breath. "Skies—have you ever been this close to one before?"

"No," Majest rasped back. "I've never even *seen* one. First Letty and the grizzly, now this. What, are bears attracted to us like fish to water? Do we smell like seals?"

The bear swam closer, and Raizu could see the gleam in its eyes—the only glimmer of light in the dark. Bears were solitary creatures—this one wouldn't single them out, attack unprovoked, would it?

Would it?

Raizu crouched low on the ground, pulling Majest down with him, and though he had seen countless bears before, even trailed them, he could not keep himself from quaking. "Maybe it won't see us," he tried.

That prospect went nowhere fast. The polar bear's ears perked up at the sound of Raizu's voice, graying face peering out from where the Bay's edge sidestepped the sky. There was something strange, something *wrong* about the way its eyes cast their lifeless gaze over the ground, but in his panic, Raizu didn't dwell on it.

"On my signal, I want you to run," hissed Majest into Raizu's ear, wasting no time. "Run back the way we came and whatever you do, *don't stop*. I'll distract it and then follow behind you."

Two beady eyes flickered between the two of them like a wavering flame, and the bear's claws moved to grip the rocky shore, a growl low in its throat.

"*Run?!* You can't outrun a bear—"

"I'm not going to outrun it. I'm going to outsmart it. Trust me; I'll give the signal."

"Alright, then what's the signal?" Raizu asked, hearing his voice crack. He trusted Majest, even if he barely knew him, but his heart still skipped beat after beat at the proposal until he thought it might just give out altogether.

"*This!*"

Majest shoved Raizu back toward the trees; he stumbled for a moment before pulling himself to his feet. There was no time to cringe at every cracking twig, no time to cower as the forest called out.

Raizu ran for his life.

At once he understood how Majest had avoided the trees—perhaps Raizu had no sixth elemental sense, but the blurry tree-shapes loomed slow-motion against his vision like paper cutouts swaying with the breeze in his wake, and he swerved without thought, without true sight, panic dominating his zigzag motion. Needles sprayed out at him; fallen branches sought to trip him, and fear was his only guide.

He did not know where he was running, but he did not stop.

And as he ran, unaware of time or thoughts or anything but the thumping feet of escape, he heard something behind him. So he ran faster, a gasp ripping from his chest.

"Raizu!" He heard the voice behind him but did not stop. "Raizy, stop! It's me!"

Raizu did not stop, did not even slow.

"*Stop!* It's me!"

Raizu's breath came in gasps. "I'm not going to stop when a polar bear is chasing us, Maji!" He felt his feet going numb under the tight leather bounds of his boots. "Where is it? Can you see it?"

"*Raizu,*" yelled Majest. "I threw a tree at its face! It's not going to be following us anytime soon!" His voice sounded distant, fainter, as if he had stopped running.

With reluctance, Raizu forced his feet to slow to a walk, feeling as if he were trying to reverse gravity, and rather unsuccessfully. Anything but the flight felt foreign and wrong. Bracing himself in case Majest was wrong, he turned around, spinning on the heel of his boot.

Quite a few paces away, Majest was grinning in the dark. "There you go. Calm down, will you?"

Raizu glared at him, panting. "Where's the bear?"

Majest laughed and kicked at a rock buried in the earth. *"Calm down*—you're going to hurt yourself. The bear is long gone."

"Where?"

A shrug. "Somewhere back behind us. I guess we'll have to continue our adventure elsewhere."

Raizu gaped at him. "You want to go back out there? Do you have short-term memory loss or something—do you want to die tonight? Is this a suicide pact you're trying to make with me?"

"Hardly," scoffed Majest. "The bear's probably swimming off with its wimpy tail between its legs as we speak. And we haven't even gotten to hunt anything yet!" He prodded a slingshot on his belt and winked. "Come on. It'll be fun."

Raizu shook his head, the night easing back over his skin. "I still don't think—"

A noise drowned whatever else he might have said. It was a deep rumble, a warning growl in the midst of an otherwise silent forest. A growl Raizu knew, and a growl Raizu feared.

"What was that?" asked Majest.

Raizu looked up, hands clenched at his sides—and immediately wished he hadn't. He felt his face go white and still, a shiver pulsing through his blood.

He lifted a quavering hand, not even daring to breathe, and pointed.

Without the same sense of fear, Majest whirled around with a curious noise—a noise that died in his throat. Looming over him with clawed mitts outstretched, its eyes orbs in the flustered dimness of moonlight, was the polar bear. There were long gashes in its side, red patterns of blood and leaves that crisscrossed in the shape of a tree. It did not look merciful.

Not missing a beat, Majest stepped in front of Raizu and knocked him out of harm's way, boots twisting in the snowy dirt. Two steady hands snagged the slingshot from his belt and loaded it with something small and green, giving the bear no time for anything but a gurgling grumble.

For a moment, Raizu forgot his terror. He had heard that sound before. And those *eyes*...

He didn't have time to brood over the thought. With a quick series of movements, Majest flung the rock out of his slingshot and hollered for Raizu to take cover, and he was running, a streak against the stilled greens, and his bullet hit the ground at the bear's hind feet.

It exploded with a velocity and volume Raizu had never known, and he was blown back with an ungraceful tumble, hands snapping to cover his ears before he was deafened. He landed on his side, locking his eyes shut and fighting for air as the breath knocked out of him.

Only a moment or two had time to pass before Majest was there at his side, pulling him to his feet and holding him there in his grasp, even as Raizu buckled against him, a cry of terror on his tongue. He opened his eyes, and found sight to be futile—the world was nothing but swirling green. His nose filled with an odor of trees and smoke and a bizarre sweetness that nearly sent him swaying back to the ground. His legs barely held their own, and he wished he had the strength to demand an explanation of what had just saved his life—but it was Majest, wasn't it? Majest had saved him.

"It's grass-smoke," said Majest, raising his voice over the hissing echoes of the explosion. "It's not poisonous, but it will give us a chance to get out of here. Stay close to me; you're not used to the effects of this stuff like I am."

"If I were any closer to you, I'd be on top of you," Raizu wheezed, choking on the thickness of the air and using Majest's side to prop himself up.

"That's the idea," replied Majest. "Now come on. We've only got a few seconds before the smoke starts to clear out, and as dazed and injured as that bear might be from the impact, that bomb won't have been enough to kill it."

Raizu shut his mouth to keep from coughing and got to his feet. He gripped the sleeve of Majest's fur jacket tight enough that his knuckles throbbed in protest—but he refused to lose himself in the blanketing maze of green and gray.

The next moments were an agonizingly-slow crawl through green darkness, and just as Raizu thought his lungs might surrender altogether, Majest's promise held true; the haze began to clear, parting like clouds to reveal the stunned bear, paces away against the blown-apart dirt. Black eyes gaped wide and it grunted with a fevered disorder, staring blankly down at the green streaks that smeared its chest in thick, pulsing veins.

Majest frowned, unfazed as always. "Raizy, do you see something off about its eyes?" he asked, low enough that Raizu almost didn't catch it.

Before he could respond, the bear's gaze drifted to Majest, the source of its perplexity and pain, and it growled loudly, yellow teeth flashing. Dried foam crusted around its mouth in a beard, illuminated by the moon as it slid out from beneath the clouds.

Exchanging a quick glance, Raizu and Majest turned and darted off in the opposite direction, leaving the confused bear to lurch after them. Its footsteps were slow; still stunned from the bomb, it could do nothing more than stagger along with frustrated howls, screams of loathing.

With a final roar of contempt, the footsteps slowed to a stop. Raizu spared a quick glance over his shoulder to see the bear lumbering away, crashing into trees as it went, rumbling like an earthquake.

Majest halted too, eyebrows up, chest heaving. "Is that it?"

Raizu's fingers still quivered as he swept hair out of his eyes. "I—I think so."

Majest laughed in triumph. "Ha! Well, that was fun."

They slowed to a walk in near-perfect synchronization, and Raizu shook his head. "Fun."

"It's not every day you get to outsmart and escape from a polar bear," Majest said with glee. "I consider this a life-changing experience."

Raizu shook his head again, and there were a few long moments of silence and walking before he said, "Well, congratulations, anyhow."

"For what?"

"You don't owe me your life anymore," Raizu noted. "You saved mine. Without you, I'd be curled up in a ditch somewhere and that bear would be tearing me into tiny, stringy pieces."

Although Raizu couldn't see it, Majest was probably rolling his eyes. "Saved your life? If it weren't for me, you wouldn't have been out here in the first place, so that cancels out any heroics. I didn't even help you cure your fear of the dark, did I? Of course I didn't. You went out in the dark, and got attacked by a *polar bear.*" He sighed. "I'm sorry. Bad luck, that's what this is. We don't even have time to hunt before the sun starts coming up."

"At least the bear distracted me from the darkness," Raizu said reluctantly, cracking a smile. "Better than nothing." He glanced around the forest, finding that it was hardly frightening now, not with a comparison of drooling fangs. "And it's easier when I'm not alone. I'm—" He broke off, flushed a little. "I'm not so afraid when you're here."

Majest grinned at him, smile barely visible. "Well, lucky for you, I'm not going anywhere. If you ever want to do this again, you just let me know, and I'll get a message to our furry bear friend." Then he laughed. "And just for the record, if I hadn't been here, you still wouldn't have been alone—you would've had the bear with you!"

Something kept Raizu from laughing along with him. "I don't think that bear was quite right," he said, confessing his doubts. "The black eyes, the foam around its mouth, the way it attacked us unprovoked…" He shuddered. "Something was strange, don't you think? You said so yourself."

"It's a bear. Bears are hungry. Maybe he just wanted something—someone—to eat," offered Majest. "And if it wasn't going to attack us at first, it definitely was after I tossed a sapling in its face. As for the eyes, who knows?"

"We should tell someone about this," Raizu pressed. "Either way, there's still a *bear* on the island. It's a danger—it could attack the village."

Majest thought on that. "I guess you're right," he said. "We should probably report this to Masotote. Especially if he's going to be expecting his currently-comatose faithful servant boy to come calling anytime in the near future and no one's bothered to give him the news."

Raizu made a noncommittal noise. "Well, someone's got to start making sense of things."

"Then Vosile Masotote it is."

XXI. DETECTION

Without Vari and Sedona's smiles, their stirring of the atmosphere, Vosile Masotote's wooden cottage held a much less inviting air than Majest remembered. He had once compared it to his childhood home far away, with the same worn walls of cedar, rasping creaks of old chairs, caribou cloths—

But now, as dawn pressed into the edges of the night, the cottage did not look like a safe haven any longer. It did not look like a home—merely another house, another building, a lifeless structure draped in security blankets. Perhaps the village had tricked him as it had tricked Letty—tricked him into believing no harm could lie in waiting on an island that feigned security so fervently.

Majest knocked on the door, the wood creaking in protest. There was no response.

"I don't think he's awake," murmured Raizu, pushing his sleeves up to his elbows in the door's warm shelter. "Why don't we come back later?"

"I'm not so sure," Majest responded, and pulled open the creaking door with one hand. Inside, the room smelled of dusty wood and faded warmth.

"You can't break into his house," Raizu scolded at once.

Majest turned back to look at him. "If we go back now, Letty will want to know what we're up to this late at night, and I don't want to cause her any more worry before we talk things over with the old man. If we tell her there's a bear on the loose, she's not going to sleep, and then she'll be a level of cranky in the morning you'll wish you had taken every measure to prevent."

Raizu chewed on his lip. "I don't want to do anything that could get us in trouble with the village. They still don't trust us—I doubt they'll like the thought of us breaking into their helpless leader's house while he's sleeping."

"We'll just wait inside until he wakes up," said Majest, and stepped over the doorframe. "It's better than sitting out in the cold."

"Maji—"

"Is someone there?" A voice like rumbling clouds called from across the house. The sound was somewhere between cranky and genuinely curious—and if Majest wasn't mistaken, a hint of something else, some dark hope beginning to fester.

"It's Majest Skylark," Majest called back. "My friend and I came here to speak to you. It's important."

There was no response, and Raizu started fidgeting with the ends of his scarf.

Tentatively Majest added, "We're sorry if we woke you up. It couldn't wait."

After another few considerate moments, there was a response—a question. "Is this about the demon going around town, terrorizing my people?"

Majest frowned. He had not known someone had come to tell Masotote of the day's events. "Somewhat," he answered. "Among other problems."

"How's my Vari doing?"

Raizu stared at the floor, clearly uncomfortable, so Majest answered again, rapidly losing enthusiasm. "We don't know when he'll be better. Jay is seeing to him. Well—metaphorically seeing to him."

Vosile didn't reply. Silence lined the walls, and with it, unease.

Majest felt compelled to break it. "But we *are* here to ask about the demon, and to bring you other news, too, of something we found when we were night hunting out in the forest. It's important."

There was a long sigh, as if just listening to young words was draining, and then the man replied, "Alright. I suppose you'd better come in. First door on the right."

Majest and Raizu exchanged a momentary glance before

obeying, following the wooden walls back into a bedroom. The bedroom was the same cedar and fur-lined chairs as the rest of the house, and in the back, a bed drowning in caribou pelts was pushed up against a wall in abandon, where it sagged against its supports. Propped up in that bed was Vosile Masotote, who stared at Majest and Raizu from within his cocoon of blankets with eyes like dust and mothballs.

"Skylark," Vosile greeted, and his voice did not hold its former rumbling cheer. "And friend. Vari told me Sedona found someone else in the forest. And now here you are—another body to house, another mouth to feed."

Raizu did not move, just stared at the floor.

Majest glanced at him with worry, then back to Vosile. "This is Raizu," he said, perhaps a little too harshly. "Raizu Capricorn. He's helping us out."

Raizu lifted his head, gaze wavering as he looked to Vosile with a near-visible veil of unease drawn down over his face. "It's not— I'm only staying until we sort this mess out," he stammered. "It's nice to meet you."

Majest found himself taken aback, like he had forgotten Raizu wasn't permanent, not as the rest of this new island world was; Raizu had his own world to return to, a horizon to disappear over until he was out of reach, onto some new curve in the earth. Majest suddenly realized he would miss him when he went.

Vosile was still staring darkly at both of them, eyes half-hidden behind the tangled bushes of his eyebrows. "Nice to meet you as well, Capricorn. I don't suppose you boys are going to explain what the problem is? You seemed fairly adamant when you stormed in here *uninvited*."

"Right, of course," said Majest, swallowing hard and feeling an uneasiness seeping out from the cracks in the walls, the cracks in Masotote's voice. "Like I said, Raizy and I were out in the forest— night hunting."

"If you've already said it, there's no need to say it again."

Majest tried not to grit his teeth. "While we were out, we came across a polar bear—or rather, it came across us. It came swimming out from the Bay and chased us halfway across the island."

Vosile's eyebrows shot up. "A polar bear on our island, you say? We haven't had any of their kind find themselves this far from the mainland in years."

"This one did," said Majest, frowning. Did he not believe him?

But Vosile didn't question the story. "We'll have to warn everyone to be extra careful when they're outside," was all he said. "Bears usually don't stay here long. They always return to their seals and their ice, in places further north than this."

"Right." Majest nodded.

"That's not all," said Raizu, speaking up for the first time. "This bear was different. Strange. It had foam all around its mouth, and its eyes were pure black—not even a sparkle to them."

"Go on," said Vosile, eyebrows still up.

Raizu's eyes shifted nervously. "Any normal bear would have left us alone until we bothered it. This one wasn't like that—it seemed almost as if it had come to the island for the very purpose of singling us out to attack. It swam across the water and came right to our feet."

Vosile seemed to consider this. "Vari's eyes were like that, too," he said. "And his mouth, and the erratic behavior. Vari had seemed rather consumed by something, whatever shadow he was screaming about—and now you say this bear is, too?"

Majest clenched his hands into fists. Who had told him all that about Vari?

Raizu made an irritated noise, kicking at the wood floor with the toe of his boot. "You think the bear was…possessed, too?"

"Are you sure that's it?" Majest asked hastily, sparing Raizu a sympathetic glance. "Couldn't it be something else—other than demons? Maybe the bear was just sick, or gone mad with hunger."

Vosile Masotote's lip curled, and Majest thought he looked rather unfriendly for a supposed village hero. "No," he said, with the coldness of a winter gust. He did not seem open to the possibility of a future argument. "The symptoms align. If your story is true, you two are lucky to have escaped unharmed. Demonic energy is not to be touched, or messed with. It is a wicked, summoned thing, and it is always on the move, as I have learned, and as I now know. You should have not let your guard down and gone tumbling into the night after what happened to Vari."

Raizu looked startled at the words, as if they were something familiar and unexpected and utterly wrong manifesting from this man's mouth, but Majest was too busy taking offense to dwell on his reaction. "I had my slingshot with me," he protested. "It's gotten me out of sticky situations before and it didn't fail me this time."

"Lucky," Masotote repeated, casting his eyes downward. "Very lucky."

Raizu was still watching the man with a wary sort of curiosity, and seemed to gather the confidence to speak up once more. "How do you know so much about this, anyway? You and Jay both seem to have the same sort of knowledge."

Then it clicked in Majest's mind—those had been Jay's words of warning, tangled up and tossed out to his crowded back room in an almost identical phrase as Masotote had used.

Muddy eyes flickered. "Stories of gods and demons have floated around long before the earth was remade," Masotote said, a note of caution to his voice. "And there are those out there who choose to harness that energy for evil, for destruction. In a village not too far from here lived a man nothing but evil, and his history collides with my own and Jay's. That is why."

"So you and Jay are from the same place?" Majest pursed his lips. "You know, that explains a lot."

At his side, Raizu's eyes were still flickering. "But not enough," he murmured with the subtle flare of a candle, too low for the man to hear.

Vosile's face was like stone, and he gave them no time to exchange further words. "I hope you all know what you've gotten yourselves into. That older sister of yours carries the same dark potential of demons, and she *will* destroy you if you let her, not to mention the number she'll do on our new world."

Majest froze. All he heard was *sister.* "You know about Lunesta?"

"Of course," replied Vosile. "Jay saw the Organization in a

dream month ago. That's old news."

Blood rose to an instant boil inside of Majest's mind. "You *knew*," he started, in a sudden rage that made his hands crumple into fists. "You knew about the Organization, knew who Lunesta was and who we were—and didn't think to tell us when we got here?"

"We thought we could keep you safe," Vosile said. "We thought this island would be too far from harm to pose any threats—we didn't want to upset you."

"'We?'" Raizu cut in, something churning in his gaze. "Who's '*we*?'"

"If you're plotting to hand us over to the Organization," Majest growled, "you've done a fine job of setting us up."

Vosile's lip curled. "Lower your voice, Skylark, and do not throw such accusations around with the lightness of snowfall. You don't know of what you speak."

Majest took a step forward. "Then why don't you tell us the truth?"

Something like a growl came from the man's throat. "There is nothing to tell. I know of the world as it is told to me, and perhaps you ought to show a little more respect for the man who brought this village to life if you want to be living in it. My word is everything here; you will do what I say, just as everyone else."

Majest, about to hurl something back in reply, was cut off as Raizu stepped forward.

"You know of the world as it is told to you," Raizu said, and his eyes were dull of any fear's shine. "Told to you by whom?"

Vosile shifted his glare to Raizu. "By the gods."

At that, as if those three words had set off a chain reaction that could have lit all the world's nerves on end, Raizu whirled to Majest, and grabbed at his sleeve with a tight but gentle force. "We have to go," he deadpanned.

The look tossing and turning against the violets and blues of his eyes was so adamant, Majest could not even protest the strange suddenness of his words. But still—"What? Why?"

"Maji, I have an idea," Raizu insisted, and he was close enough for Majest to feel his breath slide against his cheeks. "It's important; we need to go check it out right now."

Before them, Vosile's glare was uninterested and sour.

"Um, I think we need to *finish this conversation* right now," Majest noted with a crinkled brow and a glance at the man in the blanket cocoon, but then Raizu was tugging harder at his sleeve, and his expression was building bridges between this moment and some insight of knowledge Majest had not yet arrived at. "Raizy, where could we possibly have to go; we're not done—"

"It's Jay," Raizu said, and Majest could not help but trust his resolution, the rare firmness of his gaze, how his fingers kneaded into the fur of Majest's jacket. At once, Majest knew he would follow Raizu out of this house—he could have followed him anywhere on that look in his eyes alone.

"If we want to save Vari and this village from shadows, we have to go talk to Jay before we listen to another word from this man's mouth."

"Raizy," Majest protested, for what felt like the umpteenth time. "Do we have to walk so fast?"

Raizu was tugging him insistently through the black village, white breath clouding out from his lips and casting a sheen over the pebbled streets. He was still gripping onto Majest's sleeve like all might be lost if his fingers slipped, and the frigid night did nothing to impede his briskness.

"At least tell me why you dragged me out into the cold in the middle of a conversation," Majest continued, and shoved his naked hands in his pockets. "I'm supposed to be the spontaneous one without an explanation, so you're scaring me a little."

There was a glint among the dark and Raizu was turning to him with a small smile, a look on his face plastered top to bottom with determination, with a sort of new bravery that suited him, brought out the upturn of his nose, the wideness of his eyes. "No one believes in Jay," he said, with the breathless effort of his pace, "but everyone believes in Masotote, right?"

"Sure," Majest said. "Masotote's top of the food chain around here; Jay's just seen as some kid who throws around big words and ghost stories."

"Masotote claims he's *told* things—but Jay's the one with the visions. He's the prophet." Raizu's words were filled with a strange urgency.

"So?"

"*So*, Masotote has the people's opinion on his side because of what he knows. He brings them knowledge, they let him rule over them." Raizu's feet snapped harder against the stones; they were walking faster again. "But what if it's not his knowledge at all?"

"What do you mean?"

"What if it's Jay's?"

Majest nearly tripped. "What if what's Jay's?" He heard the incredulity flood his words. "Everything Masotote knows and uses to gain his respect and power? Raizy, that's a little far-fetched, don't you think? Why would Jay give him his knowledge for that?"

Raizu did not respond, and Majest realized they were at the top of a slow-winding path, in front of a house that loomed over them with disapproving eyes for windows, a door poised like an open-mouthed yawn of indifference. For the first time, Raizu was paused, and he gestured to Majest, like he had come all this way just to realize he was afraid to take one last step.

And so Majest knocked, still staring at Raizu and hearing his words replayed against the front of his mind. Raizu always seemed to see what no one else could, uncover the truth simply by shining his light. Never in all his life could Majest have pieced together what came so naturally to the boy with the arrows.

Despite the fact that night had crawled to seat itself firmly over the town, Jay was clearly still awake, for his voice called through the door, scratchy with exhaustion. "You know, some people sleep at this hour! Go away, whoever you are!"

"We have to talk to you," Majest answered, leaning close to the door until he was nearly close enough to catch his nose on the splinters.

"Is that you, idiot Skylark? You are the absolute last person on this earth I want to not see right now. Leave me alone."

"It's about Masotote," Majest insisted, and he finally found himself reciprocating Raizu's exigency. "Look, I'm not your biggest fan, either—"

"I said no," Jay snapped, and his voice sounded closer.

Majest scowled. "You know, there's a demon on the loose! What if we had life-saving information on what to do and you're just turning us away?"

"*Do* you?"

"Well, no, but—"

Raizu cut him off, slid his hand up to Majest's shoulder and stepped forward. "Jay," he tried, and his voice was yielding but firm. "This is Raizu. We don't have any new information on the...*possessions*, but this is really important. It's not some new Messenger drama—it's about you." A beat; Raizu nibbled his lip, then, "Can I come in?"

To Majest's utter amazement, the door swung open immediately, as though Jay had been standing behind it this entire time. He was rumpled and dressed in an off-white shirt much too long for him, some of his hair sticking straight into the air with a static that crackled like the electricity in his expression. He did not say a word for a long moment, seeming to gather his thoughts.

"Well?" Majest prompted, crossing his arms.

There was instantly an icy glare upon him. "Your friend can come in," he said. "He's alright. I'd talk to him, but that's not saying much."

"Excuse me?" Majest demanded.

"Only him, though," Jay noted with a dryness to his tone. "It's too late for me to listen to a whiny Skylark."

"You've got to be kidding me." Majest whirled to Raizu, but Raizu only shrugged, and moved closer to the door with eyes that seemed to take up his entire face.

"I'll talk," Raizu murmured, and gave Majest a smile that tried to be reassuring. "I'll be right back, alright?"

"Sure." Majest returned the smile, but then his eyes fell to Jay, and he was glowering again. "But the next time we need you, don't expect I'll stand here and let you shut me out in the cold like I'm some sort of stray animal!"

Jay snickered, but there was no smile in it. "Please. No one really *needs* me, do they?"

Without Majest at his side, there was a cold emptiness to Raizu's left and right, and being here alone with this stranger and his temper like a tempest had each last one of his nerves standing high at attention. The house was dark, too dark to see a thing—though, Raizu figured, there was really no point to Jay turning on a light when he was alone, was there? He did not need it.

Raizu had always been used to traveling alone into danger, and yet, being here now had him wishing with an irrational desperation that Majest had been permitted to come, too, so that he would not have to go this one by himself.

They had been walking, somewhere amongst black forms and shadows, but Raizu realized now that Jay had stopped, and it took a great deal of effort to refrain from barreling into him in all his nervous forward tumbling.

If Jay had noticed Raizu's anxiety and near-accident, he did not say a word of it. He simply stopped right there at the abrupt spot in the hall, turned on Raizu, and propped his weight up on one hip in a sudden gesture that made Raizu jump.

"So what is it?" Jay asked. Raizu had already cringed in the anticipation of a brutal snap, but Jay's voice was lighter now, not the grating rudeness Raizu had come to expect. He could see Jay's full outline now, with the faint starlight, and his face was blank and open—almost relaxed. "About Masotote, right? I stopped by his place this afternoon, told him about what's been happening."

"R-right," Raizu said, and could not hide his shock at the sudden affability. "That's why I'm here, actually." He told himself to calm down—Jay would not hurt him; Jay was standing with his head slightly cocked to one side, his former hostility wiped clean away. "Do you...know him well? He said you were from the same village."

Jay stiffened, and Raizu feared at once he had overstepped. The boy's lips pursed with a certain deliberation, something chastising itself, and then slowly, muscle by muscle, his body relaxed itself once again, as if he had determined Raizu was not a threat. "Sort of," he hedged. "I mean, he was passing through my village around the time—" He paused hastily, something flashing across his face with the fleetingness of lightning. "Well, the time I was escaping from my house."

Raizu blinked at him in the low light, and no words came from his throat.

"Masotote offered to take me across the Bay," Jay continued. "He was on his way back to the island after a brief vacation to explore, and he found me alone in the snow. He brought me here. Saved my life, probably—imagine some dumb blind kid trying to crawl his way through a Cognito winter alone." Jay gave one short peal of laughter.

And Raizu imagined; he saw Jay even smaller and colder, white fingers like icicles griping onto Vosile Masotote with a desperation only a child could have—the fear of being left alone, of being lost in the big white world before him. Jay must have been like every other child, no matter his secrets and tragedies, shrunken-in and lonely and fearing, the way Raizu had always been.

Even in front of him now, Jay was so tiny, so young in the planes of his cheeks and the curves under his eyes. He was still that blind kid crawling, and Raizu could hardly believe Jay was opening that knowledge up for Inertia-born Raizu Capricorn of all people to see—a perfect stranger.

"So," Raizu started up again, and licked at dry lips, pursing his thoughts. "You're friends then, aren't you? If he saved you like that."

Jay shrugged, the mountain-peaks of his shoulders bobbing to the sky and down again. "I suppose. I mean, I'm not really known for having friends, but he's the only one who seems to believe in my prophecies, so I don't have too many others to talk to."

Raizu's focus perked up. "Do you tell him about all your dreams?"

"More or less. He always seems to know how to interpret them, put them to their best use." Jay sounded uninterested, but this was exactly what Raizu wanted to hear.

"Jay," he said, and he knew he could have stood here all night, dancing around the subject with a refusal to unclamp it from the insides of his lips, but Majest was waiting outside with his scarf flipping in the cold, and Raizu could do nothing but come forward and say it. "Maji and I were just talking to Masotote—we found evidence of a polar bear that might be in the same condition as Vari."

"Really?" Jay's interest seamed to crest.

Raizu took a gulping breath. "Yes, but, you see—I mean, um, you don't *see*, sorry—um—well, Masotote told us almost word for word what you said earlier about demons, how they are, how they're summoned."

Jay looked almost amused, eyebrows quirking. "Like I said, Raizu, I tell him what I know. It's not my fault if he can't come up with a non-plagiarizing way to repeat it to others."

"I know," said Raizu, and tried not to let his face heat with embarrassment. "But he passed it off as something he had learned himself, something he didn't even give you credit for, and it got me thinking: what if this is something he does often?"

Jay's bemused expression paused, faded back into something somber that stretched on for miles behind his eyes. "What do you mean?" he asked cautiously.

"I think he's been using your information to gain the favor of the town," Raizu confessed. "That your prophecies, your experience, whatever it may be, are giving him the knowledge he needs to prove to the village he should be leading them. He's wielding your words like a weapon—the village would follow him through anything, grant him any of his wildest dreams, because he says he has the gods' favor. But every bit of it is a lie."

The speech seemed to jostle Jay from whatever faraway place he usually dwelled in, and a realness flashed in his eyes that gave him the illusion of staring Raizu right in the face. For a moment, Raizu was afraid he would lash out in denial or anger, but it was as if he crumpled in on himself all at once, betrayal creaking every muscle in his body to life.

"He's doing *what?*" Jay demanded, and disbelieving hurt painted dark lines between his brows. "You're not serious, are you? Is that really what you think?"

Raizu nodded somberly, then remembered it would go unseen, and rasped out a reply. "I do, but, that's just it; it's just a thought— maybe I'm just being stupid, over-thinking things—"

"No, you sounded confident there for a second," Jay persisted, with a sort of whining desperation that rang bells of misery in Raizu's ears. "And I don't think there's an otherwise confident bone in your body." He sounded as if his one pillar of support had been knocked out from under him, and Raizu wished he were better at catching people when they fell.

"If it's true, you deserve better," Raizu said all the same. "You're not like me, I don't think—you wouldn't sit by if someone's taking advantage of you, would you?"

"You don't know a thing about me," Jay noted blankly, but for once, all his walls seemed to be down. "And you don't know a thing about Masotote, either—he *wouldn't.*" His expression could have been used as a definition for misery. "But all the same, here you are—how could I not have seen this in any dream?"

"We can figure this out together…if you come back with us?" said Raizu meekly, and he wondered if there was any hope in attempting a comforting tone.

"Together?" Jay gave a startled perk of his chin, meeting Raizu at eye level. The word rolled off his tongue in confusion, as though he had never heard it before.

"Right." Raizu leaned forward, and he could no longer decipher anything in the turmoil of Jay's face. "Together we'll talk to Masotote, and together we'll figure out how to destroy whatever lies in the shadows, with or without him. Alright?"

There was a long, startled pause between the two of them, as though their worlds were suddenly shifting closer on their orbits, sliding toward each other in a gentle slope. There was something there, some understanding that flickered on and off in their eyes, as if they both were surprised at themselves and the stranger standing oppositely before them, but not a word more was spoken.

Just as Raizu was beginning to believe Jay was swinging back into his world's shadow, losing grasp on the notion of camaraderie altogether, at last, he nodded, and the air between them collided.

XXII. TRICK

Majest did not ask either Jay or Raizu what had been passed between them behind the splintered door—even as they fumbled back into Masotote's dusty bedroom, he did not dare demand an explanation. He could sense there was some newfound connection sparking between the two of them, some unlikely friendship beginning to piece together, and though Majest was admittedly the slightest bit miffed and the slightest bit jealous, he would not break the links of their new chain, not even with his voice.

Still, he kept shooting dagger glares into the side of Jay's head that he hoped the other boy could feel, even sightlessly, and shifted minutely closer to Raizu across the wooden space of the room. Raizu caught his eye and smiled, and Majest knew whatever he and Jay had discovered, it was big.

Masotote's gaze was trickling back over each of them with a syrupy stickiness, with the fed-up dejection of someone who had hoped his unwanted guests would not return—and surely would not bring another with them.

"More of this?" he croaked, and his tone was bitter, for this time, he had not invited any of them inside; their filing in had been of their own determined accord. "You've passed on your polar bear fairytale, what else do you want?" Then stony eyes snapped to Jay with a softness that implied a higher understanding between them. "And now you're wasting our prophet's time, too? My apologies, Jay."

Jay did not respond, and in fact turned his head away with a clench of his teeth. He was shivering slightly under his thin jacket,

322

and Majest realized for the first time that the top of his ruffled head only came up to just below Majest's shoulder.

"Before, you said you get told certain things by the gods," Raizu began, and his voice held a startling clarity. "So does Jay, which is why I decided to check in with him."

Masotote's eyes on Jay narrowed, and his chin jerked upward. "Of course," he said, a challenge to the words. "The gods look down kindly upon both of us."

Jay exhaled loudly through his nose.

"I don't think that's true," Raizu shot back, and Majest watched in amazement the way he met the challenge head-on, lip barely bothering to tremble.

"Oh?" Masotote didn't take his eyes off Jay, and they were beginning to look almost accusatory, weapons pointed in offense.

"Jay's the one who's a prophet," Raizu continued, and Majest's heart leapt—was he finally starting to believe? "Everything you know about demons and the old world comes from him. And you might know plenty, but Jay knows more—because he's been telling you his dreams since you first picked him up out of the snow."

Majest's jaw went slack.

Vosile merely laughed, a cruel, dry sound. "You're in way over your head, boy. Jay, won't you tell him he's got it all wrong?" That was an order, not a request. "Certainly there is nothing wrong with a sharing of intellect between two of the gods' chosen—these children are being ridiculous, right?"

"Are they, though?" Jay lifted his head, and there was fire in his eyes; though they were a milky blind, flames leapt in high towers between the lifeless blues. "Because I have to say, it would be awfully convenient if you realized when you met me that the gods' words bump around in my head sometimes, and decided to use those words to your advantage."

"Come now, Jay," Masotote drawled, and from inside his mountain of blankets, an extended hand slunk out. "What on earth would possess me to do that, when the gods' words fall inside of me, too?"

"Because they don't," deadpanned Jay, and though Majest had

seen him livid before, this was a personal sort of ire, the face not of an insolent child, but of a boy who had been wronged. "You always told me you would put my warnings to good use—not steal them in order to make the village worship you and your stories even more than they already did."

Masotote's face twisted like a screw. "You'd make accusations like that against the man who saved your life?"

"No, but I'd certainly make them against the man who *used me,*" Jay cried, and his voice was a steady, ripping current. "You caught me under your lies just like everyone else! I thought if I let you interpret my dreams, I would be helping the village, not fueling your lazy treachery!"

"You can't prove anything," Vosile hissed, and he was trying to sit up properly, to stand, but he didn't seem to have the energy. "I've always been chosen, long before any of you were born—I created this village, planted the grass beneath your feet, dug the canal that runs the fountain—"

"Is that why you can't get out of bed?" asked Majest, and he was starting to catch on. "Because you're so *tired* from the effort? I don't believe that, either. Before Jay, you might have been the leader, but you weren't their god, not yet—but Sedona said you came back from your travels a few years ago with some new god-sent knowledge that made everyone trust your word above even their own heart. Everything lines up, if you've known about Jay's dreams for that long. You'd have the perfect opportunity to convince everyone you'd been suddenly chosen by the gods, and anyone who doubted you as their leader or creator would have been stifled on the spot—and so you let them pamper you until you became little more than a loaf of bread spitting out false truths."

Masotote's mouth hardened into a thin, wrinkled line.

"No wonder I never knew," Jay hissed. "I thought you had always been giving the village advice like that—I just thought I was giving you some extra little tidbits."

"You knew no one would listen to a reclusive child prophet, so you took every last one of his stories for yourself," Raizu added. "The villagers trusted you, as the one who founded Hi Ding—

they'd never suspect you of lying, and neither did Jay. And now you've tricked them all into believing you're wise as the gods—but it's really not you who's the wise one, is it?"

Still, Masotote said nothing, and Majest knew Raizu was right.

"Did you even build the village at all, or was it like this when you came here, left over from the old world?" Majest pressed, and all at once, the island's illusion seemed to shatter into millions of knife-sharp fragments. "I assume you were never there, either. You probably stumbled into this place after the End and brought people here just like you did with Jay, claiming every building, every invention, every stone path and tree as your own. Has *anything* you've ever told the village been true?"

"Every lie stems off a seed of truth," Jay muttered.

Masotote's face broke, splitting down its lines. "The Organization," he said.

"What about them?" asked Majest darkly.

"Jay told me of their plans. To rid the world of the elemental Powers." Vosile's voice was cracked, eyes pleading and pathetic. "I really am trying to help you; that's the truth, as it always has been. In the village where I first met Jay, there was dark magic like the demon that possessed Vari. I believe your sister Lunesta has found the same energy and sent it after you."

Majest blinked, shock freezing his anger. "You think Lunesta and her Organization are responsible for the possessions?" Then he whirled on Jay. "And you knew about the Organization all along, too? You couldn't have bothered to tell us? Heavens know *you* weren't denying us that information to 'keep us safe,' so why did you?"

"I assumed Masotote told you," Jay snapped, with a certain reluctance, as though he knew he was expected to partake in the new topic of conversation, but had no desire to. His arms were folded; only a faint burning remained in his eyes. "As for your sister's relationship to the demon, it's common sense, so forgive me for not letting you know. It'd be like letting you know water is wet."

"The chances of a demonic force appearing from nowhere

and targeting one island out of thousands are slim to none," said Masotote, and confidence was rising back into his voice at the lack of opposition. "This one wants something. So does the Organization: among other things, it wants you, Skylark, you and your younger sister. And it can't track the two of you, so perhaps it sent out something that can."

"The demon," said Majest, though his voice was coated thickly with suspicion. "Alright, sure, I'll give you two that. But why attack Vari and a *polar bear* if Letty and I are right here?" He could hear his own agitation as his voice rose in pitch, peaking up like the slope of a mountain. "That doesn't make any sense. The demon is free to take me and go if it'll save the land—so why hasn't it?"

"There is a reason."

"Of course there is," Majest snapped. "What is it?"

"I think you'll find there to be a similar variable in the case of Vari Nyght and the case of your bear."

Majest slammed his foot on the ground. "Then do the one thing you're good at and use what Jay's given you and *tell us!* This is *your* village at risk! Don't you care at all for the people you've spent your life lying to? Or was that just a lie in itself?"

Raizu tapped Jay on the shoulder. "Do you know?" he asked quietly.

"No," Jay said, and he sounded as surprised as Majest did at the word that came out of him. "No, I don't. I don't know anything more than what I've already told you."

Vosile snickered. "You see, children, I am still the wisest. Only I solved this mystery."

Majest didn't move, only clenched his jaw. "Then tell us," he repeated thickly.

"Alright, alright." Vosile sighed, hands lifting in surrender before they flopped unceremoniously back onto to the bed. "The demon can only attack in pure darkness."

Majest blinked, and Raizu shifted anxiously beside him. "Is that all? Are you sure?"

Vosile glared at him with what little dignity he had left. "Darkness," he said after a while. "The garden of Quell and

Idyllice Souleia is underground in its entirely, which would place it in utter darkness if not for the lanterns." He licked dry, cracked lips. "When Vari stepped into the cavern in the wall, there was no more light. He blocked it all out with his body, covering the cracks and submerging him into a world pitch-black." His eyes darkened again, and he tried to scowl. "Is that not when the demon took him in its claws?"

"That doesn't make sense," said Raizu immediately. Majest expected a comment on the impossibility of demons, but Raizu only added, "Last night, the whole forest was dark. We should've been easy targets. But it went after a bear."

"What he said." Majest nodded, and touched Raizu's arm for reassurance. "If the demon wants Messengers, it should have taken me last night instead."

Vosile looked at him as if he were an idiot. "Night is never without its starry candle. There is always the moon and always starlight, even hidden behind clouds. It brings light to the birds, the trees, the ripples in the water. If the bear's slumber was in a deep enough cavern, the moon would not have reached it. That would have given our demon an opportunity."

Majest, with reluctance, nodded slowly, something acidic on his tongue. "I suppose."

"At last, our brave Messenger understands what comes so easily to those gifted with a higher understanding," Masotote sighed.

Majest frowned hard at him. "No thanks to your lying help."

"Well, at least you can't accuse me of not knowing how the demon attacks," Jay muttered, and he looked utterly defeated. "Everything's pure darkness to me."

"But now, we have motive, means, *and* opportunity," Raizu cut in. "My brother says that validates any theory." As three faces turned to him, he ducked meekly away and scuffed the floor with his boot.

"So you finally believe this?" Majest asked him, forcing the spite from his voice and replacing it with something gentler. "Demons and all?"

Raizu bit his lip. "Not necessarily. But whatever is out there certainly has lethal power."

Vosile cleared his throat, eyes narrowed. "That's all fine and well, but now you've got to do something about it. I've told you all I know. It's up to you to get rid of the presence. I suggest you train the villagers, or devise a trap, or—"

"Hold on." Majest felt his eyes widen again, his blood reheat. "You're asking us to go kill the demon for you? All this dancing around the truth and now you're going to sit back and watch while the villagers risk their lives?"

"You're doing exactly what we accused you of," said Jay with a lifeless rage, and Majest realized it was the first time he had addressed the three of them as a group. "You're taking what I told you about demons and using it to boss even the newest, most clueless members of this village around. Right in front of me, too, like you think I'm *that* blind enough to not notice."

"I can't fight," said Vosile plainly. "I'd be of no use."

"I can't either, but at least I'm trying to help," Raizu cut in. "I'll play my part in all of this."

"And he's not even from this village," Majest snarled, voice whipping and lashing. "You're a selfish monster, Vosile Masotote. We uncover your treachery, and now you want us to go off and destroy some unknown force at your request—and then what? You'll take credit for that too, while you lie here stagnant and useless?"

Raizu stepped forward. "Maji—"

"I swear," Majest spat, giving no one time to interrupt, "I will put an end to this. All of it. I'll destroy the demon with my own two hands and wipe the last of that crooked smile off your face. But first, I'll tell everyone what a liar you are and you'll be thrown out to the wolves like the power-hungry fox you are."

Masotote tilted his head. "I've never done anything but help our village grow. They will have no reason to hurt me—they know the truth. I am the wisest; I am their creator."

"That's what you tell them," Majest snarled, and turned away. "That's what you tell Vari and Sedona and everyone else. But even if this village might be filled with helpful, decent people like them, there are still those like you. Those greedier than squirrels in the winter time—biting and begging for attention and worship like little demons themselves."

To Majest's surprise, Vosile laughed at that, and it was a croak like a tree swaying beneath the bends of a storm, a harsh crack around the room. "You know, I like you, Skylark," he said. "You've got a lot to learn and you might be a fool, but you know who you are and that's character, that is." The laughter died, and the growling returned. "Now off the three of you go. I could lie and say it was a pleasure speaking with you, but I need my rest."

"I don't even get an apology?" Jay wondered aloud. "Not from the man who used me?"

"Not from the man who saved you," Vosile returned smoothly.

Jay lifted his chin with an immediate snap, as if he had already expected such an answer. He did not reply, did not acknowledge the man before him. Instead, in one neat motion, he stepped between Majest and Raizu, and he fit neatly there, surrounded by their bright shadows and shapes. "Come on, then, both of you," he said. "It's way past our bedtimes."

With that, Majest was cut off from anything he might have snarled to Masotote, stopped right at his roots, and he was towed from the house before he could utter another word about liars or demons.

Words could not stop those monsters, anyway.

The room was dimly lit with the sterile glow of electricity flickering in bored, hazy tiger-stripes across the ceiling, its stolen magic reflecting the light of an equally-stolen screen as Lunesta Skylark squinted at it—squinted and waited.

She was good at waiting. That was her talent, her forte—Chami and Shayming were precise, Caiter was efficient, Shatter was intuitive, but Lunesta was patient.

The screen blinked, and Lunesta's eyes bored into it until her vision was white and blotchy with pixilated monotony. How long had it been? An hour? Two?

She shifted in her plastic chair and it squeaked against the floor. The sound made her flinch, but her gaze did not falter. Her narrowed, dark eyes missed nothing, and she would not let them skip a beat, lose even a blink's worth of information. The second she tore her eyes away would be the second she needed not to miss.

Too preoccupied to think of much else, Lunesta did not notice the sudden rumbling protest of an empty stomach, or the way two heavy eyelids drooped down. She snapped them open in mindless insistence. She would not break focus.

"Lady President!" The voice came from outside the room, its high pitch straining. "We desperately need to speak to you!"

Shayming, Lunesta noted absently. She and her sister had been floating around for two days since they'd returned from their mission—waiting for instructions Lunesta did not have. She wanted nothing to do with them, with anyone, with anything but the screen.

Success came through the blinking lights and sounds of this sole object, and—as far as Lunesta was concerned—everything else could burn to the ground as long as it remained.

Lunesta did not answer the voice, did not even twitch a finger in Shayming's direction, so the psychic spoke again, with a voice that could have fragmented glass. "You haven't left your room in nearly two days! Come on and stretch your legs; come talk to us!"

"No," Lunesta muttered, hearing her voice dry and devoid of substance. "Stretching out your legs is for those who go on missions, like you. This is my mission. I must stay here."

"Ever since we restored that computer, it's been nothing but a burden on your health," Shayming noted, tone just as dry as Lunesta's but with twice the fervor. "Mental health, physical health—social health."

"I'm fine," said Lunesta distractedly.

"Whether you stare at it or not, it's going to stay the same. Has there been a change all day?"

"I'm still seeing to the calibration," replied Lunesta, gaze not shifting.

"I thought it was working just fine when we started it back up?"

"It is," snapped Lunesta, suddenly defensive. "After Caiter's tip, I find that it is of the utmost importance to learn the whereabouts of this...of this presence. If something goes wrong, you or the scientists will help me. This is our top priority right now."

"Honestly, I don't know what these scientists of yours are still doing unsupervised, after what happened," chirped a new voice—Chami's.

"Mm," said Lunesta, who had gone back to all but ignoring the twins.

Chami continued, executing a heavy, dramatic sigh that rang like metal chimes. "Malory nearly ruined everything we've worked for by injecting that boy the way he did. What if the demon had destroyed the laboratory? That's half of our old-world technology right there!"

"I don't *know*, Chami," said Lunesta, growing impatient. "Everyone seems to be telling me the same thing over and over until they're blue in the face—*Malory almost ruined us. Ohanzi could have destroyed the entire facility. Harnessing demon energy was a horrible idea.* But this screen in front of me seems to be saying the exact opposite."

"The screen's giving you results?" Chami's voice spiked up an octave.

Shayming ignored her sister. "You still believe Ohanzi could find the Skylarks? That's nonsense."

Lunesta did not respond.

"Are you forgetting the lack of credibility your sources hold?" Shayming demanded, a catlike rumble in her throat. "Are you going to trust the madman in his glass box and whatever nonsense he spills about the Skylarks on an island? If Ohanzi thought he knew something of such magnitude, he would have said so while he was still human."

"I don't trust Malory anymore. I trust Caiter." Lunesta heard her voice grow stubborn, superiority bleeding into it with a tone that made her sit up taller by reflex. "Caiter says Ohanzi had his theories about the Skylarks, and if Caiter thinks that might be a lead, then it's worth setting up a demon tracker for."

"That still places trust in Ohanzi—he was just a boy," put in Shayming.

"But it also explains how Seti lost the Skylarks at the Bay," whispered Chami. "If the Skylarks cut across the water, they could be anywhere. Ohanzi was beginning to narrow down the possibilities."

Seti's name hitting a chord hard enough to break her ceaseless scrutinizing, Lunesta cast a wary glance to the back of the room, a long black fabric covering a glass box.

"Seti," Shayming repeated, voice trembling.

Lunesta ignored her. The twins had been trying to pry Seti's fate from her grasp ever since he had disappeared, but she wouldn't let them have it. Not when she was still uncertain what Seti's fate meant for the Organization's future.

And so the twins did not ask, not to Lunesta's face. She was the President. What she said—or didn't say—was law.

"Perhaps since Seti was unable to continue his tracking, his loss of the Skylarks was due to cunning on their part and wasn't his fault at all," said Chami, her words creeping with care around her true question. Lunesta could almost hear her thoughts crying out from behind her eyes, pounding at the wrinkles on her forehead in desperation.

Each and every thought was the same. *"Where is Seti?"*

"Seti was punished not only for failing to *track* the Skylarks, but for failing to *kill* them," said Lunesta in reply, smashing the wall of ice Chami had built around the subject. She didn't have to tell them anything. "I would imagine he had plenty of opportunities before reaching the Hudson Bay. And yet he still failed. Failure is not accepted in these halls."

The twins fell silent as ash.

Lunesta cleared her throat. "So, is there something you two wanted? If you came in here just to rant aimlessly about Malory and Seti and how incompetent the workers—sans yourselves—are performing their duties, I regret to say you can just go and—"

"My lady," said Shayming softly, and Lunesta knew her eyes were flickering dark, though she did not raise her gaze to meet them. "You simply seemed sad. You won't leave your room, won't even spare us a glance. Why are you content to sit and stare at nothingness? What do you hope to find?"

"I *have* found," replied Lunesta. "Come inside and look at this."

She clicked a button on the underside of her chair and heard the door roll open behind her. Two light pairs of footsteps followed, and before long, the twins were hovering over each shoulder with a conscience-like presence.

"*That's* the screen?" Chami wrinkled her nose at the blinking box. An expanse of jade pixels greeted her eyes, mixed and matched with shades of water and sky.

"This is Ohanzi," corrected Lunesta, and she watched with a smirk as four cat eyes found the blinking dot at the top of the screen, prominent and proud. It was blood-red.

Chami's eyes lit at once, bright as the flickering greens before her. "You found him."

"I did," crowed Lunesta. "Well, we can't know for certain there isn't some other maniac in the woods setting demonic creations free, but I'd say it's a fairly solid conclusion."

"Wow." Even Shayming sounded impressed. "I know we did a perfect job of restoring the tracking device once more—but I can't believe it actually worked."

"Of course it *worked*," snapped Lunesta, crossing her arms like branches and swiveling in her chair to stare the twins down. "Caiter and Malory believe Ohanzi could find the Skylarks, and it's my duty to see that their hypothesis is explored."

"Except you're not exploring anything," said Chami, voice drooping as she pointed to the screen. "Can you even tell where he is? Northern Cognito, by the looks of it, but the map doesn't get any more specific. There's still no proof of an island—or that the Skylarks are anywhere near that red dot at all."

"I don't know anything for certain." Lunesta gritted her teeth, and debated reprimanding them for their defiance. "I know what Caiter told me and what I see on the screen in front of me. We'll just have to hope Ohanzi proves himself useful until someone comes up with a better idea of what to do in the meantime."

"A better idea?" repeated Shayming. "Like what?"

"You haven't given anyone any better ideas," added Chami in a quiet voice.

"Your mission, for instance," Lunesta snapped. "The one I sent you on—the one you returned from without even coming to see me. How did that go?"

Chami and Shayming exchanged a glance, faces shedding their uncertainty like snakeskin. Now their catlike smiles were secretive, glinting in a delighted purr. "We came across someone," they said in unison. "She wants to meet with you, and she'll be here soon."

"Oh?" Lunesta felt a grin spread across her face. Behind her, the screen flashed, red dot crawling along as she looked the other way. "Excellent."

XXIII. INSTRUCTION

"You're still not going to tell me where the two of you were?" Letty made a face, pouring herself another cup filled precariously with market tea. "You went for the night hunt after all, I presume? Did you catch anything? Find anything interesting?"

Majest and Raizu, sitting across the table and still wearing yesterday's clothes, shared a conspiring look that made Letty's hands slide instinctively to her hips.

"Nothing much," Raizu muttered. He was looking a bit flushed, and Letty knew he was lying—and that he was quite possibly the world's worst liar, at that.

Majest picked up for him smoothly. "It's almost embarrassing how boring it was," he offered.

Letty wasn't convinced. "It's a deserted forest on an island. There must have been *something* you two could find to do out there."

Raizu turned even redder. "Nope," he said, his voice squeaking with a rabbit-like frequency. "Not really."

At that, Majest put his head in his hands.

"Look, if you were out there and found something I should know about, you'd best tell me," Letty tried, lifting her eyebrows to stare the two boys down. "I don't like not knowing things. You're familiar with my incessant need to have any and all secrets shared with me the second I find out there's something I don't know, right?"

"Yes, Letty, and I've been given the silent treatment for days because of it," said Majest, exhaling in a sigh. He exchanged another glance with Raizu. "We went to see Masotote, alright?"

"Oh." Letty was a bit disappointed, thoughts of mystery and magic dashed. But still, she was curious. "Really? That late at night? What were you talking to him for?"

"We went to see him about Vari's incident," said Raizu, and took a sip of steaming tea.

"That's right." Majest put his own mug to his lips, though his sip was more like a gulp. "And he said the demon can only do its thing in complete darkness—no sunlight, moonlight, or anything. That's why Vari and the b—" He broke off, caught himself. "That's why *Vari* was possessed as he was. There was no light in the garden cavern after he covered it with his body."

Letty quirked an eyebrow, not missing the hesitation. "Is that so?"

"It's still not necessarily a *demon* force," muttered Raizu into his cup, generating an eye roll from Majest and a hint of a smile from Letty. She wondered what it would take to convince him there was more to life than what there was logic for.

"Whatever it was, I suppose that's a reasonable enough explanation," said Letty with a nod, though she still got the feeling there was something crucial her brother was making an effort to sweep out of his story. "How did he figure that out?"

"He knows a lot about these types of things," replied Raizu before Majest, making a face, could say anything. "Like Jay."

When he finished, Majest growled, "Yeah, a *lot* like Jay."

Letty blinked. "What do you mean?"

Majest looked at Raizu. "Do you want to tell her?"

Raizu shrugged. "You can tell her."

"Tell me *what?*" Letty cut in.

"That this village is built on a foundation of lies," Majest deadpanned, and now he was glowering. "The foundation being none other than 'village hero' Vosile Masotote. He's been getting all of his information about demons and the old world from Jay and using it to make the village think he's like the gods—or at least, that he can speak to them."

Letty's head spun. "Why on earth would he do that?"

"He saw a chance to put himself in control. Now the whole village is content to revere him, while he lies around in bed, wasting food and oxygen. Clever plan, actually—if it weren't so disgusting."

At that, the veil of secrecy slipped away all at once, and Letty found herself wrapped in a furious recount of the previous night, Majest's fists clenched against the table and Raizu's thoughtful notes easing some of the tension from the frame of his face. Their back-and-forth storytelling should have been an overwhelming banter, but their voices were a neat transition from one to the other, as if Letty were turning between two facets of the same boy, absorbing their words with an easy understanding.

When it was over, Letty shook herself. "You know, that makes sense at the same time it doesn't—why would Jay tell Masotote everything he knew in the first place? Jay doesn't seem to like telling anyone anything that doesn't have to do with leaving him alone."

"When no one else will listen, I guess you get desperate," said Raizu with a shrug. "He kept making it sound like he had no one else in the whole world to talk to."

"But—"

"*Anyway,*" Majest interrupted, clearly sick of the topic, "like I said, the greedy fraud told us the demon can only attack in darkness, and now he wants us to go out and destroy it while he sits back and takes the credit. What do you make of that?"

"I think it's an incredible honor," Raizu mumbled, grinning into his mug.

"It's not *funny,*" Majest insisted, thwacking his friend with a banana peel. "I don't feel honored. I feel tricked and deceived—and most importantly, bossed around. Who's this hideous liar to tell me what to do? I don't know the first thing about hunting demons!"

Letty sighed. "You can't *not* help the village," she noted. "You already told Masotote you were going to do it."

"I know," replied Majest. "I'm going to see that the demon energy is destroyed. But not for *him*, for *us*. For the village."

Letty put her head in her hands. "Alright, so what can we do to help?"

Majest stared blankly at her. "You're not going after the demon, Letty. You don't know how to fight, and you can't use your power. I don't want you getting hurt." His gaze shifted. "And Raizy…"

"I'm completely, utterly useless," Raizu said, half-smiling. "Yes, I know."

"That's *not* what I was going to say," Majest protested, looking mildly horrified. "I only meant you'd be too busy worrying about a logical way to keep everyone else safe to protect yourself if something went wrong."

"That's true," Letty put in. "When we were traveling together, all you did was sacrifice your own time and food. Then you almost died bringing us news of the Organization." She grinned. "Thanks, but why don't you look after yourself for a change?"

"I *do*," protested Raizu. "Every day, I'm worrying about myself—it's pretty selfish, actually!"

"The point is, neither of you are in any shape to take on something like this," Majest concluded over Raizu's flustered babbling. "And neither am I, for that matter, but that can't be helped."

"We have to be prepared before we try anything," said Raizu, eyes huge and stuck on Majest's face.

"How?" Letty asked. "And what about the rest of the village?"

"Masotote did tell you to get *everyone* ready," Raizu told Majest.

Majest leaned back in his chair with a hollow creak, arms folded. "I think the first step to getting everyone ready is to tell them the truth," he noted. "About Masotote, and the demon—they have to know if they're going to be safe, especially if anyone plans on wandering around their house without any lights on or windows open."

"You want us to round up the entire town so you can talk their ears off?" asked Letty, doubtful. "They're hardly going to listen to some child they don't know telling them what they don't want to hear, not if they respect Masotote so much."

"They will," said Majest, voice dripping with confidence, and Letty waited for further argument, but Majest looked as if he could fly up to the sun on nothing more convincing than his own optimism.

Letty turned toward Raizu, seeking words that would tie Majest's feet back to the ground.

But instead of an objection, Raizu just shrugged meekly. "What's there to lose? The village should be prepared." He blinked shyly at Majest. "And I can't think of anyone better to tell them how."

Majest tossed him a grin.

Letty made an exasperated noise. "Am I the only sane one in this house?"

"If whatever attacked Vari and that bear is coming after you, everyone needs to be on their guard to keep you and themselves safe," Raizu said.

Letty knew she probably should have felt a crushing sense of fear at the words, the implications of how far Lunesta was willing to go to see her fall, but she merely sighed. "Right. At least this means that if we kill the demon, we halt the Organization dead in their path."

"And they must not know for sure where you are," said Raizu, as though making a realization aloud. "If they did, they'd be knocking at the door as we speak, not sending an assailant to track you down."

Like his words had sparked fire to flip an imaginary switch, a slow pounding came from the front room, the urgency clear in its thudded intensity. A knock at the door. Letty and Raizu went still at once; even Majest flinched. For a moment, the room was silent and still as falling snow.

Eventually, Majest shook himself, clearing his throat to break the silence. "I'll get it," he said, and crossed the room.

Letty blinked with a shuddery inhale; Raizu edged backward as though an extra two inches of safety might have saved him from an unknown intruder.

Majest gave them a withering look. "You don't think the Organization is actually standing outside, do you? Honestly. Relax. Maybe the fruit cart finally has a delivery service or something. I could go for some blueberries." He yanked open the door.

"Majest!" The cry rang out as soon as the wind blew back. It was in fact not the Organization, nor any accomplice of theirs—it was Sedona, hair around her face like morning mist. She was smiling though her cheeks were flushed, as if she had been running.

Majest leaned against the opened door. "Good morning to you, too."

Letty stretched up on her tiptoes to see, and twirled a loose string on her shirt between her forefingers. "Is something the matter?"

"No, no, of course not." Sedona shook her head, breaths billowing in hectic clouds around her face. "I have something I needed to tell you."

"Good news, I hope," said Majest.

"No—it's not—" Sedona cut herself off, eyes widening until her face was a sky of blue and white. "It's a dream I had. A dream that I was running through the forest."

She looked to Majest for confirmation, and he blinked. "Um, go on."

"I kept running," Sedona continued. "Running and running—and suddenly, a gust of wind came out of the trees and blew me backwards. I tried to run through it, but it was dragging me down, pulling me with it."

Three blank stares greeted her chattering.

"Do you know what that means?" Sedona prompted.

Majest's eyebrows slowly disappeared into his hair. "That you're nuttier than a tree of acorns? Or maybe it means you shouldn't eat so much soup before bed. Honestly, Sedona—we're sort of in the middle of something. I don't mean to be rude, but is there a point in this?"

Sedona's face fell, breathing slowing. "A dream about *wind*," she said earnestly.

"If wind is her element, maybe her subconscious was trying to tell her something," offered Raizu quietly.

Letty looked from Sedona to Raizu and then over to Majest, still twisting her string.

"Yes, that's it," Sedona insisted, though she didn't even spare

Raizu a glance. Her eyes were on Majest. "It's my wind, my brand new wind; it has to be. So I thought on it for a while, and then realized—in my dream, the wind was holding me back."

"Powers aren't supposed to do that, I don't think," said Majest, though he had started to smile.

"They do if you can't use them." Sedona's voice was firm. "I've got a big enough target painted on my back thanks to the Organization—I don't need to be elementally useless on top of it."

Letty perked up, ears twitching toward the words. She knew only too well what it felt like to be poised just out of reach of the highest, brightest hill atop her mind, connection unstable, uselessness as overwhelming as a night with no stars—the kind of nights where demons of darkness lurked.

"I've been ignoring my power, not taking it seriously," continued Sedona, and she sounded worried. "So I thought of you, Majest. You can use your element like a third arm, and I want to be able to do that." She took a large breath through her nose. "I want you to train me, and get me ready to fight this demon. I want to know everything I can possibly know, do everything I can possibly do."

Letty almost laughed out loud at the irony.

Majest, a few steps away, had a similar chuckle in his gaze. "You know what, Sedona? I think that's a fantastic idea."

Sedona's expression rang with hope. "Really?"

"Really." Majest stepped forward, slung an arm over her shoulder. "Raizy, do you think she's been eavesdropping this entire time?"

Raizu shrugged with a smile. "Sure seems like it."

Sedona was bewildered. "What? Why?"

"We were just about to hold a town meeting," Majest declared loudly. "We want to help you defeat the demon, and we've got new information on it that everyone should know."

"As well as quite a few rude things to say about your leader," Raizu muttered, too low for anyone but Letty to hear.

Letty giggled.

"I could train you especially if you'd like," Majest went on, clearly having heard none of the exchange. "Me, you, and Letty—

when the meeting's over, how about we all work on our powers together?"

"Anything you can do to help me—and the village—would be great," Sedona answered.

"Good." Majest clasped his hands together with a loud noise. He swiveled around to Letty and Raizu, who were still watching him from the table. "Raizy—you come with Sedona and I. We need to find somewhere outside big enough to hold a meeting. Letty, go around to as many houses as you can—skip Masotote, of course—and ask them to come with you."

"Why do I have to be the one running around?" Letty asked of no one in particular.

"Because you're cute, and people will listen to you," Majest said sternly. "Bring anyone and everyone who agrees to the center fountain. I'll take it from there."

"When did you get so bossy?" Letty questioned wryly.

"Trust me," said Majest, spinning to face her, and his eyes were green and earnest. "This will *work*."

"Alright," Letty sighed. She knew he didn't mean to be brusque. "But that's a lot of houses."

"You've got legs," Majest told her. "Feet, too. So what's the problem?" He didn't wait for a response before grinning like a child and leaping out the door.

Letty's feet and legs had broken free of their current and swirled to and fro like water swishing around a circular cup, and she'd splashed her way from house to house until faces began to blur together, rounding up a village full of faceless spectators and friends who had come along for the ride. Majest was impressed.

Sunni and Sedona had come—of course—and so had Quell, Idyllice, and Rapple, though Rapple was too nervous leaving his partner at home with a baby due any day, and would not stay long. Cydinne hadn't wanted to come, but Jay had—Majest didn't think anyone else would have expected him to show up to a meeting like this, but he was not surprised to see the boy's black-clad shape leaning against a tree at the clearing's edge, hair drooping over a lazy blind gaze.

Sedona, though she remained as unsure of Majest's plan as anyone, was giving him the use of a favorite spot of hers: a large, snowy clearing just outside the ring of houses that looped around the fountain. It was exposed but rocky, treeless but surrounded on all sides with evergreen tassels. If lightning flashed, there was no higher figure here to strike than Majest, teetering over the crowd before him on a large stone, hands up and splayed for balance.

Majest found Sedona among the village cluster, at her sister's side. She was already looking at him, and dipped her head when their eyes met, cheeks dusted with red.

Then he realized the villagers were *all* staring at him, suspicion clouding their eyes, restless shuffling in their feet. Majest could sense they did not trust him. Not yet.

"Alright, everyone!" he called.

If there had been a face not turned to his, it whirled in that following second, and then every member of the clearing was staring him down—no greetings, no encouragement, not even a smile.

So Majest smiled at them, and lifted his chin. He reminded himself there were far worse things to fear than a bit of harsh curiosity, than judgment and scorn. He cleared his throat. "You're probably all wondering what in the heavens some young boy of seven birth-years from the mainland could have to say," he said, and let the words sing out from his chest.

Silence greeted him, and Majest saw Raizu try to duck his head into the crowd at their mutinous stares, but Majest thought the villagers looked small from his rocky podium, and he stood up straighter.

"But the truth is, I'm actually closer to eight years by now, so perhaps that will ease some of your worries." He held his gaze steady. "I left my calendar back in my old cabin, so I don't know my birthday for sure, but if you can forgive me that, we should be off to an okay start."

If Majest had thought humor would release the tension in the air, he had thought wrong. The village held its stony composure, beginning to mutter amongst itself. Jay looked—if possible—more irritated than before. Raizu's face held discomfort in each and every line.

Thinking fast, Majest went on, voice rising in harsh pitch, "I made my sister Letty bring you here today because we're all in grave danger. And it's danger I've put you in, whether I meant to or not. That's the first thing."

The muttering died in three dozen throats.

"Second," Majest continued, jaw tightening, "is that your precious leader, Vosile Masotote, is a filthy liar who's been deceiving you for years and has no intents to help save you from danger—from this danger or *any* harm that might come your way."

At that, the silence disrupted itself; wide eyes turned to wide eyes as voices began to shout Majest's way with the uncontrolled clamor of a sudden battleground, swords drawn, armor out. The crowd rolled like an angry sea, hissing and churning.

Majest turned to catch his sister's glare as she shook her head. "Take it slow," she mouthed before her face was covered by another protester.

"You've got some nerve, dragging us out here in the middle of the day to say such things!" called someone suddenly. The voice's owner was tall and lanky, with curling brown-blond hair and eyes of brooding, liquid hazel. "Who even are you, Messenger?"

"Haven't you heard about what happened to Vari?" cried Majest, raising his voice over the rumble of the village. Their gazes whipped back to him like whitecaps. "I know you have. He's not the only victim of this danger, and if you don't hear me out, he won't be the last."

From off to the right side where he stood, Jay raised a hand.

Majest looked to him in surprise. "Uh, yeah, Jay?"

Jay stepped forward warily, and Majest wondered what he was so afraid of, when Majest planned on clearing his name of any doubt. "Just this morning, I had Sharlytte's son Denrick brought in by his sister, Deras. Deras said he'd been pale as a ghost ever since he woke up, and the next thing I know, he's rolling on the floor with all the symptoms—heart rate flying, limbs twitching and flailing, gurgling like a broken fountain. Deras said his eyes were black as night. If that isn't textbook demon possession, I don't know what is."

Majest's eyes widened. He hadn't expected another villager to find themselves victim to the dark so soon. "Alright," he said after a moment, swallowing. "And where Denrick was at the time of his possession?"

"In the dark," said Jay, and he was looking at Majest so intently, Majest wondered if he had suddenly regained his sight for the sole purpose of this silent communication.

"Exactly," Majest called. "See, everyone—we're not safe."

"And I suppose you of all people are going to tell us how to *be* safe?" jeered the hazel-eyed boy.

"I am," Majest called back, voice rough around the edges. "Because I know how the demon possesses its victims. I know how you can stay out of harm's way."

"Stop babbling and get on with it!" called another boy with a snarl.

Majest closed his eyes and took a deep breath, willing patience to pump from his heart and into his veins. "It's the darkness. This demon only can attack when there is no light. When not even the smallest trickling drop of sunlight can reach your skin, *that's* when you're in danger. There was no light in Vari's cavern, and I'll bet there was no light where Denrick slept. It's the dark."

The crowd faltered, each and every face seeming to go numb and fall like an icicle from a rooftop. Silence flickered on and off, and one voice broke through the frigidness of it to call, "How do you know that?"

Majest shifted his feet, hand clenching at his sides. "That leads me to my next point—Masotote."

Another serious of distrustful muttering ensued.

"He's been lying to you," Majest insisted. "About himself, about the village—he never built the village. He's never been to the old world. He hasn't even left his bed in years, has he? He knew about the demon, how it attacked. He knew about the danger

345

my sister and I would bring before we even stepped foot on this island. But he did not tell you. He lied."

"Masotote wouldn't lie," Sedona cut in, breaking her silence with a tight voice and apologetic eyes. "He gave us a home here, a world where we're safe. He loves us. He would never keep anything from us."

"Then explain how I know!" Majest burst out, arms going up in the air. "How do I know about the demon, then, if I don't have an outside source unknowingly giving me all the information I need to manipulate each and every one of you? How does *he* know?"

Sedona's face faltered. "What kind of outside source?"

Majest drew in a deep breath, then turned his gaze back to the boy propped against the tree, who had not moved, who had not dared disturb the stillness of the air around him. "I think there's someone here who can answer that question."

All eyes went curiously to Jay, who stiffened under the pressure of their gazes.

"For every warning you get, for every story you're told, everything Vosile Masotote has ever coated your ears with—it's all Jay's." Majest's eyes were stone, marbled in resolve. "Masotote has been stealing his dreams and his knowledge for years, and he's the one you should be thanking. He's the one who should be looked up to. Er, well, looked down to, I guess." He shrugged an apology.

Jay's embarrassed glare was livid and fire-red.

"Absolutely not," someone spat. "This boy has given us nothing but grief. Is this what he's told you, that he's the true receiver of the gods' word?"

"Lies," another voice agreed. "Maybe he's the one who's been stealing from Masotote. Taking his visions and pretending they're his, so he can play the mysterious, grumpy prophet and try to win our sympathy."

Majest could hardly help but gasp as his pulse took off. "No, that's—"

"How do we know Jay's not the one plotting against us?" a girl cried.

Soon, the village was staring Jay down with eyes like needles, and he was backing further into the tree, protesting, "You don't honestly think I'm in on some kind of elaborate plan to take over the village, do you? I don't care about anything that much."

Sunni shrugged. "I think he's in on it."

"Maybe he's the one who sent the demon," a boy next to her muttered to his friends, and the words sent a chill clambering up Majest's spine. "If he's learned so much about demons from Masotote, he could have summoned one and set it against us so he could take over."

"Wouldn't surprise me," another voice agreed. Majest could not tell where the voices were coming from, but he wished he had the power to drown them out.

"The Organization sent the demon," Majest tried to insist, and he was barely refraining from yelling at his lungs' full potential. "It's not after the village; it's after the Messengers!"

"The demon wants us?" Sedona's brow wrinkled in incredulity.

"The Organization wants us," Majest said. "And if they sent the demon, then it wants us, too."

"Masotote's words, not mine, so don't go saying I've been spreading more lies around," Jay snapped, looking rather ruffled and wide-eyed, and Majest realized what he was so afraid of—the villagers hated him. They would show him no mercy, would not listen to a word in his benefit. That had been Majest's mistake.

Majest felt sick.

"What's the Organization?" called the hazel-eyed boy.

"They're a group led by my elder sister, Lunesta," Majest said, and his heart squeezed. "Specially trained to wipe out those with supernatural powers. People like me. Letty. Sedona. The Powers. *Messengers.* They've sent the demon to kill us. It's our fault—my fault for bringing Letty here. And so I'm going to kill it, because no one else will. I won't let Masotote take the glory for anyone any longer."

This time, the village merely looked at one another.

Jay stepped forward in their momentary pause, eyes flat and flinty. "I think you're done here, Skylark."

Majest wrinkled his nose. "What?"

"You heard me." Jay's voice was stiff, and he began to move toward the clearing's exit. "You've only made things worse here— now I can feel all their eyes on me, all their shadows on me. And just when I thought I might be able to trust you, too."

"You—*Jay*—"

But to Majest's complete and utter amazement, the village picked up their feet and followed him as he went, accusation in their fists swinging at their sides, muttering with the dark in their voices—ignoring Majest entirely. The meeting was over, and nothing had been done.

The only ones who stayed were Letty, Raizu, and Sedona. Majest looked to them in hope, but when their eyes met his, they held an awe and fear that filled him with dread colder than death.

XXIV. CLASH

"What?" Majest demanded again, with an attempt to ignore the unease that crawled up through his skin, the guilty rash fluttering over him every time he remembered the disappointment on Jay's face. "What's the matter? I told them everything, didn't I? Why is everyone so upset?"

Raizu cast violet eyes around, made sure the disappearing crowd was no longer in earshot. "You didn't have to go about it in the way you did," he hissed. "You gave them accusations with no proof—of course they're going to get defensive. You should have been more careful; now you've made the whole town into your enemy! Including Jay, whom we were supposed to be *helping*."

Majest refused to apologize, though Jay's eyes still flashed bitterly in his mind. "I told them how to keep themselves safe, and let them know the truth. Doesn't the truth count for anything?"

"Not when you're all talk and no proof." Letty had her arms crossed, a cloud of hair like fire around her face. "When we planned this meeting, I thought you were going to *show* them, not *tell* them."

"And I will," said Majest evenly, though he prickled with doubt. "Now that they're busy thinking through Masotote and the Organization, they can stay safe from the demon while I handle it."

"You mean while *we* handle it?" asked Sedona suddenly.

Majest's attention flickered. "Why are you still here? Don't you want to walk away, too, hearing me talk about your leader like that when I apparently can't prove a thing? Or by some miracle, do you believe me?"

Sedona shrugged as everyone's eyes went to her. "I thought we were in this together. And I thought you were going to train Letty and I."

"That's true," said Letty.

Majest let out a breath through his teeth that seemed to deflate his entire body. "Alright," he said softly. "Of course. I'm sorry. Do you want to do that now?"

"*Now?*" Raizu went pale. "Don't you want to try and fix your mess before the villagers come after you with torches?"

"*Raizu,*" said Majest patiently. "It's alright. They'll be fine; they'll come around. I'm sure they'll all go talk to Masotote, and between him and Jay, the truth will find its way out. There's nothing better to do now than work on getting rid of the demon. That starts with training, which is what I promised."

"But—"

Majest cut him off gently with a wave of his hand. "Sedona? Letty? What do you say? Here and now, a little warm-up before we start training for real?"

Sedona looked at Letty. Letty looked at Sedona. They both nodded with hesitance.

At the exchange, Raizu retreated to the edge of the clearing with a troubled frown, sitting himself down on a conveniently-placed rock and resting the heavy weight of his head atop his gloved palms, eyeing Majest and the others with a reproachful worry that made the air between them shudder.

"Don't make that face, Raizy," said Majest, taking off his gloves one by one and shoving them into furry pockets. "You get a free show; how bad could that be?"

Raizu rolled his eyes, though his face twitched upward in a small smile he didn't seem to be able to help.

Sedona stared at Raizu with an odd expression, a sudden alienating frigidness, as if she could not fathom why he was here, why he sat atop a stone in her clearing instead of making his way back to his forest pack. Then she shook herself, and tried on a smile. "Alright, well—I've already been able to access bits and pieces of my power, if that helps. I just need to find a technique that works the best."

"That's a start," Majest said with a nod. "What can you do so far?"

Sedona blinked, bit her lip, one hand scratching at her neck in discomfiture. "Not much. It's less of what I can *do*—but I can feel it there, in the back of my mind. I just can't seem to let it out."

"The key to accessing your power is focus," said Majest, folding his arms. "True focus, I've had to learn, is where you no longer feel anything but the drive, the power in your mind. You can't let outside forces distract you. It's hard to get a hold of at first—you have to focus on the doors within you and break them down with your mind."

"That sounds hard to understand, much less accomplish," said Sedona.

"I'll say," muttered Letty, though she seemed relieved at no longer being so alone in her inabilities, and shifted closer to Sedona.

"Patience, Letty." Majest grinned. "You've been staring down your own mind for so long that you never bother to see how I do it. Watch this."

Three shades of blue eyes locked on Majest as he closed his own, sky and sea and sunset and evergreen. He furrowed his brow until he felt the passageways open in his mind, and he exhaled and dropped his thoughts at the gate with a familiarity like coming home. His eyelids cracked apart, and he flexed his fingers—then flicked his wrist in a call answered by the snapping of a branch above Raizu's head.

Raizu jumped straight from his rock with a squeaky cry, and glared above him as Majest grinned and circled the branch around his head for a few moments, cheekily writing his name in the air and drawing an enormous smile in front of Raizu's face before tossing it to one side.

Sedona and Letty laughed and clapped in appreciation; Raizu made a face through a reluctant smile and sat back down, smoothing his jacket back into place.

"That would normally be flattering, but you don't have to try and scare me out of my shoes, alright?" he called in joking protest.

"I'm going to try, now," said Letty, bouncing in excitement. She closed her eyes as her brother had done, her brow breaking into creased lines that mirrored her thin mouth, twitching in focus.

Do I look that ridiculous when I do it? Majest bit his lip to keep from laughing at his sister's pinched face.

The clearing fell soundless and expectant as Letty concentrated. A few soft grunts came from her throat and then her eyes were snapping open like something awakening from a lengthy slumber, arms bursting out around her in little lightning bolts as she let out a garroted howl that shook the trees and sent Raizu's feet skipping once more into the air.

Majest almost flinched, trying to keep alarm off his face. He definitely didn't do *that*.

Sedona seemed just as disturbed, and she shot Majest a worried glanced as Letty stared down at her hands like she did not know what they were, dismay breaking out through her freckles.

With credible effort, Majest stepped toward her. "Letty, there isn't even any water around. You're not supposed to be able to use your power here."

Letty frowned angrily, still examining her hands with a persistent disdained interest, as if they were stained black. Majest could nearly feel heat radiating off her fingertips, her mind—fire in her hair, embers of sun on her face. "I thought there might be some in the air, but I guess I'm not strong enough to use it."

"That was good effort, though," said Sedona immediately.

"It was useless," muttered Letty. "It was dry, and dead, and *nothing*."

"Because there was no water," Majest said evenly, though there was something about his sister's reaction he couldn't shake.

"I think I understand how it's done," offered Sedona. "I always thought the powers were a physical thing, not that they started mentally. I never went into my head to find it. Mind if I try?"

Majest tore his eyes from his sister, still staring at herself with a curled lip. "Go ahead."

"Alright." Sedona sounded determined, and she mirrored Majest, flexing her hands, a smile on her face that seemed to oppose

Letty's maddened scowl. "Do I close my eyes?"

"It's a lot easier if you do, the first time," Majest told her.

Sedona nodded, eyelids locking shut. "Here goes nothing," she said, and clenched her teeth.

Majest hardly had time to register the words—there was only a small huff from between Sedona's white lips, and then there was a ruffle in Majest's hair, a small breeze dancing uncertainly over his face. It was just a tickle, but it had been instantaneous.

"Is that you, Sedona?" he asked with incredulity. It had taken him several tries to even sense his power there beneath his consciousness—Letty certainly had never gotten results anything like this.

Sedona did not answer, too lost winding down the corridors inside her as she fought her way through, exhaling in sighs, the palms of her hands in curved spoons, imploring the sheen of the sky above her head. Majest was watching the passageways open over her face, seeing her fight through the same walls Majest had already burned to the ground. Her lips moved in earnest.

Another gust of wind came, tougher this time. It whizzed around Majest's head with the poise of a bird, and his eyes watered with the agile force, his own mouth fluttering open. Raizu must have felt it too, because he at last seemed to leave his worries behind in his stone perch, curious enough to join his friends on the other side.

The wind grew stronger still, venerable in its insistence, the way it pushed against fur and skin until Majest had to put out his hands to keep from losing his balance. A roar sounded in his ears as if the sky were falling to its knees, and he was reminded of Komi's starry chamber, a straight shot down to emptiness.

From somewhere, Letty gasped—she had, Majest assumed, expected Sedona's efforts to mirror her own, to be in vain. But the current ventured and roared and prospered for several steady moments longer, until it faded quietly into a soft breeze, then dissipated altogether.

"She's done it," said Majest with excitement, shaking windswept hair back into place and turning to Sedona. "You did it; I've never seen anything like that before!"

"I knew I could," said Sedona, eyes shining like the sparkle off water in the sunlight. "I had it all there inside of me—I just needed a proper teacher to help me bring it out."

Majest felt oddly self-conscious. "I didn't do a thing," he said, and meant it. "That was all you. You're a natural—you got it on your first try, all by yourself."

Letty sniffed, eyes traveling up to the sky. She said, "Yes, but you were the one to tell her how. Just like you've always told me."

"And you've always listened," Majest assured her. "I promise, you'll get lots more chances to work on your water. Maybe we can bring a vat of it up by the house for you to use."

"It's not your fault there's no water here," added Raizu.

"I know," sighed Letty, visibly battling frustration. "Congratulations, Sedona," she added, managing a smile. "I suppose it's only fair you get to use your powers first. You're the same age as Majest and I'm more than a birth-year younger."

Before Sedona had time to respond, footsteps sounded from behind and Majest whirled to see Jay of all people hurtling toward them, the usual apathetic sneer wiped clean off his face. He tripped a little as he ran, the first time Majest had ever seen his blindness get the better of him.

Letty, Sedona, and Raizu spun around at the same time, elements forgotten.

"What's the matter now?" Majest demanded as Jay skidded to an awkward halt a few paces away. He was immediately on edge. *Has there been another possession?*

Jay took a deep breath, its exhale coming out as a shudder, as if he'd been running for a while. His dark hair was in complete disarray around his face, which had an angry red mark blooming on it. Majest presumed he had run into something—though with his lack of eyesight and the speed he had been going at over unfamiliar snowy ground, it wasn't surprising.

"I need you to come with me, all of you," Jay said, voice fast and urgent. "The village needs to speak with us again, and I think you'll find it doesn't look good."

Jay, much less than cheerful at being the village's courier, showed the three Messengers and Raizu to a large building behind the beguiling sparkle of the fountain. The building was a tall white glacier, paint chipping to reveal patches of gray as if stress were washing the color away.

A solemn door creaked open and Majest noted the similar dishevelment of the building's interior as Jay led them through a long, bleak hallway the dark gray of wet marble. The hall felt foreign and antique, like an underground prison from a time long past.

Majest stared at the ceiling looming high and dark above his head. He wondered how old this building was. Certainly older than Masotote or any of the living villagers—he suspected it had stood tall since perhaps before the End; it was a relic now, an artifact of another life.

But no doubt, Majest thought angrily, Masotote had claimed this place as his own invention.

Raizu seemed to notice Majest's disgruntlement. "What's the matter?" he asked, eyes and voice drifting over. Majest could tell he was still uneasy about village meetings and delicate plans, but as always, his concern was genuine.

"Just wondering how far Masotote's reign of treachery stretches," Majest replied softly. "I'd hate to see such a glorious building defaced by lies."

Jay made a noise of frustration under his breath. "Let the subject drop," he warned in a cold voice, running a guiding hand along the corridor wall. "At least for now. I don't know what exactly awaits you here, but we can be certain we're treading on thin ice. All of us."

"What, does the village really hate you now?" Majest asked, and his stomach knotted. He no longer had any contempt left to give to this boy—not after seeing the way everyone treated him. "I'm sorry, you know. I thought I was helping."

Jay stiffened. "So did I," he said.

Majest sighed. "Do you think there's anything we can do? Anything I can do, you know, to help you out?"

The hallway was reaching its end, and Jay drew a long breath in through his nose. "That's not important. I'm not important. It isn't about me. The entire village is going to be furious if you bring your accusations up again."

"Isn't there anyone else who believes you? I know Majest wouldn't lie; if he says you're being wronged, Jay, you're being wronged," said Sedona worriedly.

"They don't believe anyone about *anything,*" said Jay in a sour voice. "They never have, so don't think it's going to start anytime soon. Don't waste your breath. It was a mistake the first time."

"Then what do they want us to talk about?" asked Letty, and she did not even hesitate in the question. She must have finally realized Jay was going to be discourteous no matter how politely she spoke, that it wasn't anything personal.

"You'll see when we get there," replied Jay in a clipped voice.

"Get *where?*" Majest cut in impatiently. "Where even are we?"

"Village hall. Masotote likes to get someone to carry him in here so he can hold meetings sometimes, but it's not a frequent occasion. That's why it's such a big deal that they all flocked here after your little '*announcement.*'"

"Is it so awful to try and deliver news of a scandal?"

"Nobody treats the villagers like that, like they've been living all wrong," said Jay absently, as if he were a separate piece from Hi Ding, existing somewhere parallel. "They're awfully confused—although, they *have* come to a conclusion. And you're going to want to hear it."

Majest looked up, and realized they had arrived in front of a door. Its white wood was carved sloppily; its rough edges stuck out as if only to prick those who entered. There was no knob, only a metal bar curved in a handle like a claw.

Behind the door, Majest could hear the low murmur of voices.

The pale shape of Jay's hand, sticking out amongst the shadows of the hall, moved over the wood's surface in search of the handle. He found it hastily and gave it a savage yank; the door creaked in protest and shuddered open, hinges holding on for dear life.

Majest's eyes were met with an immediate brightness, as if the door's movement had switched on an artificial sun. The room was large and circular, rows of elevated tables and chairs in orbit around the center, each filled with a villager or two to eclipse the dry white walls.

The voices died with the shriek of the door. Countless pairs of eyes were trained on the entrance, gazes jabbing at Majest like pine needles. For once, under their lifted stares, he felt small.

"I brought the Skylarks," Jay told the crowd in monotone, as if he were delineating a rather dry set of instructions, though Majest did not miss the tremble of his fists at his sides, the way he was already poised to leave. "You can proceed with your business."

"Very good, my unfortunate Jay," said—to Majest's utmost, horrified surprise—Vosile Masotote. He was seated in the front of the room, his bony chin jutting out as he gave Majest a hard look. Those narrowed eyes were everywhere, passed throughout the room.

"Jay, what's going on? Who brought him here?" Raizu hissed.

Majest flashed his friend a quick glance. "I'm sure we'll get an explanation."

Vosile gave a little smirk. "I'm glad you could join us, Skylark."

Majest stepped forward into the bright center of the room, feeling white light buzz in circles around his face. "So, what's the deal? Have you told them the truth yet?"

He stared around the room with wide eyes, watching the steady, unwavering scowls of the villagers. They made no move to condemn their leader, to justify Majest's accusations.

Vosile's mouth twitched. "I think we've sorted the situation out," he said.

Majest blinked. "And?"

"And there has been a decision to keep you inside your house until the demon situation has been sorted out," said Masotote smugly, and crossed his arms.

Majest's face froze. "*What?*"

"Wandering the forest at night is enough to generate concern.

The fact that you came back with a story of a wild, possessed *polar bear* and a basket of lies about our village proves that such adventures may have in fact possessed *you*."

"That's ridiculous!" Majest burst out. "Don't you try pretend we never found that bear, or that we never spoke to you! Raizy can tell you. He was there, and so was Jay. We had you completely defenseless! You admitted you were stealing Jay's prophecies!"

Raizu opened his mouth, but Vosile cut him off with a wave of his hand.

"You could get your little friend to say whatever you want," he snapped. "Because you are a liar, a liar who has been listening to an even bigger liar." He snarled the last few words at Jay, a fake betrayal splattered across his face. "How could you turn on your own leader like that—trying to pretend my words are your own? I never should have brought you here."

"Really?" Jay's voice was cold, all his walls back up. "Without my warning, you never would have stood a chance against last year's blizzard. Without my knowledge of demons, you never would have figured out how this one strikes in the dark."

Masotote was barely looking at him. "You were sent to fetch the Skylarks today, nothing more," he said. "Remember that. You are not needed." His voice darkened. "Not any longer."

Jay started to flinch, then seemed to catch himself on fragile strings and wind himself back up. "I can take a hint," he snapped. "We'll see how you do without me." There was a warning note to the words, and then there was an empty space at Majest's side, and the door was banging behind him.

Jay was gone, so suddenly and unceremoniously, and an uneasy silence stuttered to life. Raizu was trembling, and hope seemed to fall to pieces.

Majest looked desperately around the room, for any signs of sympathy, any drop of consideration, but familiar faces—Sunni, Quell, Idyllice, Rapple—merely turned away, avoiding his gaze.

"As I was saying," Masotote continued, like he hadn't just essentially exiled the boy he knew to be the true prophet, "Majest Skylark, you will be put under house arrest. The demon energy needs to be dealt with, as you said, but we will not have you in our way while we do it."

We, Majest thought scornfully. *There is no we.*

"You know, the demon wants Letty and I," he said, and he shifted to fill Jay's former place, as though he could defend the boy even in his absence. "It's not going to stop until it finds us in the dark."

Vosile arched an eyebrow. "Of course. As I said—as I have *always* said."

"So what are you going to do?" asked Letty uneasily, taking a small step forward.

Vosile stared her down with eyes like a vulture's. "What do you think we *must* do?"

There was a long moment that passed by with a creeping eternalness, and the villagers were turned to Majest and Letty, unblinking, unmoving, unfeeling. Majest felt his eyes bulge wide from his skull as the full realm of possibilities struck him.

"Wait, are you planning on *sacrificing* my sister and I?"

At that, even Masotote stifled a laugh with a cough. "I see you haven't lost your good humor along with your common sense," he said. "Of course we aren't going to *sacrifice* you. We're simply going to lock you in your house."

"Letty, too?" Majest put out a protective hand in front of his sister.

"No, only you." Vosile did not blink. "Meanwhile, the villagers will find a building and turn it to shadows—paint it black, inside and out. Block the windows, the cracks in the door. When the sun rises, the demon will be looking for a place to hide, and in our black world, we'll trap it inside."

Can you really trap a demon? Majest whirled to where Jay should have been standing, but there was nothing and no one to give him an answer, just a turmoil in his gut.

"How are you going to attack it?" he protested. "It isn't human, not even animal. You don't know anything about it! At least, not without Jay, you don't!"

"The village will attack by *attacking*." Masotote's eyes were wintry. "Don't try to meddle any longer, Skylark. This is not your battle."

"Of course it's my battle," Majest protested. "I'm the one who brought the demon to the village—I should be the one to drive it out!"

"We want to do it," said Sunni suddenly, and when Majest turned to look at her, she gave him a slow, knowing nod. "It's Masotote's idea. We have to test it."

Majest looked curiously at her. *Test Masotote's idea.* It would be a chance to try out his illegitimacy, wouldn't it? Is that what Sunni meant? If the villagers could not trap and kill the demon on his trusted orders…if they were possessed, or worse…

Masotote would be seen as a failure. Jay would be free of suspicion. Raizu would be proven right.

All the same, Majest shook his head in Sunni's direction. He would not risk lives to prove a point.

"I think it's a good idea," said Raizu carefully, eyes darting around the room. "I was worried you would try to force Maji to kill the assassin by himself." Seeming to realize the size of the crowd, he turned scarlet and slammed his mouth shut.

Masotote nodded. "Even if Komi's powers brought this curse upon our village—" A glare at Majest. "—it is not the responsibility of one boy to take on the darkness alone."

"Yes," said Sedona. She held out a hand like she meant to put it on Majest's shoulder, but after a moment, she let it fall. "I don't want you—or Letty—to be hurt. We all need to do this together."

"We may not trust each other," said Masotote, giving Majest a long, hard look, "but we have to reach our grasp past disagreements to understand we are of the same Cognito blood, born or made. We fight together."

At such encouragement, the village in one entity smiled, completely and revoltingly enamored by the words.

"No!" Majest cut over their rising excitement. "I'm the one the demon wants! If I fail and it destroys me, I'm the only one who gets hurt."

Letty and Raizu both blanched white.

It was Letty who spoke first. "You can't *say* that," she gasped, and clutched at her brother's arm as if they were the only ones in the room.

"I am the storm Jay foresaw coming to the village," Majest insisted. "I brought Letty and I here. I put Sedona and her power in danger along with us. I've gotten Jay accused of treason, and I've awoken a lying beast from his bed and released him further upon all of you—so I'm going to end this."

"*I'm* the storm, too!" Letty protested; nails dug into the skin above Majest's wrist in little pinpricks of pain. "I'm just as much at fault as you. I can't let you do this by yourself. You'll die!"

"No, I won't," Majest snapped. He suddenly felt sick—with Letty, with the villagers, and with Masotote most of all, who was willing to risk his people to blanket his own bed of lies.

Shaking Letty off, he stepped to the door, threw it open. "If anyone tries to stop me or confine me to my house, I would be glad to lock *them* in my house instead."

He stormed out, just like Jay, and thunder followed him in the slam of the door behind him, feet in bolts that raced ahead. The hallway that greeted him seemed swirling with life—patterns on the stone warped in front of his eyes, scattering his vision; the gray walls bounced off one another in an avalanche of flat monochrome.

Majest blinked rapidly until the hall shifted back to normal. His heart was pounding and his blood boiled hot with contempt, but for the first time since he'd stumbled across this village, he felt something other than the lull of safety or the naivety of exhilaration. He felt brave, reckless—he felt like himself again.

With a deep breath, he strode through the rest of the hallway in a careless blur, bursting into the open air with the swing of a white door and half a smile. He trotted down to the fountain, which glistened as it bubbled and swelled up over its edges, the water plummeting to its swirling base only to find itself somehow at the top, doomed to fall in cycle.

Why should I spend my energy clawing my way into making the villagers believe me if Vosile Masotote will only push me back down when I get there? They've trusted him longer than I've been alive. The only way to make them believe me is to prove his plans are faulty and follow my own—kill the demon myself.

Thoughts buzzing, Majest sat down on the stony edge of the fountain for solace, dangling his feet just above the small pool of water. Tiny drops of crystal liquid formed on the bottoms of his boots, but he didn't care.

It seemed as if the sun had risen a few infinities ago, but even with all that had occurred under its light, it still was not setting, which was odd—this time of year, it usually took no time at all for the bright star to give up on itself and tumble through the sky, crashing somewhere else in its failure. Majest thought the sun tried so hard to bring light to its cold world that it could not bear the responsibility in the end, giving up end to shroud the world in darkness.

But the sun always came back.

Footsteps sounded behind the fountain's edge, approaching lightly like the pattering of raindrops.

Majest narrowed his eyes and balled his hands into fists, expecting someone had come from the village to fetch him, to demand that he come back inside and take back his words, return his pride.

He scowled, words wicked on his tongue. "I thought I told you all to leave me alone," he started in a snap, but when his visitor spoke, the words stopped cold.

"I knew you wouldn't get far," Raizu said, the sound of his feet stopping a short distance from the fountain. "You don't have a plan for what you're going to do now and I *know* that."

Majest swiveled and planted his wet feet on solid ground, still seated on the fountain's cold stone. Raizu was right behind it, hands clenched at his sides, eyes dark with worry.

"I have a plan," Majest said loftily, meeting Raizu's eyes with a bit of a challenge. "I'm only sitting here because I got distracted."

"A distraction can cost you your life," said Raizu, blinking. His expression was unreadable as he scuffed at the snowy dirt with one boot. "I mean, not that you've ever had a problem with risking your life before, but you might want to start preparing for the day where your refusal to ever slow down your own thoughts might be more harm than it is help."

"What?"

"You rush into things," Raizu clarified. "You leap before you look without any second thoughts."

"I have no idea what you're talking about, Raizy; you're going to have to speak in a language I understand. Are you telling me bravery is a weakness?"

Raizu's mouth pinched into a line; his eyes focused on something high above Majest's head. "There's a line between bravery and recklessness, one you and Letty seem to love to cross. Running away from home, running away from each other, crossing the Bay on a tiny wooden boat to an island that may or may not be safe…" He shook his head. "And now you want to take on an unknown force by yourself because you feel as if you owe it—to whom? The village? You don't even *like* them. You've completely alienated them—and destroyed anything that might have been left of Jay's reputation!"

"You were just as reckless as we were," murmured Majest, tilting his head to scrutinize his friend's face. "You ran away from home. You crossed the Bay on one of our boats."

"Because I had to sink to your level if I ever wanted to find you!" Raizu protested, now staring at his shoes. "I had to find you because I knew you wouldn't have the common sense to stay out of trouble yourself!"

Majest was stung. "I can take care of myself, you know. Just because you saved my sister doesn't mean I wouldn't have been able to do it myself. If I had been there, I would have protected her." He narrowed his eyes. "Besides, you didn't even save her! It was the black-haired girl!"

"I never asked you to treat me like I *did* save her," responded Raizu evenly. "I never implied that you owed me. We've saved each other's lives enough times by now and become close enough that none of those things should matter."

"Great!" said Majest, throwing up his hands. He got to his feet. "None of it matters? Sounds good to me. Now if you'll excuse me,

I have a demon to destroy and a village to save, and I don't want to fight with you. Why don't you take Letty home?"

"No!" Raizu stepped forward. "Some things do matter. You matter. Throwing away your life for this—this *thing* isn't worth it. What's Letty going to do if you don't come back? What am I going to do, just go home and forget about you, about all of this?"

"I'm not throwing away my life," Majest said pointedly. "I'm not going to die."

"But you could!"

"But I won't."

"You just don't get it, do you, Maj?" Raizu shook his head, and any trace of the calm, pleasant boy who never angered was gone; the candle was blown out. "You can't just waltz your way through the world and expect every odd to turn out in your favor just because you're trying your best. There are some things you simply *can't* do—and this is one of them. You can't manage this by yourself. If you keep digging your way through the world without any second thoughts, eventually you're going to find yourself in a hole with no way to climb back out."

Majest blinked. His next words made little sense, even to his own ears. "You'd pull me out."

"What?" Raizu's features contorted into a quizzical frown, his anger interrupted.

"I said," Majest spoke the words with care, pondering each one as he said it, "if there *were* a hole too large and vast for me to escape on my own, you'd pull me out. Toss me a rope. Like you said, we're quite accustomed to saving each other by now."

Raizu's confusion twisted into a scowl, some unreadable emotion clouding his violet eyes. "Of course," he snapped, his voice shaking with a terrifying icy fire. "Of course you'd think that. You always expect an easy answer to every solution."

Majest waited, tilting his head.

Raizu shook furiously. "As long as you assume someone—something—will be there to save you, you won't worry about saving yourself. So you'll assume, and take me and everything else for granted without any thought that someday, the world might be unable to save you."

Majest watched in bewildered shock as Raizu took a deep breath, trying to form the right words. When he found them, his gaze darkened until the blue of his eyes was like looking into midnight.

"Although, I probably wouldn't have to be the one to rescue you, because the *perfect Majest Skylark* and his *powers* would have already found a way out."

Majest flinched. "What's *that* supposed to mean?"

"You don't actually ever want anyone's help, do you? Not if it means you don't get the glory. You've made up your mind that no one else is allowed to be the hero, and you're convinced nothing could prevent you from being that hero. Well, have at it!" Raizu's arms went up in the air in a gesture of frustration; the ends of his worn coat drooped around his wrists brokenly, as if they too were defeated.

"Raizy," Majest tried, but he wasn't listening.

"If you want to get yourself killed trying to take on an enemy with more power than anything we've ever seen, be my guest. Just don't ask me to watch. Don't make me watch you die. I won't." At that, Raizu turned on his heel and stalked off, coat flying behind him like a pair of wings.

After some time of standing there in the freezing afternoon, numbed, Majest became aware of the slow descent of the sun at last, its rays searing the clouds and torching the snow on the ground until it was little more than a vibrant sea of orange against a darkening sky. The trees were on fire; the air bled ashes. It wouldn't have come as a surprise if the sudden, blinding heat of an invisible flame took over the world.

A swift wave of hopelessness washed over him. There was no one left in the whole town, it seemed—the fiery streets were empty; the village was still piled in their meeting hall, hosts to the parasitic acid in Masotote's lies.

Maybe it was true what Raizu had said—maybe Majest had never wanted or needed a hand, someone to pull him from his own reckless depths. But now that Majest was by himself as the sun's hope dwindled, he realized he had never felt so alone.

A hard, resolute feeling of desperation clutching at his heart, he turned and raced toward the light.

XXV. SHADOW

A brush whipped in a flippant flicker of a gesture, an unceremonious smack.

Black ink spurted from between its wolf-hair bristles; black ink that reeked of mud and decay slapped against a windowpane, sliding to huddle between its grains for warmth and comfort. There was a steady blackness oozing over the pane, the window, the wall, all of it—it slithered between the cracks, cast an impenetrable shield across the windows and door that glared out at the forms hooting and hollering before it, as if with a grave disappointment.

The building was surrounded in a dance—a weaving, bowing circle that moved in patterns of stitches or crochet, all spattered in paint with the muddy richness of dried blood. The walls were painted, and so were the villagers' white furs, and their bloody ink snapped against every whimpering loose end it could find, every crack and bend in the chipped wood of some abandoned storage unit. The paint was in lines, in drips, in splashes that shone like stars, though it was barely dawn.

They painted a mask over its façade, something faceless and trembling, fit for hiding some unknown terror beneath. That was the intention, of course.

There was no sunlight to these walls' night of stars—just gobs of black that sealed every possible escape. Soon, the job was complete.

Then someone, one of the painted figures, began to choke on a heaving inhale, and she sucked in her breath with a guttural gasp, limbs reeling for balance. Something frigid punched through her, snaking between the inked lines of the wood her hand rested upon.

She raised her voice, and her movements were strangled. "There!" she cried, and jabbed a finger to where the coldness had gone. "There, it's here, it's in there!"

Her words were a sudden, empirical command. Every figure, every shadow drew a knife from their belts, and held it before them with stricken obedience. Eyes were wide and doe-like, caught in the brightness of the dark.

"Go in," someone hissed.

"No, *you!*"

"We told Masotote we would—"

"I'll do it," said the girl who had felt the cold. There was a hard set to her chin, and the muscles of her jaw rippled slightly as her teeth dug into one another. She found the handle of the door, and her glove seemed frozen to it. "I'll be the first."

She pulled back the door. A slice of light meandered onto the bare floor, and dust glowed like rain suspended in midair. The girl lifted her blade, and all that reflected from it was the blackness of the ink. She stepped inside, and the door banged in her wake, though she had not laid a hand on it.

Everyone stared, faces all bugged and blind. There was silence; there was a heavy, black silence. They all watched the starry spots on each pane of wood, holding their breath, holding their knives. They were identical in their fear, in their compliance, in their knowledge they could be next.

A hiss broke through the trance, then a snapping growl that could have been words all tangled up in themselves, and then finally, a shriek high and laced together with terror. It was the kind of screech that sent birds startling from their trees in little squawks, made the fountain skip a watery beat, turned the heads of even the most apathetic clouds above.

Someone lunged for the door, and there was a struggle to pry it open, as though something were pressing vehemently in from the other side, but at last it opened, and the girl came tumbling out in a heap. Her eyes were rolling, tears sticky and hot on her face. She was crumpled, lip cracked and bleeding, and her chest heaved for air.

The man who had taken her out pulled his hat down around his ears, fixed the door with stony resolution in his eyes.

"I'll be strong enough," he said. "I'll be next. Give me the dark."

Everyone wailed after him as he joined the shadows inside, and soon he was wailing with them, and there was a swarm at the door of bodies and limbs all jumbled, prying back the wood, the inky cover already chipping, and they dragged the man back outside, his scarf askew, blade bashed into a smiling curve.

"We can't!" a woman was sobbing. "The Skylark was right, wasn't he? Isn't this impossible?"

"But it's in there, isn't it?" someone snapped. "Pull yourself together! We have orders!"

"Masotote's orders—"

They were nodding, all of them.

They trembled further, all curled in on themselves with the sunken wheezes of something rotting, but one by one, they slipped through the door with their hearts threatening to pound through the bones guarding their chests.

One by one, they were shrieking and yanked back, stumbling over their feet, skin going ash and slate until it matched the clouds. The dark was in their eyes, on their faces; they could scrub at their hands, but they could not keep their eyes from turning sky-high with fatigue, could not keep from crying.

They abandoned their brushes, the ink, the stars. In the end, morning was night.

The dark could not be conquered.

Letty could sense something was missing before she even opened her eyes. She didn't have to comb her eyes across the tables and chairs or even call out her brother's name to know he had not returned to the cottage that night, had not stumbled through the door to rest or change his mind or eat the food she had left for him on the table in some vain hope she would hear him munching between the late-night hours.

She loved her brother, knew his heart was in the right place—but once that look of radical fortitude flashed in two eyes and a dimpled smile, there would be no rest until any plan of his rang in resounding success. And as his current plan was to take on a demon unaided…

Letty chewed on her lip. She had wanted to run after him, when he had torn away and vanished—as Raizu had—but she had been swept into conversations with an involuntary impulse to listen, to become a wolf of the pack, and her ears had pricked, eyes glassy and all-absorbent.

From what she had gathered, the villagers would put their plan into action despite Majest's wishes, despite his claims and his insistence they were true. The people of Hi Ding held the same adamant urgency as Majest, but their numbers held the better odds.

That was what worried her. And Majest had not returned.

Raizu and Letty had met up later outside their own house—Raizu looking forlorn and spent, Letty with a rumbling discomfort in her stomach that squeezed painfully up into her ribs, shortening her breath into icy trembles of air that seemed to squeak.

"I tried to make him be reasonable," Raizu had told her, moving inside, slumping into a wooden chair. "I warned him he was only going to hurt himself."

"And what did he say?" Letty had looked at him closely. Though she hadn't known him for long, Raizu seemed like a steady enough light to keep her brother upright along with him. "Did he listen?"

"I don't think I helped. I think he's still going to go after whatever's out there."

"But didn't you try to convince him not to?"

Raizu had looked embarrassed. "I hardly gave him a chance to get a word in edgewise, actually."

"You? Talking over Maji? I didn't think that was possible."

"I guess I got a little upset." Raizu had scratched his head with one hand, frowning. "I was just…worried about him." A flush, a frown. "But I stormed off without him. He wouldn't listen to reason and I couldn't watch him hurt himself—so I ran, you know, like always. I don't know where he is now, and I don't know what his plans are." His face had fallen further. "I'm sorry, Letty. I should have stayed with him. I shouldn't have left him. I'm sure he must think horribly of me now."

"He would never—I'm sure everything's fine," Letty had assured him, though her twisted stomach had said otherwise, and dry eyes had begun to water, hands kneading against the stony parts of their kitchen wall. "You did your best. We just have to give him some time."

And the two of them had done just that—more than that—more than a little time.

The sun had long since struck the horizon by the time Letty's eyelids had grown heavy and her feet could no longer lift themselves off the ground. And yet, still no sign of her brother's face.

A morning later, still nothing.

"Where could he *be?*" Letty wanted to wail aloud, but she forced the words down to a harsh whisper, sitting up and smoothing the wild wave of her hair down into a low knot, tying it roughly with the string around her wrist until frizzy locks spewed around her face in protest.

She stepped out of bed, wood creaking drearily, slipping her feet into furry socks and pacing through the house until she reached the room her brother had been mocking the curtains of just the morning before.

With a shove, she pushed open the thin wooden door. "Raizu?"

Raizu was sitting on the edge of the bed, the blankets strewn across the floor in soft, helpless bodies. He looked up when Letty came in and combed through his hair with his fingers, though it hardly did him much good—it stuck up around his face like bush branches. His face looked haunted, dark circles dragging his eyes downward with sleepless worry.

"No sign of him?" Letty whispered. Her stomach tied itself back up.

"Nothing," responded Raizu, voice dead and without emotion. He looked up at Letty, and his eyes were dark, more blue than violet, as if their sunset edges had been swallowed by night. "It's been quiet as death since we got back."

Letty squeezed her eyes shut. "You don't think he's coming back."

Raizu just stared at her, and the dark pits under his eyes made the bones of his face jut unnaturally. Guilt riddled the tremble of his nose, each chapped ridge of his pink lips.

"He's gone off after the demon," Letty continued, and bit her cheek so hard she almost cried. But she held it back; she had cried enough these past few months to sail a ship on her tears, and she had to keep herself anchored.

"It's my fault," said Raizu without hesitation, snatching a pillow from the bed and setting it down in his lap, pulling at the edges until they started to fray. "I'm the one who made him run off. He thought I would stand by him even when no one else would, and I crushed that hope. I was supposed to be there for him, like I promised I would be, and I let him down."

"No," Letty said softly. "No, you were right. All dreamers need to keep their feet on the ground. That's what he tells me when I don't let the old-world stories rest. But he's a dreamer, too— he doesn't think he can get hurt; he thinks every plan can catch him from failure just because he has the will to chase after every dream; he doesn't know sometimes people get hurt when your plan goes sour, and you can't wake up with a pinch and start over from scratch like you've messed up your caribou dinner. Life's not a recipe; you can't always rely on your own directions."

"But what I said—"

"Don't you dare condemn yourself for this," said Letty. "You were just trying to pull his head out of the clouds. You care about him; that's why you said what you did. He knows that. It's not your fault."

Raizu did not seem relieved; his face only contorted to find new gaping spaces, new places to hold his mounting dejection. "I just wish I hadn't left him out there on his own. I wanted to stay, but I didn't. I'm spineless, Letty. He could die out there, and I didn't do anything to stop him. I'm weak and a coward, I am. Don't tell me I'm not."

Letty felt her face fall, lip tremble, but she didn't know what else to say. She sat down next to him and leaned her head on his shoulder, just as she would do for Majest. And she did not say a word.

They sat like that for some time, content to their own breathing, the brush of Raizu's shirt to Letty's temple, the suspension that held them in place. Letty knew any movement was futile. She wasn't Majest, and neither was Raizu. There would be no drastic plans, no willful propositions. They would not go running off. And so they didn't.

A noise cut into Letty's empty thoughts, and she sat up with a sudden flinch that made her teeth clack. The noise had been faint, perhaps not of any concern—but it had been one thing for sure: a scream.

Raizu must have heard it too, because he was on his feet in an instant, stumbling hastily across the room to peek through the hole in the wall.

"What was that?" Letty asked, and swallowed.

Raizu sighed, and took his lip between his teeth. "Mysterious sounds aren't really my forte, Letty." He made a nervous sound. "It could have been another possession, you think?"

Letty shook her head slowly, stole another glance out the window. "Let's go to the market," she said, with sudden decision, deliberately avoiding the question. She had no answer. "I could use a few more apples, and we might be able to ask if anyone's seen Majest, and figure out what's been going on." There was no fault with the idea. It was safe, harmless. She would leave the vacant house behind, pretend her brother would be there upon her return.

"Alright," said Raizu with a surprised shrug.

The door closed behind them, locking emptiness in place.

He hated it, but Majest knew he was predictable. He always found his feet molded to the same path no matter his complications, drawn along as if pulled by an unbreakable string on his mind, on his fingertips, on the soles of his shoes.

And so he found himself, once more, in the trees.

The island's forest held the harsh slant of sun as he ran through its heart, tossing trees and kicking up bare, muddy earth until his boots were stained a wet brown. The trees seemed to move and sway with him as he went in endless, rampant circles. He didn't know how many times he had crossed his own path, how many laps around the island's ring he had traveled. He didn't care.

There was no place to think but the forest. The second Raizu's coat had waved goodbye through the cottage door, Majest had torn back through the town with his eyes to the treetops, escaping sunset's flames in the one and only home he knew could not be taken from him.

The woods held no conflict, no disagreement—only the wild, erratic feeling of freedom and chance. Letty and Raizu would not follow him here. They repelled the same conflict Majest embraced.

Majest always had a way out.

But was there one here? Majest looked around the trees, feet stumbling. He knew it was morning again, but the sun was dark as any moon. And he was going in circles—trapped.

His throat ached with exhaustion, lungs grasping at what air they could find, but he could not—*would* not—go back home. He had to prove himself. He was many things—stubborn, hasty, overconfident—but he was *not* a fraud; he was not what Masotote believed him to be.

There's a way out, he decided. *And it's through what we're trying to escape.* He exhaled through his nose.

A tree appeared in front of him like a shooting star, and he swung an arm at it with one loud yell. It crashed to the ground.

He stopped running then, staring at the dark shape he had destroyed, and realized he was going to have to return to the village. The demon was in some other black place now, not these trees he had spent the night howling through.

His tired muscles protesting, Majest turned and staggered in a half-run back through the trees. He did not know which way to go, but the island was a circle, all leading to the same turn, the same village. He would have to find it eventually, and he would keep moving until he did.

After some indefinite span of time, Majest was able to make out the gray, flat tops of Hi Ding's buildings through the thinning trees. The village was still asleep. No one would interrupt his return.

As he ran forward, more impatient than ever, a faint, pain-stricken cry poured into his ears with a ring. His blood chilled. *Has the demon found someone else? Am I too late?*

Desperate, he forced his booted feet to move faster until the last tree was behind him and he found himself back on the stone path that would lead him to the fountain, the centerpiece. The place where he had heard his only doubts turn into words.

"There are some things you simply can't *do!"*

Irritated at the stab of guilt that pierced his heart, he turned away and walked deliberately in the other direction.

The new path he picked had sent him walking toward a cluster of short, wide buildings like tree stumps on the outskirts of town, and they were the dull brown-and-gray of arctic birds, matted in dirt and bitter freeze. He'd never noticed this place before, and his feet quickened at the mystery.

The buildings looked unmarked, untouched, desolate and empty. They smelled of dust and rotting wood; snow piled at the entrances in clumps stamped with footprints that ran in dizzy, knitted rings around the wood. Someone had been here—many someones.

A dark spot gleamed on the ground. Majest peered at it curiously, crouching down low on his knees in the snow. In the early morning, the splintered sun made it hard to see, but it looked like a dye or ink, black as Vari's possessed eyes.

Majest let his own eyes wander across the ground until they landed on another spot, identical to the first. "More, huh?"

Majest put a finger to the inky spot and drew it up to his face, glove stained black. He sniffed it, and it was so rank with mud and chemicals, he almost lost the food in his stomach. He flung his glove into the snow with a gag, clambering back to his feet in distaste. It lay there like something dead and fallen.

A trail of the strange black spots crawled furtively up the snow to pool under the door of a building, disappearing into hidden darkness. That building was covered head to toe in the same splatters, the blossoms of ink that cast their foul stench across the snowy clearing.

Finger throbbing in protest of the cold air, Majest took a few steps forward, black dots and mingling villager footprints luring him in, and by the time he stood at the building's entrance, his head felt plugged by the filth covering its dips and bends. He noted the windows, black as new bruises. It was all black, and he suspected he knew why.

He watched the door carefully, and suddenly, everything seemed to have a sinister air to it—this was where the village wanted to trap the demon. In a place of blackness.

The air began to sing with a buzz, and pulse with an eerie echo— Majest thought he could hear his own heart patter in aberrant fear, but still, something pushed him forward, and he found one bare hand on the door, pressure forcing it slowly open. It did not make a sound.

When nothing jumped out at him or even dared to break the morning silence, Majest's feet stepped through the threshold and into the blank room before him, mind shredding thoughts of potential danger or of anything but a rawness that seemed to move him all on its own.

If Raizu were here, he'd never let me do this, Majest realized, fingers curling on the doorframe, which felt like soot. Inside, there was nothing to look at, and the blackness of its boards and frames consumed the green of Majest's eyes. It was all there was.

Eyes wide as the outside world left his sight, Majest let go of the door.

It swung in on him with a crash that shattered the hushed stillness, smashing it to pieces.

All at once, the light went out.

The room buzzed; it smelled of the spot-stained snow, its reeking poison, overpowering the stale scent of old wood and the taste of Majest's curious uncertainty that had hung in his mouth like a bite of rotten fruit.

And he was trapped.

Majest sucked in a breath through his teeth, spinning around, hands on the door. Not a sparkle of sunlight could seep through its cracks, and Majest could not even fit his fingernails into the lines. Nor could he find an inside handle—there was none.

He pushed back at the door with the force of his entire body, battering it with his shoulder and forearms until he thought he might break in two. But it did not budge, did nothing but hold steady and dark.

"Djöfull."

Turning from the door with an irritated noise, careful not to lose his footing, Majest opened his eyes wide until they dried, begging them to find some scrap of light to see by. But the villagers had done a fine job of creating their darkness.

Majest's breathing slowed, eyelids trembled. He felt bile rise in his throat, then swallowed it back down as a sudden coldness crept under his skin. He shivered, drawing his coat tighter around him, and was conscious then that he had no weapon—his knife had fallen from his boot somewhere in the forest, and his slingshot was empty; he had used his last grass-bomb with Raizu and the polar bear.

A creak in the wood sounded somewhere in front of him and he jumped, feeling the tiny hairs on the back of his neck stand up to attention.

"Who's there?" he forced out, and his voice was weaker than he had expected. He could have slapped himself. This was what he had wanted, to seek the dark.

There was no reply, but Majest could feel his breath clot into icy clouds in front of him. It was growing colder, and frigidness eased around him, giving itself permission to dwell deep within him.

A lump rose in his throat, and that had never happened before. He knew it wasn't good, knew it wasn't any sort of trick or fabrication—he was afraid.

"What, am I turning into Raizy?" Majest muttered. "There's nothing to be afraid of. It's just a little darkness and a draft; the villagers couldn't have trapped the demon so easily. I can find a way out of here as long as I'm crafty."

He ran his hands along the door, feeling again for a knob, a latch or a lock he had missed before. But there was nothing in the slippery paint, nothing poking out from its inky grasp.

Majest let out a hiss of frustration. "*Þetta er slæmt.*"

"*Skylark,*" came a voice, but it was not *quite* a voice—it was something merely pretending to be.

Majest gasped at the wickedness of the scratching sound, forgetting his promise to be fearless, forgetting his pride and strength, instead staggering back against the wood of the door, begging it to fall back and release him.

"Who's *there?*" he called again, his voice creeping high in pitch. "Show yourself!"

In response came a loaded, injured hissing, like an animal wounded but not killed, driven by revenge, the instinct to survive and destroy what had caused its suffering. Disease riddled the sound.

Majest felt his body sink against the door, propping himself up on its greasy slant. He had heard this sound before, just last night, coming indeed from a wounded beast, manipulated by darkness and another's jealous ire.

And he knew whom he was facing.

"You're the demon, aren't you?" Majest croaked, and let go of the door. There was no use now. He would not escape. All this while, he'd imagined trapping this creature in its own rancid darkness. But this was the other way around—faceless evil had outdone him, and now *he* was trapped, lightless and without escape.

"*Ohanzi,*" responded the voice, and it might've been Majest's imagination, but it sounded closer. The word was slurred to the point where Majest was uncertain of its intention, its reality. "*I am Ohanzi.*"

"Nice to meet you," Majest breathed, trying to gain confidence through an easy tone, even if he stood in front of fear itself. "Glad you speak human, too. That makes this easier. I suppose you already know who I am." He was babbling, stalling—there was no chance he would escape alive.

"You are the gods' choice, and I was an accident," said Ohanzi's voice, and it was metallic and lifeless, sending spasms of cold through Majest's bones. *"It wasn't supposed to be this way. Our Lady never meant for power to drive out power, only for the Organization's equal world, for a shedding of the supernatural, all traces of the End. Not this imbalanced mess."*

"So it was the Organization who sent you," Majest breathed, and his hands became fists.

"It was the laboratory that started the ruin. And it isn't the first time such experiments paid their price. Before you were born, such madness bred the impossible, and it spread far, even here, to this village. I thought such a creator to be the perfect invincible god, but now I see that he is only human, and that mankind is weak. The Organization was wrong all along about how to bring greatness back to this land. It is us Powers who rule the world, do we not? And I intend to be the greatest of them all—by destroying the Messengers, of course."

Majest could think of nothing to say; his mouth felt dry, as if the sun had soaked up his breath.

"The demon was injected into me much the same way your powers were injected into you. And I knew where you and your little sister were hiding—Seti Sinestre's files told me that much, even though he had lost you. I had to meet you, since this is your fault. I am your fault."

A shiver wracked Majest's body and his teeth grated harshly together. The silence in the room was louder than thunder. "Who's Seti?" he whispered.

"I didn't come here to talk failures, Majest Skylark," hissed Ohanzi's voice in a surprising, humanlike manner. *"I came here to destroy you, to rise above you, above the Organization. Power can only seek to rise. That is its curse—mine, yours, theirs."*

"Then fight me," breathed Majest, heart pounding. "Come out and fight. That's why I'm here, in the end. Power lures power. Perhaps it means something that I've found you here."

In answer came a low gurgling noise, and Majest saw Vari, strapped to the table in Jay's claustrophobic house, twitching and howling, fingers clawing at gnarled wood, seeking escape, seeking a quenched thirst—power. He saw Letty, howling to the wind as water shed lifelessly from her fingers. It was all about power. Everything was.

A cold breath coated the room and Majest crept along the wall in desperation, fingers scratching the walls in search of a crack, a window, a weapon or hope.

He found nothing to touch but slippery, painted walls. He regretted this, all of it—he had nothing and no one here, no power at all. Raizu was right. He had been right all along.

Sounds of devils and dusk inched up his spine, caressing his skin and stabbing through bone and marrow until Majest could hear and feel nothing else. Chills ran up him and down and back again, and something pounced upon him from every direction at once, a force that knocked his breath and his heartbeat and then the rest of him in a heap to the ground.

And he fell, and he sank, and he melted, collapsing to one side as the shadows ate at his hair, chewed holes in his clothes, slurped up his veins. The bright vitality, the fresh color of life he had always held so tight—it slipped from his hands into the gloom until he was no longer just inside the dark, but part of it himself.

The noise was a grating whisper in the back of his mind, an itch he could not reach with his fingertips to scratch. Its pitch was the quintessence of *wrongness*, a devil rearing its head from some far depths to scream—softly, though. Muffled by something. It was not close by. It merely—infuriatingly—prodded the edge of Raizu's consciousness with a deadly patience, again and again, and it forced him to acknowledge that something was wrong. Right now—somewhere—the whisper was the warning.

"Raizu!" said Letty for the fourth time, voice thick with impatience. "Are you listening to me?"

"Uh-huh," Raizu replied, narrowing his eyes to squint off into the blur of a village morning—silent, just stirring. There was a buzzing in his ears, and soft voices, whispers of ambiguity. He could not stand still, could not concentrate, not when it felt as if something called to him.

"No, you're not," said Letty, picking an apple off of the market table and waving it in front of Raizu's face. "I thought the point of coming to the market was to take our minds off of things. Staring into the distance is creepy, and not helping."

"Sorry." Raizu sighed, and forced his eyes away from the morning-shrouded gray line of distant buildings. "I just keep thinking I hear something."

"The screaming?" Two familiar hazel eyes poked out from behind a fruit stand—it was the boy who had taunted Majest in Sedona's clearing. He didn't look quite so fierce alone in the light. "That's just Acillia. She's giving birth this morning—it's her first time, you know. You can hardly blame her."

"Not the screaming," murmured Raizu, though Acillia relieved some of the stressful unknown. "There's a whispering in my ears, but it doesn't sound like it's close by. It's as if it's coming from those buildings over there." He gestured to the stocky structures and their ashen gloom.

"Those?" Hazel-Eyes wrinkled his nose. "Those are old storage rooms. The old townsfolk used them to keep the materials for building houses, but they're all empty now."

"No one would go down there—for any reason?"

"Not until this morning, no."

Letty leaned forward. "What happened this morning?"

Hazel-Eyes stared at her blankly. "The painting, as the town promised. My brother and some friends went down on Masotote's request with the black dye and coated one of the buildings with it, trying to make the demon trap." He laughed, and it was a loud, harsh sound. "Apparently they think they caught the thing, but no one was able to get inside without throwing a fit. They gave up, went home crying. Who knows if they'll be valiant enough to try again."

"So no one's down there now?" asked Raizu, and felt his voice strain.

A shrug. "Nothing but the dark."

Raizu squeezed his eyes shut until he saw spots, and then reopened them. *There are no such things as demons. No such things, no such things.*

Letty, giving Raizu a curious look, finished putting apples and strawberries into a small container and held it out to Hazel-Eyes. "What do you want for these?"

The boy peered into the basket. "You can keep those for free." He gave the basket back to Letty. "Consider it a gift of apology. I'm sorry about what I said to your brother. I'm sure he was just being manipulated by that Jay kid to say what he did. I hope he comes home soon."

Letty dipped her head, mouth creasing. "Thank you," she said, but her politeness was static, expression flinty. Then she turned to Raizu, motioned back to the cottage. "Are we going home?"

Raizu's unsteady gaze slid past Letty, past her eyes, and landed back on gray-lined buildings. The whisper scratched again in his mind.

"In a minute," he said shakily, heartbeat in his ears. "I want to check the buildings out first. Find out what's making that noise."

"What's gotten into you?" Letty demanded, facing him, forcing his eyes down to hers, which were blue and stern. "You're acting like Maji—all impulsive and morbidly curious."

"I need to see, alright?" Raizu heard the pressure of his voice, heard it crack. His thoughts raged with a foreign, pooling cry for help. "Will you come with me?"

Letty stared at him for a few moments until his heart thought it might burst, and then she nodded, slow and deliberate. "Alright," she said warily. "Alright, alright. Let's make it quick, though. I want to be home in case Maji comes back."

They walked briskly through Hi Ding's streets, feet crunching in the snow, two pairs of boots marking prints along the stony path. Its snow was glowing with faded moonlight, melting further into morning. Raizu could not keep his eyes off it, as if this light would be his last.

"Raizu, look," said Letty, and pointed at the ground. Raizu looked, and she continued, "Footprints! Someone else has been here—and those look like Maji's boots!"

With one look at the ground, Raizu could see she was right. A line of booted footprints, all too familiar, led from Raizu's own toes to the low-lying buildings, unyielding and sure.

Raizu knew he should have been relieved—excited, even— to find that Majest had not gone off to get lost in the woods, but instead, his blood chilled and churned. The whispers escalated, and Raizu shivered. He did not want to associate Majest with the whisper's source. He did not want Majest anywhere near it.

Raizu picked up his pace, and his teeth found their familiar perch around his bottom lip. His heart had accelerated again, beating in his throat, ears, all around—all he could hear. And he could not calm it down. Each breath rippled out in shaky waves.

"If Maji's been here, I hope he turned tail and left," he told Letty, and his voice sounded like a stranger's. "I don't like the look of this place."

Letty frowned, thin eyebrows pushing together, but she did not say anything.

They reached the first building. It only stood a few paces higher than Raizu's head, and it was all he could do to keep from knocking his head on the ceiling as he peeked inside the open entryway. There was no door, and its inside smelled of stone and mud.

"Well, it's not this one," Raizu decided, and sneezed away the stuffy smell of empty dust.

"What exactly are we looking or listening for?" Letty muttered against his shoulder.

Raizu was about to ignore Letty's question and head for a new destination, but the whispering came again, and a shrill noise huffed out from between his teeth. The sound was no longer just a tickle behind his ear, a muffled scratch; it came from close by— close enough to make Raizu shiver up and down like ice had just rained upon his head.

He looked to Letty with eyes that felt cold and empty, and saw that her face was round with horror, pale as the seal-fur blanket that draped her bed. She had heard it, too.

"That," Raizu said in a low rasp. "We're listening for *that*."

"It's coming from over there," whispered Letty, pointing to the street's centerpiece—just another low-hanging building, but it was spattered in pitch black.

Pitch black. Stained.

Raizu's stomach churned, a wave of hysterical fear washing him into numbness. "Yes, that's it."

And he knew it, though he could not explain it—the demon was real. It had been real all along, and there it was, inside of that building, and a sickly sort of fear embraced him.

Slowly, his eyes lowered to the ground, and they followed familiar footprints to the building's door, closed black and tight.

Letty made a choked noise.

Raizu's body shook. "*Himin,* I hope we're not too late."

Letty lifted her eyes at her brother's language on Raizu's tongue, stepped forward and stared at him as if he were something she'd never seen before. Then she shook her head with some ferocity, feet shaking but moving. "Come on."

Raizu, with only a second of hesitation, followed Letty up to Death's door, watching with mute terror as she lifted her hand, pushed on the painted wood.

Then Letty flinched back with a hiss, hand recoiling.

"What? What's the matter?" Raizu demanded. Something wafted from behind the wall, some dystopic song that made his fingers curl.

"The door is *frozen,*" Letty breathed, and clutched a numb hand to her chest.

Raizu, thinking fast, noted a large stone on the ground and picked it up, lodging it between the handle and his hand to keep his fingers out of harm's way. Disregarding his usual sense of terror in favor of a different, heartbreaking sort, he pushed down and the door swung back with a violent screech.

At first glance, the room was empty. Its false darkness shimmered colorlessly, giving away nothing. There was no fight, no blood spattering the walls, no beast springing from the floorboards or victim's scream.

This was not the horror Raizu had expected. This was nothing.

Even the freezing cold and the creeping *wrongness* had disappeared with the trickle of light streaming through the open door.

"I don't understand," Raizu stammered, still clutching at the rock. His heart had stopped skipping beats. For all he knew, it could have stopped altogether. "Where's—?"

"*Maji!*" Letty finished with a scream, and leapt into the darkness, sinking to her knees somewhere beyond Raizu's line of vision.

Raizu couldn't see what or where she was running to, couldn't see her at all. What he saw and felt was nothing.

He took two steps into the room, both feet on the wooden floor of the building, and only had time to distinguish the crumpled form of Majest Skylark broken and lifeless on the ground and let out a choked gasp of horror before the door swung closed behind him, destroying the remaining light.

XXVI. RISING

Blanketed in the heavy darkness, Letty couldn't see her brother. Her hands were on Majest's cold face, stroking back his hair from his forehead with shuddering fingers, but he was invisible, merged into the black and gray that coated him like the paint on the walls, the grime in the air.

Time was at a standstill, frozen by the cold blast that pressed the door shut tight into the wall. There was nothing in the world but Majest, his body face down on the ground, unmoving, eyes closed and breath gone.

Letty's senses were muddled and blurred with anguish and tears, which both rushed down and around her face, shaking her whole body. She was reminded abhorrently of her mother's death, but that pain held nothing now—now she was losing her last piece of the world.

With some gradual crescendo to reality, she felt Raizu kneel beside her, skin and clothes cold. His breath came in ragged wheezes, and Letty realized she could hear no difference between it and her own strangled inhales. Something had lodged itself in her chest, trapping her air.

"Is he breathing? Is there a heartbeat?" Raizu's voice broke with hysteria. It cut through the white haze of numbness around Letty's brain and forced her to think with some clarity.

"I don't know," she said, the words cracking and nearly dying in her throat.

With fingers shaking as badly as her voice, she tore off her gloves and felt for a pulse at Majest's throat. Her fingertips met a wall of ice that sent spasms and chills up through her arm. "I can't feel anything! My fingers are numb!"

Immediately, Letty heard the squeaky sound of leather gloves sliding across skin and felt her hands moved aside as Raizu's took their place. They both held their rasping breath.

"What?" Letty demanded, hands jammed in her pockets where they tingled and throbbed. "What is it?"

Raizu said nothing, moved his hands, and waited.

Letty closed her eyes and shuddered. A whisper pulsed in her head.

Then came a strangled noise of distress, and Letty heard shuffling as Raizu dragged Majest into a sitting position. "There's no heartbeat, Letty," he said in such a distorted, horrified voice she almost didn't recognize it.

Her head began to spin again, threatening to send her spiraling down beneath the floorboards.

"Letty!" Raizu was grabbing her shoulder, shaking her before she could slip into her numb trance. "What are we supposed to do? He's *dying!*"

Letty's lip trembled. She did not respond. Queasiness was crawling up inside her chest from the pits of her stomach, whispering and eating its way through her.

Something was wrong. Something worse than one missing heartbeat.

"*Letty!*" Raizu said again, and his voice held a hysteria she had never heard in her life, as if the cord that tethered him to Earth had snapped. He let go of her shoulder and she heard him grab both of Majest's instead, shaking him frantically. "Letty, *do something!*"

Raizu's voice was a near-sob, an echo in the dark, but Letty through the fog in her thoughts could not hear him. She could hear only the whisper, the scratching, the *shadow*—

"The door closed by itself," she realized at once, her voice strangely solid amidst the chaos around her.

Raizu, stunned into a breathy silence, snapped his head up to the sound of her voice. How could she think of a *door* when her brother lay lifeless on the ground? She hardly believed the words had come from her mouth, but there they were.

And Raizu's hysteria stopped, and Letty heard his head swivel from side to side as if under a spell. His voice was calm without its previous frenzy, but still ghastly, and he said, "There's no light."

No light. The words sounded an alarm bell in Letty's mind, but she could not place the reason in her deadened panic, could not reach the silent scream of warning.

Raizu, clearly without a similar momentary lapse, made a panicked noise. He found a confused and hopeless Letty in the gloom and pushed her to her feet, catching at her hands to tow her up.

"What are you—?" Letty's grasp on her brother faltered, and her fingers clutched spastically at the empty air.

"We have to get out of here." Raizu's words hissed into her ear, laced with urgency and numb grief. "The demon attacks without light, and if this building was painted to trap the demon, if the village thinks they captured it—then Maji walked right into it. If the demon's still around, *we're next. Go.*"

Letty understood at once, barely registering Raizu's admission of demons, and her veins flooded with panic. If they didn't get back into the morning light soon, they could end up with Majest's same fate, broken and cold as shattered ice on the floor. All the same—

"We can't leave him here," she protested, and her arms flailed against Raizu's grip, trying to return to the floor, to her brother. She rubbed stinging tears from her eyes with her shoulders, trying to be brave like Majest. He would have wanted her to be brave, too. "I won't leave him here."

Raizu froze at that, and his grip loosened, as if Letty's words had stabbed him through the back. "No, no," he said at once. "Neither will I. Not on my life. We'll bring him with us." His words held a chord of broken notes that tore at Letty's heart, stung her icy skin. Her eyes went to Majest, invisible on the floor. She was not the only one who would be missing a piece.

A hissing noise came from the back of the room.

Raizu bent back down to the ground, moving Letty aside to gather Majest in his arms and pull his body into a half-standing, half-slumping position. Feet skidded across the wooden floor, and Letty shivered and cringed in anticipation of a fall, but Raizu held steady, staggering to her side.

"We'll have to go quickly now," Raizu said, breathless and shaky. "We can see to him once we have light to work by."

Another hiss—louder.

Letty, not wasting a crack in time's surface, ran with arms outstretched to the front of the room, nearly tripping over her own feet before her hands slapped the surface of the door. She scratched and clawed at it with near-madness, feeling for a handle, a knob, a leverage point—*any* way out. Anything to tell her there was hope of life after these few moments.

"I can't find it!" Her voice screeched to a mountain-top pitch, finding again and again only slimy paint on the wooden surface that repelled her hands, slippery as water running through her hands. "I can't even get a grip on the door! It won't open!"

Raizu whimpered vaguely from somewhere deep within his throat, and Letty knew his slender arms would not be able to hold Majest upright for much longer.

Not to mention the hissing running rampant through the room's perimeter.

And so she thrust her hands blindly to the dark door again, willing useless eyes to see, willing useless fingers to twist and pull, to grasp at what wasn't there. "There isn't a way out," she said, and her voice peaked up with hysteria. "There isn't a way out!"

Her words were drowned in the hissing gurgle and something like a laugh, perhaps a cackle—it sent a scream to her lips, buckled her knees in a horrible recollection of terror, of a boy and an underground garden and lifeless eyes, lifeless screams like the one that poured from her throat.

Letty felt her hands and knees hit the ground just as she heard Raizu drop her brother, landing in the dust alongside him. The laughter seemed to come all at once from everywhere and nowhere, from near and far and close and distance with a dread all too familiar.

"Skylark, you want power?" something snarled, and this was

not the usual voice that played between Letty's ears. *"I'll take yours first."*

"No—never!" Letty howled, and clapped her hands over her ears, crawling like a broken animal to Raizu, elbows brushing the fur of Majest's coat as she forced herself to stand again, to brace herself. "Raizu, what do we *do?"*

"I don't have a weapon!" Raizu's voice was wrecked, and he let Letty drag him to his feet, the two of them creating a barrier between Majest and the howling around them. "My bow and knives are back at the cottage!"

"A weapon wouldn't help!" Letty called back, and it was a wonder how she'd heard his words at all. "It overtook Vari within a matter of seconds!"

"So why isn't it possessing us?" Raizu was pessimistic and frantic as usual, only it was kicked up a few thousand degrees. "Why is it waiting? We're only going to die, anyway! All three of us!"

"Don't say that," said Letty, her voice breaking into a whispered squeak. Out of all the times she had nearly died this past month, it seemed preposterous she should vanish here in the darkness without a fight, without a brother, without a light or hope or even desperation. "Don't say that. Don't *say* that."

As Letty repeated the words over again, as if she could will some truth into their implication, there arose a swirling superfluity of sounds from around her. The hissing roared on, strong as ever, but there was something else above it—something high-pitched and commanding, whirring and fizzing with energy. It brought voices to the walls, their words drowned out by demons and black noise.

Letty lifted her head. She was familiar with these new sounds— an aching familiarity that shot one spark of reassurance to her chest. She hadn't heard such magic in so long, but as the roar filled her ears and folded itself over the dark, it was as if she had never lived without it.

"This is impossible," Letty breathed, but her words were lost. "Absolutely impossible."

Like a dream, she found herself lifted and carried from the ground into empty space high above her head, high above a roof and storage building that disappeared as though the heavens had erased them. Familiar starry swirls rushed under her feet, and their glittering dizziness kept both her and Raizu afloat atop nothingness.

"What's going on?" Raizu asked, voice rising up out of the cloud of whirring voices. "Letty, what's happening? Are we dead? Is this what happens when a demon takes you? Maybe dying isn't so painful, then!"

"No, we're in the realm of the gods," Letty breathed, whispering now that the roar had died away, leaving the same peaceful emptiness she remembered from the night she had received her element, the same swirling fog and stars that sang with a sort of enchantment.

Raizu turned on her, eyes wide and bright with starlight. "We're *what*?" His voice rang loud and bewildered over the night sky, and Letty remembered her own mystification and fright long ago.

"It's okay," she told him gently, though she had to pick up her voice as a low vibration brought a set of stars falling around them. "I'm sure we're here for a reason."

"*Aletta Skylark,*" boomed a familiar voice.

And appearing through countless layers of dense gray fog, cloaked and hooded in robes of starlight, stood a manlike figure with silvery skin and folded wings, blue and red streaks painted in lines over a face pulled into an expression of interest. Two blue eyes pierced through Letty's skin to somewhere deeper.

"Komi," Letty answered, head bowing low in respect. She wondered vaguely how to properly greet a god she had met before—she didn't have to ask him how he'd been, did she? "Why have you come here?"

"My job as Deliverer is to not only watch over the Powers of element, but to aid and protect them in times when their gifts are not enough." Komi's eyes narrowed. "I understand your powers have led to the rise of a great evil." He did not sound surprised. "An evil that has power from below, leading to destruction, heartache—loss."

Letty thought of Vari, pulled into a feverish shadow that did not belong to him, of Sedona, indirectly hunted for a jealous greed not her fault, of Raizu, afraid and tainted by the new world the Skylarks had led him to, and mostly, of Majest, broken and motionless on the floor somewhere far below, failed in his efforts to save those he loved and even those he did not.

"Yes," Letty whispered at last, and kept her head bowed. "Our eldest sister has made it her quest to destroy my brother and I." She bit her lip. "She sent a demon to do the job for her. It's working."

Komi's face was grave, human. "This demon was engineered by a monster who has found his way to the Shadow Energy of the darkest realms. The only way to drive it out is with Element Light. Water and earth are not light, though they thirst for it. The air and sky of Sedona Seacourt is not light. Even fire, bright as it burns, is not light, and it is not fire's time yet."

"Then what do you expect us to do?" Letty wanted to wail out loud. "My brother was killed by this monster! If we can't do anything about it, then why did you bring Raizu and I here in the first place?"

Komi tilted his head. "Quiet, Aletta, for you are mistaken in your every word. I brought you here to help you be rid of the darkness. That is the duty I am bound to, the law I must break. I will not let the lives of my Messengers be wasted—not again. I will keep you protected. Safe."

We aren't safe, Letty wanted to say. *Majest—wonderful, brave Majest—was turned into a bundle of skin and bone because of what darkness can do. We don't have a way to bring the light.*

Raizu broke his steady stream of astonished thoughts to frown at Komi. "You're the Deliverer," he said, oddly calm. "You deliver elemental powers." He blinked. "I don't possess such powers, not at all. I don't understand them and I don't envy Maji and Letty for them. So why am I here? You don't know me. I don't even believe in gods."

"If believing is seeing, I imagine such a picture before you might stir your mind," Komi said, and looked as amused as a god of the heavens could. "I know who you are, Raizu Capricorn. You think you can walk with the Messengers, prop up their power? What do you think you can do for the Skylarks that they can't do themselves?"

Raizu turned bright red. "I don't—"

"Raizu's been an angel ever since he found us," Letty argued hotly. "He's just as valuable an ally against the Organization as a thousand Messengers."

"Peace, little one," said Komi, holding up a hand. "I am not trying to bring offense. In all truths, I have watched with astonishment how this boy fought to be wherever the two of you are. For that, and because of the pure element in his heart, he will be my vessel this time, do what I am bound not to do—he will possess the light to drive out the darkness."

Raizu's red face paled. He began to shift uncomfortably, putting his hands in front of him and reminding Letty of the first time she had ever met him, tongue-tied and innocent in the woods. "I'm no hero," he stammered. "I haven't done a helpful thing since I got here, except offer my opinion. Maji and Letty—they're the real heroes, off on their own, escaping the Organization and battling everything in their way."

"You are the light," Komi repeated, and did not lower his hand. Its silver palm was beginning to glow. "Come forward, Raizu."

Raizu, stunned, didn't seem to know what to do. He opened his mouth but no words came out.

Letty elbowed him. "Go on!"

Raizu stared at her, gaze as inquisitive as Letty felt, and at last stepped forward on shaky feet, trembling with no floor beneath his boots.

Letty willed him not to fall. Somehow, her future, Majest's future, the future of every villager in Hi Ding—it all seemed to revolve around this boy, this ordinary pack boy who did not belong to the pandemonium, but *chose* it. He was the volunteer, the only one Letty had ever known to chase down his fears. He was a coward, perhaps, but he was so brave.

Komi's smoldering hand reached out through blank space to land lightly on Raizu's shoulder. The silver of his palm seemed to burn and melt from god to human in a hiss both fire and water, and Raizu shuddered, closing his eyes.

"You are not destined for elemental power," Komi murmured. Letty barely caught the words. "You do not walk the same path as my Messengers, but you have proven yourself of power in other ways. You are the sun to grow the trees; you are the sun to warm the water."

"I don't understand," said Raizu, and he was still shaking, whole body rocking with tremors. Letty couldn't see his face. "If I cannot hold one of your gifts, then what are you going to give me?"

"If the Messengers are to survive this fight, they need a different sort of power, power I can only deliver, not employ myself. It will be up to you to make use of the light I give you. You may only use it once, and therefore, you must use it wisely." Komi released Raizu and stepped back.

Letty didn't know if it was just her eyes playing tricks on her, but Raizu seemed to glow.

"I—what—?" Raizu stammered, words snapping and breaking before they could form thoughts. He turned to face Letty, and his face was wide and bright. His eyes, which were *definitely* glowing, searched Letty's frantically.

Before she could reply, Letty saw Komi nod and felt herself tumbling backward through the strange tunnel that led from the heavens to Earth, stars in reverse, air behind her in a whoosh; after an exhilarating moment where gravity ceased to exist, she landed on her feet in the pitch black storage building, finally upright again.

Her head roared like a waterfall and her body sagged, eyes widening and resetting at the world's abrupt invisibility. The hissing noise crept back around the room at once, and brought her back to the present with a jolt. Majest still lay on the floor somewhere next to her. Everything still was dark.

"Letty!" said a sudden voice from somewhere in the darkness. Raizu. "Letty, are you there? Tell me that was just a hallucination!"

"It wasn't," Letty replied, and found her heart sinking. "Komi gave you some temporary power you won't be able to use, and then threw us back into the demon's den. Any second, both of us and what's left of Maji will be torn to shreds."

"Wow," Raizu breathed, and it was as if he had not heard Letty's last words. "Gods. Demons. All real." Then he seemed to shake himself back into focus. "Letty, if Komi really gave me some kind of power—which, I don't know why he would, but he did, and it must have been for a reason—then he wants me to use the light to drive out the shadows here. The Demon of Darkness."

You can try, growled a voice in Letty's mind, and she blinked. This time, it was the voice that had flooded the stream during the caribou hunt, the same sliver of consciousness that snuck up from somewhere far down inside her.

She shook it off, remembered Raizu. "Do you feel anything? Can you feel the power?" Letty had felt different after receiving her own gift—dragged down, waterlogged. Perhaps Raizu was the same.

"I feel *something,*" said Raizu, raising his voice above the hiss. Letty could practically sense the frantic pound of his heart. "*What do I do?*"

A wave of freezing cold rushed over Letty and the demon's growl once more emerged from what had seemed only a scratchy whisper. "*So you still dare come to join your brother, do you, Skylark?*"

Letty didn't reply. She held her breath, crouching low on the ground so that she could wrap an arm around her brother's ice-cold body—as if she could shield him from further harm.

"*Lady Lunesta started this, and I, Ohanzi, will end it,*" hissed the voice again.

Raizu, though invisible to Letty in the darkness, seemed to catch his breath and hold it fast. Letty felt the stir in the air as he crouched next to her, his body radiating a hot and nervous energy.

"Do you remember what Maji told Sedona and I at the village meeting?" Letty murmured into his ear, words coming fast and low with no time to spare.

"Which part?" Raizu whispered back.

"When he tried to help us with our powers, he talked about *focus.* He said, '*The key to accessing your power is focus...where you no longer feel anything but the drive, the power in your mind.'"*

"Are you telling me that will work now?" Raizu took another breath, still shaking. "Letty, I'm not your brother, or Sedona, or you; I've never done anything like this before—"

"*Try!*" Letty pleaded as another hissing noise, this one outraged, rang through the storage building.

"Alright!" Raizu finally snapped, clambering clumsily to his feet. Letty could sense how desperately those feet itched to turn and run, but now he was not on the sidelines; it was his burden to hold the fate of lives in his hands.

"*Your brother didn't put up much of a fight, little girl,*" spat the demon's voice. "*He took what was coming to him so easily, as if dying would save the rest of you.*" A hoarse laugh. "*As if there is such thing as a peace offering. As if I could show mercy!*"

The room shook violently, and although Letty's heart rattled and screamed in her chest, she had to stall, to give Raizu time to concentrate from where he stood, breaths raspy and without rhythm behind her.

So she stepped forward. "Why is Lunesta really doing this?" she howled, and although she could not see the demon, she knew it could hear and understand. "She wants a new world, doesn't she? Is this all because she was jealous of our gifts? Because she can have them! We didn't ask to invite all this danger!"

Ohanzi laughed, but it was not a human laugh. "*Creating a better world,*" he snarled mockingly. "*It is not always about you and your insignificance. The Organization is merely a pawn to the world's games, and once I destroy you, they will not matter, for they are wrong. Such power as I—as you, as us all—is only destined to bring the world to its knees.*"

"Not if we have anything to say about it," growled Letty, and gritted her teeth. "The Organization has no way of reaching us without you, and whatever their plans are, they don't need us for a better world—there's no proof our power will ever be a destructive force. They are the destructive force. They created you—that's why we're going to destroy you instead."

"*You cannot destroy the shadows,*" Ohanzi hissed. "*The*

shadows consume everything."

"Except the light," responded Letty. Her fear was gone.

"There is no light in this place."

"You're wrong," said Raizu loudly, and he stood at Letty's side. "Even in the darkest places, there are people who bring light—however temporary their power."

"You," laughed Ohanzi again, voice screeching through layers of metal. *"You aren't even a part of this, boy. Your fear-frenzied endeavors will lead you to a death of your own choosing."*

And then Raizu was glowing again, and Letty could *see,* see the smolder of violet like fire in blue eyes, see the silhouette of a crouched shape, tense and bright in what was once total darkness.

"I don't want to be afraid anymore," Raizu said, and for once, his lip did not tremble. "I'm tired of standing behind the lines of safety. I'll never be brave, I know that—but I don't want to be afraid." He looked at Letty, then at Majest's body, and the fire in his eyes softened to burn with a gentle melancholy. "I've torn my life so far from what it's supposed to be that there isn't any way to turn back. I'm so far from where I've come from. The life I had might as well be gone—my fear should be, too."

The world stagnated to another drop in time as Letty watched her friend with wide eyes. She had never seen him like this before.

Seconds were hours as Raizu raised his hands in concentration, and if only for a moment, Letty saw a little of her brother in the set of his jaw, the steadiness in his reach, as though Raizu could command the forest with an outstretched palm just as well as Majest.

"The light will drive out the darkness," Raizu said in a low voice. "No matter how dark our nights become, the sun will rise to destroy them."

Letty could not be sure, but she thought there was a certain hollow ring to his tone, a familiar metallic pitch, and she thought she saw a flicker of Komi's starry wings flash across her vision.

But then they were gone, and Raizu was only Raizu.

Raizu reached farther, thrust his hands out as if he were trying to grasp something all the way up in the heavens, and despite the odds, Letty believed he had reached it. A stream of light burst from his fingertips, illuminating the building, and Letty smashed her eyelids together. Even with unopened eyes, she was blasted by the golden-white blaze, something pure and bright and full of skylight through the shield of her eyelids.

Then came a scream, a bloodcurdling howl of agony, and Letty swore she smelled the reek of burning flesh. She whimpered and covered her ears, not daring to breathe.

The glow died out the screams with a gradual bravado, a slow crush over each burning moan of pain; they were all sizzling out among the crackle of some gentle, living fire, and Letty squinted, eyelids creeping apart.

The flood of light had subsided into a soft halo of luster that lay in lazy clumps around the building, blanketing just enough of the darkness for Letty to see. The air was quiet; the hissing whisper had vanished.

More than anything, she felt safe.

"Where's Ohanzi?" Letty whispered to Raizu, whose silhouette was leaning over, hands on his knees, inhaling and exhaling with his entire body. Her skin still prickled, and she would take no chances, even with the softness of the light hovering over them. "Did it work? Did the light work?"

Raizu exhaled a breathy laugh. Beads of sweat trickled down his forehead; he wiped them away with one sleeve. "It must have, because I feel like I'm going to pass out."

Letty rushed immediately to her friend's side, letting him lean on her shoulder. He smelled of sunlight and leather and faded energy, and it burned her nose in sympathy. She could hear his heartbeat pounding, though it was beginning to slow.

"And so you save us again," she said. "For real, though, this time—not just stories of an Organization or finding me after I'd already been saved. None of us would be alive if you hadn't followed us here."

And that was it, Letty thought. The justification, what Raizu had been seeking. A reason to tell him he had not been a fool, that bravery was not always recklessness.

But Raizu just shook his head, and he looked nothing like a hero, just the boy he'd always been. "I didn't save anyone. Komi's light power saved us. I was the vessel, like he said. Komi acted through me, so he could interfere on Earth without breaking the gods' laws. I'm just a shell."

"Either way, we're saved, and it's because of you," Letty protested.

"Not all of us are saved." Raizu swallowed, head turning to face the still form of Letty's brother on the ground, blurred in the fuzzy light. "It might as well have been for nothing—he's gone, Letty, and I couldn't do anything to stop it."

Letty stared down at Majest. With all the heat and adrenaline of Ohanzi's darkness, she had almost forgotten.

She sat down on the floor next to him and leaned her head over his chest as though about to curl up together for a nap, but she was listening for a heartbeat, and her movements were restless and jerky. She could hear nothing but a faint murmur, as though the rest of his body tried in vain to continue life—but nothing could survive with a heartbeat painted black, and not even Raizu's light could reverse the damage that had been done.

"Nothing," Letty murmured, putting a hand to Majest's cheek. "Nothing at all." He was still so cold. Her heart hollowed out as she looked at his once-handsome face, now pale and lifeless.

Raizu sank to the ground next to her, still shaking. He had not stopped trembling since they'd entered the building, whether shaking with fear, power, or grief. "So much for Komi keeping his Messengers safe," he said, his voice bitter. "He didn't let me save Maji, did he? Only us."

Letty didn't know what to say. Anything that came out of her mouth would only tear her apart through her lips and tongue. So she leaned into Raizu's warm arm, depleted. "You didn't just save us. You saved the whole village."

"I don't care," Raizu said, closing his eyes as they began to water. "He's dead."

Letty might have tried wiping his tears before they fell, might have found something beyond herself to say, but it was as if the universe had timed itself to interrupt that moment; the door creaked open from behind with an abruptness that momentarily shattered the grief hanging in the air, flooding it with real light—sunlight.

Letty turned, not sure whom she was expecting to see, but she had definitely not been expecting Jay. But then again, with him, that always seemed to be the case.

"Morning, you two. I thought I heard some sort of racket," said the blind boy, tilting his head at Letty. He leaned against the door frame, picking at the paint absently with one fingernail.

Letty didn't know whether she was pleased to see him or not, but she was certainly startled—she had come close to believing she and Raizu and this cursed building were all that was left of the living world.

"Anyway," Jay continued, "I heard a lot of shouting, so I assumed someone was enough of an idiot to wander back into another idiot's idea of a demon trap. I decided to join you once things seemed to calm down. I didn't think I'd be any use to any of you fighting, nor did I really care to be involved in your battles in the first place."

"So why *are* you here, exactly?" asked Letty, though she didn't particularly care for an answer at the moment.

Jay crossed his arms, shook dark hair from his eyes, and for some reason, looked embarrassed. "I was in the neighborhood. These old buildings are strangely good for wandering through when your village is probably going to exile you into the Bay on a floating mat of logs, so I came here to think, to pretend that I'm alone. Unfortunately, I have ears, and so I know that not to be the case. Is the demon gone?"

"Raizu killed it," Letty told him. "We're okay, but Maji…" She blinked water from of her eyes, forbidding herself to cry in front of Jay. She would not do it, not even over this.

"Let me see," Jay said without emotion, crossing the room with an impossible fluidity. He didn't seem to recognize the irony of the words he'd said—or maybe he had, and feigning their validity was another useful way to pretend.

"Be careful." Raizu shifted away from Majest to give Jay

enough room to examine the body.

Just as Letty had done, Jay leaned over the lifeless body, listening and feeling for a pulse. After a moment he said with a decent amount of certainty, "He's not dead."

Letty's breath caught in her throat. *What?*

"But there's no pulse," she said quickly. She refused to let her hopes rise when they were only sure to come crashing down again.

"Why does no one *ever* listen to me?" griped Jay to no one in particular. "I may be blind, but that doesn't mean you all get to be deaf. I said he's *not dead*."

Letty stayed silent in her confusion, mashing her lips into a worried line.

Raizu, on Jay's other side, gave her a bewildered but hopeful glance. "*Not dead?*" he mouthed.

She shook her head. She would not raise his hopes, either.

Jay seemed to sense no one was going to respond. He drew a long, heavy sigh that made his whole body slump. "You checked his pulse?" He directed the question at Raizu.

"I did," Letty replied for him in a small voice. "There wasn't anything except a little murmur—"

"The smallest details are the most important," muttered Jay, putting two fingers to Majest's neck. "There isn't a heartbeat, but the rest of his body is alive. The demon must have stopped his heart directly, but that leaves everything else...untouched. One missing piece."

"So what do we do?" asked Raizu. His voice sounded even smaller than Letty's had, and twice as nervous. "You need a pulse to live. There's no way he's alive."

"We have to get his troublesome heart working again," said Jay, shrugging. "I'd imagine he still has some time left, though if we don't get moving, the rest of his body will give up. You can only spend so much time following a leader who has fallen."

"Well, then what are we waiting around here for?" Letty jumped up immediately, skin tingling. "Let's get him back to the village!"

Together, with the help of a jittery Raizu and a surprisingly-strong Jay, Letty was able to lift Majest up and get him outside. The opened door had *stayed* open, not closing in on anyone now that there was no demon to hold it shut, and its chipping paint seemed to welcome them back to the fresh air of the village morning.

When Letty looked up at the rising sun, she realized with embarrassment she had started to cry after all—soundlessly, tears of grief and terror and hope and confusion and everything in between. They slid down her cheeks in abandon, and she could not wipe them away, as both of her hands were around Majest's shoulders, and she could not let him fall as she could let fall the tears.

So instead, she leaned her wet face into the crook of her brother's neck and breathed in, the scent of Majest's skin and clothes just the same as it had been for years—evergreen. Home.

Letty closed her eyes, trusting Raizu and Jay to guide her. The warmth of the sunrise felt good on the top of her head, where her hair had slid out of its binding and curled around her shoulders and arms. She let it warm her, and let her hair fall, too.

For a moment, she felt like a little girl again, back at her old cottage. Back when "organization" was just a way to sort her feather collection, and she had two parents and two siblings, five wilderness survivors. There had been a time when she'd never thought she would need knowledge of how to build a fire, or find food and water. A time when gods were legends, and happiness was not. A time when everything was going to be alright.

"But everything's going to be alright now," she tried to tell herself, the words whispered into Majest's ear as if he could hear them, too. "The shadows are gone and everything's going to be alright."

XXVII. CALM

"You must have done something wrong. He's not waking up!"

"Oh, he's fine. I hear him snoring. You shouldn't be concerned about his vitality—in no time, he'll be up and prancing about with those heavy steps I always feel him taking, like he thinks he's the heavens' gift to mankind."

"Hey, you can't make fun of someone who almost *died* this morning."

"Would you rather I make fun of *you,* who almost died a few days ago?"

Majest could hear the voices somewhere far above his head, as if they were in the clouds and he lay stuck in the mud. He'd been hearing the voices for quite some time now, but he couldn't distinguish them from one another, nor could he make much sense of the words that sounded more like garbled noise than any language he knew.

He knew he had been dead. Or at least, that was what it felt like—his heart had been lost to him for only a brief hair in time, but that moment had been enough to send him hurtling down an unfamiliar path to something that was not the proverbial bright light of afterlife, but an empty hollow blankness that had seemed to him exactly as death should be.

But he hadn't wanted that path or that void, not when it would pull his freedom from his chest, so he had fought and fought, the rest of his body slammed and beating to its core in circles until he had climbed from that dark hole, or at least started to—losing ground after quite a while of the chase, slipping and tumbling until

403

something or someone had caught him tight and tethered him back to the land of the living with a sturdy rope. His heart had come back to him, stronger than ever.

Now he rested in his cumbersome state of unconsciousness, a deep slumber that kept him still and helpless as a sleeping newborn.

Except for one thing, one thing that jolted him awake. His stomach was growling.

"I'm hungry," he heard himself say. His voice was groggy and sounded ridiculous to his own ears, but it signified consciousness, and that was relieving.

He forced his eyes open, seeing blurry figures and shapes above his head. He was lying on his back on a board of hard wood. There was a cloth draped over it, and from its starchy whiteness, the faint scent of blueberry stirred as Majest did. He couldn't decide whether he was comfortable or not.

"Hungry? Is that so?" One of the figures above Majest's head moved. "You hear that? Our misfortunate hero takes on a demon all by himself, gets his heartbeat ripped out of him, practically comes back from the dead—and the only thing he has to say for himself is that he's *hungry.*"

"Be nice, Jay," said another voice, this one higher in pitch.

Another of the blurred shapes moved, and Majest's eyes strained to keep up. It took a few seconds of painful blinks and bats, but then his eyes readjusted to consciousness; he could recognize the two shapes hovering before him. They were more than shapes; they were breathing faces on human heads belonging to Jay and—Majest realized with a jolt of astonishment—*Vari.*

"I know where I am," Majest said in a daze, lifting tingling arms to rub at his eyes. His limbs felt like they were made of water, and he had to try a few times before they flowed the way he wanted them to. "Never thought it'd be me here; usually it's everyone else who ends up lying in Jay's house, unconscious with a crowd peering over them." He wasn't sure whether his unsteady voice was understandable to anyone else, but he didn't care.

"It's good you woke up," said Vari in his chipper way. He was smiling, as usual, as though this were a pleasant and normal scenario. It made Majest's forehead ache. "I woke up a couple hours ago, too, out of nowhere. Jay told me I was possessed by demonic energy and you got hurt trying to destroy it. That was really brave of you."

"Maji!" called a voice before Majest could respond. It was Letty, running toward them, her eyes alight with joy and relief. She stopped at the wooden table, which must have been the one Raizu had been put on when he had nearly drowned himself. It still smelled vaguely of salt water, and that at least was a small comfort.

"Letty," Majest breathed as his sister caught him in an awkward embrace. He patted her back to the best of his limited ability. "How are you?"

"How am *I?*" Letty's eyebrows went up above shining eyes. "How are *you?* You almost died!"

"I'm great," Majest grinned weakly, forcing his eyelids back open where they had slumped with sleepiness. "Though that demon guy was pretty creepy. Ohanzi, wasn't it?" He thought for a moment. "He's dead, right? I killed him?"

Letty and Vari exchanged a glance. Majest noticed with a surprised interest that they were standing side-by-side, their hands clasped. He narrowed his eyes. "What—?"

"Raizu killed Ohanzi," said Letty, her eyes following Majest's gaze to her hand, intertwined with Vari's. She looked away, going a pale pinkish color. "We found you in the storage building and got trapped inside of it with you. Komi appeared and gave Raizu light power, and—"

"*Komi?*" Majest couldn't believe his ears. "*Komi* appeared? And gave Raizy a *light power?*"

"You Skylarks really *are* deaf, aren't you?" Jay muttered from somewhere across the room.

"You should probably let Raizu explain," Letty said. "I'm sure he'll tell the story better than I ever could. After all, he was the hero, not me."

"Raizu. Right." Majest was confused, wondering why his closest friend wasn't there with the others. Then, with a sickening crank, his memory kicked in and he recalled their argument, Raizu's coat and scarf trailing in the wind behind him.

His face drooped into a disconsolate frown.

"He's outside if you want to see him," Letty offered. "If you think you're well enough."

Majest wasn't sure what he wanted to do. Was Raizu still angry with him for running off on his own? Was he even angrier now that Majest had nearly gotten himself killed? Had Majest lost him for good?

"I'm not letting you go anywhere until you have enough strength to move," Jay warned him before he could decide, and walked over on light feet. Somehow, he looked less irritable than usual. He was only somewhat unpleasant as he said, "You should have something to eat."

"Fine," Majest agreed. He wasn't sure he wanted to face Raizu yet, and he certainly didn't want to do it on an empty stomach, sore head, and wobbly legs. "What do you have? Caribou? Rabbit? I'm starved."

Jay snorted, though he did not smile or even smirk. Majest suspected he never did. "Like you'd actually be able to chew and digest that in your condition. I'll make you some soup."

"What kind of soup?" Majest asked, doubtful.

"Vegetable."

"*Vegetable?*"

"Yeah, you know, sort of like lemming soup, except instead of lemming, it's got vegetables in it."

"It's really good," Letty added. "I promise."

"Alright," said Majest noncommittally, closing his eyes. "Whatever you want." He felt a sudden, strong urge to simply lie where he was and forget the world for a while, and so he did.

Jay set to work making the soup, lighting a small fire under a pot in the back of the room. Vari and Letty cluttered around him in a flurry, four hands there to help when an ingredient went missing or something spilled into the fire. Jay let out an irritable sigh each time their fingers caught his mistakes, but he didn't protest the assistance.

Majest, eyes closed and ears only half paying attention, smiled to himself. Jay wasn't the type to accept help from others graciously, but Letty and Vari were persistent enough to make the best of it. Perhaps now that the danger had passed, that sort of harmony would mold the whole town together like a marbled sculpture, and Majest could finally relax, finally enjoy it.

Except for one thing.

Majest cracked one eye open. "So what about Vosile Masotote? Everyone still following him around like he's the pack leader and you're all the little minions? Does he still want to lock me up, or pretend we're a bunch of pathological liars and he isn't?"

Three figures across the room froze. Letty exchanged a worried glance with Vari.

"What?" Majest demanded, his other eye following the first. "What's the problem?"

"Masotote is dead," Jay said bluntly. "He's been dead for quite a few hours now."

That took a second to sink in. *"What? How?"*

The salty tang of cooked vegetables arose from the kitchen, and Letty appeared at his side to hold out a steaming cup. "Drink this."

Jay, behind her, leaned against the wall. "He heard about your death at the hands of his own failed plan, and he called another village meeting, out of the blue. He told everyone the truth about what he did to you, and what he did to me. Apologized for it, too. Said he could have prevented all of this." Blind eyes went up to Majest, bored through him. "Said he could have saved you, too."

Majest did not say anything. Something wormed its way through his stomach.

Jay stared back at the floor. "Everyone got really quiet, and Masotote just picked up his feet and left, walking like he'd never slept in his life. Two hours after that, someone found him dead in his room, face-down on his bed, suffocated in the blankets."

Slowly, Majest took the soup cup from Letty with a shaky hand, tiny drops raining down on his lap. "I'm sorry," he said, not sure if he meant it. "About starting all this, and if it's my fault he's dead. I'm sure it was a horrible shock to the village."

Jay shook his head with another lifeless laugh. "He was a

horrible *man*, and his greed would have gotten us all killed if not for you."

"Does the village know that now?" Majest's voice was a test, and his muscles suddenly tensed.

Jay gave a slight nod. "He told them to believe in what you said. All of it."

"Well, that's certainly a relief." Majest let out a breath he hadn't realized he was holding. "And I sure hope they believe in you now, too, *prophet*."

Jay shrugged, scuffed one foot awkwardly. "Maybe, maybe not. Finish your soup."

Majest complied, and when the last drop passed his lips, he felt brighter, well-oiled, like his joints might swing on their own. He wasn't well enough to forget his near-death occurrence, but well enough that he didn't still feel as though he could slip over that dark edge.

"I think I'm going to go talk to Raizy now," he decided. Even death could not take away impatience, wrongs that needed righting.

"Can you even walk?" Jay asked him doubtfully.

"I don't know," Majest admitted. "I haven't gotten that far."

Figuring it was now or never, he swung his legs around and off the wooden bed with a low grunt of effort. His limbs still felt watery, and his vision swarmed with black spots at the sudden movement.

Letty was at his side before he could twitch another finger, and let him lean against her bony shoulder as he set his feet on the floor with a ginger delicacy, shifting his weight downward until he was in something like a standing position. He gripped the sleeve of Letty's shirt with white knuckles, and she teetered under his weight, slouching heavily into the wooden table beside them.

"Are you sure you're going to be alright walking on your own?" she asked with hesitance. "I could go with you."

"No," said Majest through teeth mashed together, and used all his concentration not to collapse or crush into his sister. "No, I need to do this on my own."

Before Letty could protest, Jay spoke up from where he stood next to the rest of his soup, a steaming pot and a slowly-dying fire. "I have something you could use."

Every eye turned to him.

Jay disappeared down the hallway with the silence and nonchalance of a ghost, and moments later returned carrying two long wooden poles, which looked smooth and sturdy. He held them out in Majest's direction, and Majest staggered forward to take them with his free hand.

"You can use these to walk," Jay said, eyes boring blind holes into the ground. "I, ah—used to need them back when I didn't know the area so well, when I wanted to test the ground in front of me. But now that the earth seems to hold relatively steady, you can use them."

Majest raised his eyebrows. Was that *embarrassment* he'd detected?

Still, he had the decency to simply nod in gratitude. "They look like they'll work," he said. He gathered the walking sticks into firm grasps, tucking them under his arms before leaning forward, taking a step, and finding he could stand without Letty's help.

"Well?" Vari cocked his head to one side.

Majest smiled. "They're great."

Jay's eyes narrowed. "Just don't dent my floor, alright? I might trip, fall, and kill myself."

"Oh. Right." Majest balanced himself between the two wooden poles, keeping the stress off the floorboards. Once he situated himself properly, he took a breath, started for the door. "I'll be back soon. If I'm not, I've probably fallen with no one to help me up."

Letty exchanged another glance with Vari. Her face was the dark red of a ripe apple, and Vari's eyes shone with a jittery sort of resolution.

"Wait," Vari said, just as Majest turned to leave. "There's something Letty and I need to tell you."

"No, there isn't," Letty stammered, blushing furiously. "Not yet, anyway."

Now Majest was suspicious. He turned back for a moment to stare at the two younger children. Though, he figured, he couldn't call them children for much longer. They were six-birth years, and Majest himself was gaining on eight—he had to be seven and a half; he was sure of it. That was fifteen in old-world years. Letty was twelve—thirteen, maybe.

They were nearly adults.

"What is it?" Majest asked, a little nervous.

Letty flinched back. "It's nothing—"

"When I woke up this morning," Vari said as if she hadn't spoken, eyes round with faded innocence, "Letty was the first person I saw—that was a relief. She was the only one I wanted to see." His gaze drifted from Majest to Letty and softened. Majest, stomach coiling into loops, knew that look.

And Letty returned it.

"Letty told me about what happened with the demon—how she had to be so brave," Vari went on. "If it weren't for her, I would have never woken up."

"It was Raizu who killed Ohanzi," muttered Letty, and stared at her shoes.

"But I'd rather pretend like it was you who had to be the bravest," Vari told her, interlacing his fingers with hers once more. He looked up at Majest. "I asked Letty if she would be my partner."

And that was when Majest felt his eyes blow so wide that if they should have grown any further, they would have toppled out of his skull and rolled across the floor.

"Y-you," he stuttered. "You're *six.*" He knew for a fact his parents hadn't been partnered until many years later than that—partnership and love were for adulthood, not children's daydreams.

"I know," said Vari, cringing just a little. "I'm not implying we hold the ceremony *now.* But I asked her if in a couple years, if she were still interested—"

"And what did you say, Letty?" Majest demanded, cutting Vari off. He whirled on his sister, not sure what he wanted the answer to be.

"I said yes," Letty answered, and her face was more violet than red. She looked almost apologetic as she continued, "I know you don't like Vari, Maji, but this is my decision."

Majest let out a breath through his nose. He didn't dislike Vari—he wasn't sure how he felt. No matter how much or how often Vari irritated him, he obviously adored Letty. And if Majest's only reason for his aversion was that *he* had always been the one to guide Letty through the woods or wash the snow from her boots, not Vari, that was a rather petty way of thinking. Letty was not Majest's responsibility. She was young, but she was strong, stronger now than ever.

She had not almost died that morning under the cover of darkness. She was stronger than that.

"Alright," Majest said after some time, and with much difficulty. "If this is what you want."

"Yes!" Vari cried, catching Letty around the waist and lifting her into the air, the two of them twirling in a disjointed, clumsy circle that fluttered out like a flower blooming. Upon setting Letty's feet back on the ground, Vari turned to Majest. "Thank you," he said.

Majest nodded, perhaps forcibly. He pursed his lips. "Take care of each other."

"Speaking of taking care of things," said Jay pointedly, "don't you have somewhere to be going?"

Majest glanced over, having forgotten Jay was still there, a ghost in his own house. He stood by his soup pot, staring off into the middle distance with sightless eyes and a gloomy scowl, like talk of love and partnership made him inexplicably upset.

"Right," said Majest, gathering up his walking sticks. "I'm leaving."

"Good luck," Letty told him, smiling not just with her mouth, but with her eyes, the way she always did. Her expression was warm. "I know he'll forgive you. He was only angry because he didn't want to see you get hurt. He told me so himself. When you love someone, you try to protect them no matter what—that's what family is for."

Majest stared at her in wonder, wondering when she had gotten wiser than him. "I suppose we are family," he murmured.

"We are!" said Vari, beaming.

Majest rolled his eyes. "You, too?"

411

"You'll get used to it," Letty assured him. Then her eyes begin to glisten. "Now go find Raizu."

Raizu was not hard to find. He didn't have Majest's sense of reckless anger, and would never go storming off into the woods, not with his fear of becoming lost in the wilderness, stuck in the dark with no way to find his way home—whether he considered his home Hi Ding, Inertia, or any long hour of sunlight.

No, Raizu simply sat on the edge of the path to Jay's house, coat trailing in the dust, head in his hands as he traced loose patterns in the snow beside him. The path was a downward slope that led from the short hilltop to the base of the town's pebbly circle—Jay had the only house in the village without steps, and everything was smooth and winding, no rickety bumps to trip over, no chance for a tumble.

Raizu, however, couldn't have found the lack of steps any help, as it left him slumping in the snowy grit, dirt and white fluff on his boots, his pants, the cuffs of his sleeves. But he didn't look as if he minded—he looked particularly abandoned, actually, as if he had forgotten why he was there.

Majest's restarted heart nearly broke all over again. This was his fault.

"Raizy?" He hobbled over on Jay's wooden walking sticks, barely keeping from toppling over.

Raizu didn't look up—he didn't even seem to notice he was no longer alone.

"Raizu," Majest said, louder this time, waving a foot in front of his friend's face, fingernails digging into the wood under his arms until splintering prickles stabbed at his skin. "Can I talk to you?"

Raizu's head lifted slowly. His eyes, troubled, were less blue and more of their ringed violet, and Majest couldn't tell whether the sun was rising or setting inside them.

For the longest time, Majest was sure he would say nothing, but then Raizu muttered, "I'm really glad you're okay. Jay said there was a chance you wouldn't make it at all. But here you are—

already walking." He gestured to Majest, who stood while he sat in the dirt.

"Here I am," Majest agreed, and another lump formed in the back of his throat. Two in one day. "I'm sorry for everything. I hope you know that."

That snapped Raizu out of his quiet trance, lit the blue fire in two irises. "*You're* sorry? What would *you* have to be sorry for? You found the demon—I didn't believe in demons and heavens, but you proved me wrong, taught me the truth. Don't you know what that means to me?"

Majest, gripping the walking sticks, lowered himself cautiously to the ground next to Raizu, weak legs out in front of him, arms propping him up on the hard ground. "Me telling the truth, huh. That's certainly a new one." He swallowed, dropped his voice. "Letty said you killed Ohanzi?"

Raizu flushed, looking away. "That's not specifically true."

"Then what happened?" asked Majest. "She told me to ask you for the story, since you're the hero."

"She said that? I don't know why she'd say that." Raizu stared at the confused lines he'd drawn in the snow, swirling obscurity reflected in downcast eyes. "It's simple—we heard a whisper. We found the building. We found you." His voice caught. "We were trying to carry you out, trying to save you—then the demon found us."

"So how did you kill it?" Majest studied his hands, ungloved and freckled with calluses. "Letty said something about Komi and a light power."

"That's why I said it wasn't me who killed Ohanzi," Raizu replied, in the tone of someone simply delivering formalities, ignoring something darker underneath. "Komi, he...just came out of nowhere. Took us to the skies—there were stars *everywhere*."

Majest nodded. "I've been there."

"Right." Raizu nodded. "So Komi started talking about Ohanzi, said only light can destroy shadows." He took a breath, emotionless. "He told me I was the light. Then he gave me a one-time-use power, and I...I suppose that was what got rid of Ohanzi."

"You?" Majest felt himself smile. "A god singled *you* out to destroy a demon? *Hímin,* that's incredible!" He nudged Raizu's shoulder. "You can't downplay that. That's an honor—proof that you're about as far from useless as anyone could ever be."

Raizu shook his head, face almost as scarlet as Letty's had been—but distressed, red with conflict. "You shouldn't say that. If it hadn't been for me, you would have never been in there, or at least not alone. If I hadn't yelled at you like I did…" He broke off, lip between his teeth. "You wouldn't have left. You wouldn't have gotten yourself hurt."

And then Majest realized why Raizu was here, sitting out in the cold instead of a candlelit house.

"You're not angry with me," he said. "You think this is your fault."

Raizu didn't say anything in response, but he bit his lip again, and the gesture betrayed him.

"It's *not* your fault," Majest insisted. "It's *mine.* You saved my life—again, I might add. I didn't do anything but act like a stubborn fool. I thought I could save the world, but it takes more than elemental powers or reckless bravery to be a hero. It takes heart—light—and that's what you've got."

Raizu shook his head again, more ferociously, and his eyes glistened. "No, no! I shouldn't have gotten so angry with you. It was your job to destroy what was trying to destroy you. This is your fight, after what happened with your parents, and your sister. You were right. I just—" He broke off to catch his breath, like his mouth couldn't keep up with the words that itched to get out.

"Just what?"

"I didn't want you to get hurt. I didn't want to have come all this way just to lose you, lose the start of some bravery I've never had before and the one who helped me find it." Raizu buried his head in his hands with an embarrassed sound, muttered, "I'm sorry."

Majest felt his gaze soften. "It's alright," he said. "You were just looking out for me. I'd do the same for you. We're family now, right? So why don't we just agree to disagree? It's all over. Neither of us is to blame—it's the Organization. They're reckless; they're cowards. They bring out the worst in all of us, and while they're at it, they bring the worst right to our doors and make us fight it to stay alive."

Raizu wiped at his eye with one hand. "I guess that's true."

"Of course it is," said Majest firmly. "And now they're gone, right? They can't find us, and maybe they'll abandon us in their plans for good. We're safe. We can start our lives over."

Raizu couldn't help but smile. "Right, and on the note of starting life over, that reminds me—there's something I need to tell you. Something big."

"What now?" asked Majest, grinning as he thought of Letty and Vari's declaration. "Don't tell me you're partnering with someone, too. Sedona? Sunni? *Jay?*"

Raizu rolled his eyes. "*No,*" he said, "but I decided I'm going to stay here in Hi Ding instead of going back to live with my family in Inertia, if that's of any importance to you."

Majest stopped laughing. "What? You're joking. You love your pack."

"I do," agreed Raizu. "But they'll have to understand that I belong here now, because I do. Being here, tackling the world with you—that's what I want to do." He gave a tentative smile, as though some part of him feared rejection, but that was the last thing on Majest's mind as it whirled and spun—he had in fact been trying to forget Raizu had any other home at all, that there had ever been a time of only Majest and Letty without the spearhead of their trinity, the connecting piece that wove them together and tied them in a knot.

When Majest did not respond, lost in a gaping wonder, Raizu gestured to the town, the ring of buildings and curious people. "This place is starting to feel like home, more than anywhere. For the first time, I don't feel like I'm chained to myself and my fears, forced to be what my brother wanted me to be. Here, I can pretend to be brave until I start to feel its reality. I can run through the woods, I can walk through the heavens, I can face demons… I'm sure Inertia can understand that."

"But you can't just…*leave* them," Majest stammered,

immediately willing himself to stop talking before he convinced Raizu to give up the idea altogether. "I mean, I want you here more than anything—Letty does, too—but your family will think you're dead. They'll be worried sick—"

"That's why I'll go back to deliver the message."

"What do you mean?"

"I'm going to go back to Inertia, tell them I'm staying."

"And you're sure they'll be alright with that?"

"We've had a number of our packmates do the same—they find a better home, something or someone they love and they just…" Raizu waved his hands in a shy gesture, and when he met Majest's eyes, they were blue and cloud-lit again, the sun and the sky. "Leave. Maybe they're not always the leader's brother, but I'll be the first."

"It's a long way back," Majest warned him, but the giddy grin that creased his cheeks was impossible to tame. "Inertia's even farther than my old house from here. I should come with you."

Raizu's eyes lit. "Would you really? I mean, you don't have to—"

"Don't be ridiculous." Majest was firm. "Letty and I would do the same for each other and I know you'd do the same for us."

Raizu's face split into a smile wider than the forests, and then they were both leaning in with their teeth peeking out in glee. "That would be—"

"*Majest!*" came a new voice. It was Sedona, running toward them with white hair flying and a spring in her step. She came to a rushing halt at their feet, leaving snowy dust clouds in her wake, and Majest and Raizu split apart in a startled jump. "There you are! I've been looking everywhere for you!"

Majest was the first to find words and respond—"What? What's the matter?"

"Why would anything be the matter?" Sedona beamed, eyes warm and alight with pride. "You saved the day, didn't you? The village is safe!"

Raizu turned red all over again. "It was actually Komi who—"

"We're having a celebration," Sedona continued, staring at

Majest as if Raizu hadn't spoken. "An apology to you, ultimately. You were right about Masotote, right about the demon, and now we're throwing a party to celebrate the storm finally parting from our village. What do you say?"

Majest leaned on one arm. "I say, what's in a party?"

Sedona's eyes went to the sky to count. "There'll be a feast, singing, dancing, decorations, lights, more music—all sorts of things."

Majest frowned. "You're having a party to celebrate us killing Ohanzi when it was my fault he targeted the village in the first place?"

"Don't rain on the parade," Sedona told him, hands on her hips, but there was a distilled affection in her eyes that made Majest curious. "It's going to be amazing, and you're coming."

"I never said I wasn't," Majest said with touch of amusement. "It sounds fantastic and we're honored to come—right, Raizy?"

Raizu looked from Majest to Sedona with a peculiar expression. "When does the party start?"

"Tonight," Sedona answered, finally seeming to acknowledge Raizu's existence. "And soon. You might want to get some medicine for those wobbly legs of yours and wash up a bit. Come down to the fountain in a few hours. We'll be all set up. I'm head of the party organization, after all."

Majest cringed a little at the word *organization*, but held his smile. "Great. We'll be there."

Sedona's mouth formed a grin of its own, a mirror that beamed back at him. "Good," she said, and she sounded as though she'd won some sort of prize, turning with a wave to bounce away.

Once she was out of sight, Raizu turned to Majest, eyes dancing in a waltz of mischief. "You *know*," he said with some thoughtfulness, "I saw a dark brown suit in the closet in our room, shoved way in the back. It's really nice—it's got buttons up the front, and one of those old-world collars. Whoever lived here before us must have had very good taste."

"Well, you should wear that suit tonight, then," Majest told him, not understanding.

Raizu snorted. "Please. It would be too long on me." He smiled again. There was a lot of smiling today, Majest noticed. "Sedona probably wants you to look nice—she seems to really want you there."

Majest shrugged in a self-conscious way. "I don't think it really matters."

Raizu's eyes narrowed. "Wear the suit, Maji."

Majest sighed in defeat. Another smile, the thousandth smile. "Fine."

XXVIII. CLOSED

More light was tossed up into the nighttime sky than Letty had ever seen in her life. And it was not just the yellow of sun and stars, but in every prismatic hue that could have been under them—reds, blues, greens, violets, the flickering shades in between. Sedona and the villagers had managed to set ablaze the entire town center in a sphere of mottled splendor.

Strings of colored paper twined merrily around the houses in a sort of moving dance, lanterns swinging from between them and painted with frames of multicolored dye, sending color and grandeur streaking across stone paths and evergreens.

Someone had set up tables off to one side, shaded with cloth tents and adorned with platters and silverware—a village feast. There were caribou legs and rabbit breasts steaming brightly into the dark, fruits and vegetables in elegant trays, and loaves of bread so fresh they made Letty's mouth water.

Some small children toppled back and forth around the paths and fountain like fish in a stream, screaming and laughing, chasing each other in circles. A few parents looked on, but most were too busy celebrating on their own.

Behind the fountain, Rapple sat with his partner and her new baby, rummaging through a leather bag to pull from it a long wooden object, which he tucked tenderly under his arm. Strings were bound tight across its center and Rapple plucked at one gently, ringing a twang across the village center, one teasing note of song.

"It's really pretty, isn't it?" a voice murmured into Letty's ear. She whirled around to see Vari, grinning and holding two cups of a dark violet drink. "I brought you some grape juice."

"*Grape* juice," Letty repeated, and took a cup. Vari's hand was warm where it brushed against hers. "Two weeks ago I didn't know what a grape *was*, and now there's a juice of it." She took a sip and was pleasantly surprised. "This is delicious!"

"I know," said Vari, and slid an arm around her shoulders. "Quell and Idyllice make it for us. It's the best juice I've ever had."

"Do they do this often?" Letty asked, leaning into him. She remembered the shock of his partnership proposition, the paralyzing relief she'd felt when he woke up from his comatose slumber—when she had realized she felt the same way. It was strange having someone to care for her who wasn't family—or *like* family as Raizu was. Vari was a new world to discover, new spaces to fall into.

"Do what? Make juice?" Vari brought her back to the present, and his eyes were a watery glitter under the lights. "All the time. Quell's got a special machine that squeezes the fruits to get the juice out—he made the machine himself—and so they're always making it. Sometimes I go down there and—"

Letty giggled and rolled her eyes, cutting him off. "*No!* I meant, do they always have celebrations like these?"

"Oh. Um. No, only on special occasions." Vari looked out over the gathering crowd, the rising patter of conversation. "And since you helped save our town from the demon, this is one of those occasions."

Letty felt a creeping blush on her cheeks and distracted herself by following his gaze. "Sedona really outdid herself."

"Sedona isn't really interested in doing anything halfway," Vari said, something like brotherly affection in his voice. Letty imagined Sedona was a sister to the whole town—and with Sunni planning on teaching, it was if the Seacourts dedicated their lives solely to dedication.

Rapple's stringed wood rang through the streets again, in longer phrases this time, melodies and harmonies playing chase on the breeze in streams of what Letty had only just tasted before—*music*. Letty knew only of gentle lullabies and nursery rhymes—but this was beauty in its richest manifestation.

Vari visibly perked up. "Rapple's got his guitar!"

"That's what it is?" Letty attempted to brush a misbehaving lock of hair back from where the gentle wind disrupted its perch over her shoulder.

Vari caught the strand of hair and tucked it behind Letty's ear. "It's a very old instrument," he said. "Older than this village. I mean, Rapple carved his own, but the design's been around since before the world was rebuilt. His whole family can play."

Letty felt her smile blossom as the music sang on, Rapple's brown head bent over metal strings, strumming them to the beat of some unknown heart. It filled Letty's ears with a strange, elated joy.

"We should dance," Vari said suddenly.

Letty looked around, seeing couples young and old beginning to sway from side to side with the twang of the guitar, twirling around each other in graceful steps and bounds while they smiled into each other's eyes, oblivious to anything that lay beyond.

"I don't know how to do that," said Letty, feeling small and awkward.

"Neither do I." Vari shrugged, not losing the grin. He caught Letty around her waist with one arm and turned her until she was facing him. His other hand, previously on her shoulder, pulled her closer. "Let's make it up as we go along!"

Letty giggled, hair bouncing. She felt her cheeks turn pink again, and wondered how they hadn't begun to permanently dye that color. She had never been this close to Vari before, and he smelled good—like fruit and sea salt. It was different than the familiar scent of pine needles and leather boots she had grown up with, but it was not a bad different. It was a welcomed different.

"Try not to step on my feet," she teased, forcing her muscles to relax, voice to smoothen over with ease. "I need all of my toes intact."

"No promises," Vari said mysteriously, though his smile and eyes were alight with the same glow of the colors around them.

Vari moved first and they twirled in a circle, Vari's arms around Letty and her hands clasped to his neck, the ends of his dark hair between her fingers. It was soft, like seal's fur. The music was singing somewhere over and around and between them, and Letty's feet fell into its gentle rhythm on shaky muscle memory. They mingled with the other dancers, who stopped to dip their heads to her as they swayed by, passing on their poise and smiles.

"We must look ridiculous," Letty muttered as the stares continued, and some looked more bemused than enchanted. She resisted a powerful urge to close her eyes.

"We look amazing," Vari declared with supreme confidence, diminishing her self-conscious thoughts into dust that sailed away beneath the lights. Across the way, Quell was watching them curiously, and Vari flashed him a small, tentative smile. "I mean, especially compared to some of these lumbering old people."

"Sure, sure." Letty giggled, and Quell nodded to her as she passed, making a gesture to them like he was tipping his hat. "Whatever you say."

"I *do* say," said Vari in that charismatic way of his, and touched their foreheads together, absently watching as Quell sifted into the throng. "They're only staring at us because they're wondering what the simple village boy is doing with such a pretty girl like you."

Letty rolled her eyes, though she flushed deeper. "You're hardly just any village boy," she said, twisting the subject. "You're nearly as famous as I am—the medical miracle who survived a demon possession."

Vari just stared at her, blue eyes and blue eyes. His were bright as ever, but soft, too—they were pools, and they invited her to dive in. Letty was suddenly conscious of how close he was, his face just inches from hers. "I survived because I wanted to see you again," he told her matter-of-factly, and he pulled her even closer, and then they were kissing.

Letty, who had never kissed anyone before, and certainly not anyone she had feelings for, stood frozen in shock for a moment before her thudding heartbeat belted louder than the thoughts in her head and she closed her eyes, standing on her tiptoes to kiss him back, her smile all pressed to his. Her hands wove in his hair and he gripped her shoulders tightly as if to keep her there, suspended on the light-dappled stones. He tasted just like he smelled—sweet as apples with a hint of something saltier, the Hudson Bay where he made his home.

When Vari let her go, she stepped back, swaying back on her heels; the swirling colors of music mixed with her pounding heart and made her dizzy. She found herself stumbling backward, dragging Vari with her.

"Would you two watch where you step?" growled an irritated voice, one all too familiar.

"Sorry, Jay," Vari apologized, stepping back from Letty but keeping one arm locked around her waist. There was still an infinitesimal subconscious suspicion brewing in the crystals of his eyes, but Letty couldn't share such mistrust.

Jay—predictably—just rolled his eyes, crossed his arms.

"What are you doing here?" Letty asked him, and she was honestly curious. Jay didn't seem like the type to enjoy parties, especially since he was standing with a certain desolation at the edge of the spectrum of light, far away from the faded music and festivities. Alone.

Jay shrugged thin shoulders, lifted blind eyes as if trying to find the moon in the sky, the watching light of the stars. "Why is anyone here? It's a celebration. I'm here to celebrate."

Letty watched his face, watched it flicker with faint blues and greens. "Well, why aren't you with everyone else? Do they still not trust you, even after what Masotote said?"

Vari shot Letty a look as if she'd lost her mind, probably expecting Jay's temper to shatter, but Jay only sighed in immense glumness and shrugged again.

"It's not that. There's just too much commotion," he said blandly. "I don't know the layout of the party, with the new decorations and tables—not to mention everyone flitting around with cups of easily-spilled juice. I wouldn't even know where to put my feet. I'd probably end up causing injuries I'd only be expected to patch up later."

And Letty, despite the bitterness Jay had shown her, found herself sympathizing. She was realizing, again and again, that despite his skill and attention, Jay's blindness could get the best of him—he had limits, a wall around him that kept him broken off and splintered from a world that should have been in his grasp. If he didn't know something like the back of his hand, he didn't know it at all. Couldn't trust it at all.

Vari gave Letty another meaningful stare, but she ignored it, staring at Jay as he pretended to stare at the ground, locked somewhere no one could reach.

"Jay," Letty said, and it sounded like a question.

Jay's eyebrows twitched, though he did not look up or otherwise acknowledge he had been addressed.

"Just because you've put up a wall doesn't mean you can't take it down," Letty said, voice slow. "The world's not so bad in the end—people are good. I know I have no right to know anything about you, but—"

"It's alright, Letty," Jay said quietly, face still bent into the ground. "If you can't see your problems, they can't truly be there in the first place, can they?" His voice grew taut, a raw note like a tap on a window.

Letty knew she had overstepped. "Just know it will get better someday," she finished. "They're not called happy middles— they're called happy endings. You'll get one. Promise."

At this Jay looked up, jolted wide-eyed out of misery, but Letty had already taken Vari by the arm and led him back into a crowd that swallowed her whole. The celebration went on.

"Maji, you've been staring around the village for half a song with your neck all stuck out like a bird's—if you haven't found Sedona already, she's probably handling important business somewhere else. You're just going to pull a muscle or something." Raizu's face held nothing short of amusement, one eyebrow arched up.

"I'm not looking for Sedona," Majest said, fidgeting to adjust the fancy coat Raizu had forced him into. It was warm and thick, like every other coat he'd worn before, but soft and sleek and made of some foreign material that felt slippery yet dry against his skin. He couldn't decide if it was comfortable, but he had to admit, it looked good—it framed him at all his edges, drew attention to the slopes of his shoulders and the fall of his legs.

"Then what are you doing?" asked Raizu, both eyebrows now raised.

Majest peered through the crowd, finding the eye of its needle to capture a sight of dancing villagers, heads bopping in time to Rapple's music, lights spinning, the town dissolving and burning through any last memories of Ohanzi or Masotote or the Organization.

"I'm trying to find Letty," he said, distracted. "She was standing with Vari by the fountain just a few minutes ago, but now they've both disappeared."

"You can't watch over her like a hawk," said Raizu pointedly. "She's not going to stay at your side for the rest of her life. She'll be an adult soon—she's got Vari and an entire village to protect her now. Not to mention the obvious fact that she is very capable of protecting herself in the first place."

"I know," Majest muttered, forcing his eyes down and away from the crowd. "It's just that we've relied solely on each other for so long now that it feels like I'm cutting my own arm off just watching her walk off with someone else in a party that's supposed to be ours."

Raizu shrugged. "She's growing up. She's not just your little sister anymore—she's her own person. You can't control the tide."

"I know," Majest said again, but his voice was not quite as solemn. Raizu was right.

Raizu nodded with a smile, touched his arm lightly. "Why don't you stop thinking about where Letty and Vari might be and enjoy the party? It's not like you don't have anyone else to celebrate with—you've got me, after all."

"Fine," Majest replied, quirking one corner of his mouth into a smile. "Shall I go get *two* cups of grape juice for the *both* of us?"

"I think that sounds like quite the plan."

"Alright." Majest grinned in full, turning to make his way

through the crowd of celebrating villagers. They parted like a wave, flowing into new streams that floated this way and that—a natural rhythm, built into the town just the same as the stone in the ground and the fountain at its perch above it.

There was a table set up with juice cups, smaller and simpler than the feast table—which, Majest noted with a grumbling stomach, he would have to investigate later—and it was filled with a maze of violet and silver, chalices and shimmering dark liquid.

"Hi, Majest!" Sedona appeared from behind the table, teeth glimmering in a rainbow smile. Her hair was pulled in snowy lines from her face with what looked like metal pins, and she was wearing the soft, spotless white coat from the day she'd met the Skylarks in the woods—along with a long black skirt that swished to and fro as she circled around the table.

"Hello," Majest responded, shifting the collar of his shirt. "Nice party you've got yourself here. Did you do all of this yourself?"

"Not all of it," Sedona admitted, long eyelashes batting downward as she twined slender fingers together. "Sunni helped color the lights, and a few of the boys got them up on the houses. We had to make our own dyes since we didn't have enough old-world paint."

"Sounds like a lot of work to handle in such a short amount of time," said Majest, impressed.

Sedona made a self-conscious noise, and wouldn't meet his eyes. There was heat on her cheeks. "Well, it's what I do. I'm always busy doing something." She paused for a moment, flexing her arms. "So, ah, are you here for some juice?"

"Oh! Yes, please," replied Majest with a start, finding he had forgotten why he had come this way in the first place. Party lights and dazzling smiles were slowing his judgment. "One cup each for me and my company for the evening."

"Letty?" Sedona guessed, sliding two cups artfully out from the table's pattern in a delicate balance.

"Raizu, actually," Majest corrected, collecting the cups between his fingers and taking a drink out of one, delighted at the taste. It was ice-cold, rich and sweet. "Letty went off somewhere with Vari.

I haven't seen her in a while."

"They've been inseparable since Vari woke up." Sedona shrugged, as if it were only to be expected. "They're sure to be partners in a few years if they stay that way." Her voice got suddenly quiet, and she stared at him intently. "I wish all love was that easy."

Majest leaned forward, the shine in her hair pulling him in. "What do you mean?"

Under the party lights, Sedona's face turned an odd violet-red. "Well, I—was going to talk to you—about something—an idea I had—but—" She broke off in a panic, eyes jerking to something far and inscrutable in the distance, as if searching for a way not to answer.

She seemed to find something far behind Majest, and her skin looked like it was burning as she attempted to direct Majest's attention to it. "What's going on over there?"

Blinking in a bewildered silence, Majest turned away from the lights, and his eyes met the dark, and he saw it, right there in Sedona's line of sight—saw *him.*

A strange man stood at the edge of the celebration, feet just beyond the dazzle of the lanterns, so that instead of glowing under hues and streaks, his figure was a flat, dark blandness. He was tall enough to tower over the crowd, and made no move to disguise himself or a soaking wet mess of curling bronze hair—he simply stood, clutching a leather sack with a precarious concern. Waiting.

"Do you know who that is?" Majest muttered at Sedona.

"Never seen him before in my life."

Majest didn't move his gaze from the stranger, and as he watched, the man raised his chin and bored two bright eyes through the crowd—searching for something.

"There's something oddly familiar about him," said Majest. "Isn't there? Or is it just me?"

"There is." Sedona stepped out from behind the table, face wrinkled in perplexity. "He looks exactly like Raizu."

Majest stiffened. How hadn't he seen it? The gold and brown in his hair, even wet, the smooth angles of his face, the careful stance…

Casting another glance to the stranger, Majest found the violet-blue of his eyes, poignant even from afar—they stilled him completely.

"Maji!" cried a voice, and Majest was hit by a flying blur of red and white as his sister crashed into his side, Vari right behind her. "Do you see him? Do you see him?"

"Yes, I see him," Majest replied, untangling two warm hands from where they clutched at his waist, setting his juice on the table behind him. "And I'm glad to see you, too—do you know who that is?"

"I have no idea—but everyone's starting to notice him now," said Vari, and motioned to the stranger, who shuffled his feet in discomfort as the ruthless, suspicious gazes Majest knew too well landed on yet another surprise visitor.

All at once, the music stopped over one somber final note; the twirling grace of the dancers skidded to a halt in a near-collision. Every eye was turned.

"Who are you?" someone demanded.

Heart beating in his throat and a sinking feeling in his chest, Majest started to forge his way through the throng, his three companions following in pursuit. The crowd slid apart like water.

"I come without intentions of harm," the man said just as Majest broke through to the front—feet only a few paces away from the stranger, whose hands were raised in surrender. "My name is Arathiel."

Arathiel. Had Majest heard the name before? Up close, he thought Raizu could have looked through a mirror and found a smaller version of this man staring back at him.

Majest frowned. Where *was* Raizu? He hissed the question into Letty's ear, catching her by the shoulder. "Can you see him?"

But Letty, try as she might, wasn't tall enough to see over the bulky mass of crowd into the corner where Majest had left his friend, and Majest didn't want to take his eyes off the outsider.

Majest balled his hands into fists.

"How did you get here and what do you want? We have reason not to trust strangers." Sunni was demanding, somewhere to

Majest's left.

The man cringed at the harsh ring of the voice, took a step back. "I've been searching for my brother," he said. "I knew he'd come this way. He's been gone for weeks, so I tracked him—though it's been hard on my injured leg." He shifted his weight, wincing. "I rigged a few logs together to get out here. I thought it was just the place he'd end up, searching for who he was searching for." He stared around, awkward stance drowned out by a starved curiosity. The only sound Majest heard was the faint drip of the salt water from his hair onto the ground where it dissolved the snow.

"Sounds a bit suspicious to me," Vari whispered.

The man, unfazed, shook his head, drops flying. "So, is he here? Is my brother here?"

The clearing held still, each and every villager silent as stone.

Then a figure was parting the crowd calmly, hands shaking as they lifted in greeting. Raizu. "I'm right here, Rath," he said without inflection, moving to stand next to the dripping stranger.

Majest's eyes widened. Brothers? He should have guessed. He stared at Raizu, trying to get his attention, but Raizu drew his mouth into a hard line, looked at nothing but Arathiel. His eyes were oddly cold.

"Why did you come here?" Raizu demanded.

"Raizu," Arathiel breathed, and stretched out his arms in relief, leaning toward his brother with a sickening delight Raizu did not seem to share. "Thank the skies you're okay. It's a miracle you're here. I didn't think you'd be alright, or even alive—"

Raizu flinched back from the embrace. "Why wouldn't I be?"

Arathiel's face grew long and despondent. "You were gone for so long—I thought something must have happened to you."

"So you sent yourself out after me like I'm some animal you need to track down?" Raizu didn't seem to register that he was shouting in front of everyone. "You left everyone alone because you think I don't know how to take care of myself?"

"Why are you getting so upset?" Arathiel hissed, eyes darting nervously around the crowd. "I just traveled in the wilderness for two weeks simply to make sure you're alright! I risked my life for you!"

Raizu did not move. "What do you want?" Majest had never heard him sound so defiant.

This seemed to Arathiel a genuinely shocking question. "What do you mean? I'm here to take you home!"

In synchronization, Majest and Raizu inhaled sharply.

"You think you can just tuck me under your arm and take me with you?" Raizu's voice lost its strength, started to shake.

Arathiel frowned. "What are you talking about?" Behind him, the village watched in bewilderment, faces pulled to their usual group unity.

"I don't know how you knew where I was or why you can't trust me to keep myself safe, but I'm not going to pack up and leave just because you want me to." Raizu bit his lip.

"You're upset, Raizu. You don't know what you're saying." Arathiel's voice was smooth, deliberate. "I came here to take you back to Inertia, and I will. That's where you belong, and I suspect you've overstayed your welcome here. What's the matter? I thought you'd be thrilled to have an escort home."

Majest couldn't let this go on any longer. "This *is* his home," he put in, thrusting his way forward to stand next to Raizu, who looked stunned to see him there. "He belongs here. With us."

The muscles in Arathiel's face twitched; his gaze went to Majest with some reluctance. "And who exactly are you? I suppose you're one of those Skylarks."

"I'm Raizy's best friend." Majest crossed his arms. "He doesn't want to set one foot off this island. Not now, not ever."

"Don't you?" Arathiel turned wide eyes on his brother.

Raizu's eyes darted from Majest to Arathiel, losing the last of their feigned authority. "I—I was going to live here," he stammered, and the words faded out into an apology. "With Maji and Letty. Their battle against the Organization was something I wanted to be a part of, and even if the danger is gone, I still want to stay. I feel valuable here. Braver."

Arathiel's nose wrinkled. "But I'm your brother. I'm your *family*. We need you at home. You don't need to put yourself in danger for these people. Your place is with the pack. You're valuable there."

Raizu's eyes were pained. "You don't need me. I've never been any good at helping our pack."

"*We* need him," Majest put in, and had to stop himself from stepping in between the two brothers to keep Raizu from Arathiel's words. "He saved the whole village—not to mention my life a few times over."

Arathiel's blue-violet gaze froze like water, cut into Majest like a knife. They were Raizu's eyes, but Majest could not picture Raizu with such an expression. "He's my brother," he said again. "I came all the way here for him and I intend to take him back with me."

Majest glared right back, ignoring that Arathiel was older and somehow taller than him. "Well, you can't."

Raizu made an irritated noise. "Can you two please—?"

"I'm *here* to get my brother back," Arathiel said again, leaning forward on his toes until he towered another several inches above Majest. "Some silly Skylark boy isn't going to stop me. Raizu came to this place to warn you two about the Organization, and it looks as if he's done quite a bit more than that. He's done here. He belongs to his pack once more."

"Do you have to talk about me like I'm not right here?" asked Raizu, and now his voice was angry again, pulled taut like a fraying rope. "I'll make a decision, not you."

"Yes, alright." Majest stepped back and gestured to Raizu with a shaking hand. "Tell him you're not leaving."

Raizu nodded tightly, opened his mouth—

"We need you at home," Arathiel protested in a sudden interruption, voice stretching until Majest thought it would break. His eyes were more like his brother's now, wide and endless—convincing. "Kallica and the rest of them miss you desperately. They've been having a really hard time without you. I..." He bit his lip. "I don't think they've been quite themselves."

Majest saw Raizu's eyes flicker with a hint of uncertainty. "Really?"

Arathiel flashed a smirk his brother didn't see and nodded in vigorous swishes of his neck, lip trembling for effect. "Of course, Raizu. And I've missed you, too—it's kept me up at night. I don't know what I'll do without you. You have to come back."

Majest narrowed his eyes. This was a trap, some elaborate hoax Arathiel had put together to corner his brother where he could not escape, lasso him up and tow him home—couldn't Raizu see that?

Raizu hesitated, gave Majest a brief glance filled with desperate confusion. "Well, I…"

"Don't go." Majest felt himself pleading. This was not how he'd hoped to spend this celebration, not when there was feasting and dancing and laughing to be done, best friends to keep close. "Tell him he can deliver the news to Inertia that you're staying with us. That way, we won't have to travel back and do it ourselves—you know, like we planned? After you decided to stay?"

Raizu turned to Majest then, away from his brother, away from the crowd of observing villagers, away from everything else in the world but him. He looked torn, a page ripped right out of a book. "I thought I could stay," he said. "I didn't think about anything else. But my brother's here now, all the way here—just to bring me home. That means something, don't you think?"

Majest saw the glassy confusion in Raizu's eyes and knew he was falling for it, giving in, letting fear and uncertainty choke and swallow the seeds of bravery that had only just started to grow above the surface. "What does it mean?" he demanded. "That Arathiel's persistent? That he's your brother? That he's overprotective and can't stand to lose something he thinks belongs to him?" Majest grabbed the sleeve of Raizu's jacket. "You can't let yourself be such an easy target—don't you want to stay?"

"Arathiel doesn't want me to stay."

"Does that matter?" Majest heard his voice rise higher, heard Raizu slipping away somewhere below. "Don't you remember what you told me? You can be brave here! You don't have to listen to your brother anymore—you're here now, of your own accord. You're safe here. We want you here."

"We *definitely* want you here," Letty chimed in, eyes fierce and glowing as she stepped forward.

Raizu looked at the ground, and the last of his willpower dissolved, fell to the dirt like tears. "I'm so sorry," he murmured, so softly Majest almost didn't catch it.

"What?"

Raizu looked up, blue eyes meeting green. Majest tried to find that brave light he'd seen just minutes ago, but it was doused into two hollows of unhappiness that did not even shine with the stars. "My brother is right," he said dully. "How would you feel if Letty ran off somewhere, found a group of strangers and called it a home?"

"That's *different*," Majest insisted, blood freezing in some mute horror until he was shivering under his suit. "Letty and I are closer than most siblings—we never *had* anyone else. But now we have you! You have to be joking—you said your family would understand!"

"I thought they would." The pools in Raizu's eyes swelled over until they were leaking out the sides. Small, sticky tears. Unwilling. He looked back at his brother. "But I was wrong. Rath needs me. He's my family."

"Aren't we your family, too?" cried Letty, running to cling to Raizu's other arm until he was locked between the two siblings. "The three of us, we're something special. You can't walk away. What are we going to do?"

Raizu looked at her in the way Majest might have, as though she'd just awoken from a nightmare, still shaking and crying. "You could come with me."

"That's not *fair*," Letty cried. "This is our home now. We can't pack up and leave, not again."

"But I have to," Raizu told her, though he was looking at Majest. His expression was clouded, voice mechanical, like Arathiel had put it there. "I was wrong and naïve to think I could leave behind my life the way you did. I'm not brave or faithful. I'm a coward, Letty. A disloyal coward. I always will be."

Majest knew he had lost the fight, knew there was no way to save his heart from being wrenched out of place. Still, one last time—"Please don't go."

"He'll be safer with us," Arathiel said, and didn't even try to hide the sneer, the dark glint of his eyes. "Safety is always most important, don't you think?"

Raizu broke his arms free, turned to wrap them around Letty and Majest, head bent between theirs. "Don't worry, okay? I'll see you two again. I swear on my life."

Majest closed his eyes, buried his face in Raizu's shoulder. This wasn't *fair*. "You'd better not be lying," he rasped out, swallowing another lump in his throat.

All too soon, Raizu stepped back, pulled toward his brother as if tied to him by some choking string. He was shaking. Except for Sedona, the villagers around them had lost interest, no one left to say goodbye.

"Let's go," Arathiel snapped. "We can make it to the Bay before sunrise if we start now."

Raizu shook his head, still looking the other way. "It's a small world we live in, Majest. Letty. We'll see each other someday."

A sickening wave of nostalgia crashed through Majest's blood, lit it on fire. Those were the words that had first sent Raizu walking away through the forest—back to Inertia. And here they were again, at the crossroads, all three of them.

"Hopefully in better times," Majest managed to say, and though he tried to smile, to say something of gratitude—something worth remembering—he could not. He was bound by gravity, and no words were enough.

Raizu nodded, and he was crying, tears silent and glistening. Then he turned around. Majest only heard Letty's muffled sobbing into Vari's shoulder and the sounds of footsteps fading as his first and greatest friend walked away.

He was cold, but the stars were not the sun; they could not warm the ice crawling under his skin.

It didn't take long before they were out of sight, swallowed by the night. Raizu had looked back a few times—of course he had—but he was gone now. Would they make it across the Bay safely? Would Raizu be steady in the darkness, or would his fears keep him suspended from daylight? Majest didn't know.

"Majest," Sedona said, voice aching. She ran up to him and touched his shoulder. "I'm so sorry."

"Don't," said Majest, finding his sister's hand and gripping it tight. He closed his eyes. "There isn't anything you can say." And it was true.

As if on cue, the party lights flickered once, twice, and then they sputtered out altogether.

EPILOGUE

The corridors rang with an empty silence. Nothing stirred amongst white walls and sickly white floors—no patter of footsteps, no faint clink of metal and distant musings, not even the buzz and whir of electricity rising through the floor. The walls were as bare and static as the bacterial color that plagued them.

Lunesta Skylark sat in her hard plastic chair, muscles stiff and back cramped. Her presence in that chair was as constant as the paint on her walls, and just as sickly. She was diseased and destined to slouch there, to plot some futile attempt or watch screens blink on and off, off and on.

It had only been two days and seventeen hours since one vital screen had gone out, out like a candle or a fleeting blaze. The Organization was doused, too—locked in a standstill.

"He just vanished right off the map," Lunesta muttered again, numbly, rubbing her temples with the cold tips of her fingers. She stared blankly at the screen, which held an identically vacant expression. The beeping red dot that had gripped her tight, kept her tethered to some vain hope, had disappeared.

"What's that now?" asked Chami from the other side of the room.

"He's gone."

The twins crossed the floor, crouching on either side of their President as if they could shield her from the rest of her empty chamber. "Lady President, you must stop thinking about Ohanzi," Shayming reprimanded. "He was an accident all along—what more than an accident was he ever going to cause?"

"But Seti and Malory are out of commission as well." Lunesta cracked her knuckles loudly. "I don't suppose you've heard anything more from the one who wanted to meet with me?"

The twins exchanged a glance. "Not a word."

"Then we're out of ideas. Again, I might add." Lunesta let out a long breath through her nose. "Are the scientists generating ideas? Whether the Powers are on some island or right under our noses, we're going to need another plan for tracking them down, and finding a way to locate any stragglers as well. What we really need is something to track *godly* energy—what do they have to say about that?"

"They're working on it," Shayming said, voice lulling, hand patting at Lunesta's back as if she were a daughter in need of consolation. "We have Caiter. He'll think of something."

"Caiter," Lunesta repeated. "Right. Yes." She did not take her eyes off of the screen.

"No matter how many times you look at that thing, nothing's going to happen," noted Chami, though not without sympathy. She paused. "Why don't you bring back Seti? If he's still alive, I'm sure he would be able to—"

"No," snapped Lunesta, slamming a wall of ice between her and the subject. "Seti was a traitor. I have no use for traitors."

Chami swallowed, dipped her head. "Of course. I'm sorry."

Lunesta sighed, and purposefully changed the subject. "I trust you two are keeping the rest of the building in line?"

"Everyone's nearly bursting from their skin trying to figure out what's going to happen, but they're behaving," Shayming replied, her cat eyes dancing. "We made sure of that."

"Excellent," said Lunesta, tearing her eyes with reluctance from her screen to stand up.

Perfectly in time, a knock sounded at the door. Lunesta exchanged a glance with the twins. "Who could that be?"

"Are you expecting anyone?" asked Shayming.

"No," said Lunesta, and started toward the door, clicking the lock open with one finger.

At once the door flew back as though a hurricane raged behind it, shooting a wind into Lunesta's face that sent her hair fluttering behind her.

Shatter was waiting on the other side, face alert and amber eyes wary. Her usually-neat pale hair was frizzy with static and rumpled in odd clumps, though she didn't appear frantic, just concerned.

"What is it, Shatter?" Lunesta asked, leaning against the doorframe on one arm. "Is something the matter?"

"No," Shatter said in a clipped voice. "I mean—yes—" She sighed. "I don't know. But there's a woman at the door who wants to see you."

"At the *door?*" Lunesta was intrigued. The door was veiled away, concealed behind a waterfall that screamed and hissed at intruders—impossible to approach, impossible to unearth unless someone looked it dead in the eye. And there were few who knew it existed. "Show me."

Lunesta trailing Shatter's light steps, they navigated the white maze to reach the front entrance, the door to an outside world they had all nearly forgotten. There was no one to see or find poking their heads through the halls; the Organization had holed itself up in hibernation.

Several times Lunesta thought of starting up a conversation, perhaps to ask Shatter of her progress, but she could think of nothing to say. She could not even remember the last time she'd seen Shatter's face, seen anything that was not contained in the stifling chambers of screens and sleeping soldiers behind curtains.

The building was a foreign land, Lunesta a stranger in her own castle.

The front door loomed metal and thick in front of them, a solid wall of security. It let nothing in, nothing out. It took Lunesta several shaking moments to work her way through slippery padlocks and keypads that shied away from her fingers as if they could hold her inside.

Shatter stood off to one side, hands folded in front of her. She was staring somewhere far away—Lunesta could never tell what she was thinking, though it was certain she was always thinking.

"One more lock," noted Shatter as if startled, motioning to the final padlock. It was small, dark—a dare. Lunesta hadn't touched that lock since she had placed it there.

But before she could feel the cold box beneath her fingertips, the door swung backward like a cat's reflex, a loud metallic hiss rolling from its hinges.

Shatter flinched. "It did that all by itself?"

"I'm not sure." Lunesta peered into the darkness, the musty cavern that hid her whirring mechanism of an Organization. From somewhere beyond the crystallized floor, a familiar waterfall pounded.

"I don't see anyone," said Shatter with some uncertainty.

"You said there was a woman here."

"There was!" Shatter's eyes were wide. "Just minutes ago. Terrifying as all the world's shadows, but she asked to speak with you."

"But she disappears now instead of keeping her word?" Lunesta's lip curled. "I left my chambers for nothing but the smell of moldy water?"

"I am here," said a cool voice.

Lunesta disguised the startled tremor that rocked through her, squinting in the darkness to see a faint shape among the shadows of the cave. Somewhere, a stalagmite dripped from the ceiling.

"Who are you?" Lunesta called out. "I'm Lunesta Skylark, President of the Organization."

"My name is Sira Sinestre."

Footsteps echoed and the voice grew a face from the dark—a woman, as Shatter had promised, tall and slim as a ribbon with raven's hair in unbrushed tangles. Her pale face was small, not holding the beauty it should have.

Her eyes of fire were at fault for the lost beauty— they were two pulsing red hearts beating from below sleek eyebrows, clouded pupils and twisted lashes.

"Sinestre," whispered Shatter.

Lunesta ignored her. "I've been expecting you."

Sira blinked, body still and unmoving as Death. Crimson eyes flashed between Shatter and Lunesta, and Lunesta resisted the urge to shrink back like a mouse. "You were seeking assistance to your sinking ship," she said, "and after consideration, I have come to offer it. For a price."

Lunesta sucked in a breath. "A price?"

"I am going to tell you of a means to save your lost cause, and you will choose whether to accept my help or keep to your own path of destruction." Sira's face still did not change, except for eyes of fire that swam and moved as though something lived inside of them.

"The price."

At last Sira grinned, and her teeth were long and pointed like a wolf's, coated in a milky film stained brown and red. "I will show you how to create an army that will bring to an end the world of the elements, put your world in its place. It will finally finish what I once started, and for you, it may do the same. And in return..."

Lunesta waited, and a final statement rose from the gloom:

"In return, I will do as I wish with this new world."

A.L. Mundt—known to some as Alaina, and others as Letty, though there is no connection to a certain Letty Skylark—has been putting stories to paper since she was just three years old. Admittedly, though, they weren't any good back then. Now a full-time, pizza-guzzling, nineteen-year-old student, she studies creative writing and frequently authors in St. Norbert College's *Graphos*. A love for the sublime in the northern wilderness fuels the Messengers trilogy, with *Water and Earth* marking her first installment and her first publication. Aside from writing, she dreams of one day owning a pet squirrel named Daniel and a kitten named Mika, witnessing Eyjafjallajökull (and its proper pronunciation), and learning how to stop getting sucked into unpopular television shows.

CPSIA information can be obtained
at www.ICGtesting.com
Printed in the USA
LVOW11s2010050417

529720LV00004B/840/P